MW00615004

THE WATCHERS OF MONIAH
BOOK ONE OF
THE WATCHERS OF MONIAH

Barbara V. Evers

New Mythology Press
Virginia Beach, VA

Copyright © 2020 by Barbara V. Evers.

All rights reserved. No part of this publication may be reproduced, distributed or transmitted in any form or by any means, including photocopying, recording, or other electronic or mechanical methods, without the prior written permission of the publisher, except in the case of brief quotations embodied in critical reviews and certain other noncommercial uses permitted by copyright law. For permission requests, write to the publisher, addressed "Attention: Permissions Coordinator," at the address below.

Chris Kennedy/New Mythology Press
2052 Bierce Dr.
Virginia Beach, VA 23454
http://chriskennedypublishing.com/

Publisher's Note: This is a work of fiction. Names, characters, places, and incidents are a product of the author's imagination. Locales and public names are sometimes used for atmospheric purposes. Any resemblance to actual people, living or dead, or to businesses, companies, events, institutions, or locales is completely coincidental.

Cover Design by J Caleb Design.

Ordering Information:
Quantity sales. Special discounts are available on quantity purchases by corporations, associations, and others. For details, contact the "Special Sales Department" at the address above.

The Watchers of Moniah/Barbara V. Evers -- 1st ed.
ISBN: 978-1648551048

To Mom and Dad, who gave me the joy of reading and education.
I wish you were here to see this.

Acknowledgments

So much goes into the writing of a book, and this one is no different. First and foremost, I must thank my husband, Bruce, who never doubted I could write and publish a novel. You never questioned this and put up with me disappearing to write or attend conferences, leaving you to handle things on the home front. I love you.

My beta readers, Tina, Linda, Sarah, Christina, Roiselyn, and Chris gave me encouragement when I needed it and became this book's first fans. Thank you for loving this story before anyone else saw it. Also, special thanks goes to my writing tribe, the members of the Greenville chapter of SCWA including Marcia and John, Bob, David, Susan, Phil, Adrienne, Valerie, Roiselyn, Larry, Jim, and Jim. You helped make this book better and kept me writing.

A special thank you to my author friends, Faith Hunter and David B. Coe for never doubting I had a publishable book inside me.

And I don't think this book would be anywhere near as good as it is without my editor, Rowe Carenen. You love these characters as much as I do and helped me develop a fuller story. I doubt I'd be here without your enthusiasm.

A special thanks to Jake Clark at J Caleb Designs for creating an amazing cover and making Adana and her world so beautiful.

And, last, but definitely not least, thank you to my publisher, Chris Kennedy, who saw the potential of this story and opened the door to publication for me.

Map of the Four Kingdoms

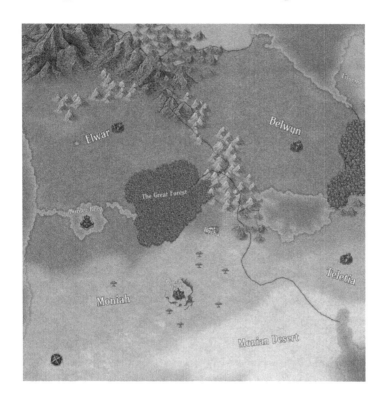

* * * * *

Prologue

Queen Chiora of Moniah leaned back on her throne, her gaze steady on the traitor, Maligon. The sight of her once truest friend tightened the knot in her stomach. The gathered nobles hushed as he strode past them, head held high, escorted by two women of the queen's Watchers. The heat in the air lay thick as a blanket. The silence matched it. Chiora resisted the urge to shift in her seat as sweat pooled inside her uniform, the leathers chosen over ceremonial dress to remind him she was a soldier, not just a figurehead.

Sunlight poured into the open courtyard and radiated across the landowners' formal robes of glimmer cloth, creating a rainbow of iridescent color around them. Normally, she enjoyed the play of the sunlight on their clothing, but today she couldn't. Today, they waited to witness the sentencing of the man who dared bring destruction to the kingdoms.

The Watchers and Maligon came to a stop below Chiora's Seat of Authority. He wore the plain clothes of a prisoner but still stood tall and well-muscled, his dark hair tied back in a fighter's tail. His black eyes once caressed her in love, but now they radiated hatred so pure it shimmered in the air.

"Maligon," Queen Chiora spoke, her voice firm and strong, "you betrayed me. And so you betrayed us all. And for what? Power you didn't need."

Maligon's black eyes didn't blink. He sneered at her. His injured hand twitched. She watched it with dispassionate interest. He'd never wield a sword again, a satisfying bit of knowledge even if he was about to die.

She took a focused breath, centering her mind and soul. "I sentence you to wear the oxen head into the desert."

A low murmur of approval hummed through the onlookers.

Maligon continued to stare venom at her as she gestured to the Watchers. "Take him from my sight."

The two Watchers, dressed in the tanned leather tunics and leggings of Chiora's all-female guard, escorted Maligon from the hall. He walked between the tall soldiers, head still held high.

Chiora drew a deep breath, the tension in her muscles easing as the air spread into her chest and throughout her body. She took another breath, and another. With each controlled inhalation, she drew her focus inward, preparing to bear witness as her soldiers carried out Maligon's sentence outside the walls of her fortress. The sentence would finish him. The heat, even this far from the desert bordering her lands, baked the air.

As her breathing settled into a steady rhythm, she sent a tendril of thought into the telepathic link with Ju'latti, her royal giraffe. Tension slid from her neck and shoulders as the noble beast embraced the connection. Through this link, Chiora looked through the animal's eyes and saw a throng of tribal villagers gathered outside the walls of the fortress. They stood near the horses where the soldiers led Maligon, but not too close. She couldn't blame them after the devastation the traitor and his followers wreaked on their lands.

Two Watchers lashed Maligon to the back of a donkey, securing the bindings so neither traitor nor beast could dislodge the man.

Then they handed a large skin bucket to a squad of First Soldiers, the male branch of Moniah's military. At the edge of the desert, the soldiers would remove a water-soaked oxen head from the bucket and secure it over Maligon's.

Chiora squinted at the sky. The sun, now a short distance above the horizon, promised a scorching day. Just before it reached its pinnacle, the First Soldiers would place the suffocating weight of the oxen head over Maligon's. A few hours later, the soldiers would stab the donkey's rump, driving it farther into the desert. In the heat, the wet oxen head would dry and conform to Maligon. Suffocation would kill him long before the donkey collapsed from exhaustion.

And if he survived? Chiora shook her head. No one had survived this sentence in hundreds of years.

The thought of this torturous death repulsed her, but Maligon made his choice when he defied Moniah and her allied kingdoms of Elwar, Belwyn, and Teletia. He didn't deserve the pity that rose in her throat.

As the soldiers and Maligon disappeared beyond the fortress walls, Chiora released the remaining tension in her shoulders and let the giraffe's gentling influence wash over her. Only Ju'latti truly knew her thoughts and feelings on this ominous day, and in the way of their long relationship, the animal sought to comfort her by cutting off the sharing of sight and focusing on the soothing sounds of the large, life-giving fountains in the Great Hall.

The queen focused on the gentle bubbling and ignored the stream of sweat trickling between her shoulder blades. "Send in the champions."

The assemblage shouted their approval as two foreigners walked forward to accept the accolades they deserved. The men's lighter coloring no longer startled Chiora unlike the day she and a squad of Watchers found them at the bottom of a muddy cliff. The man on the right, Micah, saved her life during the war with Maligon. Her gaze ran over his tall, lithe build in appreciation. Light hair, bleached white from the sun, glowed against his Monian-kissed suntan like bones on the prairie. Clear blue eyes gazed at her with startling familiarity, stuttering the pulse in her neck.

She drew another calming breath as his companion knelt before her. Unlike Micah, this man's fair skin had blistered and burned in the harsh sun of their land, a point that favored the reward she would grant him.

Micah maintained his focus on her and nodded in acknowledgement before kneeling. Chiora breathed deeper to suppress the shiver of excitement prompted by his forthright behavior.

"Our dear champions." Her low-pitched voice echoed throughout the huge open hall. She thanked the Creator that it came out strong and clear, with no hint of the emotions tumbling her soul. "Your journey from beyond the northern mountains came at a fortuitous time. Your courage in the face of our recent struggles brought peace to our lands. As reward, the kingdoms have decided to grant you titles and property." She turned to Micah's companion. "Donel, you will be known as Sir Donel and receive land as a vassal to Queen Roassa of Elwar."

A glimmer of a smile ghosted his face. She suspected his pleasure stemmed from admiration for Roassa rather than the title and cooler climate. Her sister queen shared this interest and had suggested his placement in Elwar rather than Moniah.

Whereas, Chiora could not stop thinking about the other man before her. Micah.

She stood and approached him, placing her hand on his shoulder in the formal greeting reserved for one of her subjects. "As for you, Micah—"

As her fingers settled on his rough, leather vest, the bond with Ju'latti surged into her mind in a flash of light. She gasped, closing her eyes. An image appeared. Micah stood by her side. Between them stood a young girl, her skin a blending of Chiora's amber-colored skin and Micah's pale complexion. The child's hair was twisted into a Watcher's braid the shades of a lion's mane. In the image, the girl walked away from her parents. With each step, they faded from view, first Chiora, and then Micah. The girl continued to walk forward, alone.

The landscape around the child changed, first the flat plains of Moniah, then the mountains and forests of Elwar. With each step, the girl matured. She halted at the top of a hill, now a young woman dressed in leathers, a quiver of arrows strung over her back, a sword at her side. The shadow of a man emerged from the forests and stood beside her. A divided path lay before them, one route blocked by a monstrous blazing fire, the other by a wall taller than the eye could see. The young woman raised her head, blue eyes blazing, and stepped forward, aiming for the point where the two paths merged together in a wall of conflagration. The man's shadow followed.

Chiora bent over, gasping for air, as the vision faded. Two Teachers of the Faith rushed to her side, their green robes swaying in their urgency to support their queen, but Chiora remained upright, her fingers digging into Micah's shoulder. He rose to steady her, a look of concern in his eyes. She gazed back at him, the warmth of his touch flooding her veins.

The Creator had not only sent her a champion to help defeat Maligon, he had sent her a partner. They would make a strong child together, an heir to Moniah's Seat of Authority. A child who would face insurmountable struggles.

* * * * *

Part One

Chapter One

Moniah, 20 Years Later

Adana believed deep within her soul that her actions today could save her mother. The familiarity of the dirt-packed ground of the archery arena and the blazing Monian sun beating down on her did little to distract her from the haze of incense hovering over the fortress. Incense that proclaimed the illness of her mother, Queen Chiora of Moniah.

Tiny rivulets of sweat trickled down the contour of Adana's back. She focused on the damp track as it ran beneath her leathers. Anything to pull her mind from the weight of grief hanging over her and the kingdom.

She couldn't lose her mother. Not yet. Not when she still needed her guidance, teaching, and even scolding when she forgot her training as a soldier and acted like a princess.

The work of a soldier came first. Not the princess. And definitely not her future as the queen. Even the laws of the land knew this. Three years until she could rule at eighteen. Too soon.

She glanced at Montee, the Watcher assigned to work with her today. Montee hadn't moved, standing still, arms hanging by her side, attention focused on the young princess. Adana expected her to say something. She had taken too long to make this shot, but Montee waited.

As did everyone, today. Waited for their queen to die.

If she met this challenge, passed this test, would the Creator reward her and heal her mother? Give her back the time she needed, the parent she craved?

She drew an arrow and nocked it to her bow.

Nine arrows in a straight line pierced the scarred target wall in the distance. A significant feat and cause for jubilation for most trainees, but she didn't rejoice. Not yet. Not until she fired this last shaft. Sent true to its mark, she prayed it would prove her worth to the Creator and save her mother. She didn't care about the promotion in the ranks of the Watchers, the fact that no fifteen-year-old had ever passed this test. She only needed to please the Creator.

She inhaled. The noxious fumes of the incense, thick and cloying, settled around her. She wanted to run, to shake her head, to escape the reminder, but instead she raised her bow.

A nudge at her mind disturbed her focus. Am'brosia, her royal giraffe, offering assistance with this last shot. The animal had hovered in the background of her thoughts all morning, seeking to connect, to comfort Adana, but she'd closed her internal eye and ignored the contact, unwilling to risk the joining of their vision. Afraid Am'brosia might show her the reality of her mother's illness.

Focus.

She set her stance.

The white sun beat down. Beads of sweat pooled beneath her Watcher's braid. Adana inhaled and closed her eyes, seeking a center within her breathing, extending her mind and ability. Each inhalation spread through her chest, down her arms and legs, giving life to her focus. She breathed again. Again. Again.

Heat, sweat, and incense faded from existence. Adana envisioned the target.

She let loose the arrow.

Thunk.

The shot penetrated the wall at a perfect interval from the other nine arrows. Most Watchers released their control and shouted with joy after succeeding in this trial, but Adana dropped to her knees in thanks.

Heart pounding, she fought the urge to weep in relief. The Creator would save her mother. Save them all. And save her from this grief.

Montee studied the target, her green eyes squinting in the bright sun, then turned toward Adana. "Good," she said. That brief word rarely crossed Montee's lips.

With the heightened awareness brought on by her focused breathing, Adana found her gaze drawn to the deep lines etched within the golden skin around Montee's eyes. The premature wrinkles combined with a warrior's height and hard, muscular stature, proclaimed the Watcher as a member of the elite female branch of Moniah's military. Some day this soldier, and all the women honored to be trained as Watchers, would serve Adana. Not today, she reminded herself as she rose to her feet, waiting for further instruction. They still served her mother, as it should be.

"Aim for the spot between the fifth and sixth arrow," Montee said.

Adana nodded but wondered at the new challenge. Did Montee think she could do it? Or did she seek to remind her of the humble nature of her position?

No matter. She would succeed. A year of practice, that's what it took to pass the straight line of arrows test, but she could do anything now that the Creator would heal her mother.

Heart racing in anticipation, she set her stance.

"But first connect to Am'brosia."

Adana faltered at Montee's words. Dread ran down her spine like cold water. Lowering her bow, she stared at Montee.

What if Am'brosia chose to show her what she'd avoided all morning, Ju'latti, her mother's giraffe, suffering from the same illness? Clear proof of how deep the connection between the royal and giraffe went.

Doubt crept into her mind. What if the Creator wasn't pleased? What if he demanded more?

"Please, not today…"

Montee narrowed her gaze, silencing Adana's objection.

Adana faced the target, took a breath, and drew an arrow. She took another breath and raised her bow. Only royals sensed the presence of the bond. If she appeared to connect, Montee wouldn't know she hadn't.

"Adana." Montee's warning tone invaded her thoughts. "You will be the only one linked to a giraffe in battle. You must master this."

What small motion gave her away, hinted at her disobedience? With another Watcher, her defiance might have worked. But not with an attentive and experienced Watcher like Montee.

She whispered a brief prayer, "Please Creator, heal Mammetta." Then she inhaled. As she exhaled, she sent a tendril of thought toward the giraffe and gasped at the strength Am'brosia used as she seized the connection, not the gentle embrace Adana had grown accustomed to.

Please don't show me Ju'latti.

The pressure along their tie relaxed, cradling her, giving Adana time to settle her breathing and accept the link, but, after a few moments, Am'brosia tightened the hold and expanded their view. A distant image of the paddock appeared in Adana's mind. The scene becoming clearer, more troubling.

Adana closed her eyes but couldn't avoid what the giraffe chose to reveal.

Ju'latti, lay on the ground. The animal labored with each breath just as Adana's mother did in her chambers.

The Creator hadn't healed them.

Nearby, a bull giraffe hovered—Va'lent, the one bonded to her father.

Adana fought tears and attempted to release the connection. It held tight.

In the year since their bonding, Am'brosia had never forced the union. Neither of them had. Her parents never told her what to do in this case. Wasn't Am'brosia supposed to cooperate?

A sharp burst of mirth streamed down the tie.

Let go, Am'brosia.

The tie between them remained, strengthened.

Frantic, she envisioned a knife and pictured herself severing the invisible line of force between them. Would it work? Am'brosia kicked the knife away.

Eyes wide, Adana fought back, shoving her view of the archery grounds and the sky bleached white from the sun into her mind's eye.

Am'brosia tossed her large head, their vision bouncing around the paddock. The sudden movement rocked Adana, and she braced her feet. The scene in her mind moved over the paddock grounds toward the sheer cliff beyond the southern wall of the fortress. Adana's stomach lurched as they plummeted over the cliff. They raced toward the ground. She braced for impact. What would happen if they hit?

But they didn't. Moments before the expected blow, their sight leveled out. Am'brosia turned their gaze across the barren plains.

A Watcher ran toward them, her leathers blended with the tans and browns of her surroundings. She wore a red stretch of glimmer cloth tied across her forehead. Red for danger. Forgetting who controlled their sight, Adana turned to check the signal tower, to see if the guards saw the warning. Her view did not change. Am'brosia still controlled the direction.

Instead their gaze raced toward and past the approaching soldier. Dust and dirt swirled around them as they traveled farther into the plains. She tried to identify the running Watcher, but the soldier sped past too quickly for her to gain more than the awareness of serious intent on the woman's face.

Adana cried out in shock as they collided with a giraffe in a herd facing south.

Am'brosia stop this. Please. I don't feel well.

For a moment, everything before her wavered, and she hoped Am'brosia would release her. Then, the scene cleared. They were looking through the other animal's eyes. Then the sight jumped. Adana's stomach churned as they sprang to the mind of another giraffe, and another, and another. She lost track as they traveled far to the south.

Finally, they stopped, looking through the eyes of an old male. A village stood a short distance away. Fire raged from thatched roofs of several huts and the people ran, their mouths open in unheard screams.

Where are we?

Horror coiled in her belly as soldiers swarmed the village brandishing axes and swords. The farmers fought but fell before their attackers. Bile rose in her throat. Why would men do this? She sucked in air through her mouth, trying to ease the shock.

With an unsettling sweep of his head, the giraffe they inhabited turned his gaze toward a lone man astride a horse. This man watched the village's destruction from a distance, a ferocious smile on his face. Am'brosia drew Adana's attention to his hand, its deformity suggesting an impossible name.

Maligon.

As if he heard her thoughts, the man's head jerked up. He squinted at them then shouted an order, pointing at Adana.

"Turn," Adana shouted, unsure how to direct this distant beast. She pictured herself turning her head to the right. "Turn."

The giraffe's head swung in an arc to the right. A man ran toward them, closing the distance. He stopped and drew an arrow. Alarm skittered through Adana's brain. She raised her own bow and shot just as the giraffe wheeled to the left and ran.

A sense of shock and pain reeled through her.

The bond snapped.

Adana tumbled to the ground.

Her stomach heaved. Everything spun when she tried to lift her head.

"Adana." The pounding of running feet approached her.

She shuddered and shrank from the sound.

Montee's shadow fell over her. "My lady? What happened?"

Adana struggled to raise her head and choked out one word, "Maligon."

"What?" The woman squatted beside Adana, her shadow providing some shade from the unbearable heat. Adana swayed as her stomach gave up its fight. She hadn't eaten that morning. Little came up. A cool hand drew the braid back from her neck as she continued to heave.

When the spasms stopped, Montee offered her a water skin. "Don't swallow, just spit."

The water was warm, but she welcomed it, rinsing the sour taste of acid from her mouth.

She upended the rest of it over her head, the water washing away the frantic energy of what she'd experienced. "Thank you."

Taking the water skin back, Montee frowned at her with concern. "My lady, this is why I suggested you not attempt this trial today. You're under too much strain worrying about the queen."

Adana shook her head and moaned as it throbbed. "No. Something else." She struggled to stand, but weakness flooded her legs.

Montee rose and reached out a hand to help Adana rise.

She accepted the assistance and stood but stayed bent over, hands on her legs, taking in deep breaths. The pain and weakness subsided some. How to explain?

Had Am'brosia really carried her beyond their own sight? Outside the fortress? To the edge of Moniah? It might be a prophecy of warning. It looked so real. Real enough for her to shoot at someone leagues from here.

She drew a breath and tried to focus on one point. "I saw Ma-ligon."

"Maligon?" Montee wrinkled her forehead. "He died twenty years ago."

Adana shook her head. "I saw a man with a mangled hand."

Everyone knew how her father injured the traitor, left his hand crippled. That her mother sentenced Maligon to his death in the desert.

"But—"

"It was him. I know it. Don't ask me how. I just do."

"Is that why you shot an arrow?"

Adana looked down at her bow and back up, the motion making her head throb again.

The soldier following Maligon's command had shot at them. Giraffes were sacred. To harm one meant death. "He ordered a man to shoot at the giraffe. I was there."

She wasn't making any sense.

At that moment, the warning bell on the south tower clanged. A shout interrupted them. "Red from the south."

The Watcher they'd passed on the plains.

It was real. Am'brosia had taken her somewhere. Struggling with this realization, Adana glanced at her mentor, tried to form the words, but the Watcher's attention was on the guard tower. Montee's high rank required her to respond. The warning bell continued to clang, and the guard continued to shout the warning.

"Go, I will be fine," Adana said.

Despite the urgent summons, Montee studied Adana closely. "Are you sure? You're still unsteady."

"I'm fine. Go."

The older warrior motioned to Suru, a young Watcher of low rank who waited on the far side of the field. The woman trotted over and bobbed her head toward Adana. "My lady."

"Please escort the princess to her chambers. Make sure she's safe, then summon the apothecary. The princess became overheated and needs water and rest."

Without a backward glance, Montee hurried toward the south tower.

Suru turned toward the fortress, took a step and turned back when the princess didn't join her.

Adana straightened and pushed her shoulders back, years of deep-rooted training helping her hide any weakness. "Not yet."

She needed answers and going to her chambers wouldn't provide them. The ease at which Adana re-opened the bond with Am'brosia told her she'd anticipated her return.

Show me the red Watcher.

* * * * *

Chapter Two

The connection with Am'brosia burst to life, more vivid than before.

Soldiers atop the cliff at the southern end of the fortress rotated the crank of a rope and pulley attached to the only access from the south. The Watcher from her vision sat on a round, wooden seat attached to the thick rope as the guards hauled her over the edge of the cliff. The moment her feet touched the ground, she shoved away from the seat and trotted toward Montee who waited by the gates. The two Watchers shared hurried words then rushed toward the barracks.

An urge to follow them overwhelmed Adana, but a different question stopped her. Am'brosia showed her the attack, but how?

That question might help her understand the warning better, so she hurried toward the paddock, instead.

"My lady? Princess?" The quick footfalls of Suru sounded behind her.

Adana raced through the gates without looking in the direction of her mother's giraffe.

Am'brosia stood by the timbered fence of her own corral. A little over three years old, she was not full grown but stood at least twice Adana's height. The golden animal lowered her long neck until they were almost face-to-face, the large, liquid-brown eyes expressing anguish.

"How?" Adana placed a gentle hand on the side of the animal's neck. "How did we see that attack?"

Am'brosia nudged Adana's shoulder, turning her toward the next pen. An animal knelt in a tiny spot of shade, his head drooping almost to the ground. This giraffe, Bai'dish, was bonded to Adana's betrothed, Prince Serrin of Elwar. The same illness sapping the strength of Adana's mother and Ju'latti afflicted him. Although only first-level bonded with Serrin, the connection was strong enough for them to share illness and death.

The meaning hit Adana in the heart, pain choking one word from her. "No."

Unable to face more misery, she turned and ran from the paddock and its disturbing truths, preferring to hear the Watcher's bad news than face her own troubles.

* * *

Adana slid along the cool sandstone wall of the barracks. She'd roamed this fortress and its winding corridors from the day she could walk. Knew every path and secret doorway. Losing Suru had been easy.

The clamor of voices echoed down the corridor as soldiers responded to the warning. If she could get close, she might learn if the man on the horse truly was Maligon. She shivered despite the heat and tiptoed to the corner, listening.

One of the Watchers was speaking, "...several leagues south, on the border. It will take half a day."

Montee spoke next, her voice firm and clear. "Send for Joannu and Halar. They must lead our forces this time."

"No," an angry voice protested. "If Maligon lives, we must go."

Montee's voice sharpened with command. "The queen lies on her deathbed, Samantha. We must remain to attend her. To bear witness. You know that."

Adana slumped against the wall unable to listen further. Two words stuck in her mind—deathbed and Maligon.

All high-ranking Watchers must remain at the estate in case her mother died. One of them would rise to the highest rank, the First Vision, the one chosen to command the Watchers and advise the next queen. That meant her.

"But I'm not old enough yet," she whispered. "Creator, please don't let Mammetta die."

Maligon should be dead, too. No one survived an oxen head sentence. But she'd seen him.

The quick running of feet on the stone flooring signaled the departure of Watchers and soldiers heading for the armory. When the chamber grew quiet, Adana peered into the room and scanned the empty corridor beyond.

The Creator must expect more from her. But what?

She scurried after the troops.

The armory smelled of leather and oil, the silence broken only by the clanking of steel. Watchers struggled into heavy leathers and coiled metal armor designed to protect them from an enemy's blade, but one warrior spotted Adana and approached, a question in her eyes. "My lady, why are you here? Has the queen sent you?"

Adana ignored the question. In the voice she'd been trained to use as a royal, she said, "Tell me of the warning. Is it Maligon?"

The Watcher, her face a controlled mask, stared at Adana unblinking. "You should return to your chambers. We will handle this threat. No need for you to worry." The woman waited, arms hanging by her side, a posture that on any other person would appear relaxed.

Adana hesitated but retreated, aware of the Watcher's continued attention. Down the hallway and around the corner, a series of cloaks hung on the wall. Rare attire for a Watcher in Moniah's heat, but useful to conceal a uniform and identity.

It might help her now.

She grabbed a heavy cloak and raced for the stables. If she couldn't control Mammetta's future, then she would control her own. Eliminate Maligon and maybe the Creator would heal her mother as a reward.

* * * * *

Chapter Three

Montee entered Queen Chiora's darkened chamber, feeling older than her thirty years. She'd known this day would come but had hoped they'd misinterpreted her vision. She paused, her eyes straining in the dim light, and fought off the claustrophobia that overcame Watchers in enclosed quarters. Chiora, the Seat of Moniah's Authority, lay pale against the pillows on a low chaise, her dark-brown hair tumbling around her in a luster-less tangle. Micah, her husband, knelt by her side, formal blue robes shoved back to his elbows as he caressed his wife's forehead.

The sight made Montee pause. The queen would have enjoyed the news of her daughter's successful trial this morning and then would have set that joyful news aside as she learned of the new threat to the kingdom. If she wasn't dying.

The news must be delivered to Kassa, the woman standing at the foot of the chaise, her mouth compressed in a thin line. Did Kassa realize today was her last day as First Vision?

Montee sent a prayer to the Creator for healing of the queen and help in dealing with the report of Maligon. Even as she did so she knew the prophecy of death would prevail.

The queen stirred at the sound of Montee's approach and murmured, "Light."

Micah paused in stroking her brow. "Your pain."

Kassa moved to stand over Micah, her Watcher's braid appearing to bristle with repressed emotion. Along with her countenance of authority, Kassa wore the brushed leather tunic and leggings of a

31

Watcher, the colors blending into the sand-colored walls of the darkened room. She spoke with an even tone, "The Princess Adana must not see her mother in this way—hidden in a closed room, separated from the sight she treasures."

Micah rose to his feet, exhaustion in his eyes.

The First Vision faced him, steadfast in her stiff posture. Her hawk-like gaze created unease in many who dealt with her. Micah did not appear fazed.

"Micah?" Chiora reached out, fingertips brushing her husband's hand. "Please."

With a resigned air, he took her hand in his and sank back to her side, gesturing for Montee to open the heavy fabrics closing out the sun.

When she pulled back the cumbersome cloth, Montee breathed a sigh of relief. Sunlight poured into the room, revealing a spacious chamber furnished in sparse elegance. As in most Monian buildings, the walls were made of a thick mixture of sand and desert rock, giving buildings warmth in the short, rainy season and coolness in the hot, arid climate of the land. The opening led to a courtyard with a sparkling fountain. The air in the chamber lay still, but the thick cloud of incense burned by the Teachers of the Faith dissipated some.

Chiora struggled to sit up in her chaise and face the light. After a few shallow breaths, she fell back against the pillows and turned her gaze on Montee. "My daughter?"

Montee stepped forward. "Your Majesty, your daughter passed her trial today. You should be proud."

Chiora grimaced a small smile of pride before closing her eyes. "Bring to me."

"Yes, Your Majesty." She bowed then gestured for Kassa to follow her from the chamber. Montee pulled the doorway curtain aside and allowed the senior Watcher to proceed her into the corridor.

"The alert?" Kassa asked in hushed tones as soon as they stood alone in the corridor.

"An attack on a village near the southern border. Possibly Maligon."

Kassa's mouth compressed into a thin, straight line. "Who did you send?"

"Joannu," Montee said, and hesitated before adding, "and Halar."

Kassa turned her gaze southward.

Halar, Kassa's husband, was expendable as second in command of the Soldiers of the First Sight, but Montee regretted the necessity of sending him at a time when Kassa might need his comforting presence. Linus, her own source of comfort, and the commander of the First Soldiers, remained in the fortress like her, awaiting the shift in power for the kingdom.

"Samantha?" Kassa voiced the name of her only daughter, also a high-ranking Watcher.

"She waits," Montee said, seeing no reason to share that Samantha argued about the decision.

"Very well. Bring Adana. We have little time." Kassa ducked back through the curtained entry of the queen's rooms.

Montee headed toward Adana's chambers. She chose not to tell Kassa of the strange trance the princess experienced in the archery field or that she'd claimed to see Maligon. The girl was too young for visions, but a spark of hope ignited wonder within the warrior. Maybe the Creator gave her visions early to prepare her for what was to come.

At least the time of secrecy would end. Today, the queen would die.

The weight of Montee's dark braid swayed across her back, beating time to her steps as she considered how others would respond to the news.

* * *

Adana was not in her chambers. Montee rushed across the Great Hall, frustration pounding in the echoes of her footfalls. Where might the princess go? She turned into the Watchers' wing and pulled up short, as Samantha almost collided with her.

Samantha jumped backward, a look of anticipation flashing across her face.

"The queen calls for the heir," Montee said. "Have you seen her?"

Samantha shook her head, and excitement sparked in her eyes. "Should I go up to witness?"

"Yes, but first summon the Watch. It's time." Montee hurried away, disturbed by the look in Samantha's eyes. As the closest of friends, they often chose to relax their Watchers' composure and reveal their thoughts to each other, but that brief glimpse of emotion hinted at joy over this sad news.

She checked the temple where Adana often spent many hours beseeching the Creator for her mother's health, but for once, the princess wasn't there. Nor was she in the paddock, the archery field, or Watchers' quarters. Mind racing with concern, Montee went in search of Linus. Unable to lead his troops, he would be in the south tower, watching the horizon for news. Maybe, he or the tower guards had seen Adana.

As she approached the tower, the sight of Linus scanning the distance through a looking tube released some of the tension in Montee's shoulders. The burly, square-bodied man turned toward her as she ran up the steps. He rubbed a hand over his bald head and gave her a sad smile. "How is she?"

Montee shook her head. "Not well." She glanced around at the two soldiers and the single Watcher in the tower. "I can't find Princess Adana. I asked a Watcher to accompany her to her chambers, but they're both missing."

"Blazes." Linus ran his hand through the red-brown beard trimming his chin. "Sound an alarm if she's spotted," he said to the soldiers, then rushed to descend the steps to the yard below.

Montee followed, matching him stride for stride. In the midst of her worries, an awareness hit her. Linus would soon know of her prophetic vision of the queen's death. It would be a relief to have it told.

* * * * *

Chapter Four

Adana saddled her horse and paused to pull the hood of the heavy cape over her head. She peered into the stable yard to ensure no one lurked there, then ventured into the open. The cloak wrapped her in suffocating heat, a discomfort she embraced if it meant saving her mother.

Near the western gate, she mounted the horse. Just a little farther, and it would be too late for anyone to stop her.

"Exciting, isn't it?"

The voice caught her by surprise, and Adana jerked around to stare into the brown eyes of Glume, the giraffe keeper. Suru, her Watcher escort, followed him. The quiet and hefty older man bobbed his head in deference to her rank, but a frown creased his broad forehead. "M'lady, now isn't the time for a ride outside the gates."

Adana sagged in frustration and rolled her head back on her neck. "I need to, Glume. I must stop Maligon."

"No. Not yet." The man shook his head.

Suru studied her with curiosity, the unhidden emotion a clue to her low rank. A more advanced Watcher would study Adana discreetly. It would be hard to detect the interest.

At that moment, Montee and Linus rounded the corner.

Adana sagged in the saddle and shoved the cape off her shoulders. So close. What would they do if she kicked the horse into a gallop?

Montee quickened her step to grab the horse's bridle.

How did this Watcher always know her thoughts?

"Where are you going?" Montee asked. "The queen summons you."

Adana glanced toward the gates. Could she make it?

Montee tightened her hold on the bridle.

Could she convince Montee to ride out with her? They could stop Maligon, please the Creator, and save her mother. She opened her mouth to suggest it, but one look at Montee's firm composure told her the truth. Montee would never agree. Hope drained out of her heart as she slid from the horse and handed the reins and cloak to Glume. The man clucked at the animal, and he and Suru led the horse away.

Montee waited until they were gone. "I shouldn't have left you with an inexperienced Watcher." She bowed her head in brief apology. "Where were you going?"

Adana considered responding but didn't know how to explain. Where would she start? The giraffe's odd journey? The sight of Maligon? The fear of her mother's illness? None of it mattered. Montee would never understand the compulsion to go after Maligon in order to heal her mother. Driven by her fears, not training, the idea lacked logic.

A sudden frenzy of emotion throbbed along her connection with Am'brosia. Adana opened the bond. A tumult of misery spilled into her soul. She fought the urge to cry out in despair, and, without a word, ran toward the paddock.

Behind her, she heard Montee say, "Inform the First Vision that we come, soon."

Relief filled her heart. At least, Montee allowed her this act of defiance.

When she passed through the high sandstone archway of the paddock, Adana faltered. Ju'latti, lay on the ground, sides heaving. Her father's powerful giraffe hovered over her, nuzzling the ill giraffe with his nose. Glume appeared at Adana's side. He patted her hand then attempted to approach Ju'latti, but Va'lent kicked out with his large hooves, keeping the man away.

Swallowing grief, Adana turned away from her parents' giraffes and climbed up and sat on the fence of Am'brosia's enclosure. The giraffe shone golden in the sunlight, the spots along her long neck creating a mottled pattern. With graceful steps, she glided toward Adana. This animal, powerful enough to kill a man with one swift kick of her plate-sized hooves, radiated a gentle comfort as the two drew closer in mind and body.

The gentle beast's shadow covered Adana, and she remained in it for several moments.

Am'brosia's large eyes brimmed with tears, and Glume, cradling a small vial in his hands, crept toward her with the caution of a man approaching a skittish colt. The vial contained giraffe tears, specifically Ju'latti's. The scarce fluid held the secret to her family's connection to the animals, a gift given in appreciation for their protection at a time of near extinction.

Glume cupped the vial under Am'brosia's brimming eyes. The animal blinked and tilted her head, as if she understood Glume's need. Tightness squeezed Adana's chest. Later the mixture would enhance her bond to Am'brosia and awaken her gifts from the Creator to the level a ruler would need, not the needs of a daughter but of a queen.

Adana turned away from Glume's task and leaned her forehead on Am'brosia's large flank.

After some time, she heard Glume walk away and felt a mental nudge from Am'brosia. *Go.*

If only Glume hadn't stopped her from seeking out the enemy and destroying the horrible Maligon. The Creator's blessing for such a daring task of faith most certainly would be her mother's health. And Serrin's. And time.

She needed time. The Creator could give it if she sought guidance in the temple.

* * *

Adana's evident struggle made Montee's mouth go dry. The day she dreaded more than anything had come. The prophetic vision, *her* vision, played out in harsh reality. The prophecy had come to her in a dream, warning of illness and death for many including Queen Chiora and Adana's betrothed, Prince Serrin of Elwar. It left no room for other interpretation. She, Kassa, and Chiora recognized the warning—Adana and Am'brosia would lose their mothers and their prospective mates too soon. Today.

How would Adana react to the rest of the vision? The part that threatened her life. The part that moved the queen to write a decree of protection sending Adana to Elwar until she turned eighteen and could sit on the Seat of Authority as queen.

Montee turned at the sound of Adana's approach.

"Come," the young girl said and walked toward the gate.

"Of course, we must hurry." Montee fell into step, relieved that the princess appeared ready to go to her mother.

Adana shook her head. "The Creator will give us time."

Heart heavy, Montee followed her through the deserted Watchers' wing. When they entered The Great Hall, Adana's steps faltered. The remaining squads of the all-female guard of Watchers stood in ordered ranks—a death watch for the queen. Although close to five thousand waited there, stillness reigned. As Adana marched forward, they parted in a wave, bowing like stalks of wheat as she passed. The only defect in this ripple occurred when Adana veered in an unexpected direction toward the temple instead of the queen's chambers.

Withholding more objections, Montee hoped the Creator might guide the girl toward her mother.

The aroma of incense permeated the wide corridor leading to the Temple, becoming stronger as they entered the round receiving room and climbed the stairs to the sanctuary. At the top, Adana turned to Montee. "Wait here."

As she approached the altar, Princess Adana looked older than her fifteen years, her tawny-colored braid falling between strong, determined shoulders. Montee sent a prayer of thanksgiving to the Creator for Adana's strong faith, a quality important to the duties of Moniah's Seat of Authority. She would need this faith.

Adana knelt and bowed her head. A Teacher of the Faith glided over to her and knelt. Their heads bowed low for several moments. Then, Adana rose and returned to Montee, confidence curving her young mouth. "All will be well. They will not die." Adana's eyes shone bright. "I know the Creator hears my pleas."

Montee said nothing. She knew the Creator's answer this time would be no.

* * * * *

Chapter Five

Sunlight drenched the corridor outside Queen Chiora's chamber. Several Teachers of the Faith knelt before the entry curtains, their green ceremonial robes clouding the floor. Adana slowed her steps. The confidence she gained in the temple faltered at the droning sound of their prayers of departure, the dirge resounding throughout the hallway. "Release, release, protect, accept, release."

Commander Linus stood behind them. He bowed toward Adana. When he straightened, his gaze lingered on her face. She blinked in surprise at the compassion reflected there. Had he forgotten her failed attempt to flee?

Six high-ranking Watchers flanked the entryway. They stood alert, eyes focused in the distance even though walls blocked their sight. Each wore the brushed leather tunic and leggings of a Watcher, a giraffe standing in a field of green grass embroidered on their shoulders, the emblem of their rank. One of these women would become her primary advisor, the First Vision. Her stomach churned as her gaze fell on Samantha, the harshest of the six. The lines around the warrior's eyes made her face harsh, not kind like Montee's. Many assumed the queen would choose Samantha as First Vision, allowing the title to follow the lineage from Kassa to her own daughter. Kassa's mother had served before her, so the assumption made sense. Adana breathed another prayer to the Creator as she swept through the curtain, trying to sweep her worry away with the action.

Mammetta reclined on her chaise, dark-brown hair unbraided and fanned out over the pillow in a riotous tumble. She turned toward Adana, her weakened green eyes seeking her daughter's gaze. Tightness squeezed Adana's chest, and she fought to breathe. The cloying stench of incense saturated everything.

Father Tonch knelt to one side of the chaise, his white robes ballooning around him. Her father rose from beside her mother as she approached. His mouth, normally jolly, turned down with sadness. The somber mood reflected in his eyes and squeezed the fist clenching Adana's heart.

A flush painted Queen Chiora's cheeks as she attempted a welcoming smile and extended her hand toward her only child. Adana rushed to the bedside and buried her face in her mother's arms, anxious for her touch, wishing the incense didn't cloud her mother's natural scent of lemon and mint.

Mammetta stroked her head, the pressure so light Adana wondered if she imagined it. The strength in her mother's hands, her countenance, her firm jaw, all gone. Their absence told her what she refused to believe. Mammetta was dying.

The chanting from the teachers on the other side of the curtain rose in volume, and Adana closed her eyes, wishing for a way to close out sound, too. She felt, more than saw, Linus and the Watchers file into the room.

The First Vision knelt beside the queen's chaise, her body warm beside Adana's. Adana peeked from below her eyelids and saw the older woman unwind the cord in her Watcher's braid.

A chill of fear ran down her neck as the other Watchers followed Kassa's lead and unbound their hair. Adana's heart pounded in fear and protest. Their unbound hair stated that they weren't at war with the queen's departing spirit.

Montee stepped forward to unwind Adana's braid, but she jerked away. "No." She clutched her mother's hand. "You will get well. I've prayed unceasingly." She turned toward Father Tonch. "Have I not? Tell her."

"Dear child, you have been most faithful in your prayers, but we must accept the Creator's plan."

"No, I—"

"Adana!" A short burst of energy surged in Queen Chiora's voice. "Unbind your braid." That was an order from the queen, not her mother.

Adana drew back, unable to defy the tone of command and tore at her hair until it spilled out of its confining braid. The cord lay tangled in her fingers, and she wove it around them, pulling it tight, reveling in the sensation of pain followed by numbness.

"Kassa, the scroll please." Mammetta's voice sounded quiet, but firm, giving Adana a moment of hope.

The First Vision approached the queen's trunk at the foot of the chaise. The chest, covered with intricate carvings of giraffes, was an artifact from the holdings of the first Monian queen. Kassa slipped the trunk's lock, her body blocking the secret access, and removed a scroll. She handed it to Father Tonch.

"Read it to them," Queen Chiora said.

Father Tonch's face remained impassive as he scanned the directive.

Adana straightened, holding her breath. None of the traditions mentioned a scroll. Could this be a healing ritual? She leaned forward, waiting in the interminable silence for the man to speak.

Tonch began to read:

"Due to infallible Watcher vision, the knowledge of my death has been foretold. The Princess Adana still requires several years of training before accepting the mantle of rulership, and Moniah still maintains its heightened security due to rumors of Maligon's survival and return. The kingdom lies at risk. For this reason, I lay down these decrees and my signature has been witnessed by the First Vision and by Montee, the Watcher who provided this foretelling."

Adana reran the words through her mind. Had she misheard? Her mother's death foretold? By Montee? The kingdom at risk? Rumors of Maligon?

Father Tonch paused and laid his hand on Queen Chiora's shoulder. He turned and studied each person in the room. As his brown-eyed gaze fell on her, Adana shook her head, fighting the tears choking her throat. It could not be. Her mother knew she was going to die and said nothing, did nothing to warn her? Montee spent days, weeks training her without a word?

"The Princess Adana must still embark on her planned journey to the kingdom of Elwar. The education and protection she will receive from King Donel and Queen Quilla will be of utmost importance. Since Queen Chiora will not be present to guide her in court protocol and politics, her stay in Elwar will be extended until her eighteenth birthday."

Adana gasped and grabbed her mother's hand. "Mammetta?" Tears welled in her eyes. "Please don't. I will suffocate there. I'll die."

Her mother turned toward her, sorrow naked and real in her gaze. She had chosen not to hide her grief as a Watcher was trained. Adana gulped and turned away, thinking of the dark spaces that made up Elwar's castle, its high walls surrounded by mountains and forests. How could she live without her mother? How could she survive Elwar, a place so closed in, so different from the open plains of Moniah?

With an unyielding will that had typified her reign, Queen Chiora tugged her daughter's arm until Adana turned back. The queen's gaze bore into her soul.

"You must." She struggled to turn toward her husband. "This must be." Spent, she sank further into the pillows. "Continue, Father."

"Prior to her departure, the Princess Adana must be raised to Phantom status in the Watchers and bonded by the Second Degree to the giraffe, Am'brosia. When the princess departs, Am'brosia must remain in Moniah. The giraffe's well-being will provide insight to Princess Adana's welfare while she is far from home."

Adana gasped and dropped her mother's hand. Her father stroked her hair and knelt beside her, but she felt the tension of his displeasure in the stiffness of his fingers.

The Second Order Bonding forced a stronger link, one that should help her find Am'brosia if separated in battle. Separation became stressful, painful with distance. They both would suffer. She felt a glimmer of awareness from her link to Am'brosia. The giraffe showed her Glume, earlier, collecting the tears. Even Am'brosia understood and accepted this plan.

Father Tonch continued to read the lengthy document while Adana sat frozen in shock. Mammetta would die. The face she knew so well lay before her, eyes closed, breaths drawn with slow, agonizing gasps. The worst had happened. The Creator had chosen to punish her. Take away all she loved—her mother, her father, Am'brosia, the Watchers. In the back of her mind, she overheard the decree designate her father as Moniah's regent, guided by the First Vision, until she returned at the age of eighteen.

Emptiness opened up inside her. A large gaping hole of nothing. How could she survive without her mother? Who would teach her essential Watcher skills and prepare her to lead the kingdom?

It had been years since she'd been to Elwar, and then only as a toddler when Queen Roassa died. Prince Serrin visited Moniah four years ago, and … Serrin. He had lost his mother, too.

She glanced at her mother struggling to breathe, her color fading. A cry stuck in her throat, and she stifled it, refusing to give in to the loss, yet.

Serrin would understand, he would know her pain. He was all she would have after today.

She grabbed her mother's hand and clung to it as she clung to the promises of her betrothed, Prince Serrin, her deliverance. If only the second son of Elwar knelt beside her now.

* * * * *

Chapter Six

Montee followed Father Tonch's gaze around the room after he finished reading the decree. The droop of Adana's head and the sag of Micah's shoulders stabbed her with guilt. The day she shared her dream with the queen, Kassa had stood by her side in support. The two women warned her, then, not to feel responsible. They assured her the Creator had chosen to give her the message because of her strength, not to cause her hardship.

Linus, lost in his own grief, didn't look up. The other waiting Watchers stood at alert, but the glint of tears shone in the eyes of four of them. Samantha did not cry. She glared at Montee, mouth pressed in a firm line. The queen's command of silence prevented her from sharing the prophecy with her closest friend. She had hoped for Samantha's understanding.

The rest of the witnesses stood in uncomfortable silence, the gurgling of the fountain in the courtyard beyond filling the silence. After several tense moments, Adana slid closer to the queen and laid her head on her mother's shoulder. "Mammetta."

Queen Chiora reached up and laid her palm along her daughter's cheek. "My little one." A tremor shook her hand, and it dropped to the chaise. "Micah?"

Falling back on her heels, Adana pulled away as her father moved to embrace his wife. The princess stared at them, her shoulders rising and falling with obvious effort to take calming breaths. Her hand fluttered toward her mother's arm, but she drew it back, a sign of doubt evident in her inability to keep still. After one large breath, the princess stood and turned away from her parents. She met no one's gaze as she walked out of the chamber, her hands reaching up to re-braid her hair.

Montee swallowed her own grief and turned to follow her, but Kassa placed a restraining hand on her arm. "Keep watch for the queen."

Micah kissed Queen Chiora's lips and held her hand to his heart. Tears streamed down his face. Montee dropped her gaze, embarrassed to witness this intimate moment.

Kassa nudged her, again. "Keep watch." She quietly commanded all of the Watchers to remain vigilant. Each woman straightened and focused on their dying queen.

Comforted by the presence of her sisters in sight, Montee looked back at the chaise and gasped. A golden mist hovered around Queen Chiora's body. She stared as golden droplets rose into the air. Their glow cast a beautiful light over the queen, and for a moment, the mist coalesced into the queen's face. The golden image smiled at Montee, and then, the face faded back into a haze of gold.

Kassa studied her. "Do you see it?"

Montee nodded, unwilling to take her gaze off the mist as it began to pulsate inches above Queen Chiora's body. She stared mesmerized, until she felt the First Vision's hand on her arm. "You've seen. Go to Adana."

She took one last look at the beautiful mist and hurried from the chamber. Behind her, Samantha whispered, "Seen what?"

The memory of the queen's golden spirit filled Montee with awe as she hurried along the corridor. Death, although something she didn't fear, seemed less threatening if the soul became so beautiful once released from the body. She felt joy for the queen's release from pain, while a heavy mantle of grief and guilt weighed her down. The two emotions didn't go together, but at this moment, they felt right.

She found Adana struggling to reach Ju'latti, but Va'lent still stood guard over the near-motionless animal. Each time Adana inched forward, the bull kicked out his lethal hooves and swung his long, muscular neck in deep arcs.

"Please, she must live." Adana's voice broke as she scurried back from Va'lent's threatening stance.

Dodging hooves and neck, Glume managed to pull the young girl away from danger. Tears poured down the keeper's face as Adana lurched out of his hold and ran toward Montee, who wrapped her in her arms, swaying to and fro like a mother soothing a small child.

In just a few breaths, Va'lent ceased his violent actions. He stretched his neck toward the body on the ground and nuzzled Ju'latti's still form. In a long sweep of his neck, he raised his head. An eerie bugling rose from the king's giraffe, its tone loud, grief-stricken, and haunting.

A golden mist shimmered above Ju'latti's body. It stretched tall and floated over the timber fence to Am'brosia. The younger giraffe straightened and tilted her head upward, her nose reaching toward the sky. The mist twinkled around Am'brosia and then spiraled away until it disappeared against the sunlight.

Montee squinted into the brightness. Quiet descended. She hugged Adana closer. "It's over."

Adana stilled.

She turned to face the paddock. A cry choked from her at the sight of the giraffe's still body on the ground, and she began gulping in deep breaths, muted whimpers intermixed with each inhalation. After a dozen breaths, a weak Watcher's calm sustained the girl. With slow steps, she approached Bai'dish's enclosure.

Montee braced for the inevitable, unable to turn and witness this second death. The vision promised the Elwarian prince's death, so Bai'dish would die. If he hadn't already.

"Montee!" Adana's voice rang with relief not despair.

Montee turned and searched the yard, noting the impression in the grass where the animal had lain earlier. Where had the giraffe gone? Had he died and been removed?

A glance toward Am'brosia's pen revealed another empty space. Where had the giraffes gone?

"There!" Princess Adana climbed up the fence and pointed toward the trees along the edge of the field.

Moniah's fortress housed a small number of giraffes to protect them from extinction, an agreement made to the giraffes centuries ago when the first queen discovered her ability to bond with them. These giraffes gathered in a grove of acacia trees at the top of a hill within the walls of the fortress. The animals raised their noses toward the sky and echoed the haunting lament bugled by the king's giraffe. The sound raised the hairs on Montee's neck and arms as she searched the herd for Bai'dish or Am'brosia.

Glume pointed toward the trees. "There. The two of them. Underneath the branches."

One of the trees moved. Not a tree, Bai'dish, standing strong and steady. Am'brosia stood beside him.

"Look at the new little queen and her prince. Praise be!" Glume exclaimed at the sight. "Something good has happened this day." His gaze traveled back to the body of Ju'latti, and his voice dropped to a whisper. "We'll have new giraffes tonight."

"New giraffes?" Montee shook her head convinced she had misheard the quiet man. Around them, the giraffes' lament continued, carrying on the silent, still air as all living creatures turned toward the song.

Glume cast his serious brown-eyed gaze toward her. "Hear their song? The giraffes of the plains will come to pay homage. Some will stay and become part of our numbers. Others will return to the savanna. It's part of the promise." Glume leaned on the fence and gazed with wonder at the gathering giraffes. "Somehow they always know."

Adana slid off the fence and approached Montee, a weak smile on her face. "The giraffes cry for Ju'latti and mother. The Creator healed Serrin. I will not be alone in Elwar."

Montee nodded, her mind scrambling to understand. Overwhelmed by the poignant cries of the giraffes, she questioned her vision. Had they misinterpreted it? It seemed so clear at the time—images of the queen and her giraffe as the stem of a sunflower reaching toward the sky. Nearby, a strong, but young, sapling wore the prince's face. Bai'dish's image resonated in the leaves on the fresh branches. Around them, flowers and grasses bent in the wind. Without warning, the sunflower and tree wilted and sagged toward the ground. Several of the other flowers and grasses wilted with them, turning into dried, brown debris. An angry ox trampled the plants and tree under his feet. The tree's leaves scattered on a sudden breeze.

Princess Adana's voice interrupted Montee's thoughts. "Will you accompany me to Elwar? I will need someone to help me, to stay with me." The young princess' eyes were dry, but red-rimmed.

The sight of her pain clutched at Montee's heart. The request honored her. The queen's decree called for four Watchers to attend Adana while in Elwar. Could she withstand the claustrophobic world of Elwar to serve Moniah's heir? Maybe the Creator gave her the vision so she could aid the young queen.

Before she could reply, Kassa's voice sounded behind her. "No, child. Montee must remain here as First Vision. I will accompany you."

Montee turned and stared at Kassa. "First Vision? But Samantha?"

"The queen chose you. Only you saw."

"I saw?" Montee frowned. The mist was a sign? A declaration?

For the first time since her arrival as a twelve-year-old candidate, Montee felt a twinge of doubt. The First Vision held more power than anyone, save the queen. Queen Chiora had placed the kingdom's needs on her shoulders until Adana returned from Elwar.

From behind Kassa, Linus watched her, his face a mixture of pride and sorrow. Montee's heart thudded in her chest. As the commanders of Moniah's two military forces, their love could never be. It became forbidden in a momentary glimpse of the afterlife.

* * * * *

Chapter Seven

The Kingdom of Elwar

The room stank of sour bodies and infection. Prince Kiffen of Elwar slumped in a chair beside his brother Serrin's bed. He fought to keep his eyes open and alert, struggling against the same malady attacking his younger brother. Exhaustion overwhelmed him, but he refused to believe his body would succumb to the disease.

Serrin lay in the bed like a dying leaf, a shadow of his former exuberant self. The fair blond hair he inherited from their father stuck to his forehead in sweaty clumps. A high flush bloomed on his cheeks, evidence of his fever rising as the sun set in the distance.

Kiffen suppressed the urge to cough, unwilling for his father, who finally slept in the chair on the other side of the bed, to learn of his own illness. Clattering footsteps rang on the stone floor in the corridor, and his half-sister, Leera, raced through the door, her eyes bright with a thirteen-year-old's enthusiasm. She halted just inside the entry, her face losing its excitement as she studied their beloved brother, Serrin.

"Kiffen?" Her voice squeaked as she uttered his name.

Kiffen took a deep breath and pushed himself upright, hiding the weakness in his limbs. He beckoned, and she stumbled to his side, tears welling in her eyes.

"Will he die?"

"I don't know," Kiffen told her, unable to lie anymore. He stroked his hand through the soft flaxen curls framing her face.

Leera's lip trembled as she looked across the room at her father. The last few days had aged their portly parent. The king's exuberance, rare since Kiffen and Serrin's mother died fourteen years earlier, had faded even more.

"Is Papa sick, too?"

"What? No." Kiffen smoothed the ringlets that ran down her petite back. For him, death wasn't new, but to Leera, it invaded the castle like a stranger. "He's asleep."

Leera seemed mollified, but she crept away from Kiffen's side and poked her father's hand. King Donel snorted but didn't wake.

Kiffen's heart ached for this strange little sister produced by his stepmother. Leera had the misfortune of being born into a difficult time in Elwar's history. Her mother, Queen Quilla, did not endear herself to the people. Many thought Quilla a grasping opportunist, marrying the widowed king so soon after Queen Roassa's death.

Somehow, the kingdom had weathered the upheaval of their beloved queen's death. With the foresight typical of her reign, his mother declared her husband, a foreigner, as her successor, followed by Kiffen when the time came. Kiffen shook his head. The weight of the crown and Elwar's expectations dragged him down in ways he could not describe. His father's determined effort to hold onto the throne the first year after Queen Roassa's death only pushed Kiffen further into the hole that gaped before him as the future king.

What a difference birth order made. Serrin, as the second son, earned freedom and love through his betrothal to the young and lanky Princess Adana of Moniah. A few years earlier, Kiffen accompanied Serrin to Moniah and witnessed the two playing together, unaware of the fate life held for them. They radiated a joy that, even in his young years, Kiffen knew must be rare. He moved to his brother's bedside and rested his hand on Serrin's forehead. "Don't give in, Serrin. Moniah and Adana await you."

A slight frown appeared on Serrin's face.

Kiffen froze. "Serrin? Serrin?" He turned to Leera. "Fetch the apothecary."

Leera scurried to Serrin's side, the excitement lighting up her face.

"Hurry." Kiffen's voice turned sharp. "Go!"

The child's eyes flashed anger before she flounced from the room. Kiffen spared little thought to the behavior of his spoiled sister before he turned back to his brother. "Serrin?"

He took Serrin's cold and clammy hand, a contrast to the feverish heat in the boy's cheeks.

"Kiff." Serrin croaked the nickname in a light whisper. One of his fingers pressed against Kiffen's hand as if Serrin sought to squeeze it.

"I'm here, Serrin. You must get well."

Serrin shook his head, a slight motion on the pillow, and his eyes fluttered open, gazing unfocused at Kiffen. "No." His throat convulsed. "Adan…"

Kiffen leaned closer to his brother. "Yes. Adana. You must get well for Adana. And Moniah."

"Watch," Serrin whispered, his voice raspy. "Protect."

"Yes," Kiffen said. "You must protect her."

Serrin didn't respond. His hand slipped from Kiffen's grasp.

"Serrin?"

A shallow breath rattled in Serrin's chest.

Kiffen grabbed Serrin's hand again. "Serrin?"

"What? Is he awake?" King Donel started up from his chair.

His brother's next breath, delayed and agonizing, tortured Kiffen's soul.

"He spoke," Kiffen said, fighting tears. "He said he needed to protect Adana."

King Donel sank to his knees beside the bed, hope lighting his eyes. "He's improving. Look his color is high. He's not so pale."

Kiffen glanced at the flush of fever in his brother's face and watched Serrin's chest rise and fall. After a long pause, it rose and fell again. Then his body fell still. The next breath never came. Through a blur of tears, Kiffen watched the color seep from his brother's cheeks.

Leera rushed back into the room. "I found mother."

On Leera's heels, Queen Quilla entered, stiff, regal, and alert.

"Where is the apothecary?" Kiffen searched the empty doorway, aware it was too late.

Quilla pressed her lips together in a frown. "I thought it best I come. We can call for him if necessary."

The skin on Kiffen's arms turned cold. Quilla, once again, took control where she shouldn't.

His father rose from the bed. "Serrin spoke. I think he improves."

Quilla turned an impassive face toward Serrin. She blinked once, twice, and Kiffen saw a flicker of satisfaction cross her face. He glanced at his father, who still looked at his son with hope.

"Father," Kiffen whispered, "he's gone."

King Donel's head jerked up, and he stared at Kiffen in disbelief. Quilla slid in beside King Donel and caught his arm as he sagged against the bed. She smoothed graying hair off his forehead, murmuring comfort. She dabbed at her eyes, wiping away nonexistent tears.

* * * * *

Chapter Eight

Moniah

Adana stared at the cup Kassa held out to her. It held the tears of Am'brosia, collected in preparation for this day. Second order bonding. She and Am'brosia linked closer, a tight awareness of each other always. Her gaze drifted toward the window where servants and soldiers bustled about their duties, preparing for her departure. That tight awareness would stretch to the point of agony, soon.

"Why must I leave today?" She ignored the offered cup. "I want to be here tonight to present Mammetta to the four corners of the land."

The funeral frightened her, proof that Mammetta really had died, but the idea of missing it weighed heavy in her center where her focused breathing couldn't ease the pressure. She hadn't stopped Maligon, and now the Creator was punishing her for it. Maybe if she honored Mammetta's passing, the Creator might find pleasure in her again.

Kassa put the mug on the table and sat in the chair beside it. She looked up at Adana, her gaze compassionate. So accustomed to the stern visage of the woman, the look, though kind, still made Adana's skin prickle with unease.

"Adana, you know we must not wait. Your safety relies on a quick departure. If Maligon truly lives, we must send you to Elwar before he learns of our plans." Kassa pursed her lips in thought. "With the second order bonding, you will gain the ability to share and see through Am'brosia's eyes at any time you wish. She can share the funeral with you through your bond." The old Watcher picked up the mug and handed it to her. "If you wish."

Adana hesitated before accepting the mug. She had seen more than she expected through Am'brosia's eyes already. Did she want to watch the ceremony that way? No. She wanted her mother alive, this nightmare ended. She shuddered as she sipped the milky-colored substance. A bitter and sharp aftertaste coated her tongue. Holding the cup back out to Kassa. "It's salty and smells musky."

Kassa pushed Adana's hand and the cup back toward her. "You'll get used to it. Your mother said she didn't mind it so much after a while."

Adana sipped again and tried to swallow without the liquid touching her tongue. Bracing herself, she up-ended the mug and drained the viscous fluid. A prickle burned through her body and, without warning, her link with Am'brosia exploded to the forefront of her mind. The animal looked into her soul and wrapped her presence around the heavy weight in Adana's center. The pressure didn't go away, but the giraffe's embrace lightened it, gave her room to breathe.

After a few deep breaths, Adana sent an image of herself standing in the giraffe's shadow, leaning against her comforting flank. *Thank you.*

Unlike the first order bond, the second order didn't require her to be facing the outdoors to link with Am'brosia, but she wandered over to the window out of habit, anyway. In the courtyard below, Montee strode across the grounds, determination in her step. The purposefulness in the woman's stride and shoulders gave Adana a small sense of relief. Mammetta chose well. She turned back to Kassa. "Montee will make a good First Vision."

Kassa nodded. "I'm glad the queen's choice pleases you. You will have nothing to fear with Montee in charge while you're away. And, of course, your father and Linus will be here to aid her."

Her father. Where was he? She hadn't seen him since that moment by her mother's bed. She studied the courtyard, hoping to see his reassuring bulk, but he wasn't there.

Several Watchers slipped through the bustle of activity and headed for the barracks, their purposeful strides matching Montee's. "Something's happening," Adana said turning to find Kassa beside her, gaze intent on the Watchers, too.

"Yes, my lady, there might be news from the troops we sent yesterday." The woman turned and took a step toward the corridor but stopped. For a moment, Adana noticed the older woman's shoulders go slack, then Kassa turned to face her. "I'm confident the First Vision will alert us if it's of importance."

Awareness dawned on Adana. "They won't report to you, anymore, will they?"

Kassa shook her head. "No child. That time is over."

"Does it bother you?"

Kassa tilted her head and regarded Adana with a hawk-like stare—a curious hawk, not a predatory one. She might not be First Vision, but her behavior would always be seeking information from those around her.

"Old habits die hard," the older woman finally said. "I will accompany you and start a new role in life." She laid a hand on Adana's arm. "We will help each other see among the walls of Elwar."

The walls of Elwar. Just the thought increased the weight in Adana's chest. She tried to imagine the closed-in quarters of the castle. Despite the rising heat of the day, an icy chill crept over her. The idea of high walls as protection rather than the Creator's gift of sight baffled her. But those very walls were her mother's reason in sending her to Elwar. Protection of a different kind. How did the people in Elwar survive?

The curtain of Adana's room swished aside, and Montee walked through. She bowed, then straightened, her gaze on Adana, eyes flashing between worry and compassion before settling on compassion.

Adana straightened. Watchers, especially ones as skilled as Montee, didn't show their emotions unless they felt it necessary, or sometimes out of respect or honor. She'd seen too many Watchers drop their masks in the past days.

"What is it, Montee?" Her voice quivered. A flood of well-being washed through the link from Am'brosia and massaged the burden in Adana's chest. "Have the troops returned? Was it Maligon?"

Montee glanced at Kassa and shook her head before turning back to Adana. "We've received a message from Elwar."

Hope leaped in Adana's heart, releasing the weight in a flash. Maybe they would decline her mother's decree, refuse her extended visit.

"I'm sorry, Adana. There is no easy way to tell you, but—" Montee paused and turned toward Kassa. "The vision was true. Maybe you should explain."

"I see." Kassa paused. She faced Adana, her shoulders held back. "My lady, Montee's vision prophesied of two illnesses. The other in Elwar, and ending with the same result."

Adana glanced between the women. She shivered again despite the sweltering heat of the day. Am'brosia tucked a cushiony swirl of security around Adana. "What has happened?

"If I understand correctly, Montee has received news of the prophecy's fulfillment."

Montee took Adana's hands and looked into her eyes. "Prince Serrin has died."

The cry refused to come to her lips. She stood, her mouth moving but nothing to say. Those awful words echoed around the room, and the dissipating stench of incense invaded the few safe corners of her mind.

Adana grasped for the link with Am'brosia. If Serrin died, it meant his giraffe, Bai'dish would die. The bond wouldn't allow any different outcome. She sent an image of Bai'dish to Am'brosia. The image returned to her showed Bai'dish, healthy, but facing northward, toward Elwar.

"Bai'dish is alive?" She whispered the question but knew it to be true. "How?"

"He lives." Montee frowned, a look of concern on her face. "We don't understand why."

* * *

Just before noon, Adana stood in the outer perimeter of the fortress, waiting to mount her horse and ride away from her life. She opened her senses to everything around her, absorbing the warmth of the white heat, the images of the sandstone walls reflecting the sun, and the tanned leathers of the Watchers as they went about their business. She wanted to be sure to recall all of this when the high walls of Elwar closed her inside. No longer could she hope for any peace or comfort in Elwar. Serrin's death left her more alone than ever, and the weight in her center pressed down harder than it had when she arose this morning. She tilted her head up, toward the unrelenting sky, aware that the Creator still punished her for her failure to seek out Maligon and kill him.

When she looked back down, sun glinted off the golden armor of the Soldiers of the First Sight, and she blinked a moment until things came back into focus. Around her, Watchers, soldiers, and servants secured items to horses and wagons, checked inventory, and said their good-byes. A few people glanced her way but kept their distance.

Where was Papa? She turned full circle, searching for his graying blond head above the crowd. Would he let her leave without a good-bye?

Through the throng, Montee headed in her direction. The Watcher stopped before her, face set with stoic control. "Do not fear, Princess Adana. I will ensure nothing happens to your kingdom in your absence."

Adana studied her, uncomfortable in the shift in their roles. Just the day before, Montee directed her in training. Now this teacher represented Adana in all Moniah's interests. She stood for Moniah until Adana took the Seat. "Have we heard from the troops sent out yesterday?"

"Yes, my lady." A flash of concern blinked in Montee's eyes. Adana almost missed the quick change in the woman's face, her Watcher's control was so strong. "Didn't your father, the king, tell you?"

Adana fought to maintain the same composure as her teacher and mask her thoughts of betrayal. "No. I haven't spoken to my father since Mammetta died." The words, spoken aloud for the first time, sliced through her.

Montee stared at her for a moment, then turned and searched the crowd. "I thought he was here. I will find him for you." She turned to Adana, again. "Your troops report that the villagers didn't see anyone matching Maligon's description."

Which was more disturbing? That no one saw Maligon or that Montee said 'your troops?' Ignoring that thought, she asked, "What about the attack?"

"Marauders overwhelmed the village at sunrise and took food stores. The troops have remained to help them clean up."

"And the giraffe? Was he found? Is he well?"

"No sign of an injured giraffe, yet. We sent our best tracker, Kalara, to search the vicinity for the giraffe and the marauders. She still searches, but a sandstorm covered the tracks."

"Kalara?" Adana couldn't place the Watcher, but there were close to ten thousand women in the ranks. "Is she skilled at tracking after a sandstorm?"

Montee nodded. "She grew up in the desert. If anyone can trace them, it's Kalara's squad."

One last worry burned in Adana's mind. The prophecy indicated danger, and every story she'd ever heard of the traitor said danger followed him. "If it is Maligon, what will you do?"

The First Vision's gaze bore into Adana's. "The traitor won't take Moniah. I promise you." She gave a formal bow and struck her right fist across her chest. The salute surprised Adana, but she honored it with a deep nod of her head. Montee didn't have to place such conviction on her words. Her skills as a Watcher and leader were well known to all. There was no one Adana trusted more.

"My lady, if that is all, I will find your father for you." Montee glanced around, then went in search of King Micah.

"You will want this."

Adana jumped at the gentle sound of Glume's voice behind her. The man handed her a small, leather vial.

"What is it?" She hefted it in her palm, surprised at its weight.

The man leaned in close. Adana strained to hear his response. Glume always made her feel safe, but his ways were strange.

"I can't tell you where this comes from, but this vial holds tiny crystals. They will help with the pain of the bond separation. Pinch two or three grains into your water and drink it when the discomfort becomes unbearable. Only then, never before." He nodded at her, turned and walked away, but stopped and turned back, causing one of the Soldiers of the First Sight to swear and pull up short rather than run the round man down. "Never take it more than once in three days, m'lady. It's very powerful."

Adana stared after him. Crystals to help with the pain? What were they? She opened the vial and studied the tiny white stones. They resembled salt, but as she studied them, sunlight revealed pale pink ripples of color within the crystals. She stuck the stopper back in and gave it an extra push to ensure it didn't come loose. Hopefully, the crystals would work. Nine seasons was a long time.

The crowd began to part, people stepping back, their heads bowed in reverence. Her father marched through the throng and stopped before her. Relief washed through her at the sight of him, and she looked up into his eyes. Blue, like hers. This was the most obvious trait he shared with her, and it set them apart from other Monians. His posture lacked its usual vigor, his eyes their shining humor. She'd never seen the weight of time on her father's face before. In spite of his sad state, her heart lifted.

"Papa." She threw her arms around his middle and felt him hesitate before wrapping her in a tight embrace.

His lips brushed the part at the top of her head. "Little one," he whispered. "If I could change this I would. Donel is my closest friend. He will keep you safe. He is a good man." He hugged her again and, without another word, turned and hurried away.

Loneliness washed over Adana. Her father's retreating back told her something she feared already. When she lost her mother, she lost her father, too.

"Time to mount up, princess." A young soldier appeared beside her, a pleasant grin on his face. He laced his fingers together and bent over before her. "I can offer assistance."

Adana scowled at the man. If her parents had left her, she needed to take care of herself. Ignoring his offer, she hauled herself into the saddle. She looked down on him, her eyebrows raised in unspoken challenge.

"My apologies, my lady. Of course, you don't need my assistance." He nodded and walked away, his brushed golden armor reflecting the sunlight. She watched as he positioned his horned helmet on his head and mounted his own horse.

The crowd backed away as the train of horses and wagons began to move forward. All too soon, she rode through the massive gates on the northern side of the fortress. Am'brosia's mind embraced her in a sad farewell, the emotions welling through the link. As they rode down the steep incline that protected her home from invaders, Adana turned and looked over her shoulder at Chiora's View. No, she corrected herself, it was now called Adana's View, named after her as the current ruler, even if in name only.

The high sandstone walls shone white in the noon sun. The air shimmered with the thick heat. At each tower along the walls, black flags bearing the golden giraffe hung limp in the still air. Hundreds of Watchers lined the ramparts, their vigilant gazes on the horizon, a reminder of their ever-watchful role. The sight comforted her, and she closed her eyes to burn the image into her memory.

At the bottom of the incline, the plains stretched out before them leading to the northern hills. Adana pulled on her mount's reins and halted. She turned back to the walls and lifted her right hand in farewell.

A cheer rose up from the walls. It didn't dissipate until she was far from their hearing.

Moniah now lived in her memory.

* * * * *

Chapter Nine

Near the Desert

"The queen is dead." The Watcher who delivered the news to Maligon stood in the doorway of his small cottage. A fire burned in the large fire pit in the center of the room. It cast flickering shadows over the woman's face, her dark-brown hair catching the light with streaks of red. Maligon couldn't help but recall how firelight used to do the same in Chiora's hair.

This young Watcher, Kalara, was his prize, his wonderful find in the desolate land of exile. When she found the donkey with Maligon strapped to its back, parched and barely breathing, she soothed the animal and gave it water from her cask. Her sweet, childlike voice comforted Maligon, urging him to relax while gentle hands eased him off of the beast and a knife sliced through his bindings and cut away enough of the oxen head so he could breathe.

The rank carcass removed, he had squinted in the bright sun. Before him sat the vision of an angel, an aureole of light surrounding her. He had rubbed his eyes in disbelief. The child resembled a young Chiora. From then on, every time she entered his presence, he looked for that similarity, comforted by the familiar. He often wondered if he would have recognized her Watcher's gifts at such a young age if it hadn't been for Kalara's coloring, so similar to the queen's. Those gifts allowed him to infiltrate Chiora's court again, but in those years before she joined the Watcher trainees, she never left his side.

The news of Chiora's death hurt more than he had expected. Could he still feel something for her so many years later? Maligon stared into the fire, his thoughts meandering through the past. At fifty, he was old by fighting standards, past the vigor of life, but excitement raced in his veins. He ran a scarred and emaciated hand through his hair. The dark locks still fought off the gray of advanced years, even though his face, lined and weathered, labeled him a much older man. At one time, he had been found handsome by the ladies, at least most of them. But the ones who truly mattered never succumbed to his charms and turned to filthy foreigners instead. Now his daughter brought news of one of those women. Could Chiora really be gone?

Maligon beckoned to Kalara. "Come closer."

She knelt before him, and he reached out and ran his long fingers through the tight curls of her hair. Today, more than ever before, she reminded him of Chiora at that age, as if the queen's soul had found rest within his adopted daughter. Maligon paused, his hand entwined in Kalara's hair, unbound as he commanded her to wear it whenever in his presence, a reminder that this Watcher never fought his plans.

He sighed. "Welcome home, child of my heart."

The young woman rose and hugged him hard. When she pulled away, he saw tears in her eyes.

"Are those tears of mourning, Kalara?" Maligon said. "Or joy because the time draws closer?"

She sat on the raised hearth and, from her seated position, met him eye-to-eye, her unusual height an essential characteristic of a Watcher and a sign of maturity.

Where had the time gone? His exile felt like an eternity, but his life as Kalara's father had flown by.

"Father, I weep for Queen Chiora." She wiped at the tears in her eyes. "And for you. Is that wrong? The queen was always honorable and courageous."

Maligon understood. As his childhood friend, Chiora always remained fair in disputes. The first time her judgment sided with him, he fell in love with her. When moments later, she led their band of friends into the off-limit depths of Moniah's dungeons, he loved her even more. Some nights he dreamed that she sided with him on that last day. The two of them sending Micah into the desert under the oxen head. But he always awoke. Now, Chiora waited for him in death, may it be a long time in coming.

He clasped Kalara's hands between his. "Now you understand some of why she captured my heart for all eternity. That is why our plans must succeed. To honor her memory." For a few moments, Maligon bowed his head and stared at their entwined hands. Anyone interrupting this scene, he mused, would think they were praying. They would be wrong.

With a sigh, he sat back. "You have other news?"

He listened to the elaborate plans that Chiora, and no doubt Kassa, had devised to place Adana safely on the throne. Although the young heir's lengthy excursion to Elwar altered his schemes, he could not help but feel pride in Chiora's ability to surprise him.

"So Micah is the regent for now." The words tasted foul in his mouth.

He pondered this and the opportunity presented by Adana's departure for Elwar. "When does Adana depart?"

Kalara bowed her head again. "I fear she already has. The day after Chiora died." She looked up at him, an apology in her eyes. "I was sent with the troops to the village you attacked, or I would have come sooner."

Maligon smiled at the irony of his own daughter tracking his little band of thugs. "No one, of course, followed you here?"

"A sandstorm erased your tracks. I sent the others back and said I would stay another day to look for signs."

So clever she was. Maligon cogitated on the situation a little longer. "And the new First Vision?"

Kalara's head snapped up, disgust crossing her face. "Montee."

"Montee?" A shiver of surprise and excitement trickled down his spine. "Not Samantha? Very clever, Chiora, very clever."

"Montee saw something." Kalara shifted uneasily. "No one knows what, but Samantha did not see it. The old ones say the First Vision must see. They agree with the decision."

"Interesting." Maligon rose, walked to a small table, and struggled to pour himself a glass of wine. What had Montee seen? Not the sight greeting him every day, the sight of his damaged hand and arm. Micah would pay for this and other indignities. But it seemed he was not the only one usurped by the man. Samantha would have been a fourth generation First Vision. Was she angry, humiliated, ashamed?

"How many Watchers stand with us?"

"Twenty-three."

"Do they support Samantha as First Vision?"

"Of course. It's in her blood to be First Vision. But father, she wasn't chosen."

Maligon smiled and waved her objection away. "Have you recruited Samantha?" His question casual, he sipped the wine, waiting in anticipation as the dry vintage tingled on his tongue.

Kalara's eyes widened in astonishment. "She's the First Vision's daughter. To do so would be dangerous."

"Not anymore. Montee took her birth right." He swallowed another mouthful of wine, enjoying its fruit and woodsy essence. "How did Samantha react to the news?"

Kalara's mouth twisted in thought. "Harsher than normal. Even other Watchers avoid her, now."

"Chiora's decree gives us time." He poured another glass of wine and handed it to Kalara. "She can help our cause. Let's drink to your newest recruit."

Kalara took the glass and sipped, her eyes focused on Maligon.

"Something troubles you?" He put his glass down and paced to the fire.

"Forgive me, Father, but shouldn't we act now? With Adana gone? Adana's View stands without its Seat of Authority."

The smile that stretched across his face felt superior. "My daughter, you don't yet see it, do you?"

He approached her, his arms spread wide. "I could strike at any time. Even now, if I choose. But timing. Timing is important. Micah must know, without a doubt, that I have beaten him."

"Surely, he will."

Maligon nodded and sipped his wine again, letting the liquid roll across his tongue in ripples of pleasure. He swirled the deep red liquid in his goblet a moment. "Yes. He would suspect. They whisper my name in connection with the attack?"

"Of course. You are hard to hide." She glanced at his shrunken hand and arm before whisking her gaze elsewhere.

"Good." Wine splashed on the table as he slammed the goblet down. "I want Chiora's daughter on the throne, my child. I wouldn't take that from her."

Kalara frowned. "I know that's what you say, but I always thought—"

"What did you think, daughter?" He advanced on her, his tone turning cold and sharp. She no longer backed away like the child of old. Good. She needed spirit.

"That you would kill her some day."

He sighed. "I hope not. She will take the Seat." He turned and smiled at his daughter again. "But she won't rule. I'll rule through her. Moniah will be ruled as Chiora wished. She discussed it with me many times. A foreigner like Micah will never honor her visions, and Adana carries half of his foreign blood. The people will appreciate a true son of Moniah at her side. "What do you know of her betrothed? The brat, Serrin?" Maligon didn't try to hide the sneer in his voice at the idea of two half-breeds ruling Moniah.

"A messenger arrived at the village before I left. He died, too."

Maligon clapped his hands together in glee. "Excellent. One less worry. Now we need to find our child queen a suitable husband."

The way Kalara stared into the fire, he knew she still had concerns, but he waited. In time, she would voice them. Meanwhile, he stared at her sun-bronzed skin glowing in the firelight. She stood so tall. He wondered, again, at her parentage. Her memory of her life before her parents' death was scattered and hazy. No doubt they died in his first effort to gain the Seat. People must die, sometimes, to aid a cause.

"Father?"

"Yes, my child?" He smiled at her, satisfied in his place in her life.

"Shouldn't we attack Adana's caravan? Maybe nothing large, just something to keep the worry in their blood? More of a warning than a true attack."

The idea held a certain appeal to him, but he couldn't risk too many men, yet. His forces, although loyal, still were small and poorly trained.

"What about the forest?" Kalara said as if she read his doubt. "Send some snipers in to pick off a few soldiers."

"Or Watchers?" Maligon said.

Kalara blinked at him in surprise. "Soldiers are easier to target. You know they will send some of the best Watchers to protect her."

"True, true. But we must attempt to strike at the Watchers. If we succeed, the Watchers and Adana will learn they are not invincible. If we strike at a Watcher, they will learn fear."

Kalara nodded and stared back into the fire. Maligon allowed her a few moments. "Do you wish to protect your sisters in the Watchers? Is that your concern?"

She jerked her head up. "Only those true to our cause are my sisters. None of them accompany the heir."

"Good. Then I will arrange for a small attack. Come now. Let's dine. We have much to celebrate my lovely daughter."

* * * * *

Chapter Ten

The Journey to Elwar

Five days into the journey, the forest loomed before Adana's caravan. Tall, massive trees lined the horizon as far as the eye could see. The air turned cooler, and a crisp smell tickled Adana's nose. She recognized it as the fresh, invigorating scent of the tree cones burned on Moniah's hearths during the short, rainy season.

Adana reined in her horse and studied the heavy woodland. Trees taller than the walls of Adana's View crowded in on each other. She tried to examine the landscape and discern the small details so important for a Watcher to maintain a safe lookout, but the complexity overwhelmed her. How could she recognize any change signaling danger in so much chaos?

Behind her, the prairies sank below the rolling hills. Clouds of dust rose above the horizon. This sign, evident to a Watcher's enhanced sight, signaled large herds of grazing animals roaming the prairie. She longed to wheel her horse around and gallop back into the flat lands, racing into the midst of a herd of wildebeest just to watch them scatter as far as she could see. Then she would keep galloping until she reached the place where her sight never failed her. Home.

As if in response to her desire, the horse beneath her stomped a foot and tossed his head. Kassa rode up beside her and nodded toward the forest. "Pick one point and study it."

When Adana looked at her in confusion, the woman pointed to the north, away from Moniah. "The forest. We must prepare to enter it. No Watcher can absorb all of the details. You pick a spot and learn it. Then you pick a second spot. No more than two spots. I will do the same. Each of us does this."

Adana returned her gaze to the stretch of forest. Her Watchers had fanned out in front of them forming a long line facing the edge of the woodland. Behind them, the Soldiers of the First Sight straightened in their saddles and their bodies tensed in vigilance. Men might not possess the gift of a Watcher's sight, but when a Watcher dropped into her focused breathing to access her stronger visual abilities, the soldiers stood guard. A Watcher's sight became so focused that something or someone from another direction could attack without their knowledge. Linus, the top commander of the soldiers, drummed this responsibility into his troops from the first day of training.

"I wondered how we managed with so much to see," Adana said.

"No one takes on the whole forest, my lady. We divide and share the task."

Adana nodded and forced herself to ignore the itch to turn toward home, again. "It's bigger than I remember."

The old Watcher swung her hawk-like gaze toward Adana. "I'm surprised you remember. You were not even two the last time you traveled this way."

And there it was. A reminder of her last, and only, trip to Elwar. The death of Serrin's mother, Queen Roassa. Although Serrin was three when his mother died, she felt sure that he would have understood her loss. He could have helped her mourn Mammetta and given her a reason to hope for the future. Sadness threatened to envelop her, and she pushed it down where Am'brosia's presence lurked at all times. Ever since she began drinking the giraffe's tears for bonding, the animal's presence relieved some of the deep numbness in her heart. Still, the farther she traveled from Moniah, the less Am'brosia helped and the more the link stretched like the tension in her bow just before she released an arrow.

Glume's crystals might help ease the pain, but she ignored the urge to use them yet, aware the necessity would increase as the distance between them grew. Focusing on the task at hand, learning the forest, might provide enough distraction for now. "What section should I study?"

Kassa pointed straight ahead. "There. We will enter through that gap in the trees. You should know that area best."

Even from this distance, Adana's Watcher vision discerned the narrow path in between the trees. Leaves danced in the breeze above it, and the ground, hard-packed from evident use, stood bare of foliage. She glanced sideways at Kassa, but the old Watcher conducted her own study of the forest, her face an intense frown of concentration. Adana studied each tree, each branch, fixing the image into her memory. Any slight shift in the shadows, odd twist of a leaf or the angle of a branch turned differently could warn of an enemy's presence. She must not miss anything.

It turned out Adana had plenty of time to learn her range. The caravan stopped a short distance from the forest for a mid-day meal and to rest the horses. Around her, soldiers and Watchers moved at a steady pace, their actions less fluid than normal. Many cast glances toward the forest, most with a frown of concern on their face, especially after an advance line of Watchers crossed into the tree line.

After the meal, everyone moved to their horses and advanced toward the forest. Adana recognized the similarity to battle preparation in the purposeful way each person approached the trees with confidence, displaying none of their earlier unease. Adana rode along the path and soon found herself under the canopy, ducking even though the lowest branches rose high above her. Dimness settled around them, and she shivered in the immediate loss of the sun's warmth. Small rays of light pushed through the heavy foliage only to evaporate as soon as they appeared. She pulled the folds of her cape around her, for once appreciative of its thick layer of covering.

About half of her Watchers, along with the Soldiers of the First Sight, maintained a tight, attentive boundary around her. The Watchers who entered the forest first wandered farther into the trees, their bodies moving in slow, fluid motions, each foot placed with precision and care.

Gloom settled over the caravan with each step Adana's horse took. She continued to study the line of trees around her, casting her sight deep in the shadows. The sense of being watched tickled at her neck, and she twisted around to find nothing unusual.

"All will be well, my lady." A young soldier rode up beside her, a smile on his clean-shaven face. "I've ridden through this forest many times."

It was the soldier who offered to help her mount her horse the day they rode out of Moniah. A flush of shame over her behavior at the time surged up her neck. She pulled the cape tighter in hopes of hiding the blush from his gaze.

"How many times have you been here?" she asked him.

He settled back in his saddle and glanced around, a look of peace and comfort on his face. "Quite a few. My father used to bring me hunting here."

"Hunting? How would you ever find game here, with all these trees hiding everything from sight?"

The man laughed. "It is good that you will spend some time in other surroundings, my lady. You may have a Watcher's sight, but Moniah makes it easy for you."

"Easy?" Adana snorted at his ignorance. "What's so easy about…" She had been going to flaunt her archery successes in his face, but the knowing look on his face cut her short. "Forgive me. I'm unaccustomed to the forest and my senses are on edge. I'm sure you meant no disrespect."

Satisfaction slithered down her spine when the soldier jerked his chin in a slight motion of surprise over her assessment. "No, my lady. I only sought to lend you some comfort." He dipped his head in a brief bow. "Forgive me if I overstepped."

Before she could respond, he reined his horse around and rejoined his men. Adana turned in the saddle and scrutinized him in the lines. "Some queen you'll make," Adana whispered to herself. He only meant to help, yet every time he offered, she had responded like Kassa reprimanding a new recruit.

Struggling to think of something appreciative to say, she sought to catch his gaze, but he surveyed the forest and didn't glance her way. She promised herself to seek him out and thank him for his concern when they made camp.

To her left, another line of First Soldiers marched, and she spoke to the one closest to her. "Officer?"

His head swiveled toward her, his eyes never losing the attentiveness of their surroundings. "Yes, my lady?"

She nodded toward the helpful soldier further back in the line. "Do you know that soldier? His name?"

The First Soldier glanced behind him and chuckled. "You mean Hunter?"

Adana tilted her head to the side. "Hunter? That's an odd name."

"Truth be told, it's not his name. It's how he's known though."

"And why would that be?" Adana stepped her horse closer to the soldier, intrigued. Nicknames weren't common in Moniah. The honor of one indicated great respect for the person

The soldier grinned. "Our squad eats well, no matter where we are, thanks to Hunter. He can find game where there is none and can single-handedly bring down large animals."

"Really?" Adana glanced back at the young man. He rode with less tension in his body, but his gaze never wandered from the forest. "What sort of animals?"

"Well, there are the common ones, antelope and hare. But once, on a scouting trip, he brought down a lion that had been tracking us. He was the only one who sensed the animal's presence. We ate lion meat for dinner that night."

Adana wrinkled her nose. "Lion meat? I've never tried it. Was it good?"

The soldier shrugged. "Don't recall the taste, just the thrill."

Adana looked over her shoulder at Hunter again. She did owe him an apology if he'd cared for her men so well. She would find him after they made camp and ask him to tell her about his hunting trips with his father in this forest.

* * * * *

Chapter Eleven

Early in the afternoon, Kassa called the caravan to a halt. "Darkness falls before the sun does in the forest."

Adana looked around the clearing. The path broadened enough to accommodate a small camp and fire, nothing as big as her caravan required. The soldiers and Watchers spread out, seeking space in the close gathering of trees.

After attending to her horse, Adana scanned the camp in search of Hunter. Soldiers not on guard duty gathered in small groups, either tending to horses or setting up camp. A third of her Watchers fanned out on the edges of the clearing focused on their scouting responsibilities. Everyone else settled in to make camp.

Adana wandered through the groups. Hunter was nowhere in sight. She stopped the soldier who had answered her questions earlier. "Where is Hunter? I wanted to speak with him."

The soldier grinned. "My lady Adana, you will soon see the proof of my story. We're in for a good meal tonight. He spotted boar signs and took a small hunting party to flush him out."

Adana's mouth watered at the thought of fresh meat after days of bread and dried fruit. "I will be pleased if he succeeds."

A loud bark of laughter erupted from the soldier. "Then be prepared to be pleased. I've never known him to not bring back spoils."

Curious to learn how a man like Hunter could track anything in the darkness of the forest, Adana glanced around for any signs of his departure or clues to a boar's presence. Perplexed, she studied the edges of their group but couldn't detect the hunting party's path.

She turned back to the soldier. "Which way did they go?" Normally, she would have continued to pursue her search for clues, but the confines of the forest left her muddled and disoriented.

The soldier bent to tend to his pack and nodded to the right of the path. "That way."

Adana took one step in that direction and peered through the trees.

"I wouldn't assume he'll come back through there. A boar can lead a merry chase." The soldier hefted an ax to his shoulder. "Forgive me, Your Highness, but I must get firewood."

Adana stepped out of his way and turned to peer again into the woods. She glanced around, checking the layout of the camp. Kassa stood at an angle to her, able to detect her movements out of the corner of her eye. Adana meandered back toward her horse, nodding to soldiers as she went. When the older Watcher's back bent to clean the hooves of a horse, Adana scooted over to their belongings and retrieved her bow and quiver. She glanced around again. Kassa still cleaned the dirt from the horse's hoof.

Another Watcher glanced in her direction, a light-brown eyebrow arched in question.

Adana glanced upward and around her trying to convey her discomfort with the forest. "I feel safer armed." She shrugged with a sheepish smile on her face. The Watcher returned the smile and nodded in acknowledgement before she returned to her duties.

Adana breathed a sigh of relief and slipped into the woods, angling her path toward the direction Hunter took.

With each step, the forest closed in around her. The trees towered, branches hanging in midair, ensnared with their neighbors. It felt unnatural, and Adana fought a rising panic through her focused breathing.

In. Out. In. Out. In. Out.

Each breath spread throughout her body, easing her anxiety. The tension in her shoulders gave way, and her nerves calmed.

She might be composed, but the sinister nature of the forest forced her to stay on alert. Bow readied for the unexpected, she inched forward, seeking signs of the men's passage. Unaccustomed to drawing on hearing rather than sight, she attempted to hone in on the sounds of the forest. Except for the murmurs from the camp at her back and the occasional stamp of a horse's hoof, she heard very little.

After a while, a tree limb bent askew and tiny scuff marks in the ground coverage indicated the path of someone or something. She smiled triumphantly and followed the slight disturbances in the ground clutter. The noises from camp faded. Except for her own breathing and the creaking of the trees around her, Adana heard nothing else.

Ahead in the trees, a flash of movement caught her attention, and Adana crept toward it, her gaze traveling over her surroundings as well as the position ahead.

"Yah! There he goes!" The shout sounded off to her left, and the woods erupted in sound as men crashed through the undergrowth. A deep, long grunting drowned out the shouts of the men. Adana hurried toward the chase, careful to stay behind the fray. She still couldn't see anyone in the waning light, but their path was obvious as the trees shuddered with the hunting party's passing.

The pounding of the men's feet and jubilant shouts came to a sudden halt. Ahead of her, hidden in the trees, the boar squealed and growled its anger in both shrill and deep grunts. Adana envisioned the men spread in a wary circle around the boar, waiting for the perfect time to thrust a spear or shoot an arrow. She hesitated. The desire to draw closer and watch this battle between man and prey clashed with the need for safety. If she moved in closer, made herself known, her presence could distract and endanger the soldiers. Or worse yet, they might strike at her before realizing they faced their next ruler.

She glanced around, noting a heavier darkness settling in. Disappointment mixed with her earlier unease from the forest. She backed away, studying the ground to follow her own tracks back to camp before full dark fell.

After wandering a few moments, she stood at a point where several tracks mingled and crossed over each other. Was this where she crossed the route of the soldiers? An awareness of being watched enveloped her. Adana held her bow at the ready and searched the growing dimness. A few careful steps backed her against a massive tree trunk. The cursed foliage made it so difficult for her to use her Watcher's skills. A breeze ruffled her hair and sent the leaves in a dance. Everywhere she looked held movement. What was danger? What was forest? Was there a difference?

"Take care, my lady." A man's voice whispered beyond her left ear. She spun toward him, but he grabbed her arms, forcing her bow down. Hunter shook his head, worry in his eyes. He nodded in the direction Adana had been staring. "Someone is out there."

* * * * *

Chapter Twelve

Adana nodded to the soldier, ashamed to admit how grateful she was to see him and turned to look back through the trees. After a few moments, Hunter whispered, "Ah, your Watchers have you in sight, too."

She felt an upwelling of surprise followed by thankfulness when Kassa and Veana, the Watcher who observed her in the camp, stepped into the small clearing. They moved in a protective wall in front of Adana while they helped Hunter search the forest beyond.

In those brief moments, the last inkling of daylight evaporated. Hunter pressed her behind him. "I don't think they know we're here. They followed our boar hunt."

The scaly bark of the tree pressed into her back. Adana stared at the man's broad shoulders before her eyes, amazed at how large and muscular he was up close. The scent of horse and sweat seeped from his body. She couldn't recall when she'd stood so close to any man before, except for her father. It wasn't unpleasant to have a man positioned between her and danger, the feeling a vast contradiction to her Watcher training.

The thought annoyed her, and she pulled on all of her Watcher's instincts to ignore the physical distraction of Hunter and focus on the forest around them. The darkness beyond the small circle felt thick, like a substance.

In the hope of observing how to use her skills in the forest, she glanced toward Kassa in time to see the Watcher's head whip around to their left. Sound erupted from that direction, the soldiers tracking the boar. A great melee flew their way, and Veana pulled Adana to the other side of the tree. Hunter drew his knife and crouched, his eyes glinting in the dim moonlight peeking through the trees.

The boar crashed through the undergrowth, its tusks dripping blood. The howl emitting from its mouth echoed in agony throughout the forest. Adana raised her bow, but with a quick flick of his wrist, Hunter hurled his knife toward the boar, hitting it in the throat. The massive beast faltered as the knife struck but it continued its forward charge. It rushed toward them, stumbling on its feet. Adana prepared to loose her bow as the animal crashed to the ground mere steps from Hunter's feet. Several spears and arrows bristled from the animal's hide. Its sides heaved once, twice, and shuddered to a halt.

No triumphant howl greeted the hunting expedition's success. The soldiers prowled forward, bodies tense and alert. Someone still lurked beyond them in the forest. Several blinked in surprise when they spotted Adana, and without a word, they added their own protective wall around her.

Adana heard the whistle and zing of the arrow moments before Hunter fell. Veana and several soldiers raced after the shooter while others closed in the space around her. Within moments, a disquieting stillness fell over the forest.

At Adana's feet, Hunter wheezed in pain, his hand clenched around the arrow protruding from his chest. His proximity to the slain boar hit Adana in the gut with startling reality. She crouched to his side, fighting the bile that burned in her throat. The arrow penetrated close to his heart. Blood bubbled at his lips as he whispered his last words. "It will be good for you to learn, my queen."

Hunter gasped his last breath.

Adana's hands shook as she touched the face of the man who stood between her and danger. He still felt warm, but she knew the chill of death would overtake him soon. The arrow in his chest looked different from any she'd ever seen. She pulled it from the man's dead body, unable to stand the similarity to the boar's death. Red, blue, and green spiraled along the shaft. "Who?"

One of the soldiers near her spoke. "His name is Hunter, my lady. He was one of us assigned for your protection."

"My protection?" She straightened and stared at the three men surrounding her. Then she turned toward Kassa.

"Yes, my child." Kassa reached out and took the arrow. "First Soldiers provide a second layer for your protection on this journey. Hunter led those assigned to you."

Adana's stomach cramped as awareness threatened to claim her senses. Hunter sought her out because of duty. She stared at his silent form, aware that the physical distraction of just moments earlier would soon fade into nothing. He served her more than she understood, even with his life. "I didn't know," she whispered to his soul. "I'm so sorry, Hunter. I didn't know."

A gentle hand touched her shoulder, and the soldier who spoke earlier said, "You weren't to know. It was part of your training. We wanted to see how long it took you to realize." He nodded toward Kassa. "I suppose we ruined that test."

Kassa shook her head. "No one ruined the test. We wanted to know how well your skills worked in a foreign environment. Especially under your current agitated state."

Anger surged through Adana. At Kassa. At herself. At Hunter for making her curious. At the boar.

And at…her mother. If Mammetta hadn't died, Hunter would still live. The world would be safe, for now.

"The others return." One of the remaining soldiers pointed through the trees.

The soldier was correct. While Adana stood in a haze of confusion, her protectors returned, frustration rimming their eyes. "We lost him."

"Him? Just one person?" Adana fought the urge to scream. "One person did this?"

Each man stood before her, shoulders back, eyes intent on her face. "In the dark, we can't be sure."

She glared at Veana, the one Watcher who joined the search party.

"The woods are dark. It's a challenge for anyone. We have scouts still looking, but they won't go far in this dark. It's not safe. We need to get you back to the camp where it's easier to protect you."

One of the men shouldered his bow and gestured toward the boar. "Let's not let Hunter's last kill go to waste. We will follow you soon, my lady." Several of the men moved to prepare the boar for transport, while one man lifted Hunter's body on his shoulders.

Adana stumbled after Kassa and the man carrying Hunter, not even bothering to use her Watcher's sight in the dim light. Instead, she listened intently for any sound of warning or approach…or the whistle of an arrow.

Their return to camp created a stir of joy replaced by dismay when the others saw Hunter's body. Grief lay bare on the faces of men and women alike. This man, the very man she slighted, had not only saved her life, but he had endeared himself to the Monians of her home. Unsure of her welcome, Adana stayed back as they mourned and dealt with his remains. No funeral pyre for the man, just a quick hole dug among the trees of the forest he loved. When they finished, they piled rocks over the grave.

Kassa found her, and handed her the arrow that killed Hunter, a scowl on her face. Adana, still focused on listening to every sound around her, thought she heard Kassa mutter, "Maligon." When questioned, the old woman wouldn't speak, her mouth a firm, thin line of anger.

"You are angry with me," Adana said. "If it helps, I'm angry with myself. I was rude to Hunter earlier. Now, I can't apologize for that or his life." The weight of the day and the looming trees pressed down on her.

Kassa dropped to the ground beside her. "I'm not angry at you. I allowed you to wander into the forest."

"What? I made sure you didn't see me."

Kassa grimaced. "You know better than to try and fool a Watcher. I saw you go, as did Veana. We allowed it but followed you."

"Why? If you'd stopped me, he might still be alive."

"Might. Might not. You will never know."

When Adana stared at Kassa, unspeaking, the woman continued. "You had the privilege of wandering in Moniah. You will have that privilege in Elwar. Watchers don't intrude on the ruling family unless necessary."

"But you knew it was dangerous." Adana grabbed handfuls of the blanket she sat on to control her frustration.

The look Kassa gave her was the look all Watchers feared, head tilted forward, eyes peering into hers like a hawk studying its next meal. "You knew it was dangerous, too. You took your bow."

"I'm a fool," Adana said.

"No. You're the next queen of Moniah. You have much to learn, but you won't learn in a cage. What did you learn from this?"

Adana recalled her brief interactions with Hunter. While not rude, she had not treated the soldier with respect. "All who serve me agree to die for me. They deserve my kindness, gratitude, and respect."

Kassa nodded and stood up brushing dirt from her leggings. "For safety, tonight, we will sleep in the trees." She grinned at Adana. "I doubt Queen Quilla will allow that practice once you arrive in Elwar."

Adana rose and followed her mentor toward the gathering around Hunter's grave. The soldiers began to hum the song of death, and the Watchers echoed them in a haunting refrain.

Later, the roasted boar served an opportunity for the travelers to share stories of Hunter's exploits. Adana choked down the meat, determined to honor the man's efforts and memory. The more she heard, the more she knew she'd lost a superior First Soldier. A man who one day could have succeeded Linus as Commander.

At the end of the evening, she glanced around those gathered in Hunter's honor. "I didn't know Hunter well, but your homage does him great honor. Word must be sent to his family. They know this forest. Tell them where he is buried, so they can honor him as he should be."

She rose and followed Kassa. Her limbs and heart dragged as the other Watchers selected trees, chosen for their natural climbing nobs and Y-shaped formations. She ascended the tree without thought and settled down, gazing through the lower branches at the other Watchers clustered below. Above her, the moon skulked across the night, playing hide and seek in the branches.

* * *

They emerged from the forest late in the afternoon of the next day, the scouts on high alert for any other signs of their attacker. Adana breathed a sigh of relief when the trees parted, and she rode into daylight again. The dark shroud of death and fear fell away, and she raised her face toward the sun. The air held no warmth, but she relished the return of her sight.

Her relief lasted a brief moment. The northern mountains, the same ones her father crossed when he left his homeland and came to Moniah, rose up in an imposing array. Would she ever see the horizon again? Half the sky hid behind the great behemoths. Somewhere in their foothills, the capital city of Elwar nestled like a secret kept from view.

Adana shivered.

* * * * *

Chapter Thirteen

The Kingdom of Elwar

Prince Kiffen of Elwar stared at the histories spread out on his desk. Maligon's Treacherous War. At least, that's how his mother had referred to it. Recent history, but of no interest to many today. The sounds of people gathering in the streets outside the gates to the palace floated up to him. The people were excited to see the Watchers enter their city. Many had never laid eyes on the warrior women, and for those who had, it was many years ago.

A steward rapped on the door and entered. "Prince Kiffen, the Monians have arrived in the city. The king and queen request your presence."

He nodded without looking at the man. "Of course."

As he stood and pulled on his thick, quilted doublet, his gaze fell on Serrin's books, still stacked on the adjoining desk. Kiffen figured he should remove them but wished someone else would take that final step, an admission to his brother's death.

"She's here! She's here!" His half-sister, Leera, burst into the room, excitement dancing her across the floor. "Come, Kiffen. She's here."

He smiled at her and tousled her curly, blond hair, a gift from her father that she had shared with Serrin. Leera scowled and patted her hair in a gesture so like her mother's that Kiffen felt sorrow for the child. Would she grow up to be her mother? Or would their father's kinder nature embed itself in her soul?

"Go on, Leera. I'll be along soon."

Leera giggled and ran out of the room. Kiffen felt a stab of irritation when Quilla's sharp reprimand echoed down the hallway. "Ladies do not run. Please act with decorum."

Kiffen thought he heard Leera giggle again. For some reason, her mother's scolding never seemed to faze the girl. Maybe she would come to follow their father's personality, after all.

People said Kiffen looked like his mother, Queen Roassa. He managed to dredge up faint memories of her when he tried but nothing significant.

From far below in the city, cheers rang out.

He walked from the room. Serrin should be here to greet his betrothed. Kiffen remembered a little girl, infatuated with giraffes and learning swordplay. Three years younger than him, he never paid her much attention during his only visit to Moniah. A few years had passed, so he supposed she was a little older now. Maybe all giggles and pouts like Leera. As he started down the stairs, Serrin's last words echoed in his footfalls, "Adana...watch...protect."

King Donel met Kiffen in the courtyard's gatehouse. "Son, I have a favor to ask of you." The boisterous man glanced through the gates as Quilla led Leera to the raised platform in the waiting arena. "I would have asked this of Serrin." Tears misted the man's eyes, and Kiffen fought hard not to comfort his father in front of his subjects. "I need you to keep an eye on Adana. You must protect her. She knows nothing of our ways, and Queen Quilla..." The king lifted a penetrating blue-eyed gaze toward Kiffen. "She might not know how to handle Quilla's sharpness. Watch out for her at all times, son."

Kiffen nodded. He would honor Serrin's request, as well as his father's, no matter how boring and annoying the child might be.

* * *

The city walls loomed above Adana before she realized it. One moment they were winding along the road, the next, they rounded a curve and there stood the capital city of Elwar, hidden in the hills like she imagined. The walls rose high above her. A cleared area ran the length of the fortifications, and her caravan lined up along the walls in preparation to enter the city. As Adana's horse moved forward, she looked to the sky, seeking some distance in sight. Everywhere else, trees, people, hills crowded over her. The sky, a brilliant blue, gave her scant comfort, but at least it was clear today and not overcast, adding another layer of obstruction to her soul.

Inside the gates, buildings rose along both sides of the street, two and three stories high, crammed next to each other. Adana shuddered and fought the urge to reach out and part them, give them room to breathe. Lining the road, villagers gathered five and six people deep cheering and chanting her name. A little girl reached out to one of the Watchers on Adana's right and gave her flowers. The Watcher accepted them and passed them up to Adana. Adana inhaled their foreign fragrance and turned to thank the child, but the throngs had absorbed her. Adana nodded her head in the general direction and rode forward.

Agony roiled over her as Am'brosia stretched across the link, trying to calm her nerves. A hazy image of the paddock shimmered through the connection, but the effort was too much to hold, and the pain, like a muscle stretched beyond endurance, fogged her senses. She pushed back and ignored the giraffe. It didn't help much. The crystals provided better comfort, but she'd taken them already.

Kassa rode up on her left side. "Breathe, Adana. Make sure you breathe. It won't be so bad when the crowds go home."

Adana inhaled and let the air spread through her lungs and into her abdomen. She coughed. The stench of too many people and animals assaulted her.

Kassa stayed by her side, a knowing look on her face. "You will learn to ignore the odors. Find your focus. Breathe. Focus on the action of breathing, not the smells."

Adana tried again. She gagged but forced her mind to center on the swelling in her lungs followed by the gentle rise and fall of her abdomen. She let the breath rise into her head and held it before releasing it through her lips in a slow, silent breath.

"Good. Again." Kassa talked her through several breaths until her body relaxed, and the pain of the stretched link with Am'brosia lightened.

The castle gates stood open before her, and the crowds fell back as her caravan approached the entrance. Two more breaths should get her there, away from the crowds.

But still trapped inside high walls.

Breathe. Focus. Breathe.

Like a wash of cool water, the shadow of the gate fell across her, and Adana breathed a sigh of relief. The courtyard held a smaller group of nobles, and no one clamoring for attention. Everyone stood in quiet, but alert, reserve, awaiting her approach. On a raised dais at the end of the courtyard stood the royal family.

King Donel resembled her father in his lighter coloring, but where her father was tall and angular, Donel had grown portly. He sported a bushy, white beard, trimmed to just below the chin. As she approached, his face broke into a welcoming grin that helped dissipate some of her fears.

She smiled back and turned toward Donel's wife, Queen Quilla. The petite queen stood beside her husband, the top of her head only reaching his shoulder. She wore her glossy brown hair in an artful arrangement, a center piece rising above the small crown perched on her head, while the sides cascaded down her cheeks in ringlets. The welcome from King Donel didn't spread to the queen, who glared at Adana.

Prince Kiffen had grown taller than his father since the last time she saw him. The sensation she experienced in the forest when confronted with Hunter's broad shoulders flowed over her. Kiffen hadn't reached the full musculature of a man, yet, but his shoulders showed the promise. He wore his brown hair shorter than most men, just long enough to touch his collar, and he regarded her with sad, deep-set, brown eyes.

Beside him, the young Princess Leera stood, bouncing on her feet. She was a tiny duplicate of her mother except for the blue eyes and blond hair given to her by her father. She stood a little farther from Kiffen than she should, the slight gap proof of a presence gone, but not yet acknowledged. Serrin's siblings hadn't found a way to stand closer, yet.

* * * * *

Chapter Fourteen

Swaths of cloth enveloped Adana's legs as she stumbled along the twisting corridor of the castle. She kicked at the material, unable to feel her legs under all of it. "How do they manage?"

"Did you say something, miss?" A startled maid stood, mop in hand. Eyes widening in recognition, she dropped to a quick curtsy. "My apologies, Your Highness. I didn't recognize you without your uniform."

"Me neither," Adana said, unable to escape the snarl in her voice. She kicked at the layers of petticoats and finally reached down and grabbed as many hems as she could and pulled them up.

The maid blanched at the sight and turned away.

"Blazes," Adana said and dropped the skirts again. It wouldn't do to ruin propriety on her first days in Elwar. She rushed down the passage, kicking her anger out on the thick underskirts each time the material ensnared her legs.

After three wrong turns, Adana stood before the door to Queen Quilla's torture chamber, known as the small dining room. She took a deep breath and pushed the door open. Kiffen turned toward her, his eyes a mixture of concern and regret. Leera's blond head popped up, a look of vicious glee on her face. She slanted her gaze at her mother whose back straightened, if it was possible to be any straighter. A frown of displeasure darkened the queen's face.

Breathe. Adana entered the room, each foot placed with careful precision. "I apologize for my tardiness, Queen Quilla. The halls still—" The skirts swirled in odd directions, catching her off balance. She stumbled and caught herself on the back of the chair closest to her.

Kiffen half-rose from his seat before Quilla stopped him with a look. Crimson bloomed in splotches along his cheeks, and he returned to his seat, head bowed. Adana watched a muscle flex in his jaw.

"Clumsy savage," Quilla said, a sneer stretching across her features. She laid down her fork and studied Adana. "I guess it's no wonder, I've heard the horrid details of your uncivilized kingdom."

The chair took the pressure Adana squeezed into the wood without complaint. She pushed and shoved the skirts, lifting them just enough to slide around the legs of the supportive chair and settle in its seat.

Quilla raised an eyebrow. "You plan to break your fast way down there?"

Several seats separated her from Kiffen and Leera.

"It seemed best." Adana picked up the napkin and spread it in her lap with as much decorum as possible. "Again, Quilla, I apologize for my tardiness. I'm still learning the twists and turns of your palace." She shrugged, unwilling to show how much the queen's taunts angered her. "It's just so different from home."

"I can help you," Kiffen said, a slight lift to his voice. The crimson seeped higher in his face, but he held her gaze with a friendly smile.

"Thank you." Adana nodded and accepted a cup of tea from a servant. The poor woman had waited at first, her face showing confusion on whether to serve Adana at the foot of the table or wait for her to move.

When Adana turned back to thank Kiffen, she noticed Quilla studying him, a speculative look on her face. Kiffen stared back, his jaw muscle working harder than before.

"Hmm." Queen Quilla sipped her tea. "As long as you don't forget your studies, Kiffen." The cup clinked as she placed it in the saucer. "As for you, Adana..." Her scrutiny blazed down the length of the table. "You may be informal in Moniah, but here I am Queen Quilla or Your Highness. Understood?"

Adana nodded but fought the urge to smile. Quilla might enjoy lording it over her, but she had already learned little ways to jab back. "Of course, Your Highness. My deepest apologies."

"Well, now that's settled, I'm afraid you're too late to eat. Come, we have studies."

Adana grabbed a biscuit from her plate before the servant swept it away. Unable to keep up, she hitched up the skirts and trotted behind Quilla and Leera. Their skirts swayed in perfect rhythm to their stride. How would she ever learn to do that?

A throat clearing to her left drew her up short. Kiffen stood beside her, an apple in his hand. He tossed it to her, winked, and walked away.

* * *

Twelve times Adana stumbled over her skirts that day. Twelve times Quilla lashed out at her and called her names. Twelve times Leera watched. Adana knew Leera tripped her at least two of the times, but you didn't accuse Quilla's little darling.

Nine seasons of this torture was too long. Across the distance, she felt Am'brosia's concern. Thanks to the crystals, the pain was less, but she was almost out of them. She had relied on their cushion too much. Maybe if Quilla had shown her kindness, she could have managed the pain, but for now, the crystals gave her the means to deal with at least one of many stressors.

When Quilla dismissed them from her rigorous instruction on the proper way to set a table, Leera followed Adana back to her chambers. They entered the suite of rooms to discover them unoccupied. The young girl glanced around, disappointment clouding her face. "Where are your Watchers?"

Adana shrugged, hiding her own dismay at their absence. "I imagine Kassa has duties to attend to. She might have the others on a practice circuit."

The more she thought about it, the more Adana suspected they were practicing, running free and unencumbered in their leggings and tunics. So far, Quilla had kept her from continuing her Watcher training. Not that she could do anything in these skirts.

As if she read her mind, Leera said, "Why do you wear those tight breeches? It's so vulgar."

Silence echoed in the room while Adana bit down on her tongue to avoid a quick retort. Once she gained control over her thoughts, she spread the skirts, as Quilla had taught her, and perched on the edge of the bed. Still the sticks that forced the skirts into a bell shape stabbed her in the rump. She shifted but gave up.

"How do you run in these hideous skirts? It's so dangerous. How do you climb trees? Or hunt?"

Blue eyes blinked at her in surprise, but only for a moment. "Ladies don't do those things. It's unnatural."

Adana raised her eyebrows at the girl. Leera glared back. When it became obvious that Adana would no longer discuss the topic, Leera bounced a few times on her toes, then hurried toward the door. "Mother wants us early in the morning. Don't be late." Her voice lilted over that last statement, and she laughed in delight before prancing through the door.

To Adana's surprise, Leera appeared at her door early the next morning.

* * * * *

Chapter Fifteen

Adana sat on the floor, skirts billowed up around her, while deep in the trance-like state created by the connection with Am'brosia. The animal relaxed their trance with a slight nudge, warning of another presence in the room. When Adana opened her eyes, she stifled a groan. Bent over, a curious moue to her mouth, Leera's blue eyes stared into Adana's face.

When Adana continued to stare back, Leera jumped back, clutching her hands in her skirts. "Oh! Oh dear."

Adana jumped up and tripped over her skirts. Again.

Leera smirked as Adana stumbled around to get her footing, and then said, "Why did you have such a blank look on your face? I thought you'd gone quite loony."

Adana considered her options. She needed to find some common ground with the princess, so she sat on the edge of the bed and studied Leera a moment. Most young girls in Moniah mooned over the giraffe herds. The tall, gentle beasts might be exotic enough to draw the girl's interest. "I was connected to Am'brosia, my giraffe."

The answering sparkle of interest in Leera's eyes warmed Adana's heart. The princess, only a couple of years younger than Adana, might be just like the girls back home. "Your giraffe? The one called Am'brosia?"

"I miss her." Adana sighed. Stretched over such a great distance, their connection burned raw like a wound pulled wide open. Am'brosia suffered, too. Leera had managed to interrupt Adana's

107

efforts to find out if Am'brosia knew the source of the crystals or something else to soothe their pain.

Leera walked over and patted Adana's hand in an elaborate show of sympathy. Her voice resonated with the comforting tone she used with her horse. "Of course you do. Mother says savages feel more at home with animals than people."

"Savages!" Adana shot out of her seat and towered over the young girl. "We're not savages. The giraffe is a nobler beast than your beloved horses. At least I can talk to mine. Can you talk to your horse?"

A flash of irritation crossed Leera's face. In a waspish tone, she said, "Of course I talk to my horse." She laughed, a bright tinkle incongruous with her behavior. "I don't expect her to speak back, though. Only people can communicate. And at least my horse can carry me where I want to go. You have to walk beside your pet."

"Pet?" Adana reared back to blast Leera again when a warming sensation rolled over her mind. Am'brosia advised diplomacy. Leera had never seen a giraffe, so Adana relaxed her stance and changed tactics. "The giraffe is a noble animal. It exhibits intelligence beyond your imagination. We learn of danger from the giraffe, first. That's why the Watchers copy the giraffe's behavior."

A look of delight crossed Leera's face, giving Adana hope. If Leera began to show interest, she might even share with her the secret of the unusual journey she experienced with Am'brosia on the day her mother died. She'd make sure Leera understood the honor. She hadn't told anyone about jumping from one giraffe's sight to the next.

But, Leera pounced forward, excitement in her eyes.

"Copy? You copy giraffes? Show me. Do you stretch your neck like them? Do it." Leera began to prance around the room, her neck extended, her nose stuck high in the air. "Is this how? Show me." On the last word, the girl whirled around to face Adana. She stomped her foot and arched an eyebrow in challenge. Then she smiled and started walking around with her nose in the air again, humming a silly tune.

Adana watched Leera waltz across the floor in the ridiculous posture. The girl exhausted her with her questions and quick shifts in mood. Still, Leera's behavior wasn't that far off from some of the more excited Watcher candidates on their first days of training. Many used the same tactics in an attempt to appear taller than the other trainees. It made them look ridiculous.

As a child, long before her own training, she had witnessed Kassa's approach to this nonsense. Any young trainee, eager to stand out, slinked back into the ranks, head hung in shame after Kassa tripped her, adding the admonishment, "You can't see anything with your nose in the air!"

Choosing Kassa's version of reprimand over regal indifference, Adana stuck her foot into Leera's path. "If they walked like that, they would break their necks!"

Leera tumbled forward with a shriek and landed in a heap of yellow skirts and petticoats. Not wanting to endure the sure wrath of Leera and her mother, Adana hitched up her own heavy skirts and ran from the room, seeking open air. She clattered down the hall, spun through a stairwell entrance and flew across the great receiving chamber. Following the only path she knew out of the castle, she raced for the gardens.

* * *

Kiffen stared after the girl fleeing down the hall, her feet pounding out a frantic pace. He jumped from his desk and trotted after her, a grin spreading across his face. When his father commanded him to watch Adana, he accepted out of duty. In truth, it was fun. Who knew the Monian princess would contribute so much entertainment to the tedium of life in the castle? Servants chattered about it when they thought he wasn't listening. They loved her. And, the added pleasure of observing Adana spar with Quilla increased everyone's enjoyment.

Kiffen followed Adana out of the castle and into the gardens. She disappeared in the maze of bushes, trees, and arbors. He glanced down the pathways. The crunch of gravel to his left led him in his pursuit. At another cross path, he paused, scanning the area. She was a fast girl. A gardener straightened from a patch of flowers and touched his forehead in salute.

Kiffen nodded in acknowledgement. "The lady Adana?"

Humor lit up the man's creased face as he pointed down a path.

"My thanks," Kiffen said and ran after her.

Before long, he realized she followed a path leading outside the gardens. He slowed and took a shorter route, hoping to not lose her once she burst free from the plants and arbors. At the entrance to the estate's lands, he paused in the shadows of a large bush and stared after the racing princess. She held her skirts high above the ankles and ran like a young hunting dog getting its first taste of freedom. He smiled even broader and watched her race toward a nearby hill, wondering how close a foot race between them might be.

When she hiked her skirts higher in order to tackle the hill, a strange feeling tumbled in Kiffen's stomach. Even at this distance, her legs tantalized him. Ladies didn't expose their legs. Her actions would scandalize Quilla.

* * * * *

Chapter Sixteen

The gardens rose behind Adana in green, gurgling quiet. She lurched out of the maze of trails into the massive estate encircling the castle. Running, even in the cumbersome skirts, soothed her nerves. A hill rose before her, and Adana hiked the skirts higher, surging up the slope. At the crest, she paused, winded, but exhilarated.

Dropping to the ground in a sprawled heap of skirts and petticoats, Adana gazed around her. The hill stood higher than the rest of the grounds, providing a better view of the surrounding area than any place she'd found in the castle. A glance back toward the gardens confirmed that no one beat down her trail, but a movement in the shadows of the garden gate caught her attention. A closer study revealed a person standing beside a large rose bush, hidden within the shadows. The person watched her, and her heart pounded at the notion of Quilla sending someone to punish her.

After a few moments, it became obvious this observer wouldn't follow, and Adana relaxed. One of the Watchers might be assigned to follow her at a distance.

A pond shimmered below, and a small rowboat beckoned from the shore. Adana released a sigh. This might provide the escape she desperately needed.

She stretched out on the grass and studied the sky. Light clouds scudded across her sight driven by the breeze. The wind never blew in Moniah, except for during the violent sand or rainstorms. A waft of air danced over her skin in a gentle caress. The grass beneath her tickled and Adana giggled at the sight of her skirts, forced into a bell-like projection, poking up toward the sky.

"These stupid skirts," she said. Struggling upright, she decided to get rid of the petticoats. A quick glance back down the hill revealed the person in the garden still stood watch. The more she studied the person, it became obvious it wasn't a Watcher. When the clouds moved across the sun and then set the light free again, she could make out the colors of the person's clothing. They didn't blend in with the background like a Watcher's would.

Still, she wanted rid of her skirts. She stood and walked down the hill toward the pond until the slope hid her from view. A studied survey of the area proved she was alone, and Adana hefted up the outer skirt of her dress and yanked and pulled a petticoat off along with the wooden stays. She kicked the skirt toward the pond, hoping it would land in the water while terrified that it might. She yanked off another, and another, until one petticoat remained.

A sigh of release flew from her lips as the last shift tumbled down the hill. The wind whipped her dress skirt around her legs, and the cool embrace eased her senses. Adana plopped back down on the hill and waited. Someone would come searching for her, soon.

She felt their presence before she saw them. First Kassa, then Veana, then two other Watchers appeared at the top of the hill. Kassa's eyebrows rose as she took in the disarray of Adana's clothing. The others chuckled.

Sinti reached her first. "We laid bets on how long it would take you to dump those contraptions."

Unsure how to respond, Adana stood and waited for Kassa's reprimand. The Watcher wandered down to the water's edge and picked up the only one that managed to make it into the pond. Brown water seeped along the pure white hem.

"Tsk, tsk. Queen Quilla will be most displeased." Then Kassa cackled loud and long. Tears ran from the woman's eyes. "My lady Adana, you are your mother's daughter! The Creator be praised."

"You're not angry?" Adana stared at Kassa in confusion as the woman ambled up the hill toward her.

"Angry?" Kassa chuckled. "No, child. I can't stand these death traps either. Quilla will rant and rave, but you don't need to worry."

Relief washed over Adana as the breeze danced around the five of them. "Then I don't have to wear them anymore?"

Kassa straightened and the smile vanished from her face. "No child. You must while you are in Elwar, but I have managed to re-claim some of your training time. We can't let your Watcher skills go to waste while you learn to set a table. With me, you can wear the uniform." She bent and picked up another petticoat. "And I'll see if the lessons provided by King Donel might allow less cumbersome layers." She shook the grass out of the petticoat and gestured for the others to gather the rest. The five of them walked back to the castle, each carrying a flouncy white undergarment in their arms.

The person who had stood in the shadow of the rose bush had disappeared.

* * *

Later that morning, Adana stood, her head held high, while Quilla berated her and railed at Kassa for not teaching the young princess some respect for fine clothing. The look of disbelief followed by horror on the queen's face when they encountered her as they entered the courtyard, petticoats in tow, made the tongue lashing worth it.

The woman had stiffened as they approached, a mask of reproof settling over her features. "My chambers, now. All of you."

Once inside the queen's chambers, Quilla had settled in her chair of office with care, ignoring the six towering soldiers before her. Her eyes dark with venom, she raged at Adana—her clumsiness, her disregard for clothing, her lack of proper manners. Although her Watchers controlled their emotions over the queen's disregard for Adana's royal position, their shoulders stiffened and eyes narrowed in on Quilla.

Surrounded by these protectors, she fought the urge to harass Quilla's temper more.

Kassa waited, her face never changing in composure until Quilla took a breath, then she interrupted. "As you have said, Your Highness, my lady Adana is unaccustomed to the fine clothing you provide. For a Watcher, they are cumbersome, and to some degree, dangerous."

Quilla sputtered and opened her mouth to speak, but Kassa plowed on. "That's why I'm asking that you only require her to wear proper dress when she is in lessons with you or participating in functions under your directives. When the lady attends my training, I need her to wear something more practical."

Quilla closed her mouth and frowned, nostrils flaring, as she glanced from one woman to the next, her final glare landing on Adana. Adana stared back, unwilling to show any weakness.

"Very well," Queen Quilla announced as she sat back in her chair, an ornate, carved structure less in stature than her throne but imposing, nonetheless. "You may have one day a week. The rest of the princess' time will be mine, and she will dress as I say."

"Every other day." Kassa relaxed her stance and crossed her arms.

"Absolutely not. Two days a week. No more."

"Done." Kassa bowed her head toward the queen and nodded toward Adana, a tiny beam of triumph on her lips. "She will join you today, and I will have her for the next two. Agreed?"

A frown crossed Quilla's face, and Adana wondered if the queen worried whether she had given in too easily. After a few silent moments, she nodded. "Agreed. But your Watcher dress upsets my household. From now on, you must wear more suitable clothing, too."

Kassa turned around and took a long stride toward the queen, the hawk-like glare pinning Quilla to the chair like a cat with a mouse under its paw. "We are soldiers, not ladies."

Shrill laughter rang from the queen's lips. "Of course, you're not ladies, but our servants dress with more dignity than you. You will wear simple skirts and blouses befitting your station."

Adana watched, horrified as Kassa continued to glare at the queen. The other Watchers stood at alert. Quilla held Kassa's stare without blinking.

"I will accept your terms, but only me." Kassa stepped closer to the queen, drawing near enough that Quilla had to tip her head up in order to maintain eye contact. "I am an old soldier, so I accept. Adana's Watcher guard will continue in uniform and try to remain unnoticed."

"See that they do." Quilla settled in her chair and gave them a pleasant nod. "You are dismissed. Adana, change and return here forthright."

Hours later, after several more humiliating trips and falls in the queen's presence, Adana sought refuge in the far side of the stable yard. She held her skirts up higher than allowed as she walked. To survive Quilla, she must find a way to navigate in these impossible skirts.

She still couldn't believe Kassa agreed to Quilla's demands. In response to Adana's questions, the older woman said, "I have done far worse in service to Moniah. If it maintains the queen's desire for control, it's a small thing."

At the far end of the stable yard, Adana spotted bales of straw and a few wooden crates. She dragged several bales and crates into an obstacle course and began walking around the objects, placing each foot with care. The dust from the crates gathered on her dress and the sweat of her exertions soaked through the valuable material. It might make Quilla angry, but Adana refused to trip over her skirts in Quilla's presence, again.

She'd spent the whole morning studying the sway of Leera's skirts, unable to see her foot placement, only able to guess at how the girl managed to navigate with all of that material clogging her path.

The sun eased lower in the sky and began to cast deep shadows in front of Adana. She lost count of the number of times she traversed the course, but her efforts began to improve. A thrill surged through her and she quickened her pace, testing her abilities. Her ankle hit one of the crates and she tripped, tumbling over a bale of hay.

A high-pitched laugh rang out behind her. Leera.

The girl stood in the shadows, a hand muffling her mirth. She couldn't contain herself when Adana jumped up from the ground in a fury.

"Mother will kill you when she sees the mess you've made."

Adana shook her head at the girl. "Do you think I care?"

The girl cocked her head to the side, the speculative glee on her face so like her mother's that Adana cringed. "You must care. Why else are you out here practicing how to walk?"

"It's important I learn how to do this because I'll be queen, not because of your mother." The words rang sharp in the afternoon air.

Leera frowned in displeasure. "You should care what mother thinks."

Defeat sagged Adana's shoulders. Leera may be young, but she knew enough to read the obvious signs of Adana's behavior. "Of course, I do. It's just not the only reason why I need to learn this." Adana turned away and started through the maze again.

"You're doing it wrong," Leera said. "Here let me show you." The girl lifted her skirts and carefully placed one foot in front of the other, toe to heel, toe to heel.

Shocked, Adana watched the petite girl navigate the path with no problems. Toe to heel. Toe to heel. When the girl completed the circuit, she swept her hand in a grand gesture toward the obstacle course. "Now you do it."

Toe to heel. Toe to heel. It worked. Skirts swirled around her, but the small steps kept her feet clear of their snatching hems. Adana laughed and did it again.

Leera applauded.

Pausing, Adana studied the young princess. "Why are you helping me?"

Leera pranced over and sat down on one of the bales, spreading her skirts out in order to keep them from bowing up. She picked at a piece of straw, not meeting Adana's gaze. "The days are so much more interesting with you here. You make me laugh."

Skeptical of the young princess' reasons, Adana sat down beside her. "So, why show me? If I don't make mistakes, how will I continue to entertain you?"

Leera broke into a grin. "Because it will aggravate mother when you don't trip anymore." The girl slid her satin slipper in the dust.

"Won't you receive punishment for ruining that slipper?"

Surprise flashed in the girl's face. "Mother never punishes me."

Laughter bubbled up in Adana as realization dawned on her. "It will annoy the queen if you befriend me."

Leera giggled.

* * * * *

Chapter Seventeen

Wooden swords cracked against each other in the practice yard as Kiffen battled his closest companion, Pultarch, the son of the Earl of Brom. The two matched their styles well, having trained together for years. Some days Kiffen won. Other days, Pultarch. It never mattered. They laughed and went at it again the next day.

During a short break, Pultarch brushed his long brown hair out of his eyes. The boy stood a little shorter than Kiffen, but where Kiffen was tall and lean, Pultarch was broad-shouldered and muscular. With a full sweep of thick, brown hair falling over his large brown eyes, the Earl's son already attracted many admirers, Kiffen's younger sister among them. Pultarch glanced down the yard where Adana stood, her bow drawn, lean form held predator-still as she sighted along the arrow's shaft toward the target.

"What do you think of her?" Pultarch asked as he wiped sweat from his forehead.

Kiffen had spent all morning fighting the urge to stare across the yard at the young girl. Today, she wore a Watcher's uniform, reminding him of her legs as she trotted up the hill the other day. He swallowed and cleared his throat. "She's young. A lot like Leera."

A bold lie, but he couldn't bring himself to say anything different. He sat on a barrel facing away from the archery practice. What kind of man showed interest in his deceased brother's betrothed? It alarmed him how much she filled his thoughts, especially last night when he couldn't sleep.

Pultarch leered. "In that uniform, she doesn't look like Leera."

Kiffen jumped up and smacked Pultarch's head.

"Ow!" The boy glared at Kiffen. "Why did you hit me?"

Kiffen struggled to find an explanation, not sure himself.

Across the field, Adana let loose another arrow as accurate a hit as each one she'd fired that morning. "Try to exhibit some respect. She's the next queen of Moniah, no matter how she's dressed, or what she's doing."

"Easy, easy," Pultarch said, examining his friend's face. "If I didn't know better, I'd say you were in love with her." He punched Kiffen in the arm.

Kiffen jerked back in surprise. Love? It was unheard of. He would one day rule Elwar, she would rule Moniah. Thanks to Maligon's attempts to create one huge kingdom out of four, current customs forbid the two heirs to marry.

When Kiffen didn't reply, Pultarch laughed out loud. "You are in love with her aren't you? That's hilarious. Elwar's heir able to love any woman he wants except the one he does."

"I'm not in love," Kiffen ground out between his teeth.

He turned toward Adana again, watching her fluid motion as she pulled an arrow from a line of shafts stuck in the ground. She notched the arrow and drew her bow. The stance left little to his imagination, and a strange feeling rose in his chest. "I promised Serrin I'd watch out for her." He squinted up at his friend. "To protect her from scum like you."

"Ahh. Well, I think it's the fair lady's decision on who she chats with. She must believe differently, because she's walking this way."

Adana beamed with pleasure as she approached the two men. Kiffen considered turning away and snubbing her just to keep Pultarch from an introduction. The idea of Adana falling prey to Pultarch's charms bothered him. The idea that it bothered him, bothered him more.

It didn't matter, to not provide an introduction went against all protocol, but her approach violated protocol, too. She had so much to learn, and only Quilla to drum it into her.

"Prince Kiffen," her voice rang clear as she drew near. "Good morning to you. How was breakfast with your mother, this morning?" The girl laughed a carefree sound on the air.

"Fine." He had worried when she missed breakfast. "Did she punish you for missing it?"

"Oh, no. Kassa and Queen Quilla came to an agreement about my training. Today and tomorrow, I'm a Watcher. Then the queen gets me for five days straight."

Kiffen chuckled as Adana wrinkled her nose in distaste when she said five days straight. "So you have a reprieve each week?"

Before Adana could speak again, Pultarch cleared his throat. Annoyed, Kiffen turned to his friend and, fighting to keep a polite tone, introduced the two. "Princess Adana, may I present Pultarch, son of the Earl of Brom."

Pultarch bowed, his thick brown hair draping across his forehead in a practiced gesture as he straightened. Bile roiled in Kiffen's gut, but he proceeded with the introductions. "Pultarch, the Princess Adana of Moniah."

Adana smiled at Pultarch, a relaxed and open gesture. Kiffen's heart pounded out a protective beat as Pultarch swept his hair aside and glanced up at Adana from a shy bow. He wondered if Pultarch even thought about these actions anymore. He used this ploy so often. And it worked. Girls, young ladies, even older women, flocked to his friend's charms. He wished he knew why.

"Sir Pultarch, it is a pleasure to meet you. The Princess Leera has mentioned you a time or two."

Kiffen wanted to groan at the thought. His sister swooned over Pultarch. If Adana knew of him through Leera, she had heard whatever it was that drew women into his friend's net. He wished they could hear how his friend talked about them later. Pultarch had no intention of settling down with one woman. Not yet, no matter what his ailing father desired.

The light dazzled off of Pultarch's teeth as he flashed his most charming smile on Adana. "The pleasure is mine, Princess Adana. I trust Princess Leera has been kind in her comments?"

"Oh, of course, but," she turned toward Kiffen, "please call me Adana. We are not so formal on names within the landowners of Moniah, except for when I'm queen." She smiled at Kiffen. "Do you practice here every day, Kiffen?"

Surprised when the attention turned in his own direction, and over her use of his name used so informally, Kiffen stumbled over his words. "Me, um, yes. Most days."

"I'm glad," Adana said. "Maybe we can spar together tomorrow. That is, if you're not committed to practicing with Pultarch." She arched an eyebrow in the other man's direction.

Spar? With a girl? Kiffen swallowed and fought back his immediate response. What if he hurt her? What if …

"It would help us with my lady's training." Kassa had approached them, catching both men off guard while they stood mesmerized in Adana's presence. "She needs to spar with men in order to strengthen her arms. We thought you might be an agreeable partner."

An agreeable partner? Kiffen nodded. "Of course, if you think I can help. But," he fidgeted a moment, "I wouldn't want to harm you."

A sharp cackle broke free from Kassa's stone-hard face. "I'd be more concerned that she might harm you, Prince Kiffen."

Adana tittered and blinked a quiet smile in his direction. "Don't mind Kassa. It's her job to build me into a warrior."

"Excuse me, Your Highness, er, Adana," Pultarch interrupted the conversation. "I would be honored to offer my sparring services to your training, too."

Kassa snorted. "I might let her take on the both of you at the same time. See how that goes. Come my lady, we have more to do."

With a quick dip of her head, Adana turned and walked away. The sunlight glinted in the tawny hair of the precise braid stretched down the length of her back. Her tunic swayed as she walked in quick, purposeful strides, while the leggings embraced her muscular calves.

Kiffen swallowed and grabbed his practice sword. With a shout he lunged at Pultarch. The other man scrambled for his own sword and blocked the strike at the last possible moment.

* * * * *

Chapter Eighteen

Days bled into nights, week after week, and Adana adapted to her new surroundings. Two days with Kassa's training, one to two days in King Donel's receiving room while he made judgments over his subjects' problems and disputes, and the remainder of the week with Queen Quilla. When she expressed doubt over why she needed to know the proper setting of a table or the correct order to seat people, Quilla's voice rang shrill in her ears. "You might not be the one to set the table or assign the seats, but it's your responsibility to ensure your servants do it correctly. It reflects on you, not the servants, if you err in the etiquette of court."

Chagrined, Adana submitted to Quilla's admonishments and did her best to please the queen. By her side, the now faithful Leera whispered her own complaints but never within her mother's hearing.

At night, at least for the first few weeks, Adana wished for Serrin's calming presence. How different would her experience in Elwar be if he had lived? The pain of those evenings burned raw like the sudden sandstorms that rose unexpected along the horizon in Moniah. Some days, she found a spare moment to herself and wandered back through the gardens, up the hill, and down to the pond. After a few failed attempts, she managed to guide the rowboat out onto the pond, where she lay down in the bottom of the boat and drifted, her thoughts wandering.

On one such day, she noticed the letters S-E-R-R-I-N scratched into the boat and found comfort in the knowledge she'd found, and now shared, his own sanctuary. She remained longer than normal in the boat that day, seeking to find some hint of Serrin's presence. As the sun began its downward path in the sky, she ambled back toward the gardens.

In the shadows of the large rose bush at the garden entrance, Kiffen waited for her. "The king and queen request your presence." He glanced down at her Watcher uniform. "You should wear appropriate attire." Kiffen stalked away.

Adana stared after him, trying to grasp the moods of the prince. When they sparred, she knew he held back until she came after him in such a fury, he had no choice but to use his strength and skill against her. When they shared breakfast, he displayed the kindest of manners to her, but always with a cool indifference. Just then, when his gaze wandered down the length of her uniform, she'd felt an odd shame intermingled with a thrill she couldn't identify. What had she done to receive such an unfriendly reception? At least, Leera remained her steadfast, if not trying, friend.

Annoyed, she traversed the castle hallways, now a familiar route, in search of Kassa or Veana to assist her in dressing. Along the way, she sought out the connection with Am'brosia. The giraffe's agitated excitement surged into her mind in an excruciating burst of energy, and Adana fought to not stumble at the force. Across the link, the giraffe shared the image of a small, green-leafed plant with tiny red berries dangling from the stems. A treatment for their pain? The positive energy glowed along the connection in affirmation. Adana studied the image again, careful to note the tiny details. Leaves serrated on one edge, smooth on the other. Berries, tiny, but plump with juice. The stems a dark, dark, brown, smooth in texture.

She arrived at her chamber content that the end of the painful days might be upon her. All she had to do was find the plant.

"There you are," Leera said as Adana entered her chamber. "I've been waiting for you all afternoon. A message arrived from Belwyn. I did my best to eavesdrop, but mother and father spoke too softly this time."

Leera knew of many places in the castle to eavesdrop. A small alcove above the Great Hall provided a concealed hiding place to observe the great dances and dinners deemed inappropriate to the thirteen-year-old Leera. As for her father's receiving chamber, a recessed part of the corridor a short distance before reaching the massive entrance doors did the trick for overhearing court discussions. A little less practical if the king chose to close the doors, but it still gave Leera more information than her parents or brother did.

"I've been summoned." Adana said, unsure what to think of this news. "Do you think something is wrong at home? My father?" She reached out to Am'brosia, but the giraffe couldn't provide any clues.

"I don't think so." Leera wandered toward the door and glanced along the corridor for a moment. When she returned, she lowered her voice and leaned in close to Adana. "I think we're going to have a Kingdoms Council. I couldn't make it all out, but I think they want to meet you."

"They?"

"Empress Gabriella of Belwyn and King Ariff of Teletia."

Adana pondered this as a maid bustled into the room and began the tedious job of transforming her into an Elwarian lady instead of a Monian Watcher. An excruciating amount of time later, as the maid completed the finishing touches to the cascade of curls that now rippled down Adana's back, Kassa entered the room. "Good. You are almost ready. We need you in the Receiving Room, now."

Adana obliged by standing very still as the maid hefted a vibrant blue dress over her head, avoiding the precious curls, and settled it over the multitude of petticoats. It swirled to the floor in iridescent shades thanks to the rare Monian glimmer cloth used in its design.

Before the last button was hooked, Kassa started out the door, Adana quick to follow her.

As they rushed along the hallway, Kassa turned toward her. "Don't you have questions?"

Years of training still held Adana's tongue in Kassa's presence. As rising queen, she knew she should discuss more with her mother's former First Vision, but the habits of childhood still silenced her. "No."

The well-known hawk stare creased Kassa's face in displeasure.

Clearing her throat, Adana tried again. "Yes."

"Good," Kassa said, the contours of her face relaxing into her stoic Watcher's face. "What do you want to know?"

"Why am I summoned?"

"You received a message today. Against my orders concerning any missive addressed to you, the chamberlain delivered it to Queen Quilla, who opened it. Otherwise, you would have received it in private in your chambers."

The queen opened her message? The person determined to teach Adana propriety and decorum? Was that treason or an overextended attitude of superiority? Unsure of how to respond or react to this news she waited for Kassa to explain.

"Fortunately, it was nothing the queen shouldn't know." Kassa's jaw flexed as she paused before continuing, the words ground out between her teeth. "Even so, it caused quite a bit of concern on Quilla's part. She summoned King Donel, and he, rightly so, summoned me."

"So what was the message?" Adana asked while noting that Kassa rarely referred to Quilla by her title but always honored King Donel with his.

"Except for our encounter in the forest, no one has seen or heard anything about Maligon. Since you are connected to the last two events possibly related to him, the kingdoms ask for a council, here, with you present."

Adana saw again the arrow sticking out of Hunter's chest, his life trickling away, blood bubbling at his lips. Kassa later had confirmed the arrow's markings belonged to Maligon. It lay in her trunk upstairs, a constant reminder of Hunter's sacrifice for Moniah.

"Why should this concern Quilla? I would think she'd be pleased to entertain a Kingdoms Council in Elwar." Adana asked the question, although she suspected she knew the answer.

"You are not queen, yet, so Quilla objects to your participation."

"And King Donel?"

"He summoned you."

The stiffness in her shoulders relaxed. She tried to recall if she ever felt so tense in Moniah. It must be part of being in Elwar, and even more so, something to attribute to Quilla.

"Then let's hear what he has to say."

Kassa rewarded Adana with a smug smile of satisfaction. She had given the right answer.

* * * * *

Chapter Nineteen

The Kingdom of Moniah

Montee entered the regent king's chambers to find him stretched out in his chair, legs extended and head turned to stare out the window. Micah's listlessness hovered around him like a cloud of bitty bugs over a bog after the heavy rains. Even an entire season after the queen's death, he displayed little interest in his surroundings. Montee glanced at the missive in her hand. Maybe this was what the king needed.

"King Micah?"

Micah roused and brushed a hand over his eyes before sliding back into a more upright position. "Yes, Montee? What is it?"

She stepped forward and handed him the message. "This came from Belwyn."

The note shook in the king's hands as he scanned it, but his eyes cleared a little as he looked back at Montee. "A Kingdoms Council? In Elwar?"

"Yes. Belwyn and Teletia find the recent rumors of Maligon disconcerting. Whether he still lives, or the remnants of his supporters have rallied to continue his madness, they want to gather and strategize."

"Why go to Elwar? The attacks occurred in Moniah. Why not meet here?" Micah rose from his seat, a familiar vigor returning to his stance.

Montee's heart beat faster at the king's alertness. For weeks, she had sought to find a way to bring him out of this depressed state. What he needed was a call to duty. A call against his most hated enemy, Maligon. She thanked the Creator for creating a diversion even if it was this disturbing rumor of the traitor's survival.

"I believe Belwyn and Teletia wish to meet my lady Adana and acknowledge her as her mother's heir."

Micah turned toward Montee, his eyebrows raised in surprise at that statement. "Recognize her before she's eighteen? Before the Recognition Ceremony? Why?"

"Adana was present for one of these attacks. Both occurred within our borders. She may never have the chance to rule if we don't extinguish it now. It makes sense to include her."

The man's voice rumbled up from his chest in the gruff, protective manner reserved for matters dealing with his only child. "She's fifteen. It's not how we do things. She's too young."

"She turns sixteen soon."

The king stood by a window staring across the Monian plains. In the distance, she could see a disturbance, the patterns of swirling dust indicated the presence of a herd of antelope close by. "Sire? When you look to the horizon, what do you see?"

He glanced at her, an eyebrow raised in annoyance. "The horizon."

"No, Sire. Look harder. What do you see?"

Micah stared out the window for a long time, his brow wrinkled in concentration. In exasperation, he turned to Montee, and said, "Chiora used to test me like this. I see nothing, so why don't you just tell me what it is you want me to see."

Satisfaction slid over Montee's shoulders. A rise out of the king was better than the melancholy he wore like a mantle. "I see a disturbance, a swirling haze on the edge of the horizon. It runs along this line." She showed him a stretch of horizon spanning a great distance. This was a large herd. "The disturbance tells me that a herd of animals, most likely antelope, travels nearby."

"And?" Micah stared out the window, a frown crossing his face. "What's the point?"

"Although it's far away, I can see it. If the animals were to turn, I would recognize the signs. I could warn us before they came too close to our grounds, endangered our livestock." Montee turned her gaze on the regent king. "Adana may be a few years from her time as queen, but it is coming. It's better she sees what might be headed toward her reign, now, rather than learn of it on her eighteenth birthday."

The regent king nodded. "You sound like Chiora. And Kassa. They had an annoying habit of speaking wisdom." A small huff of mirth escaped his lips, followed by a look of surprise at the sound. "So, who shall we send to this council?"

"I've called an advisor's meeting. We await you in the small receiving chamber."

The regent king grunted but didn't object. His strides matched Montee's as they descended from the royal chambers into the Great Hall. Off to one side of the Great Hall, the smaller receiving chamber provided privacy for less formal meetings.

When they entered the chamber, Linus rose from his seat, a look of pride darting toward Montee. Even now, with their fates sealed by position, she couldn't stop the flush of heat his attention gave her. Next to him, Samantha rose as well as Kalara. Who better to send than the Watcher who spent an entire week tracking Maligon's attacking vigilantes?

Micah settled into his seat at the head of the table and gestured for them to do so, too. A cask of watered wine sat on the table, and he helped himself to a goblet before speaking.

"You have been alerted to the contents of this message?" Micah placed the parchment on the table before him.

Each of them nodded.

"Who goes?" Micah leaned forward and stared into each of their faces. "Who should stand for Moniah since it's evident my daughter will not know enough to conduct our affairs?"

"Sire," Linus leaned forward as he spoke, "we're in agreement that you should go."

Dismay etched across Micah's face at this pronouncement. For several moments no one spoke, and the soldier and Watchers held their breath during the silence.

At last, Micah spoke in a quiet voice. "I would prefer not to visit Elwar."

"But Sire." Montee tried to mask the plea from her voice. "It's logical you would go."

Eying the king, Linus ran his fingers through his red-bearded chin. "Your daughter would want to see you. Who else would you send?"

The tragedy of the last few months shrouded Micah's face, his head bowed, lips pulled tight. "I would not prefer to see her." He slumped in his chair, his fingers spread out over the parchment on the table. "At least not yet. I'm not prepared."

Montee knew how Kassa or Chiora would deal with his reluctance. The approach, still foreign to her sensibilities, rankled her nerves. Before she could sway her mind, she rose, quick and agile, from her chair and leaned over Micah. She spat the words at him the same way she spoke to unruly trainees. "You must go as regent king. You do not wish to see Queen Chiora's likeness in your daughter's eyes, but you must."

Kalara gasped as the sharp words snapped from Montee's lips.

Montee didn't pause or hold back. "She is not Queen Chiora. She is your child. You are all she has left. Will you abandon her, too?"

For a moment, anger boiled in the tenseness of the king's shoulders, in the set of his jaw, and Montee thought he might storm at her. Instead he rolled his neck on his shoulders, the tension visibly melting from neck and jaw as he did so. He glared at Montee, the only continued sign of his displeasure, but nodded. "Who will you send with me? It's time to rotate out the Watchers attending to Adana. It can't be you if I'm to go."

Montee nodded. "Both Karyah and Ostreia were part of the troops sent after the attack on the village, and they are known to Belwyn and Teletia, so they will go. I will find a new honor guard, but I intend to send Samantha and Kalara, too. They are the most knowledgeable in what we've seen from Maligon's supporters as of late."

Micah nodded his approval. He stood, resignation in his voice. "When do we depart?"

"Tomorrow."

Montee registered his dismay at her answer, but she didn't dare give him time to slip back into his depression.

* * * * *

Chapter Twenty

With Quilla frantic over arrangements for the Kingdoms Council, Adana began to fear she might never find time to search for the plant Am'brosia assured her would stop their pain. The longer she waited, the stronger her headaches from the stretched connection became. She doubted her ability to maintain a regal composure in the face of Quilla's treatments, much less with a full royal entourage arriving from three other kingdoms. The news her father would be in attendance brought some relief. Somehow, she felt his presence might ease the discomfort, although she didn't know why.

Meanwhile, the only relief she found was in her focused breathing during archery or sword practice. If she could maintain focused breathing all of the time, she would, but the exercise presented its own dangers from prolonged use. The most obvious being inattentiveness to anything but the exercise of focus.

After a grueling afternoon with Quilla's shrill voice hammering into her skull, Adana begged for a reprieve. "Kassa, the council arrives in just days. Would it matter if I skipped one evening at dinner?"

The hawk-like stare swiveled her way, but as Adana continued to spend time in Kassa's presence, it unnerved her less and less. As usual, the old Watcher's face softened into a kinder visage after studying Adana for any clues. "Quilla has pushed rather hard these last few days. Why don't you relax for the rest of today and tomorrow?

You will need to play courtesy to her demands even more as the council draws closer."

The idea of Quilla pushing harder propelled Adana into hurried action before Kassa or someone else might remove her new freedom. She dumped all but one petticoat. A spiteful temptation to don an old, worn uniform pricked at her mind, but today was not a day for Watcher dress. With reluctance, Quilla allowed Adana to wear fewer petticoats when not in attendance to her or the king. This would have to do.

All she needed was time to find this plant. Even though embracing the connection meant agony, she linked with Am'brosia for assistance in her search.

The gardens held nothing even close to the image of the plant, so Adana trekked up the hill to her pond, her alert gaze sweeping across the slope as she climbed. Nothing. She wandered along the shoreline, longing to climb into the rowboat and float her troubles away with the water's gentle rhythm.

Concerned, she stalked along the rolling hills of the castle grounds, wandering farther from the castle than she'd ever ventured. At the sound of hoof beats pounding up behind her, Adana paused to check the approaching rider.

With flamboyant motions, Pultarch halted his horse and vaulted down at her feet. Adana shook her head, surprised and disappointed to find him before her. How could one person find so much motion in their body? Watchers used economy in their actions to remain hidden in plain sight, plus it minimized the effects of the Monian heat during a long day of scouting.

He executed a perfect bow, and rose, laughter glinting in his brown eyes. A smile quirked at her lips when she thought of Leera's response to this unexpected visit. The girl would turn it into a lover's tryst given half the opportunity to employ her vivid imagination.

"Sir Pultarch, you have discovered me."

Brilliant white teeth gleamed in the sun as the young nobleman laughed. "I'm pleased to do so, my lady Adana." He stepped forward and reached for her hand.

Quilla's instruction resonated in her mind. A gentleman kisses the hand of a lady when he encounters her presence. She allowed him her hand, uncertain of this custom. It seemed silly to her, but she was in Elwar.

The absurd practice completed, Pultarch glanced around them, his eyes searching the hills. "What brings you so far afield? Where are your ever-faithful Watchers?"

Adana shrugged. "I sought solitude. They understood and complied."

Dismay crossed Pultarch's face at her response, and she realized her error. A lady never made a gentleman feel unwelcome. A stranger or ruffian, yes, but never a gentleman, and especially not a nobleman destined for a title some day.

Elwar's rules of decorum confused Adana. She longed for Moniah, where she already understood what others expected of her. Of course, came the unbidden thought, these lessons explained her mother's reason for sending her to Elwar in the first place. Long before the changes to that plan wrought by Montee's vision, she had known she must spend two seasons here learning Elwarian culture and practices.

"Of course," Adana forced brightness to her tone, "your presence is more preferable. So thank you, Sir Pultarch, for the welcome distraction."

The words melted the man's frown, and Pultarch's demeanor relaxed as he flashed his bashful grin, again. He always managed to duck his head, so he could look up through thick long eyelashes at the woman graced by his smile. It sent most hearts aflutter, Leera's included. Adana hadn't determined why.

"Tell me, what brings you and your horse this way?"

"I arrived at the castle to invite Kiffen for a ride to my father's estate, but I find the castle all alert, preparing for many esteemed guests, your father included." Pultarch picked up the reins of his horse and began strolling alongside Adana. "How did you escape the frantic preparations of our Queen Quilla?"

Adana laughed in surprise at his forthrightness. Pultarch chuckled and leaned in to whisper in confidence. "No disrespect meant, of course. The queen is dedicated to this kingdom."

"Dedicated?" Adana repeated the word, rolling it over in her mind. "On that, I will concur with you, Sir Pultarch."

At that moment, Adana's keen vision spotted a patch on the hillside that might match the plant she sought. She rushed over to it and bent to examine the leaves and stem. Serrations ran along one edge, but not the other. Small, juice-filled berries hung from the stems of dark, dark, smooth brown wood. She glanced around, excited to see it covering the entire hillside.

Pultarch hurried up beside her and scowled when he spied the plants. "Drunkenberry."

When his horse leaned its face down to graze on them, he yanked it back. "Be careful, Adana. These plants cause strange behaviors in the animals that eat them."

Disappointment flared in her heart at his words. "Drunkenberry? Does it intoxicate?"

Pultarch shrugged and pulled his horse to an area spread with clover. "Sometimes. Birds swoop and dive in crazy patterns if they eat too much. I've seen horses fall to the ground and roll in the stuff. Those are the harmless effects. Other times, a beloved dog might snarl at you and bare his teeth. We should alert the groundskeeper of this patch, so he can destroy it."

Alarm pulsed through Adana. "Destroy it. Surely, it's not dangerous?"

"Dangerous?" A look of surprise crossed Pultarch's face. "No. I suppose not. It's just a nuisance."

Adana still knelt in the patch running her hand along the leaves. When Pultarch glanced toward his horse, she yanked a few from the ground, roots and all, and stuffed them in a bag she carried for just such purpose.

The young man missed the action and turned back to Adana with a smile on his face. "I've had a wonderful idea. Since you've managed to escape the bonds of the queen and your fascinating training, why don't you accompany me to my father's estate? He's been asking to meet you."

Propriety aside, Adana felt sure this proposal wouldn't be met well by Kassa. It was one thing to wander the grounds, another to disappear to the Earl of Brom's estate. "Sir Pultarch, how kind of you to alter your plans to support my need to wander. Unfortunately, a visit to the earl requires a bit more preparation. Why don't we discuss this with the queen and plan a formal outing someday soon? We could include Leera and Kiffen as well. Make a day of it."

Shock flashed in Pultarch's brown eyes for a moment.

She wondered how often ladies turned him down. Surely, he knew his invitation was ill-conceived. "As free as I may seem to you this far from the castle, I am still within the reach of my Watchers and the queen if she needs me. I can't wander off as I see fit."

"It appears to me, my lady, that you should be able to do whatever you please. You are destined to be queen. What good is your rank if you can't use it?"

Irritation flickered across Adana's mind at the boy's simplicity. Did he really not understand? "I assure you," she said, her tone sharper than she meant it to be, "my rank is the very reason why I do not gallivant off on a whim."

The irony of her attempt to do that on the day her mother had died struck Adana as she corrected Pultarch. With a proud smile for her own growth in this area, she started back toward the castle. "Now, why don't we locate Leera? I'm sure we can find some refreshment or games to play for the rest of the afternoon."

* * *

Kiffen's strides clicked on the stone paving as he hurried across the courtyard. Adana had managed to elude him once again. He had checked the gardens first, but she might have gone there while he wandered the endless corridors searching and snarling at the inconvenience. Just moments ago, he had turned down an offer from Pultarch to go riding. All because he promised his father and brother to keep an eye on Adana.

On a whim, he swung around and hurried toward the stables.

Relief ran through him, releasing tension he didn't know he held in his shoulders at the sound of Adana's laughter ringing out from the yard. In response, he heard an all-too-familiar chuckle, deep and practiced. He knew it was practiced because he had been the unwilling recipient to Pultarch's continuous practice to develop just the right laugh for a man courting ladies. At the time, he thought it was funny, and unlike Pultarch, he laughed loud and hard every time the boy tried a new method.

Once Pultarch started using it on the ladies, Kiffen couldn't help but hide a smile each time they fluttered around him. Today, the sound grated on his ears. He balled his fists in anger. While he took the time to search everywhere, Pultarch managed to locate her without trying.

At the edge of the stable yard, Kiffen slowed his steps, not wanting to alert the pair to his presence. He'd gotten good at this part, the quiet sneaking up to avoid notice. Not an easy task when dealing with a trained Watcher. Still, he felt he'd improved over the weeks. He couldn't imagine what she might think of how well he followed her activities.

Pultarch and Adana strolled toward the barn, smiles wreathing their faces. A young boy raced forward and took the horse's reins from Pultarch. The man didn't even acknowledge the boy, but Kiffen approved of Adana's immediate response. She smiled down on the stable hand and spoke something, too soft for him to hear, but the boy's reaction, an immediate straightening of posture and confident swagger as he led the horse away, told Kiffen volumes.

Pultarch laid his hand on Adana's arm and leaned in to whisper something to her.

A knot tightened in Kiffen's gut. The feeling confused him. Did a brother typically feel such displeasure when his sister flirted with a friend? Leera flirted with Pultarch all of the time. He just laughed at her childish efforts to gain the young noble's attentions. But Adana was a different story. She was of an age for Pultarch.

Which meant she was of an age for Kiffen. He stumbled at the thought. With her sixteenth birthday just days away, she would not be a young girl in the eyes of Elwar's court anymore. Confused, he turned and wandered away.

For once, he didn't want to honor his brother's wishes.

* * * * *

Chapter Twenty-One

A Kingdoms Council required a lot of work. That was the first point Adana learned. And that work included her. Still, she couldn't help but enjoy the excitement of monarchies seeking her introduction, wanting to know what she knew about the Maligon situation.

In the midst of it all, she managed to gather some more of the drunkenberry.

Cautioned by Pultarch's brief lesson, she left the berries alone and tried to steep the leaves in a tea. A rough night with a cramping stomach rewarded this effort. When summoned for breakfast, she groaned and begged a leave of absence.

Quilla, herself, stormed into her chambers and yanked the covers off of Adana. "What ails you child? What mischief are you about today?"

The Watcher assigned to her for the morning had gone for the apothecary, so Adana faced this intrusion alone, curled in a ball, fighting nausea.

Leera rushed in behind her mother, took one glance at Adana and objected. "Mother. Look at her. Does she look like she's lazing away the day in bed? She's *green*, Mother."

Touched by Leera's ferocious rise to her defense, Adana missed Quilla's reaction to her daughter's outburst.

Moments later the apothecary arrived. He stood in the doorway surveying the scene, his gaze radiating concern.

"Find out what's wrong with the princess," Quilla said in a sharp voice. When a Watcher followed the apothecary into the room, she changed to a sweeter, gentler tone. "We mustn't have her ill with so many expecting to see her in a few short days."

Of course, that was the problem. Not that Adana might be lazing about, whatever that was, but she might ruin Quilla's Kingdoms Council. No matter what the others thought, Adana knew this was Quilla's show. Her lessons came just short of that proclamation. Quilla wasn't known for subtlety.

The apothecary, a slight, young man, skinny to the point of starvation, approached her, a guarded look in his eyes. Adana couldn't blame him.

"Your Highness, I'm called Suban. What ails you?" He asked almost the same exact question Quilla asked earlier, but the differences between their approaches resonated in Adana's mind. She found herself wanting to help him.

"My stomach churns."

"What did you eat at dinner last night? Anything different? Anything special?"

Adana grimaced. "I ate what they served us."

Suban glanced at Leera who still hovered nearby, chewing a thumbnail, a deep wrinkle dividing her forehead. "And you, Princess Leera, did you eat the same meal?"

"Of course." The girl straightened and raised her chin a little as she spoke.

Suban nodded. "Have you experienced any discomfort?"

The girl shook her head, curls bouncing with the motion.

After some uncomfortable prodding at Adana's stomach and a few more questions, Suban disappeared to his pharmatorium. In a short while, he returned with a white, chalky liquid. "Drink this, Your Highness, and rest. It may be your constitution isn't as strong as Princess Leera's."

Adana would have laughed at Leera's gasp of indignation if it wasn't for the remedy. She gagged and coughed on the grainy substance, suddenly aware something could taste worse than the formula used to enhance her bond with Am'brosia. Leera rushed to her side with a goblet of water. After sputtering and guzzling the girl's offering, Adana curled up on the bed, pulling the covers up to her chin.

"Thank you, Suban," she whispered and rolled away from Leera and the skinny man.

Sometime later, Adana woke to the afternoon sun streaming in the window. Veana sat by her bed, her face deep in concentration. In her lap, she held needlework. Adana sat up and stretched forward, trying to glimpse the cloth. A line of golden giraffes stood sentry along a ridge.

Veana glanced up and winked at Adana. "I grew up the daughter of a landowner, my lady. It troubled mother that my talents with the needle would go to waste once the Watchers identified me as a candidate."

"It's lovely." Adana studied the cloth. "Is that the ridge above the east wing of the fortress?" A lump formed in her throat at the sudden longing drawn by the image.

"It is." Veana pulled the thread tight and wrapped the cloth with care. "I saw my first giraffes lined up on that ridge. It was my first day of training."

"It's beautiful. I never could manage a straight seam."

Bell-like laughter pealed forth from Veana. "Oh, my lady, I've seen your efforts. Do not worry. Your ancestor didn't possess needlework ability either." She tucked the cloth into a basket on the floor. "Are you feeling better? Your color has returned."

Recalling the incident leading to her stomach discomfort, Adana stirred uneasily on the bed. "I'm fine. I hate how much trouble I must have created. Quilla was irate."

A straight-lipped frown settled on Veana's face. "Do not concern yourself too much with the queen, Adana. She is a small ant who wishes to own the oasis in the desert. She might make your life difficult while you are here, but she will not harm you."

"Harm me?" Adana shook her head at the notion. "The thought never occurred to me. That would mean war, for sure."

"Precisely." Veana rose and offered Adana a goblet. Chalky substance swirled in the cup.

"Again?" She slumped against the pillows. "I feel better."

Veana crossed her arms. "Suban left specific orders. You must drink this when you wake."

Resigned, Adana downed the cup and groped for a goblet of water on the table beside her bed. Cool water rinsed some of the grit away, but the bitter flavor stuck to her tongue in a thick coat of white.

She opened up her connection to Am'brosia as wide as possible and slammed her reaction to the taste across the link.

Humor trickled along the bond mixed with a small amount of sympathy.

Next, she sent an image of the plant, the leaves, the disastrous tea, and the result. Am'brosia showed her the berries.

* * *

The berries were sweet, the juice gushing out in a light flavor, a drastic contrast to Suban's stomach aid. Adana chewed three of them and waited.

She sat in the rowboat on her pond, the sun beating down on her. With the arrival of the Belwyn and Teletian rulers eminent, she had employed her Watcher techniques to slip away undetected. Quilla probably raged down the hallways, now, threatening servants, but Adana couldn't bring herself to meet Empress Gabriella of Belwyn or King Ariff of Teletia without some aid to her pain.

After waiting long enough for the boat to drift across the entire pond, Adana felt no different. Her head pounded and her neck muscles constricted in an effort to hold up her heavy head against the pain of the stretched connection.

She ate a handful of berries. The light, sweet flavor danced along her tongue.

* * *

Whatever was happening on the pond, Kiffen found it hard to explain. Adana lay back in the boat, giggling a high girlish squeal. She sat up and trailed her fingers in the water, then splashed herself. The hysterical giggling bounced off the water and encircled the pond.

Next, he heard a thump, and Adana lurched forward. She grasped the sides of the boat and snorted as she tried to get her feet underneath her.

Kiffen swallowed hard when her rump rose in the air, and the boat tipped sideways.

Loud laughter came from the girl, her face now lost in the folds of her skirt. Moments later, Adana straightened, hands reaching towards the sky. She let go of the sides of the boat, wobbled and flung her arms wide. The bow of the boat rose out of the water, flew into the air, and flipped over. A family of ducks, resting in the reeds of the far bank, burst into the air on a raucous wave of complaint.

Kiffen raced down the hill.

The girl floundered in the water, splashing about in the same way puppies did the first time introduced to water. To his relief, she managed to stay afloat.

As she splashed about, Adana noticed him. "Prince Kiffen." She pronounced his name in a deep voice, then cackled. "Will the perfect prince come swim with me?"

He paused on the bank. Perfect? A cold certainty ran over him. The princess disliked him.

She still flailed about and splashed water everywhere. "When a lady asks a gentleman a question, he must answer, Kiffen. What would your queen mother say? Really." She rolled over in the water and slung one arm out while her back leg, entangled in her skirt kicked up out of the water. A moment later, she sank from view.

Shirt and boots came off quicker than he could have imagined, and Kiffen plunged into the cool water. As he swam toward her, Adana's head bobbed up above the surface. She smiled, water running down her face, tiny droplets sparkling on her eyelashes.

"Oh valiant prince," she announced in a high, sing-song voice, "I don't believe I know how to swim." She sank again.

Kiffen straightened his feet and met ground, standing chest high in the water. He plunged a fist under the surface and grabbed at the girl's cumbersome clothing. He heaved, and she popped out of the water, arms wheeling around her. Long fingers clamped onto his arm.

"Oh, oh. Help." She giggled again, then straightened her face into a frown. "Don't let me drown."

"Ballene's fire, Adana. Stand up. The water's not deep." He let go of her, but since she still clung to his arm, she pulled him underneath the surface with her.

Water seeped into his nose, and Kiffen fought upward, head breaking the surface. "Adana. Let go." A quick yank of his arm freed him from her grip. He stood and stared down at her.

She flailed in the water, light purple skirts floating up around her.

"Adana, stand up." Agitation sharpened his voice, and the girl's laughter ceased at his words.

Long strands of light-colored hair floated around her head as Adana gazed up at him. With her skirts floating in the water, she resembled a strange flower, waiting for him to enjoy its fragrance. Kiffen stumbled back a step, clearing his throat. "You are in no danger, princess. Please stand up."

His words appeared to sober her, and the girl stood. The water's depth came to her chest and damp clothes clung to her body, while her skirts continued to flirt around her in the water. Kiffen inched forward a step and slid a thick strand of wet hair back from her soft cheek. He stepped back two steps but wondered how she'd look if the water wasn't chest-high.

Convinced she had gained her footing, Kiffen led her, still giggling, from the pond. He averted his eyes after a brief peek revealed the tantalizing image of her dress plastered against her chest, her long, muscular body.

Adana flopped down on the ground and flung her arms wide. She chuckled and chuckled.

"What is wrong with you?" Kiffen squirmed, his gaze darting about the pond. He stood over her and fought the draw of her body stretched out on the ground before him.

"Drun...drunk...drunkenberry," Adana snorted. She sat up, brief alarm on her face. "Shhh. Don't tell. Oh, my head." The princess pressed her palms into her scalp, tears springing to her eyes. "The pain. It's supposed to stop the pain."

* * * * *

Chapter Twenty-Two

Whispered voices woke Adana from a fuzzy sleep. The massive bed enveloped her in soft luxury.

"Why would she do this?" Kassa's voice sounded bewildered and concerned.

"The prince said she complained of headaches." Veana sounded less bewildered, more loyal to her future queen. "Someone must have told her the berries might help."

"The apothecary says the residual effects of this berry cause headaches. How long has she been eating them?"

"Just once." Adana's voice croaked, unable to rise to a volume the Watchers might hear. She peered through one eye, winced at the light, and slid her body up into a reclining position, keeping the other eye closed.

Across the room, Kassa and Veana turned toward her, worry creasing their brows.

"You're awake." Kassa stalked over to the bed. "How do you explain yourself?"

The woman's angry tone rang a gong inside Adana's head. She inched back against the pillows, covering her eyes with her arm. "Just once."

"Just once what?" Kassa's voice drew closer and Adana sensed a shadow falling over the bed.

"Kassa. I hurt. Be quiet."

Silence.

"Thank you."

Silence.

Light blazed into her skull as Adana peeked through one eye again. Kassa stood beside the bed, arms crossed, her features scrunched into fury.

Adana struggled to sit up, rising slower this time. The pounding increased the higher she managed to lift her head, but she closed her eyes and fought through it. In the distance, she felt Am'brosia's caress. It grew stronger the longer she sat up. "Blazes. It didn't work."

Silence. The imposing figure of Kassa still glowered at Adana, so she turned to check Veana's mood.

The woman nodded once and wandered over to the trunk at the foot of Adana's massive bed. She lifted the lid and removed the carry bag with the drunkenberries in it. "So what are you doing with these?"

* * *

Shock and amusement warred on Suban's face when Adana and Veana sought out his assistance. "You made a tea out of the leaves of the formissa berry?"

"Formissa berry?" Adana shrugged. "I was told this is called drunkenberry."

When he raised his eyebrows at Adana, Suban's face became longer and thinner, resembling the face carvings sometimes found in the village elders' walking sticks. "That is a common name, mostly used by the peasants. Who identified it as such?"

"Just a stable boy."

"Ah, that would explain it. I imagine he warned you off of the berries?"

The plant sat on the apothecary's long compounding table, the berries glistening in the candlelight. "Yes. He told me of many side effects that sounded unpleasant."

"Of that, he was correct." The man pinched one of the berries between his fingers, a pinkish fluid leaking across his palm.

"But…" Adana stopped herself from admitting Am'brosia's involvement in this caper.

"But I imagine, the berries are the source you seek." Suban rose from his bench and consulted a large book on a raised pedestal. "Let me experiment for a while."

The odd little man turned his back on the two Watchers and began plucking berries from the plant, rolling them in his hands. With a start, he realized his error in protocol and turned back to Adana. "Forgive me, my lady. Now if I may? I will endeavor to find the concoction you seek."

She nodded her thanks and turned to leave.

"But please, do not attempt to use any more of this plant without my guidance."

Adana spun around, stunned at the terseness in his voice. "Of course not, Suban. I'm in your gratitude for this. The pain of separation leaves me lost in agony."

Sadness crept into his gaze. "We will find a way."

* * * * *

Chapter Twenty-Three

Adana lurched awake, gasping for air, the remnants of her dream drowning her. She had been lost in the rapids of a river, bounced along by the current. She blinked at the dim firelight in her chambers in Elwar's castle. Veana stood over her, shaking Adana's shoulder with urgency.

"My lady Adana, wake up."

The dream floated in Adana's memory as she struggled to sit up in the bed. The lush mattress and pillows gave her a wonderful night's sleep, but the same comfort made it difficult to reach an alert position. "What's wrong?"

Veana shook her head, eyes reflecting concern. "You must rise and get dressed. We've received a messenger. I'll explain as you dress." Without waiting for a response, the Watcher grabbed Adana's arm and hauled her to the edge of the bed.

She swayed in response to the unexpected adjustment but slid off the bed and shuffled over to the wardrobe. The door creaked as she opened it. Sleep confusion melted away, replaced by straight confusion. She turned back to Veana. "What do I wear? Monian or Elwarian? Tell me what's happened."

Veana strode across the room and pulled a Watcher's tunic from the wardrobe. "You represent Moniah tonight."

As Adana began to pull on a matching pair of leather leggings, Veana grabbed her boots and set them beside her. "A runner from

159

the Teletian guard arrived a short time ago. King Ariff's caravan was attacked."

Adana halted in her dressing and stared at Veana. "The king? Is he?"

"Two soldiers dead. Several are wounded, including Queen Morana and the prince. King Donel sent a squad to escort them in. Suban went with them. Kassa wants you prepared to greet the king and his family when they arrive."

Adana adjusted her leggings. Once they were in place, a dread crept along her spine. "Father?"

The Watcher shook her head. "We've heard nothing from King Micah's caravan. We sent a runner to warn them."

Relieved, she pulled the tunic over her head and yanked it into place. After tugging on her snug boots she began to straighten her hair. "Hand me my comb."

The comb, carved from the ivory of an elephant's tusk, slid through her hair as she divided it into three sections and braided it. "How badly are the queen and prince injured?" Adana tried to recall the age of Prince Navon. Morana had lost so many babes over the years. Navon was the only surviving heir to Teletia's throne.

"We don't know," Veana said, handing Adana the cord to tie her braid back.

"What of Belwyn? Has Empress Gabriella arrived yet?"

"Just before midnight. We've awakened the empress, too."

"Not the introductions Quilla planned." Adana frowned, aware Quilla might try to pin the blame for the ruined plans on Adana's young shoulders. Somehow, everything managed to be her fault if one asked Quilla.

A gentle hand touched Adana's shoulder. She turned and looked into Veana's green eyes. "I've told you before, forget the queen. She can try to make things difficult, but she can't harm you."

A cord hung around Veana's neck, a small flask hanging from it. She lifted it over her head and handed it to Adana. "Suban said to have you try this. He thinks he's gotten the proportions right, whatever that means."

The small, black flask felt cool in Adana's hand. In response, she checked her connection with Am'brosia, the pain roaring to the forefront of her mind. It always started this way when she woke, dulled senses until she checked the connection. At one point, she thought that might be the answer…to not check the connection. Although a good idea, it didn't work. The connection remained a significant part of the two of them. If she didn't check it first, Am'brosia did. She asked Am'brosia to stop once, but they found the task impossible. The connection drew them to connect whether they desired it or not.

"We trust this one? It will keep me alert and sober?"

Suban's last three concoctions didn't succeed due to the apothecary's hesitation to use large quantities of the formissa berries. She hadn't suffered any side effects with his efforts, but the formulas didn't work, either. He promised her he would make a stronger formula this time.

"He assured me you will not act unusual."

The man's willingness to predict this with such confidence concerned Adana, but she shrugged and unstopped the bottle. "How much?"

"All."

A sensation of sparkly sweetness swished over her tongue and trickled down her throat. The flavor, although pleasant, tasted odd, something sharp in contrast to the sugar. The two of them stood waiting. After several focused breaths, Adana chuckled. "Look at us. All on edge over a small drink."

"You feel fine?" Veana studied her face closely. "No dizziness or strange sensations?"

"No. At least, not yet. Will you hand me my cloak? It's sure to be cool outside, but I want to be there when King Ariff arrives."

* * *

Torches lit up the main courtyard at the castle's main gate. People milled around preparing to assist with the injured or relieve the other travelers of their burdens. Adana paused on the edge of the gathering, surveying the area. A petite woman, an overabundance of brown curls spilling across her shoulders and back, stood on a raised platform beside Kiffen and his father. She wore a deep purple colored gown, much simpler in design than Elwarian fashion. As Adana moved toward the platform, the woman leaned in toward Kiffen, laying a gentle hand on his arm. The young prince inclined his head toward the olive-skinned beauty. Adana halted. A flash of irritation pulsed through her. Kiffen obviously preferred dark-haired, tiny women. Not that she could blame him after her drunken episode at the pond. Adana had sought every opportunity to avoid the prince since that afternoon.

The two of them turned as Adana mounted the steps to the platform. Kiffen smiled at her and gave a short bow. Either his best manners were on display, or he was mocking her. She tried not to frown as King Donel introduced her to the woman.

"Empress Gabriella, may I present my lady Adana of Moniah."

New shame washed over Adana as a warm, friendly hands grasped hers. The empress smiled. "You are right, Prince Kiffen, she is as beautiful as her mother."

"My mother?" She choked back her confusion and looked into Gabriella's face. The friendliest brown eyes she'd ever seen twinkled back at her.

"Of course. I had heard you'd grown into a lovely young woman, and the prince was just confirming the information for me." Gabriella glanced sideways at him and tilted her head in a coquettish way. "And now that you join us, I see he did not exaggerate."

Adana stared at Kiffen, a flush rushing over her body.

The prince looked away and cleared his throat.

Footfalls mounting the stairs interrupted the awkward moment, and Adana turned to greet Kassa.

"You have been updated?" The old woman glanced between Adana and Veana who both nodded.

"Good. Horses approach."

A flurry of activity at the gates confirmed Kassa's information. Servants went into action, helping the exhausted troop from their horses, wrapping blankets over the shoulders of those who had carried or assisted the wounded, and offering warm mugs of cider. Adana breathed a sigh of relief at the sight of King Ariff astride his stallion with his wife and son riding beside him on a small, dun-colored, mare.

"Oh, there's the dear one." Gabriella rushed toward the queen's horse where the small toddler slept in his mother's arms, a bandage encasing his arm. The queen sported a gash on her face, but except for dark circles of exhaustion, she appeared fine.

"Gabriella can't have children." The hot breath of Kiffen's whispered information spun along her cheek. "She dotes on Prince Navon."

Adana turned toward Kiffen. He smiled at her like he had done in her first few days in Elwar. Why had he changed? Was he seeking Gabriella's approval? Although the empress was beautiful, she was still old enough to be his mother. She frowned at him and turned away, satisfied to see confusion settle in his eyes.

King Ariff dismounted and clumped up the steps toward King Donel. The two men grasped hands and forearms and studied each other. "My thanks for sending your troops to assist us," Ariff said. The slim man turned a loving gaze toward his wife and child, now dismounting from their horse. "And my special thanks for sending your apothecary. The queen and prince are fine thanks to his quick ministrations."

The two men spoke a few more moments, then Ariff assisted his wife up the stairs, taking the two-year-old prince in his arms. Adana watched the thick muscles of the king's upper arms bulge and flex as he hefted his son to his shoulder. The man stood slim and angular, but his shoulders and arms spoke of great strength.

The young prince awoke and stared around, his brown eyes wide and owl-like as he took in his surroundings. Like his father, he had curly hair, but his was brown while his father's grey.

The queen stepped forward and brushed a curl out of her son's face. "Sir," she addressed her husband, "we must not ignore Moniah's heir." She smiled at her son and spread the sweetness of that smile in Adana's direction. This woman stood closer in height to Adana than most women, but still not as tall as a Watcher. Her long, straight hair shone silken brown in the moonlight, making Adana wonder what it might look like if woven into glimmer cloth.

"Forgive the kings," she said to Adana. "The urgency of this evening's events has them distracted."

At that point, Queen Quilla mounted the steps, a deep scowl on her face. "My Lord, why do you allow our guests to stand about in the chill of the night? We must bring them in by the warmth of the fire. A small meal awaits them as I'm sure they are hungry."

The friendly atmosphere evaporated as Quilla turned and led the way into the castle. Unable to reject him without appearing rude, Adana accepted Kiffen's offered arm and followed the procession into the large dining hall.

Fires roared in the hearth on the far end of the large stone room, and the group gathered by the welcome warmth. Adana shed her cloak and draped it over the back of a chair. As she straightened, she caught Quilla's gaze on her, a thin line of disapproval to the woman's mouth, her brows arched inward. She turned her back on Quilla without acknowledging the stare, knowing Veana had provided the right wardrobe for meeting the other royals.

When she turned, she found Kiffen's eyes on her legs, a confused expression on his face. The prince started in shock when he caught her gaze. His lips twitched into a frown as he strode over to Gabriella's side. Adana fought the heat of anger toward his opinion of her uniform and turned toward the travelers, instead.

Quilla presided over the gathering. As her role demanded, the queen ensured that Adana gained her proper introductions to the king's family and to Empress Gabriella. Only after the introductions and proper nourishment crossed the travelers' lips did Quilla allow King Donel to inquire about the attack on Teletia's caravan.

Ariff set down his goblet and glanced around the room, his gaze resting on each person before moving to the next. "Where is King Micah? I'm told he will join us in this council."

"He should arrive soon," Kassa said. "By late morning if not sooner. We sent a runner with your news, so I suspect he will press on through the night."

Gabriella smiled at Adana as she breathed a sigh of relief over that news.

"I regret his absence, but we should discuss this now." Ariff set his goblet down on the table and pushed on the edge of the table, rising. "One of us can update Micah after he arrives. For now, I'll give you the details. Then, I suggest we sleep and discuss this in our scheduled meeting later today."

Agreement rippled along the table.

Adana glanced at Queen Morana. Her hair hung over her shoulder in disarray, and the small boy, Navon, lay against her body, his arms limp and hanging by his sides, a biscuit clutched in his tiny fist. The queen smiled down at him and loosened the fingers on the biscuit, placing it on the table. Her face transformed as she stroked the small boy's face with a gentle finger, but once King Ariff began, her mouth tightened and wrinkles of concern formed around her eyes.

"We'd settled into camp for the night. As close as we were, we didn't set up the tents in order to gain a quick departure in the morning. Shortly after I retired, a cry sounded from the south. I could hear the horses neighing and shouts in that direction. I jumped from my bedroll and joined my men. We ran toward the noise. Men crept out of the dark, most of them armed with knives. No swords, thank the Creator. We fought them off, but as quick as they struck, they retreated. We found two guards on the south end of camp, their throats cut."

Adana listened to his report, recalling the sudden attack on her men in the forest. It happened fast and was over, too. She glanced at the queen. "If you fought them at your camp's perimeter, how did the queen and prince become injured?"

Morana turned and studied Adana, her mouth pursed in thought. After a moment, she said, "We ran to the horses to calm them. The horses were frantic. Navon's touch often gentles the animals. We succeeded, but not without injury." She gazed down on her son and caressed the bandaged arm.

The group sat in silence, each studying the small child in the queen's arms.

"Was it Maligon?" The question came from a man Adana had only seen from a distance. His name was Simeon, King Donel's advisor and, according to rumor, the man who saved the king's life during the war with Maligon.

As she watched the dark-haired, dark-eyed man, he rose in a fluid motion and walked toward the fireplace. Once there, he turned his back to the fire and regarded the group. "The attack concerns me, yes, but was it Maligon?"

Ariff shook his head. "I don't know. The men fought but didn't shout any names or any battle cry."

Another silence fell.

"They didn't fire arrows?" Kassa leaned forward to better see King Ariff. "Or leave any weapons behind? The markings on an arrow can indicate."

The King of Teletia shook his head, but his wife interrupted the action. "There was an arrow near the horses. I believe it's what set them off at first." From the folds of her skirt, she pulled an arrow.

Red, green, and blue spiraled along the shaft.

* * * * *

Chapter Twenty-Four

Was it the sunlight streaming into her chambers or the tickling sensation under her nose that woke Adana a short while later? She rubbed her nose and turned over, stuffing her head under a pillow. After Kiffen's strange behavior in the middle of the night, she had found sleep difficult, only drifting off as the sun peaked over the horizon. The tickling sensation offended her nose again. She groaned and swiped at it, but a strong hand grabbed hers and held it tight.

She bolted upright, yanking her hand, unable to release it from the firm grasp.

Her father's chuckle greeted her. "You've become lazy in Elwarian luxury, I see."

"Papa!" She threw herself into his arms and held on tight. Unlike the last time he saw her, the king wrapped strong arms around his daughter and didn't let go.

Tears watered her eyes, but she clung to her father until she had them under control. After a season in Elwar, she didn't want him to decide she'd become soft. "When did you arrive?"

The king released her and closed his eyes, rubbing a hand over them. "Just before dawn. When we received news of the attack, we struck camp and pushed through the last few leagues."

He studied her, his red-rimmed, bleary eyes focused on her face. "After seeing the site where you buried Hunter," he wiped at his eyes, "and then getting the warning..." The distinctive blue in her

169

father's eyes shifted to steel, his mouth compressed into a straight line. The old vigor flowed through his body, the straight-backed posture returning despite any exhaustion he might claim. "I knew I must get to you soon. Make sure you are safe."

Joy soared through Adana's heart. The memory of their short parting festered in her soul, declaring the loss of both parents, not just her mother. "I'm so glad to see you, Papa. There's much to share."

"Of course, of course." He leaned against the bed post, and his eyes fluttered closed.

Adana tucked her feet under her. The vigor had returned to her father's body, but travel fatigue sagged his shoulders, nodded his chin toward his chest, and erupted in a sigh from beneath his beard.

"You've not slept." Shoving the covers aside, Adana rang the bell by her bedside. When she first arrived in Elwar, the maid explained the use of the bell to her. She had laughed at the audacity of ringing for a servant.

A maid bustled in the room, eyes wide, cap askew. After never ringing the bell before, Adana guessed its commanding peal surprised the woman.

"Where are King Micah's quarters?"

The maid glanced at the king and bobbed a quick curtsy, even though the man didn't see it. "Just down the corridor, my lady. Would you like a footman to..." The maid glanced back at the large form of the sleeping king, her expression like the face of a doe surprised at the edge of a wood by a hunter.

Adana considered the slumbering giant of her father. "King Micah must get some rest. Fetch someone to assist him to bed."

The maid nodded and scurried out of the room. In a short moment, barely a few breaths, two muscular footmen entered the chamber and helped the king to his feet.

The king roused enough to glance around at her and nod his head. "Wait, wait." He reached into a pocket and withdrew a small leather bag. "Glume sent this to you. Said you needed it." Errand completed, King Micah staggered on his feet and the footmen caught his arms again. "Night, daughter. Sleep well."

The words, muffled by his drooping chin, echoed from her memory and sent a sharp stab of longing into Adana's heart. Every night of her childhood, if present in the estate, her father sent her off to bed with those words.

"Night, Papa. Sleep well."

For a few moments, Adana watched the door where the footmen had escorted her father from her chambers. She held the small pouch in her hands and eventually turned her attention to it. She felt something oblong and hard inside the bag. "What have you sent me, Glume?"

Euphoria trilled along the link with Am'brosia as Adana dumped the contents of the bag on the bed, finding a small vial of crystals. A leather cord tied a note around the vial. She unrolled it and read it, then read it again.

My lady Adana,

I fear you may be experiencing more pain than expected while in Elvar. Here are more crystals. Remember only use a pinch in liquid every three days. No more! These will run out. I regret the need but share the formula below with the apothecary. This will help when the crystals are gone, but use it sparingly, miss. I would regret if the potion prevented your bond to develop.

Your servant, Glume

Adana stared at the valuable treasures, tears of relief pooling in her eyes. How had Glume known? The potion last night eased the pain some but not enough. The giraffe keeper's concern over the bond's interruption surprised Adana, though. She would never abuse this comfort. Still, she tucked Glume's note away before delivering the formula to Suban.

* * * * *

Chapter Twenty-Five

The morning sun slanted through the doors of the barn while Kiffen saddled Barlo, his horse. The late arrivals meant most of the castle still slept. He could enjoy several hours respite before the council meeting. After tossing and turning the remainder of the night while his thoughts tumbled over the memory of Adana in her snug Watcher's uniform and the scowls she bestowed on him, he gave up on rest and decided to clear his mind with an early morning ride.

The well-worn saddle welcomed him in its familiarity, and he clucked to the horse as they eased through the barn doors. Once beyond the stables, he stopped and looked around. A chill hung in the air, soon to be burned off by the sun. Exhausted servants moved in slow motion, starting the day. Birds sang above, and, across the fields, a hazy mist hung close to the ground. The yard remained caught in the shadows of the stable and other outbuildings.

A slap of the reins sent Barlo trotting across the fields and past Adana's pond. Just over the rise, Kiffen slowed the horse to a walk and returned to the hill overlooking the spot where he had observed Adana many times.

The pond stood still and empty. Disappointment clouded his mind. With the sun just above the horizon, he should have known not to expect her to be there, but thanks to his father's and Serrin's request, the habit of watching out for Adana became a natural part of his daily actions.

Images of Moniah's heir crept into his thoughts without prompting. He might be studying Maligon's War or practicing swords with Pultarch or wandering along the streets of the city, and, unbidden, she would materialize in his mind.

Kiffen spurred his horse onward, galloping across the fields, the wind ruffling his hair. Try as he might, he never could outride the pull of the girl. Why did thoughts of her plague him? If only Serrin had lived. He drew the horse to a slow walk at that thought.

Kiffen never would have thought of Adana as more than a sister with Serrin here. Did he love her as Pultarch teased during her first weeks living in the castle? The horse snorted, and Kiffen patted his neck. "I know, Barlo. It doesn't matter if I love her. She and I are forbidden to marry."

After the ancient king of Yarada divided his kingdom between his twin daughters, Elwar and Moniah, a tradition grew over concerns of the twins' kingdoms losing their identities. The heir to the throne of Elwar could not marry Moniah's queen. Only a second son, if he forfeited his rights to Elwar's throne, could do so.

Unbidden, memories of Serrin's anxious excitement over meeting Adana for the first time rose in Kiffen mind. The two of them traveled with their father three years earlier to learn about Moniah and introduce Serrin to Adana. Serrin chose his giraffe for bonding, Bai'dish, during the same visit.

"Or was it Bai'dish who chose Serrin?" Kiffen's voice sounded muffled and thick in the stillness of the dawn. It didn't really matter now; Serrin was gone, and, for some reason, Bai'dish survived him.

As the two boys and their father had ridden toward the huge plateau where Moniah's fortress estate rose above the plains and marked the last stretch of the savannah before reaching the desert beyond, Serrin had chattered on about Adana. At thirteen, just a year younger than Kiffen at the time, his brother had just begun to notice young girls, and Kiffen recalled a certain jealousy over his brother's marital decisions being already made for him.

"What do you suppose she's like?" Serrin's voice squeaked in one of those embarrassing transitions to manhood, and Kiffen smiled at the memory as if the boy sat astride his own horse alongside Barlo on this particular morning.

Not waiting for an answer, his brother had plowed on. "Father says she's tall and slim. Not tiny like mother or Leera."

Kiffen never understood how his brother managed to call Quilla mother. She lost interest in both of them once their father married her. From then on, her thoughts and comments centered on Leera, the small baby who arrived ten months later.

Still, his brother had rattled on. "Do you suppose she'll like me? She's only twelve. What do you think, Kiffen?" He'd turned his serious blue eyes on his brother, concern crowding the excitement from his face like the clouds rolling in to block the sun.

Kiffen had laughed at him. "What's not to like? She's a child. You're a child. I'm sure you'll run and play and become great friends together. Then you'll do some bizarre ceremony with the giraffes and be happy together."

Serrin kicked at his brother, unable to reach the distance when Kiffen danced his horse sideways with another laugh.

Serrin's voice dropped almost to a whisper, and he sidled his horse closer to Kiffen's. "What if the giraffes don't like me? Or I don't like them?"

Drawing his horse to a halt, Kiffen had looked at his brother. "Serrin, everyone loves you. You're fun; people always prefer you."

Kiffen shook his head and started his horse forward again. "It's me they don't like. I'm too quiet. Hard to get to know."

The memory faded as Kiffen recalled those last words. Maybe that had been his problem with Adana. He held back. He didn't speak. He watched. He listened.

The words of his mother echoed in his ears, "Your brother is so like your father, friendly and chatty." She'd cupped Kiffen's childish face in her palm and gazed down into his eyes. "I'm afraid you've inherited my quiet and solitude, dear one. Don't let it hold you back."

A few weeks later, she had died, consumed by the eating-away sickness.

Kiffen shook his head, and Barlo whinnied and danced around in a circle. Around him, the mist rose from the ground. "Begone," he yelled toward the sky. "Take these ghosts with you."

His troubles no better, he spurred the horse back to the castle where spirits knew to remain hidden.

* * * * *

Chapter Twenty-Six

Adana studied the thirteen faces of those gathered around the table—King Donel alongside his advisor, Simeon, Kiffen, Empress Gabriella with one of her knights, Sir Jerold, King Ariff and Queen Morana, Adana's father, and three Watchers familiar with the attack on the Monian village. On either side of Adana sat Veana and Kassa.

"How do we know it's really Maligon?" King Micah's voice echoed in the cavernous receiving room. "I was there when Chiora sent the despicable traitor to his death. Surely, this is the work of one of his disgruntled followers seeking to frighten us with his memory."

Adana looked up at her father's familiar but determined face. He filled the room with his presence, and all listened when he spoke. She recalled many meetings before Mammetta fell ill where her father *and* her mother exhibited such strength and confidence. The three Watchers beside him—Ostreia, known to the Teletians as the Monian emissary, Karyah, Belwyn's emissary, and Kalara, a gifted tracker—reflected the same determination.

Did Kalara recall her last meeting with Adana? On the day of the border village attack, when Adana lurked in the barracks eavesdropping, this was the Watcher who noticed her and sent her back to her mother. If she hadn't listened, if she'd managed to sneak away, the Creator would have saved Mammetta and Serrin.

A sharp pang sank into Adana's chest, and she laid her hand over it, breathing in, then out in focused breathing. The simple motion must have alerted Veana. The Watcher shifted in her seat, the gathering ignored, while she studied Adana, a question in her gaze.

Adana shook her head and placed her hands on the table, but she continued the focused breathing. Now that she had the crystals, the comfort Am'brosia might lend her lay just beyond her grasp. Constant pain or occasional comfort? Such a tough choice she must make between the two.

Kassa rose and all turned toward her. "We can speculate on whether or not this is Maligon, but it doesn't matter. Someone, a follower still caught up in his treachery, or a newer kind of enemy seeking to destroy us, has attacked us three times. We should discuss what we know, first."

Empress Gabriella nodded. "As much as I fear the return of my cousin, it is not the most pressing question. Kassa speaks wisdom as always." She turned toward the Watchers seated alongside Micah. "What can you tell us of the attack on your village?"

The darker-skinned Karyah answered for the three of them. "Ostreia and I went with the first troops sent in. Running at top paces, we reached the village late in the afternoon. Most of the buildings were gone, burned out, their food and livestock stolen. A few of the old and young were injured, but no one killed. Whoever attacked did so at dawn, without warning. No one saw a man resembling Maligon, but some of the villagers thought they heard the marauders mention him."

Silence settled over the group. Adana, through a weakened connection to Am'brosia, relived the strange trip they took that day, seeing, again, the disfigured man astride a horse overlooking the village attack.

Into the silence, Kalara spoke. "My tracking squad followed the attackers. We searched a wide area around the village, but a sandstorm wiped out any traces before we could arrive. I remained and conducted a search of a larger perimeter, hoping to find something. After several days, I found this not far outside the village." She dropped an arrow on the table. It clattered against the wood like the failed bowshot of a Watcher in training.

Red, green, and blue spiraled along the shaft of the arrow.

Adana heard the whistle and zing of the arrow striking Hunter. If she looked down now, would he lay at her feet, wheezing out his last breaths? Her hands itched to pick up the arrow and examine it. A twin remained tucked in her trunk. Kassa had identified those markings as Maligon's when she gave Adana the arrow that killed Hunter.

"I saw him." Adana spoke the words, not meaning to give voice to her revelation. She paused at her own words and checked to see if those around her heard. Everyone stared at her in curiosity.

"You saw who?" Kassa squinted at her in confusion.

"A man on a horse overlooking the village. His hand was shriveled and useless. One shoulder drooped with weakness." Adana licked her lips as all the moisture left her mouth. Everyone still stared in confusion. Except for Kalara. Her intense stare made Adana feel pinned to the wall for study and dissection.

"You had a vision?" Kassa's expression shifted to the one she used during training, the hawk-like stare. "At your age?"

"I don't know if it was a vision. Am'brosia took me."

In the silence, Adana sought a friendly face around the table. Her father steepled his fingers and looked over them, not at her, but at a point on the far wall of the large room. Ostreia and Karyah tilted their heads sideways and studied her like a challenge target on archery day. Kalara's gaze continued to strike deep in Adana's heart, an accusation she couldn't name or comprehend.

Around the table, the others appeared silenced in shock. Gabriella tapped her fingers to her lips. Sir Jerold copied her, his taps in syncopation to Gabriella's. King Donel stroked his white beard and sat back, his gaze focused on Simeon, his advisor. King Ariff leaned forward on his elbows, scrutinizing her like an odd bug who suddenly landed in their midst. Kiffen was the only one not looking her way. He frowned, his gaze following hers around the group.

"Perhaps you should explain," Veana said.

Adana scrutinized the table. She couldn't find the strength to share the story while reading the questions and doubt on everyone's faces. Why had she spoken? She hadn't planned to reveal this experience to anyone but Kassa.

"That day. The day Mammetta…The day the red warning came." Adana squeezed her eyes shut trying to recall the strange way Am'brosia jumped her from giraffe to giraffe. "I saw the Watcher before she arrived. Montee told me to connect to Am'brosia during my archery trials. I did, but Am'brosia took control. It felt like she jumped off the cliff and flew across the plains. I saw a Watcher running toward us."

Dryness stuck Adana's lips to her teeth. Without a word, Veana handed her a goblet of wine. As she gulped, Adana glanced around the table. Donel and Kiffen reflected the same confusion from moments ago, while the rest leaned forward, gazes intent on her.

"Am'brosia jumped into another giraffe's head." She turned to Kassa and shook her head. "I don't really know what she did. We just kept jumping from giraffe to giraffe. I could see through their eyes. Then I saw the village. The attack. People running, screaming."

Adana swallowed, reliving the shock of the scene. She turned toward Empress Gabriella who sat forward, the rest of her body gone still. "That's when I saw him. Not with the attackers. He was on a horse on the hillside watching. I couldn't see his face, but he had injuries to his hand and shoulder."

"Maligon," Empress Gabriella whispered. "It's not possible." She turned, wide-eyed, to Sir Jerold and grasped his hand, her knuckles turning white in her grip. The young soldier covered her hand with both of his. "What do we do now?"

* * * * *

Chapter Twenty-Seven

Adana's revelation created havoc in the council until King Donel's advisor, Simeon, stood and slammed his hands down on the table.

People jumped in their seats, but the man's actions silenced them all. He spoke in soft tones. After the chaos of moments earlier, the room remained still, so all heard him. "My lady tells an interesting story. There are other men with such injuries, but I'm inclined to say the evidence points to the traitor's survival." He focused on Adana, his mouth parted in a regretful smile. "We still need to hear the story of the forest attack. And, then we need to discuss last night's attack on Ariff's troops."

Once again, everyone focused on Adana, expectation in their faces. She did her best to meet their gazes as she spoke this time. Kassa's presence to her left gave her comfort as she recounted trailing Hunter's party into the woods and the sudden awareness of being watched. Everyone listened, their faces thoughtful rather than speculative, until Adana mentioned her narrow escape from the arrow.

"The arrow would have found me if Hunter hadn't stepped in front of me when he did. He died instead of me." Tears clouded her vision, and she sought out her father's face through them. He wiped at his eyes, too. She turned away from his loving gaze and saw Kalara frown, a thunderstorm of emotions flitting across her features.

"I'm sorry, Kalara. Was he close to you?" Adana flashed back to the grief and mourning of her troops that night.

183

The Watcher blinked and all emotion washed from her face, a stoic Watcher's mask falling over her features. "No. I didn't know him well."

Confusion over her mistaken interpretation of Kalara's body language silenced Adana. She considered the Watcher further, but the woman maintained her silent mask, not revealing any more thoughts.

"After the arrow shot," Veana said, "several First Soldiers and I pursued the shooter through the forest. It was too dark, and we couldn't find any tracks without more light. We don't know if it was one or more, but the arrow was the same."

"As it was with us," Queen Morana added, her soft voice barely audible in the cavernous room.

After King Ariff recounted the details of the attack on his camp the night before, everyone sat in silence. After a few moments, all turned toward Kassa.

The woman frowned and shook her head. "I am here in Montee's absence, but many of us lived through the last war with Maligon. Empress Gabriella, I know for you this news is hardest. His return jeopardizes your life and throne, but he won't stop there. History proves he wants more. He wants all of us. I believe we should think on this and meet again tomorrow. Maligon's had twenty years to plan. We don't have that luxury, but we can take one night."

* * *

Adana stood as the others did, but no one left the room, instead gathering in small clusters, discussing how Maligon's plans might unfold. Across the table, Kiffen nodded at her and motioned her to the end of the room. She wandered around the others and reached the spot at the same time as Kiffen did.

His face, for once, didn't look on her with contempt, but he reminded her of the way Serrin said farewell the last time she saw him, the day he departed Moniah. The resemblance was so striking, at first she thought she heard Serrin's voice instead of Kiffen's. "My lady Adana, I want you to know that I'll be here for you."

Unable to separate the two brothers in her mind, she tilted her head and waited, thinking he must have more to say. When he said no more, she touched his arm. "Thank you, Prince Kiffen. It's important that you and I work together. If we can stop Maligon, that is."

Fire lit his eyes and his jaw muscle flexed. "We will stop him, I assure you. The Creator will not leave us to this evil."

"I hope so." Adana watched Kiffen stalk away, his shoulders set with tension. Maybe the Creator still aided Elwar's heir, but she knew better than to rely on their god's help.

Gabriella joined her at the end of the room, her gaze following Kiffen as he left. The empress had shown nothing but kindness to Adana, but she still fought the urge to strike at the woman, to remind her of her age against Kiffen's.

"Empress, you wish to speak to me?"

"Yes, Adana. May I call you that? And you stop calling me empress?"

"Of course." A flush of embarrassment over her previous thoughts spread up Adana's neck. In the muted distance, she felt Am'brosia's heart flutter with approval.

Gabriella turned and walked toward a window, Adana following her. "You know of the events of my cousin's birth?"

Adana lowered her voice, aware of the sensitive nature behind Maligon's connection to the ruling family of Belwyn. "I know of your aunt's rape by a vagrant. She died giving birth to him." Adana knew many things about Maligon's life. His family squired him sooner than normal due to his unsavory beginnings. He came to Moniah as a young boy where he befriended her mother. For years, the two were inseparable, until his true nature surfaced.

Gabriella looked out the window as night fell on the castle. Adana saw the shadows of guards moving along the walls, their calls to each other ringing on the night air. "Then you know he murdered my entire family in the first war? In his quest for Belwyn's throne."

She could only nod, unable to voice the truths of Gabriella's life.

The empress' brown eyes pleaded with Adana. "Your mother sought to protect you the way my family protected me. My parents hid me. That's why I live. I never should have been empress, but…"

The similarity of their situations had never occurred to Adana before. "But you are the only legitimate heir. Just as I am the only heir to Moniah."

A gentle hand, not unlike her own mother's, smoothed a hair on Adana's brow. "Your mother loved you more than you'll ever know. Every decision she made was for you to follow her to the throne. I know it's hard to be here, to be in a foreign place, among strangers, but it will grow easier. You will rule wiser because of this."

With a wistful smile, she patted Adana's arm then turned away. She walked straight across the room to Sir Jerold. The young knight watched her approach, a mixture of concern and devotion in his eyes. After a few shared words, he escorted the empress from the chamber.

Adana remained by the window, listening to the sounds of night settle around her. Somewhere a horse stamped its foot, a young boy laughed, pots clattered. The sounds weren't different from home. Just those who made them and the places they inhabited.

She turned away from the window and found Kassa standing a few steps behind her, waiting. "We must discuss your vision. There is nothing in the former queens' journals of such a journey. No one knew a giraffe might be capable of such an action."

* * * * *

Chapter Twenty-Eight

After a sleepless night, Adana stumbled from her bed and prepared to join the Kingdom Council again. When Veana pulled her leathers from the wardrobe, Adana shook her head. She couldn't take another day of Kiffen's eyes on her, distaste turning his eyes flat. She would heed Gabriella's advice and embrace Elwar as home until her eighteenth birthday. If that meant wearing the overworked dresses, she would do so. Maybe she could find a seamstress to cut a few of the more cumbersome dresses down to match the simpler style worn by Gabriella.

Veana raised an eyebrow at Adana's objection but didn't question it. "Let me locate your maid. These dresses are beyond my ability."

Adana laughed. Watchers weren't known for their fondness of fine things. Life, out of necessity, remained simple.

The council gathered, breakfast spread on a table along the wall. Adana found she couldn't manage a morsel of the breads and muffins, so she cradled a goblet in her hands, sipping the watered wine with care. The memory, or in truth, the lack of memory from her one bout with drunkenberry, provided the caution she needed.

To her surprise, Simeon yielded the floor to Kiffen. The prince nodded his thanks and addressed the table. "I've considered the ramifications of Maligon's return. It's a speculation that Simeon and I have entertained during my education for years. We don't know where he is. He has struck on the southern edges of Moniah. He struck in the forest just inside our border, and he struck not a day's journey east of us. His reach is large."

The truth of Kiffen's words surprised Adana. She had spent the night before mulling over the details of the three attacks. None of it made sense. Now, she knew why. The three attacks covered a wide area.

"We must assume that Maligon has relocated or recruited followers throughout Moniah and Elwar. I doubt he participated in any of these attacks, save one." Kiffen's serious blue-eyed gaze captured Adana and held her still, not breathing. "We have my lady Adana to thank for that knowledge."

When Adana found her breath again, she laid her palm across her abdomen, seeking the focused breathing that might calm her jumping pulse. For just a moment, she had seen a reflection of the ruler this boy might become, but something else delighted her insides. Something astonishing…and pleasurable.

The Watcher, Kalara, sat forward. "What do you propose, Prince Kiffen? How do you suggest we fight an enemy we can't recognize?"

"We don't." Kiffen turned to face the Watcher. "That's what he wants us to do. He seeks to draw us out. To pull us apart, scatter us. We must remain vigilant, step up our security, but it's not time to seek him out. Let him come looking for us."

* * *

K iffen's assessment ruled the rest of the meeting, and everyone agreed to his wisdom. When they exited the chamber around noon, Queen Quilla swept down on her husband, a gleam in her eye. "Have you resolved your discussions? Made your plans?"

Dark circles weathered King Donel's jovial features, but he took his wife's hands in his and nodded. "We have."

A victorious smile stretched the queen's features. "I look forward to hearing your plans, my lord. Now, I can send the invitations out for our celebratory ball."

Adana halted in the stone hallway, one foot not settled on the floor. To her side, Kiffen froze in a similar position. In fact, the entire Kingdoms Council paused and stared at the queen.

Quilla glanced around at each of them, amusement on her features. "We have several royal guests in our midst. We would be terribly impolite if we did not provide a feast in your honor and introduce you to our noble families. You mustn't return home believing Elwar is run by savages." As she spoke those last words, Quilla swept her gaze over the Watchers, but her triumphant smile faltered as she encountered Adana, attired in Elwarian dress. "It seems I've proven that to at least one of you, anyway."

Quilla's smile returned as she nodded toward Adana.

Adana did not enjoy it.

Next to her, Kiffen made a humphing sound. Wary of her earlier, unexplainable reaction to the prince, she chose to remain facing forward, but observed him through her peripheral vision. His perpetual frown lingered while his gaze traveled back and forth from his stepmother to Adana.

Adana walked away, head held high, toe heel, toe heel.

Clattering footsteps rang down the stairs toward Adana as she climbed them, prepared to return to her chambers. Leera rounded the corner and drew up short, her blue eyes sparkling. "Have you heard? There's to be a dinner. With dancing. Mother says I may attend, and I'm to have a new dress. As are you."

Adana nodded and trudged past Leera. "So it seems."

Spinning around to trail Adana, Leera said, "Aren't you excited? We get to select materials. Mother summoned the best seamstress in the city. Her gowns speak volumes."

Adana paused and regarded Leera. "Speak volumes? Dresses don't speak."

The girl's sudden trill of laughter never ceased to surprise Adana. Leera found so much of Adana's thoughts amusing. "Have you never noticed how people act in response to your clothing? Don't people respond to you a certain way when you wear your uniform?"

Quilla hated the uniform, and based on his glares, Kiffen did, too. In Moniah, a Watcher's uniform commanded respect. "Of course they do. It's a soldier's uniform, not a dress." Adana stiffened her shoulders and continued up the stairs.

Leera rushed after her. "But a dress says something else. It announces your beauty, your feminine grace."

The dress Adana wore swished around her on the steps as she turned back and forth, studying it. "These skirts? Do you recall how I tripped over them for weeks? And they hide everything."

Kassa came up behind them on the stairs. "My lady, you walk with a regal grace now that you found a way to navigate those skirts. Men notice. And women have teased men for centuries by hiding their bodies under material."

"Queen Quilla disapproves of my uniform because I don't hide my body from the eyes of men?"

Her mouth in a straight line, Kassa nodded. "In part. But, she also seeks to conform all within her reach to her own ideas of propriety, not ours."

"I see." Adana turned to Leera. "Do you think this seamstress can make a gown cut like one of Empress Gabriella's? I dislike these petticoats, and if we're to dance, as you suggest, I doubt I can manage in a dress like this."

Leera pouted. "The seamstress is renowned in the four kingdoms. If it can be made, she'll make it." She flounced up the stairs, leaving Adana and Kassa behind. "You should wear a proper dress, though. I already asked her to make us matching ones, mine in green and yours in peach."

* * * * *

Chapter Twenty-Nine

Kalara whipped her horse into a frenzy, racing across the land of Elwar. When the Kingdoms Council adjourned, she fabricated an urgent message from an outpost and departed.

Once beyond the hills and into the flat lands leading into Moniah, she left the horse at an inn, and ran. The rhythmic pounding of her feet released the anger in her body. Father would have to kill the ones who went into the forest. Their orders had been plain. What fools!

Three days later she arrived at her father's home. He stood in the doorway of the simple, sandstone dwelling, squinting in her direction. How many times had she returned to find him waiting on her, as if he sensed her arrival?

"Daughter? What brings you in such a rush? Did those fools at the Kingdoms Council surprise us with a great plan?"

Kalara shook her head and stalked over to a barrel of water by the door. She scooped up handfuls, gulping the warm liquid. Even in the shade, water remained warm, but it was wet, and that was what mattered. The last handful she used to scrub her face clean of sand and sweat. Water trickling down her front into her tunic, she shook her head again. "We must speak. Inside."

Maligon's eyebrows rose in surprise. She knew he preferred all requests phrased as a question, but the urgency of the situation and her overwhelming exhaustion pushed the prescribed behaviors from her mind. Rather than apologize, she pushed past him and entered the small room. A fire burned in the hearth, the heat unbearable after her run, but she poured herself a glass of wine and sank into her designated chair awaiting her father.

Maligon meandered after her, ignoring her for a moment while he poured himself a glass of wine and took several moments to settle in his chair. She couldn't help but smile over his show of indifference. Now that she fought better than he, he used behavior to make his points.

"Now, Kalara, what pressing news brings you barreling to my side? Surely, nothing creative occurred in this meeting?"

"No father. It's as we expected. They are on high alert, but they choose to wait and see what your next move will be."

"Hmm. No troops sent into the areas of the attacks? No recruiting of more soldiers? I'm disappointed in Micah. I hoped he'd prove to the kingdom what a fool he is."

"The one you need to watch is Prince Kiffen. He was the first to speak wisdom, and all listened to him." Kalara sipped the wine, the warm liquid sparking flavor along her tongue. A Lisseme vintage for sure.

"So, the young pup favors his mother in strategy does he?" Maligon placed his goblet on a table and rose, ambling toward the fire where he held his hands over the flames as he might do on a day in the rainy season. He turned his back to the fire, hands tucked behind him, delight stretching his lips into a smile. "That will make our plans all that more fun to execute, my dear. If the boy shows promise, now, imagine how well they will listen to him when Adana returns to Moniah. I do hope he continues in that vein. Winning without effort is not worth the battle."

Kalara nodded. She'd heard Maligon brag on the scheming minds of Queen Chiora and Queen Roassa, even Kassa. Although she never met Roassa, she would agree that Chiora and Kassa possessed keen minds when it came to strategy.

"So," Maligon seated himself again, "what caused you such great concern?"

"The attack in the forest, sir."

Leaning back in his seat, feet stretched before him, Maligon regarded her from under lidded eyes. "As I recall, you suggested that attack."

The response was expected. She'd had little else to think about in her three days of running. At least Watchers learned how to maintain a fast pace, or she'd still be days away, rolling this problem over in her head, her stomach churning with each footfall.

"Yes sir, I did. You recall we determined they should try to hit the soldiers, but if an opportunity presented itself, to try for a Watcher?"

"Yes. The archer who fired the shot bragged that he almost got a Watcher, too. I rewarded him with a small patch of land."

"You what? How could…" Kalara bit back the retort. If she planned to remain loyal to her father, her loyalties to the Watchers must not get in the way.

"Father, the Watcher he almost shot was Adana."

"What?" Maligon burst from his chair with a roar. "The idiot. How could he brag about that?" He stalked to the door to a back room. "Soldier!"

A large, bearded man wearing a sleeveless leather vest over filthy brushed leather pants appeared at the door.

"Fetch Patiken. Bring him here, now." Maligon roared the last word, spittle flying from his lips.

The soldier wiped the spittle from his face without flinching, nodded once, and trotted out the door.

"The fool. The idiot. The scum." Maligon paced the room, the purple robes he'd taken to wearing flapping around his legs. After two laps, he turned to his daughter. "Was Adana harmed? If he lied about that, he could lie about anything."

Kalara rose and offered a fresh goblet of wine to her father. "No. We would have known in Moniah if he struck her."

When he stopped and looked at her over the rim of the goblet as he sipped, she said, "For what it's worth, I doubt he knew who she was. True to her nature, she wasn't where she should be. She followed a hunting party into the woods. By herself."

He grinned at that, then he laughed. "Oh, she is Chiora's daughter, isn't she?" Patting Kalara on the shoulder, he gestured for her to sit. "So what else can you tell me of this significant gathering of power?"

Kalara laughed at her father's sarcasm and shared the details of the Kingdoms Council. When she had finished, Maligon sat back, his eyes lidded again, hands resting on his flat stomach. "What of Samantha? How goes your effort to recruit her?"

"I've planted seeds of doubt in her mind. She and Montee are not speaking to each other, and she complains to those who already follow us. She'll be ours, but it will take time. She was nursed at the breast of a Watcher, after all."

"Yes. Yes. We have time, still." He leaned forward, his gaze penetrating into Kalara's soul. "But we need her."

* * * * *

Chapter Thirty

Elegant string music played in the background as Kiffen descended into the Great Hall. People mingled throughout the room, dressed in their finest clothing. Across the room, he spotted Pultarch chatting with a swarm of young ladies, their dresses blooming around him like a flower garden. As Kiffen made his way through the throng, Pultarch flashed his well-rehearsed smile and a high-pitched titter erupted from his admirers.

In unison, the group turned when Pultarch waved to him. In an instant, several of the ladies rushed to his side, etching quick curtsies, and rising to chirp silliness. He nodded, not really listening, while he scanned the guests for Adana. Pultarch searched the gathering, too.

"Oh! There she is!" One of the bevy of girls said. "She's so tall. And what is she wearing?"

Kiffen and Pultarch swung around and followed the young women's gazes. Adana stood on the stairs, her hand placed on her father's arm as she descended. She wore a gown made from blue glimmer cloth, Moniah's most valuable export. As she moved, the exotic fabric shimmered between the shade of the pond's waters when mid-day sun hit it and the darkest blue of the evening sky before the sun dropped below the horizon. The dress clung close to her body, revealing a slight, but tempting dip at the neckline, until it reached her hips, then it flared into a dramatic sweep of skirt that fell to just above the floor. Her hair fell in a tawny curve around her shoulders.

Both men excused themselves from the flower garden of ladies and moved toward the stairs. When Adana's gaze fell on them, she tipped her head in acknowledgement while the beginnings of a smile quirked the ends of her lips. Something in her eyes struck Kiffen as different.

While he tried to understand the meaning in her look, Pultarch seized the opportunity to greet her and relieve King Micah of his escort duties. Adana accepted Pultarch's arm and allowed him to lead her away without a glance at Kiffen. Quickly, they disappeared among the guests.

"There you are, Your Highness." One of the earlier flower ladies had managed to follow them and now stood before him, expectation plain on her face.

"I'm sorry, my lady. May I be of service to you?"

Her smile never faltering, the girl took his arm and led him across the room. "Your mother, the queen, has selected me as your seating partner this evening, Prince Kiffen. I hope you will find my attention suitable."

Dismay rocked over him, but Kiffen maintained their forward direction. He glanced down at the tiny woman beside him, aware the top of her elaborate hairdo of black curls didn't reach his shoulder. "Forgive me if I was distracted before, but whose daughter are you?"

Bright hazel eyes smiled up at him as she tapped his arm with her closed fan. "Your Highness, you do not remember me, do you?"

"I fear I may have offended you, but, in truth, I do not. Perhaps it's due to your elegance, tonight." Kiffen breathed a sigh of relief when the girl's smile grew even wider.

"Your Highness, we used to ride together as children. I'm, Contina Lord Sarx's niece."

"Contina?" Kiffen stopped and searched the girl's face. "You've changed since we last rode together."

The girl flipped open her fan and hid a pleased smile behind it, peering at him over the edge of the hand-painted instrument. "I hope the changes please you, Your Highness."

Tongue-tied, Kiffen stared into those eyes. He fought every urge to search the crowd for Pultarch and Adana. "Mistress Contina, when I first saw you tonight, I thought you resembled a flower. Now, if we are to be seat partners, you may as well drop the formalities and call me by my name."

"Yes, Kiffen." She breathed the words in a hot rush of air which managed to rise up and scorch his neck.

"Very well." He rubbed the spot on his neck before extending his arm to her again. "I believe we should join the others in the Banquet Hall."

As Contina promised, his stepmother had matched the two of them for the evening. Meaning he must offer her the beginning and ending dances as well as one more. As he assisted Contina into her seat, his gaze sought out Adana and Pultarch seated across the table but down a few chairs from them. His sister Leera appeared, breathless to take the seat across from him, while a young boy trailed her, his eyes following her every move like a puppy.

Kiffen swallowed a groan. Not only did he have to watch Pultarch play the charms on Adana, but he needed to ensure his sister and her beau came to no mischief for the evening.

* * *

Adana managed to maintain a running conversation with Pultarch and the couple across the table from them without allowing her gaze to wander to Kiffen and the young lady seated by his side. The girl reeked of ease and charm with the prince, and her laughter came often enough to grate on Adana's nerves.

Once the dancing began, she found it easier to ignore Kiffen. Pultarch led her to the floor and swept her around the room with such grace she barely knew her feet touched the floor. Not once in Quilla's dance instructions had Adana managed the intricacies of this dance without stepping on her partner's feet.

In surprise, she gave Pultarch her full attention for the first time of the evening. "You dance well, Pultarch."

Small red splotches blushed on his cheeks. "Only due to the lovely woman in my arms, my lady."

"I assure you, Pultarch, it is not due to me." As his blush faded, Adana looked deeper into his face. The charming façade had evaporated sometime during dinner. For the first time, she suspected Pultarch gave her a glimpse of the true man instead of the flirting boy.

They whirled around the floor with the music swelling in her ears. The dance carried them in sweeping circles, preventing Adana from even recognizing other dancers as they twirled by. When the music stopped, she staggered from dizziness. Pultarch grabbed her around the waist and pulled her to him. "I won't let you fall."

When the musicians paused for a break in the dancing, Leera sidled up to Adana. "For someone who didn't care about a dance, you hide it well. Or has Pultarch claimed your heart?"

Adana looked down her nose at the girl and laughed at the hopeful expression. "Your mother seated me with Pultarch."

Satisfaction lit up Leera's face.

Adana wasn't sure whether to thank Leera or smack her. "You suggested Pultarch as my partner?"

"Of course." Leera sipped from a small glass cup of punch. "I had to do something. You were never going to give him a chance as long as he pranced around showing off."

"So, you know his behavior is a farce?"

Leera tilted her head sideways and glanced at Adana. "I've known Pultarch my entire life."

When Adana only nodded, Leera leaned in close and whispered, "Forget Pultarch for the time. Have you noticed how the Empress Gabriella acts with Sir Jerold, her knight?"

"I haven't had the opportunity to observe them."

The musicians began another dance number, and this one moved at a slower pace. Gabriella and Jerold danced together not far from where Adana and Leera stood.

The couple spoke and laughed, their heads nodding in toward each other. Adana followed them with her eyes, studying each movement, the placement of their hands, the way they gazed at each other. "What are you thinking, Leera?"

"He's her lover."

A tingle of shock ran up Adana's neck at the thought. She turned and watched the couple again. "He's much younger than her. Surely, you're mistaken." In the back of her mind, Adana remembered how Gabriella had laughed with Kiffen on the night they gathered to meet the Teletians' arrival.

Mischievous glee radiated in Leera's smile. "Why not? She's unwed. She's unable to bear children. If I had Jerold as my most trusted advisor, I might—"

"Leera!" Adana pressed her hands to her burning cheeks. "You should not know such things."

The girl straightened her spine and gave a toss of her head, curls bouncing everywhere. "I listen. Servants talk of the things mother never tells me."

With one last glance toward the dancing couple, Adana grabbed Leera's arm and dragged her through a door onto a large stone balcony overlooking the gardens. At the balustrade, she stopped and turned on the girl. "Leera, you are young—"

She held up her hand to stop a retort when Leera's tiny mouth popped open in protest. "You are young, and you hear things you shouldn't. Your mother condones your mischief, but you should still take care of what you say. Just because you suspect something, doesn't mean you have to speak of it."

The cool night air settled down on Adana's neck and shoulders while she watched Leera's mouth work. It opened and closed several times, while thoughts galloped across the girl's features. Eventually, the girl giggled.

"Why do you find this funny?" A fury over Leera's disregard for manners tightened Adana's shoulders.

"It's not," Leera said, her words leaking around the giggles in short snorts. "I'm trying to imagine how mother would react to you, the savage, correcting my behavior."

A chuckle escaped Adana's lips as she pictured the queen's mouth working in the same open and closed confusion as Leera's had just done. She pushed the chuckle back and shook her finger in Leera's face. "You will get us both in trouble. We better return before someone comes searching and finds us giggling like the little girls they think we are."

After the cool evening air, the warmth of bodies and bright glare from thousands of candles lighting the room almost suffocated Adana. Just for a moment, outside on the balcony, she had forgotten that Elwar surrounded her with high walls and hid the horizon from her sight.

The two girls stood at the edge of the dance floor, searching the guests for their partners. Instead, Kiffen emerged from the crowd. He bowed before the two of them and offered his arm to Adana. "I believe they expect us to dance at least once together this night, my lady."

She took his arm and followed him onto the floor. As his arms enveloped her, a strange pressure built in her lower abdomen and warmth flooded her belly. The sensations set her off-balance, and she stumbled into Kiffen's arms, breathing in his scent of sun and leather, smells associated with their few opportunities to practice swordplay together. Adana closed her eyes, fighting the acute awareness of his closeness.

Kiffen held her without any hesitation and led her through the dance in precise motions. She stepped on his feet at least four times.

* * * * *

Chapter Thirty-One

The season of warmth faded into the cold time of the year. The heavy clothing Adana loathed earlier became a welcome addition to her wardrobe when the winds blew through the cracks in the castle walls or she ventured outdoors. Along with the departure of the warm season, the threat of Maligon disappeared. There had been no more attacks or sightings in the four kingdoms.

Today, the royal family deemed it safe to travel to the Earl of Brom's estate to celebrate the Twin's Festival. Since the earl's household would conduct the celebration, for once Adana had not been privy to all of the planning. She wondered how Elwar's celebration might differ from Moniah's. Both twins were to be celebrated, but in Moniah, the majority of the stories belonged to their first queen, Moniah, not her twin sister, Elwar.

In the early morning, a light snow began to fall.

Adana stood by the window mesmerized by the specks of white floating down to settle on the courtyard. At home, it would be the short, rainy season, with severe, but necessary, rains and floods. It never grew cold enough to snow.

The stones of the courtyard transformed from grey to a fine coating of white in just a few breaths. In twenty more breaths, no hint of stone appeared below the accumulation of white powder.

"Will we have to cancel our trip to visit Pultarch's father?" Adana turned away from the window.

Leera sat on the edge of the bed. She wore a green dress cut in the clinging style of the gown Adana wore to the Kingdoms Council ball. Ever since that night, the fashions in Elwar had shifted from the heavy, puffy layers of petticoats to the simpler dress styles of Belwyn. Becoming a fashion leader still surprised Adana.

Quilla's pleasure over Adana forgoing her uniform for dresses shriveled up and disappeared with the advent of the new style. Although the queen didn't approve of Adana's ability to start a trend, she had acquiesced and ordered a new wardrobe for herself and Leera.

Leera bounced up from the bed and crossed to the window. "Because of the snow? That's hardly worth worrying over. We'll use the sled and glide all the way there."

A sigh of relief escaped Adana.

"You were worried," Leera said, surprise and amusement in her tone. "Do you miss Pultarch so much?" It had been two weeks since the earl's son had last visited the castle.

"No," Adana said, clipping the word. "I don't want to disappoint the earl. Pultarch has told me so much about him, and he has asked to see me."

After breakfast, the girls and Kiffen met the sleigh in the main courtyard. Adana, wearing thick, fur-lined boots as well as a fur-lined cape, gasped in amazement when her feet sank in the soft ground covering. She examined the snow, toeing it and reaching down to feel its texture.

Splat! Cold snow trickled down Adana's neck. She straightened, squinting around for the culprit.

Leera stood by the sleigh, laughter echoing in an odd muffled way, reminding Adana of the day she had caught her practicing how to walk in skirts.

"That's what you do with snow. Here let me show you again." The girl scooped up another handful and hurled it at Adana, who sidestepped.

The snowball whizzed by her and hit Kiffen who stood with his back to the girls. He spun around, a big grin on his face as he yanked off his gloves, scooped up snow, and began patting it into a round ball.

He winked at Adana. "She lacks finesse. Let me show you how it's done."

Adana scooped up her own handful of snow and began forming a ball while eying both Kiffen and Leera. Out of the left corner of her eye, she spotted Leera at work on her own missile. The two girls exchanged knowing smiles.

Kiffen reared back to throw his ball, and both girls hit him square in the chest with theirs.

Moments later, the courtyard rang with squeals and laughter, while servants stopped in their duties to watch the three at play.

Both girls, cornered behind the sleigh, peered underneath their transport and spotted Kiffen, both hands filled with weapons, his gaze intent at the top of the sleigh. On a finger count of three, they jumped up and flung their balls at Kiffen. He threw his and ducked just in time for King Donel and Queen Quilla to come through the doors of the castle.

All activity in the courtyard ceased as Quilla stared down at the icy sludge on her cape, her face impassive. Donel stifled a laugh, his face turning red with the effort. After a moment, the queen brushed the snow from her shoulder and gave each one of them a cold stare before stepping up into the sleigh. "Are the three of you ready to depart? We must not keep the earl waiting. And I have need of a warm fire."

The three dusted off their hands and climbed into the sleigh, their lips twitching.

Huddled under a blanket with Leera, Adana regretted their romp long before the Brom estate came into view. Remnants of snow leaked icy tendrils down her back and into several unmentionable places. The unexpected chills sent shivers throughout her body, and she began to think this endless trip might kill her from the cold. When she thought she couldn't take one more frigid breath, the sleigh emerged on a tree-lined roadway. Ahead, gray against the snow, Brom Manor promised a warm welcome.

A footman ushered the group into a huge foyer, the floor gleaming in black, polished stone. Portrait-covered walls rose several stories high and displayed countless members of the earl's ancestors. Adana felt a sad ache in her heart at the multitude of Broms, now reduced to two, the earl and his son, Pultarch. Everyone knew the earl pinned the hopes of his family crest on Pultarch.

Two stairwells rose up the sides of the room, and at the foot of one of these stood Pultarch in a heavy, quilted surcoat, stitched over with gold thread forming the family crest of a bear standing on its hind feet, head lifted in a roar. Beneath the surcoat, he wore a fine linen shirt of white and trousers in a deep brown, matching the surcoat. Except for the celebration feast after the Kingdoms Council, Adana had never seen him dressed so elegantly.

Beside Pultarch, an old man stood, his posture straight, although the strain in his shoulders and face hinted at the great effort it took.

The man and Pultarch dropped in a bow before the king and queen. King Donel approached the two of them and reached a hand out to assist the elderly man to rise. "Thank you for inviting us for your celebration of the Twin's Feast. I can think of no one I'd rather spend the time with on such a poor weather day."

The Earl of Brom smiled, adding to the wrinkles and crevasses of time marked on his face. "It is a great pleasure, Your Majesty." He turned toward the rest of Donel's party and his bright eyes inspected Adana. "Would you be so kind to introduce me to the young lady my son speaks of night and day?"

Donel barked an echoing laugh and motioned Adana forward. "My lady Adana, may I present to you Conrad, the Earl of Brom."

The old man took her hands in his cool, calloused ones. "I knew you the moment you crossed my threshold, my lady. It took me back to the days your mother visited us here. She was a welcome guest, as I hope you shall be, too."

"Thank you. I'm pleased to know my mother knew you. Maybe you can tell me of her adventures with you some time?"

After introductions and salutations, a chamberlain, dressed in Brom brown, escorted them to their chambers in order to change and prepare for the evening's festivities. To her dismay, Adana discovered she and Leera would share their accommodations with Contina. A trunk lay at the foot of one of the beds, but the young lady was not in sight.

Leera paced around the room, evaluating the size, the furniture, the bed coverings, eventually proclaiming the chamber acceptable. Bemused, Adana wondered how Moniah's simple offerings might hold up to such scrutiny.

As Adana envisioned the possibility of Leera in her home, the door burst open and Contina rushed in, cheeks rosy from the cold.

She hurried over to the fire, dropping her cape and gloves where they landed and held her hands toward the flames. "I'm so pleased you've arrived." She paused in warming her hands and gave the two of them a brief curtsy. "It's so cold outside, and my only companions have been the boys." She wrinkled her tiny nose. "All they want to do is build snow forts and have snowball fights."

Adana and Leera exchanged private smiles behind Contina's back.

"Princess Leera," Contina turned to warm her backside, "I saw one of your mother's servants. She said your mother has need of you in her chambers. Ta ta." The young lady gave a tiny finger wave.

Shoulders drooping, Leera trudged toward the door. "We only just arrived. What can mother need of me, now?" When she left the room, the door swung shut behind her with a bang.

"Perfect." Contina grinned, her teeth sparkling in the candlelight. "Now that Leera is out of the way, I want us to be great friends." She approached Adana, capturing her hands in cold, icy ones. "As friends, we can share all of our secrets and dreams."

Looping her arm through Adana's, she wandered back over to the fire. "I'm dying to know more about Prince Kiffen. You spend a great deal of time with him during your studies, don't you?"

Adana gulped and unhooked her arm. "I have no idea what I could tell you. Why don't you ask Kiffen your questions?"

Contina's bright laughter tinkled on the air just as Adana recalled it doing at the dinner last season. "I'd heard Monians were forthright, but come now, my lady Adana." She glided across the room and sat on the window seat. "If I'm to be his queen some day, I need to know more."

* * * * *

Chapter Thirty-Two

Elwar's Celebration of the Twins consisted of a lavish dinner laid out before the nobles gathered around the earl's table. Besides Adana and the royal family, the evening included Contina's mother, Lady Suppina Sarx, a portly widow with an eternal frown, and uncle, Lord Frank Sarx, a thin, dark-haired man. She found them presumptuous and grasping and wondered if she might like them if Contina hadn't spent every spare moment with Kiffen by her side. The petite, young lady's light, sparkling laughter grated on Adana's nerves, and she fought the urge to clout Kiffen over the head when he chuckled every time the lady laughed.

Pultarch, on the other hand, never left Adana's side, a fact she took great comfort in. After her initial reaction to his braggart behavior, she had found a kind man hidden underneath. Conversations with him weren't as stimulating as with Kiffen, or even Leera for that matter, but his gentle wit eased her nerves, and he possessed a keen ability to recognize the perfect moment to employ it.

After dinner, Adana waited for the festivities to begin. In Moniah, the story of the twin sisters inheriting their kingdoms would be told by a Memory Keeper, but she had yet to spot any of those jolly men in their multi-colored cloaks and conical hats. After the Memory Keeper's story, Adana's mother would tell the story of when she established the first link with Ju'latti, her giraffe. If Adana had been home, she would stand before the Watchers, landowners, and First

213

Soldiers telling the story of her connection with Am'brosia. She sent a tendril of thought toward the giraffe, but the potion prescribed by Glume created a haze which dulled her ability. She sensed Am'brosia stirring, peering toward her, but neither could access the other's thoughts or sights.

When the earl rose to adjourn the meal, Adana followed the group into a large sitting room. Two fires blazed in large hearths. Scattered around the room, sumptuous furniture created the opportunity for small, private gatherings. Contina led Kiffen to the farthest corner of the room, gripping his arm in possession. He went without a word.

Dismayed, Adana sought out Leera. "Where is the Memory Keeper? What about the traditional story-telling?"

The young girl glanced around the room, bouncing on her feet as if anxious to seize her own seat. "I don't know what you're talking about. We had a feast. Now we mingle."

"Nothing else?" Adana turned to follow Leera's retreating back as the young girl settled in with others of her own age.

"Nothing else?" Pultarch appeared at her elbow, an inquisitive smile on his face.

How could she complain in the face of such kindness? "I was curious about Elwar's traditions for the Twin's Festival. It appears we do things differently in Moniah."

"Remarkable." Pultarch took her elbow and guided her toward a love seat. "Why don't you tell me how it's done in Moniah? I hope to attend your festivals at the royal estate, some day. That is, if you'll welcome me?" He peered up at her under long lashes, an errant lock of hair falling over his forehead.

Adana gave in to compulsion and combed the hair back with her fingers. Pultarch grabbed her hand and pressed it in his as he gazed into her eyes. "Does that mean you will invite me to stay in Moniah?"

The room felt incredibly warm at the moment, and Adana searched the other guests for a diversion. Divided into small, private gatherings, no one noticed her discomfort, except when her gaze ventured in the direction of Kiffen and Contina, she found Kiffen's cold, disapproving stare aimed her way. Returning to face Pultarch, she inhaled a breath, two, then three, before trusting herself to speak. She smiled, more for Kiffen than for Pultarch. "I would love for you and your father to visit my home."

Once the opportunity arose, Adana escaped through two tall glass doors and found herself on a balcony overlooking a vast expanse of white. She breathed in the cold, crisp air, and welcomed the shivers accompanying it. If she ignored the cold, she could imagine she looked out across the landscape of home. Nothing but white for as far as the eye could see.

After a few moments, someone draped a warm cloak over her shoulders, and she turned to find the earl beside her. Together they stared across the glistening landscape, not speaking for some time.

Once warmth returned to her limbs, Adana found it easier to imagine she stood in Moniah. "It reminds me of home." Her breath fogged the air, the only deterrent to her wishes.

"So your mother used to say." Conrad smiled up at her, his attempt to carry a straight posture gone as the day progressed.

"She visited here?"

"Many times." The man stared across the snow, unseeing.

"What did she do here? Was she here in the cold season or the warm?"

The man chuckled. "All three seasons. We rode horses. We hunted. We played games. I loved her in my own way. We all did."

"Loved?" Adana turned toward him. "As a ruler?" As she asked the question, she knew he meant different. Her mother was not his ruler. Roassa had been.

The gentle, calloused hands patted hers and gripped them in a warm embrace. "No, my child. But once your father arrived, we all knew she was destined for something greater." He frowned. "Except for Maligon." Conrad's clear, intelligent eyes scrutinized her again. "Never forget, he instigated his war because your mother rejected him. He wanted a crown. And your mother. No matter the cost."

A different chill ran over Adana's skin.

"I've frightened you. My lady, I apologize. You look so much like her, I forget your age."

"No. No." She shook her head and bent forward to peer into his eyes. "You tell me nothing new. But this is the first time I heard it from someone who was there besides my parents. From you, it feels more real."

He gazed at her, unblinking. "It was real, my child. It was."

* * * * *

Part II

Chapter Thirty-Three

Adana kicked her feet free of the ensnaring covers and slid to the edge of the enormous bed, pausing as it squeaked beneath her. Watchers slept in the next room. She didn't want to wake them. With her eighteenth birthday a few days away, sleep eluded her most nights.

The fire burned low, so she padded over to the hearth and poked at it, trying to coax more light and warmth into the room. As flames licked up the logs, Adana gathered a coverlet of Monian glimmer cloth around her and curled up in a wing-back chair, staring into the fire's glow. The glimmer cloth's smooth sheen against her skin lent a small sense of security in the quiet hours of the night.

Nightmare images danced through her mind: the crown of Moniah floating in a raging river, the crown of Elwar somewhere underground. She watched the flames, mesmerized, eventually nodding off.

Adana gasped for air as her head broke above the river rapid's surface. Water washed into her mouth, choking her. Kicking her feet, she fought the current and tried to swim to the shore. The undertow pulled her under. She flailed and fought to get her head above the choppy surface.

"Your Majesty!" A Teacher of the Faith ran along the riverbank, his eyes wide in panic. Another Teacher pushed past him and thrust a long branch toward her.

Adana kicked toward it. The water sucked her under again. She fought panic and the fast current. All went dark. She thrashed her arms, grappling for any handhold. Lungs burned as she fought toward the surface and burst above the water, gulping air. She let her body go limp and drift on the current, hoping to remain afloat. The water dragged her under again.

Something sparkled on the river's surface above, and she kicked upwards. The shining object bobbed just out of reach—her crown! An overwhelming desire to grasp it overcame her, but the crown danced in the rapids, slipping away each time she lunged.

"Your Majesty!" the Teachers called to her. They thrust a larger tree branch within her reach, but the crown taunted her and floated farther away.

She plunged after the golden image of her station. Roiling water splashed her face, and, as she sputtered, a large shaggy beast waded into the river and scooped up her crown. "No," she cried. A large rock loomed ahead of her, and everything went black.

Gasping, Adana stumbled then froze. Firm ground lay below her feet. She patted her clothes and found them dry, but she still felt chilled to the bone. Darkness enshrouded everything.

Adana brushed against a cool, stone wall and inched tentative hands forward. Fingers skimmed over slime, and she recoiled at the thought of what lay beyond. No sight, no vision, no sound. "Don't panic," she whispered over and over again while counting each breath, trying to focus and find a calm to fight down her terror.

After some distance, a faint glow appeared ahead. She gave a cry of relief, stumbling toward it. The light sparkled, blinding in the midst of blackness. A crown!

But not her crown. The crown of Elwar. She reached for it, and it vanished.

Adana jerked awake. The smooth feel of glimmer cloth spilled over her arms. She stared around her bedchamber in the north tower of Elwar's castle. Dim firelight flickered on the walls of the room, and its comforting glow reflected in the large square window on the opposite wall.

Could this dream be a vision? Watchers never had visions until becoming a Unit Leader, a rank the queen skipped in order to take the Seat. She felt sure visions began with the coronation, but then, what was the journey she took with Am'brosia the day her mother died? Kassa referred to it as a vision.

Sighing, she rose and moved to the window seat, replaying the new part of the dream, the animal. It appeared two nights ago. Unsure of its meaning, she hadn't shared this new detail with Kassa.

Not the only information she withheld while in Elwar. Glume's note warned of problems if she overused the potion he had sent to control the pain. He advised three days between doses. She never went more than two without taking it. Until recently. Suban stopped making it as her birthday approached. Am'brosia and her father were traveling toward Elwar, but the pain wouldn't subside until they drew close.

Without the potion, her dream returned, too. She'd blocked her own abilities. Had it stunted other Watcher skills?

She rested her forehead against the cool glass of the window. In the darkness, two guards walked the parapets on the median wall.

Faintly, on the night air, she heard them call out to each other, "East Gate, all clear. North Gate, all clear. "

She had been in Elwar for nine seasons, yet it still sounded strange to hear the deep voices of the guards instead of the female voices of the Watchers who guarded her own estate.

"My lady?" A Watcher's voice whispered at the door. "Are you well?"

Adana turned, thankful to see Sinti and not Kassa. A Strategist in rank, Sinti had arrived a month earlier with Veana, Joannu, and Samantha, the Watchers chosen as her Honor Guard to escort Adana back to Moniah.

Joannu had trained Adana in her first year as a Watcher candidate, but Adana did not know Sinti who was recently raised to a higher rank.

"I'm fine," Adana said. "Just unable to sleep."

The sinewy brunette crossed the room. "This is the fourth night in a row. Should I contact Suban to see if he can offer a sleeping draft?"

A shudder ran up her spine at the thought. The only thing she wanted from Suban, he refused to provide. "No. I'd rather sit up for now." She fidgeted on the window seat and pressed her hand over her eyes. A tendril of agreement floated back through the weak link with Am'brosia.

"Shall I join you?" Sinti said.

Adana nodded, and the young woman sat beside her. They stared out the window.

The link with the giraffe felt strange after such a long separation. The potion hid the pain, and for the most part, stifled Am'brosia's questing contact. She sent a hesitant query southward, seeking to see the caravan's overnight camp.

Am'brosia's joyful response jolted through her body, and she stifled a cry of pain mixed with joy. The caravan must be closer than she realized. The link hummed with a strength she'd forgotten.

Sinti looked up at Adana's choked off cry, brow wrinkled in concern, but said nothing as Adana returned her forehead to the leaded glass of the window.

Dismay from their separation leaked across the connection. In the last few days, Am'brosia's pain had grown less, but sometimes it flared like a fire catching hold of a pile of twigs.

I'm sorry.

Forgiving warmth spread into her body. She didn't deserve it.

Adana closed her eyes and sought to see through the animal's eyes. A few scattered fires lit the camp. The bedrolls and sentries represented a large number of First Soldiers and Watchers. More than normal. She focused on the huge forces, showing Am'brosia an image of the numbers she had expected.

A vision streamed back to her of peasants trudging toward Moniah. They carried possessions on their backs, led livestock and families, leaving burned out villages behind.

Adana frowned and sat up straight. "Sinti?"

"Yes, my lady?"

"Why are refugees headed for Moniah?"

The Watcher jumped up, her gaze searching Adana's face. "How do you know of that? Kassa told us not to concern you."

Adana took a slow breath, seeking a majestic calm. "Am'brosia showed me. There's no reason to withhold the information now.

What do you know?" She raised an eyebrow in the same way she'd seen Quilla do when she expected absolute obedience.

Sinti studied Adana for a moment, then nodded. "You should know."

A brief thrill of satisfaction ran through Adana's limbs, but it dissipated with the Watcher's next words.

"There have been attacks. On small villages near the border of Moniah and in the kingdoms of Belwyn and Teletia."

One name crept into Adana's heart and started it beating faster. "Maligon?"

"We don't know." Sinti met Adana's gaze head on. "Rumors say it's him."

Adana fought the urge to bang her fists on the window. Rulers, especially those who were Watchers, did not reveal frustration when receiving disturbing news.

Since the Kingdoms Council, there had been no more attacks or signs of Maligon. Or at least no one reported any to her. She had hoped some small faction had been responsible and given up, unable to maintain any order once the four kingdoms increased their security.

"How long has this been happening?"

"About a month, my lady. The First Vision and Regent thought it best to bring additional forces to escort you home."

Home. Adana missed Moniah, its flat, sparsely vegetated land, the heat of the prairie sun on her skin, the grit of sand between her teeth. Elwar made Watchers uneasy, a fact she'd adapted to over the years. But what joy to finally find her sight again, to not suffer blindness created by mountains and forests.

"It's a good thing father and King Donel are friends." Adana frowned, thinking of the number of soldiers revealed through Am'brosia's link. "Or Elwar might think we march on them in war."

"King Donel knows and agrees with our plan. He has provided an area outside the village for the extra forces to camp."

In a short time, she would rule a kingdom she had not seen in nine seasons and only then as a child. Peasants sought refuge in her land. Would Monians follow her, a stranger to her own land and customs? They may as well follow Princess Leera.

Adana leaned against the glass, again, seeking comfort from Am'brosia. A strange image came into focus. It took her a moment to recognize Bai'dish covered in leather and other foreign gear. Something dark draped over the giraffe's back, covering most of his sides and upper legs. On his rear hooves, metal glinted in the fire-light.

She focused on the gear, sending curiosity through the bond. Am'brosia returned an image that still haunted Adana's dreams, the man firing an arrow at the old giraffe they inhabited on the day her mother died.

For years, Moniah protected the giraffe, made it sacred, illegal to hunt or kill. Would this be her legacy? Protect them with armor or risk their destruction?

"You're shivering." Sinti retrieved the glimmer cloth blanket and tucked it around Adana.

She fought to hide her emotions from the Watcher's keen aware-ness but pulled the blanket tighter, anyway.

So much had changed since she left. Could she handle the in-creased security of her home? Every morning she woke, reminding herself that freedom waited at the end of this journey. She looked forward to leaving Queen Quilla and her rigorous demands, but now another kind of demand awaited her. One she couldn't refuse or ignore.

Worse, responding to that demand meant leaving Kiffen.

She shut her eyes and burrowed into the blanket, trying to push him from her mind. Unbidden, Serrin took over her thoughts. His death, so soon after her mother's, hurt more than she had imagined possible, especially when his giraffe, Bai'dish, continued to thrive. To love Kiffen, besides being an impossible match, felt like a betrayal to Serrin's memory.

"Sinti," she said, "did you ever meet Prince Serrin?"

"You have felt his presence while here, haven't you?"

"Some." Adana turned back to the window. The moonless night matched her mood.

"I saw him once when he and Prince Kiffen visited Moniah. I was a trainee then." Sinti laughed. "We swooned over Prince Kiffen. No one dared look at Prince Serrin, knowing he was your betrothed."

"Many women find Prince Kiffen attractive." Adana swallowed the jealous lump forming in her throat. She had watched young women and girls flock around him for three years, especially Contina.

Her thoughts wandered to an impossible future with Kiffen by her side, where politics and death did not reign. These thoughts vanished when she sensed a shift in the darkness below. Sinti's body tensed beside her, indicating she had seen the same thing. The guards on the walls didn't react.

Adana stared into the shadows until her Watcher's vision detected the outlines of the shape. A man.

"Who would be sneaking into the castle at this hour?" Sinti said.

The man slid along the walls toward a door. When he reached it, he rapped it once with his fist. The door cracked open in a brief shaft of light. The man slid into the castle, the door closing behind him.

Adana and Sinti jumped to their feet.

"Could you see who let him in?" Sinti said.

"No. I think he slipped by the guards unnoticed."

No one came inside the walls of Elwar without a guard admitting them, especially in the dead of night. Unless he was already inside the walls. But why lurk in the shadows if you were already inside the walls?

"I don't like it." Sinti backed toward the door. "Not this close to the celebration. Should I check this out?"

"Wait. Let's watch. Maybe it's a lover's tryst between a maid and stable hand." Adana doubted her suggestion but also did not want to risk waking Kassa for now. The old woman would see through her and know something more bothered her.

Adana's insomnia worked in her favor. During the guard change, the same door opened, a slim shaft of light announcing the exit. This time, two shadows moved into the night, the second identifiable as a soldier by a momentary gleam of light off his armor. When the light spilled through the doorway, Adana glimpsed a third person within the castle, a twirl of green skirts before the door closed.

The soldier escorted the visitor through the middle of the courtyard. No secrets now, but why. It was the same man even though, now, he walked briskly, almost charging, with a swagger.

"I know that walk," Adana said. "Who walks like that?"

* * * * *

Chapter Thirty-Four

A short time after dawn, Adana awoke, still seated on the window seat. Kassa stood before her, hands on her hips. "Child, why are you here? You only have a few more nights to sleep in such luxury and you choose this uncomfortable bench?"

Bird song and the distant voices of servants in the courtyard counterbalanced Kassa's scolding tone. Groaning at odd aches earned from her makeshift bed, Adana stood. "I was unable to sleep, so I kept watch for awhile."

"Hmph! Some Watcher you make. Sleeping on the job. So what did you see? Rats or mice?"

"Actually, I think I saw a rather large rat. Maybe three. Quite big." Adana held her hand to the height of the average Elwarian male.

Kassa crossed to the window. "What?"

The woman's surprise shocked Adana. Sinti had not told Kassa of her late night problems or the mysterious visitor. She related what they saw. "Do you know where that door leads?"

Kassa shook her head while she handed Adana a small cup of liquid.

"More?" Adana grimaced. "I can feel Am'brosia without this." Now that she couldn't drink the potions from Suban, the link grew stronger as the giraffe approached.

"Even so, your bond lost its momentum during the separation." Kassa's gaze returned to the door in the courtyard.

Adana swallowed the musky fluid of Am'brosia's tears wondering if Kassa suspected that Suban's potion might have hurt the bond. She set the cup down as Samantha entered the room. A maid trailed behind the Watcher and reached for the cup.

"I will take care of this." Kassa snatched the cup out of the woman's startled grasp. "We will dress the lady this morning."

The maid nodded, her gaze darting between the three tall women, and scurried from the room.

Kassa shoved the cup under Adana's nose. "A few drops remain. Do you want the maid to bond with Am'brosia?" She shook her head. "You know these cups must be cleansed in my presence."

"Of course. I was thinking about the man."

"Man?" Samantha took the cup and rinsed it in the basin, handing it back to Kassa. "What man?"

Adana struggled into a pale yellow dress trimmed with pink rosettes, while she related the details of the night visitor.

Samantha stood by the window, arms crossed, studying Adana. "You recognized this man's walk?"

"Yes, but I can't tell you who he is." Adana grimaced in annoyance. Why couldn't she identify the man?

"Never mind for now. You must be presentable for Quilla this morning." Kassa dragged a comb through her hair. Before she came to Elwar, she never imagined her mother's strict First Vision would style a lady's hair. Yank on a braid, yes, create styles appropriate for court, never.

Samantha's green eyes reflected disbelief in the mirror as Adana watched the woman glance at her, pace to the window, and pace back. "The person inside wore a green skirt? You're sure of this?"

She twisted on the seat earning a gentle slap from Kassa to turn back around. Adana rubbed her fingers together. "It caught the light like glimmer cloth. I'll remember who walks with that swagger soon. If I can find some time alone today—"

"Glimmer cloth. The color and material rule out a servant." Samantha wandered over to the window, again.

"Adana." The singsong voice of Leera called from the corridor. "Are you awake? I'm coming in."

Princess Leera sashayed into the room, violet-colored skirts rustling as she walked.

"Good! You're awake and dressed." Leera's blue eyes twinkled as she took in the cluster of Watchers in the room. They regarded her with mother-daughter hawk stares of suspicion. "I thought we'd go to the dressmaker's this morning."

Kassa dropped the comb on the table with a clatter. Hands on her hips, she sought Adana's gaze in the mirror. "My lady, need I remind you that your father's caravan arrives today or tomorrow? You do not have time for excursions." Shaking her head, she muttered, "Or disappearing to find some time alone. Just like your mother. She always disappeared if she had a puzzle to work out."

"Puzzle?" Leera angled closer. "I adore puzzles."

Adana slumped in the backless chair but straightened when Kassa's mouth thinned in disapproval. "Leera, I'm afraid I have other priorities today."

Leera's sharp gaze darted between them, the young princess' ability to sniff out a mystery revealed in the intensity of her observation.

There would be questions later. "Of course. Maybe this afternoon." She sauntered out of the room causing Adana to smile.

"Yes. Maybe this afternoon."

Kassa rounded on Adana, dropping the pretense of using the mirror's reflection to communicate. "Your father is close. You know you do not have time to disappear."

Samantha closed the door. Adana knew she had waited until the princess vanished from sight down the corridor. "Queen Quilla commands your presence this morning. Afterward, Joannu and Sinti must evaluate your archery skills. You've not practiced as much as I'd hoped. When the First Vision arrives, we do not want to reap her displeasure if you do not meet expectations."

Sighing, Adana nodded in reluctant acceptance. Quilla would be hard to escape, but the features of Elwar which discomfited her nine seasons ago also confused other Watchers. That truth allowed for occasional escapes from duty. She wondered what kind of ally Sinti might be. Would she allow Adana the opportunity to escape? She had not reported on last night's conversation or Adana's insomnia.

At least, the afternoon's archery practice would allow her to free her mind and become centered. Many times, answers came to her after such an exercise.

* * * * *

Chapter Thirty-Five

The pond lapped against the rowboat's side as it rocked in the slight breeze rippling the surface. Lulled by the water's melody, Adana lay back in the boat, hands folded across her stomach. Thank goodness Sinti, showing a level of loyalty Adana approved of, agreed to shorten the archery practice, allowing time for her to escape.

"Your skill appears adequate," Sinti had said. "Get the rest you need."

And so, she had fled to the pond.

With a deep inhalation of breath, Adana began focused breathing, seeking true calm. Although she used this during archery and sword practice, it also helped her focus on issues, puzzle out a problem, or deal with a threat. Thanks to Elwar's walls, Quilla's furies, and Pultarch's exhausting attention, she excelled at this skill.

With each breath, Adana felt the presence of Am'brosia drawing closer. The link bubbled with excitement. Once her father arrived, events would tumble into place with little chance of peace or quiet. She struggled to focus on the man's identity from last night, but the warm sun and rare opportunity of privacy tempted her thoughts to drift with the boat.

The previous evening, she had walked with Leera in the gardens after dinner, the sixteen-year-old repeating one of her favorite topics, Adana's future. Leera complained over the imminent change in their lives. "Elwar is dull. Who will I chat with when you're gone? I wish I could be a Watcher. Throw away these old dresses." She pinched a piece of her blush pink skirt, her nose wrinkled in distaste.

Adana had smiled at her. "You loved that dress when the seamstress delivered it."

"It's just a dress. I have hundreds of them." She turned and pouted. "I'd trade all of them for your life. You get to rule an entire kingdom and without wearing dresses." They reached a curved, padded bench painted a bright green shade, and the girl crossed her arms and plopped down on it. "It's not fair. I'll be stuck here under mother's wing. The best I can hope for is to become a Lady in Waiting to Contina when she marries Kiffen."

The words stabbed Adana's heart, but she kept it to herself. The two shared a dislike for Contina, discussing her annoying laugh and bright smile many times, but she never shared her feelings about Kiffen with Leera.

Wound up and ready to burst, Leera continued her rant. "Kiffen gets to be king. You get to be a queen." She looked at Adana, seriousness deep in her gaze. "I don't know who I'll marry, but it won't be a royal. The only eligible heir is Prince Navon. He's six years old."

The complaint was familiar. Even if Kiffen did not produce an heir, Leera wouldn't wear Elwar's crown. The royal blood followed Kiffen's line through his mother's family not his father's. A distant cousin stood in line to the throne, his descendants well-established.

A slight breeze rocked the boat, pulling Adana from her thoughts.

The night visitor, she reminded herself, sitting up to cool her skin in the gentle draft. The warm season in Elwar provided pleasant temperatures without the unyielding heat of Moniah. Leera and Quilla complained of the heat, but in Moniah the scorching season was upon them. Would she find it unbearable after so long in a milder climate?

Closing her eyes, Adana leaned back and listened to the rustling leaves and the songs of birds. Water plunked against the wood of the boat, and she placed her hands on the smooth, warm wood memorizing the gentle rock of the craft.

Elwar, with its tight spaces, taught Adana to look beyond sight. Hunter's final comments flashed in her mind, "It will be good for you to learn, my queen."

All Watchers knew how to move beyond sight to sound, smell, and touch, but, out of necessity, she learned to hone them. She doubted she had perfected the skill, but she noticed more than most Watchers.

The breeze against her skin was cool, not cold, but she shivered like she always did when remembering Hunter. The fragrance of sweet flowers budding on the hillside caressed her nose, and she drew her attention to them instead. A hint of leather intertwined with the floral scents.

From where? She opened her eyes and scanned the stillness. Nothing appeared different, and the smell dissipated. The wind, swirling around her, might have carried it from the stables.

Adana lay back in the boat, the memory of the pond stored in her mind.

A flash of pain shot through her head and cramped her stomach. Am'brosia's link demanded attention, the animal's presence an increasing pull. Did the growing link harass her or the lack of the potion? In response, she saw the formissa plant ground to pulp under Am'brosia's large front hoof.

The frustration tumbling through the connection didn't surprise her. She realized the mistake they'd made, now, even if the potion made life bearable.

Soon Am'brosia would be here. She promised the giraffe to never leave her for so long.

The giraffe's arrival, as well as her father's, would signify the beginning of a celebration, Elwar recognizing her as the rising Queen of Moniah, the Seat of Authority. The ancient tradition held less importance than in older days, but the tradition kept both kingdoms happy in their alliance.

Then, Leera's worst fears would be realized. Adana would depart for Moniah and her coronation. Elwar's celebration should have included the official beginning of her one-year engagement to Serrin.

Leera speculated daily on Adana's potential betrothed claiming Pultarch's obvious attentiveness would win him Adana's hand. Over the seasons, he sought out every opportunity to visit her. She returned the visits by spending innumerable hours at the Brom estate, Leera and Kiffen in attendance.

Late at night, when sleep eluded her, Adana thought about Kassa's lessons on the feelings of attraction. "Here," the woman had patted her lower abdomen. "Just one touch from the right man, and it flutters. Then it's as if something hooks you to him and pulls you from deep inside. An unanswered yearning comes over you, until you satisfy it." The old woman, a distant smile on her face, patted Adana's hands. "Don't worry, my child. You will find this."

She had, just not with Pultarch.

Tradition prevented the one match Adana desired, so it was best to be comfortable with the handsome Pultarch, even if he didn't create even a slight tug inside her. Of course, Leera relished Pultarch's presence. "He's so masculine," she had said. "How can you not be attracted? He just enters the room and my stomach flutters."

"Yours and everyone else's," Adana said. "I can't help what I don't feel."

She groaned, her thoughts an ache in her chest.

"Didn't Quilla teach you that a lady never groans?" A deep voice spoke from above her.

Adana's eyes flew open. She jerked upright, heart pounding and reached for her knife. Her rowboat had drifted to the shore. A man on a horse loomed over her. With the sun behind him, she could not distinguish his features.

The man jumped from his horse and grabbed the edge of the boat, dragging it toward shore.

Adana gasped, drawing her legs up under her, and scooted backwards in the belly of the vessel. The scent of leather had been a warning. A warning she ignored.

The sun's glare still hid his identity, but the young man frowned, and the familiarity of this expression made her shade her eyes and squint upward at the familiar face.

Kiffen. As if summoned by her thoughts, he leaned over the edge of the boat, his hand unfolding toward her.

The urge to respond to the invitation overwhelmed her, and she reached out, her gaze on his face. Kiffen's gaze dropped to her fingertips as her nails grazed his palm, but doubt stretched between them, and she slid her hand away, his fingers folding to grasp emptiness.

Adana gathered up her skirts and tumbled over the edge of the boat, splashing through the shallows at the pond's edge. "What are you doing here? I'm not drunk or drowning. I don't need your assistance."

Annoyed for letting her daydreams distract her, she stalked up the bank and away from him. "Will I never find any privacy?"

"I was sent for you."

His voice came to her timid and hurt. She turned, knowing she imagined it, but eyes downcast, he wore an expression of regret and pain, his deep-set eyes clouded in sadness. She'd seen that look before, whenever Quilla sought to embarrass him.

With a raised eyebrow, he nodded toward her hand. "Would you mind putting your weapon away?"

Adana glanced down surprised to find she still held her knife. She sheathed it, never turning away. Focused breathing came in short pants, a complete failure, but the exercise never worked in the prince's presence.

"Who sent you?" She wanted to ask how long he had been there.

"Kassa. Your father's caravan arrived on the outskirts of the city."

Embarrassment fled. She must return to her chambers and dress. She could run the distance in a matter of minutes if she wore her leathers. Running in this dress meant hiking it up to expose her legs and risking Kiffen's disdain at her impropriety. Cool as the afternoon might seem, a run meant sweat and disaster to her hair. What a fool she'd been to sneak away.

Kiffen's horse stomped his foot. Could she ask him to loan her the horse?

"Adana, we must hurry." He stepped closer, his gaze searching hers in a way that went beyond a flutter in her stomach. She leaned toward him, drawn by something unexplainable. "It would not do for you to be absent when your father arrives."

"I know, but I need your horse." She held her breath and waited to see if he would offer to help her.

* * * * *

Chapter Thirty-Six

Kiffen hesitated. The moment the guards sighted the Monian caravan, he had saddled his horse and ridden to the pond where he knew he would find Adana. Many times in the past, he sat just over the crest of the hill and guarded her. In the beginning it was out of duty to Serrin's last words and his father's request. At first, the request seemed odious, but he enjoyed this duty and found himself watching her when it was not necessary. He couldn't have her, but the desire to touch her just once, engulfed him.

"Of course, you can ride my horse," he said, swallowing when his mouth dried up.

Concern crossed her face. "But what about you? Will you be able to prepare in time if you walk?"

Heat blew through him. "I meant share the horse. Ride together."

"Oh!" Adana said. "Oh." Her cheeks flushed a gentle pink. "It's not allowed," she whispered. "A lady only rides with her betrothed or a relative."

He hung his head.

He was asking her to ignore three years of Quilla's strict training for one brief moment of pleasure. It was selfish, however much he wanted it, but this might be his only opportunity to be close to her. Desire outweighed reason, and he presented his practiced excuse. "I think it can be overlooked this once. Under the circumstances. Distantly, we are related."

Many generations in their families had passed since the twin sisters ruled Elwar and Moniah, but common ancestry did exist. Kiffen searched Adana's face for horror or disgust while she stared back at him, her face poised in a Watcher's impenetrable mask. He swallowed hard, willing himself to not betray his feelings, praying she would accept his offer.

When she smiled and nodded, relief flooded his limbs like the release of tension after a difficult but successful sword practice.

Kiffen rushed to help her mount the horse. She straddled the saddle, her skirts riding up on her calves. The temptation to touch a gentle curved leg pulsated through him, but he jumped up behind her and wrapped an arm around her waist. The angle of the climb up the hill pressed her body closer to his. She smelled of fresh air and sunshine, and he held her tight, exhilarated over the opportunity presenting itself.

At the top of the hill, he kicked the horse into a gallop, the curve of her hips under his hand. Her hair, unbound, tickled his cheek. He wrapped both arms around her waist, pulling tighter than necessary. She towered over Elwarian women, but with her body pressed up against his, he discovered how slight and feminine she truly was. Joy surged through his body, and briefly he considered turning the horse into the forest never to return.

As they approached the stable yard, he slowed their mount to a walk. "I'll try to bring us in so no one will see," he whispered in her ear.

She shivered, and he experienced a thrill, hoping he had caused it.

They emerged in a small clearing behind the stable. She twisted to smile at him, her gaze taking in the privacy of the spot.

Unfamiliar sensations threatened to overtake him as he stared into the blue depths of her gaze. The horse stomped its foot and shuffled sideways, impatient to lose its saddle and bridle. Kiffen jumped down from the horse and reached up to lift her down.

Reluctant the moment was over, he kept his hands around her waist longer than he should, and she made no move to turn away. They gazed at each other, a tiny smile curving her lips, until a shout from the other side of the stables broke them apart.

"I should hurry," she said but lingered a moment longer. Eventually, she turned and walked away. At the corner of the stables, she paused and smiled back at him. "Thank you, Kiffen."

Kiffen willed her to come back, but she floated around the corner and out of his sight.

* * *

In Adana's chambers, Kassa waited. She laid out the filmy, iridescent blue dress robes, marveling at how closely the seamstresses matched the iridescent glimmer material to the ceremonial robes Chiora wore when she presided over formal hearings and appearances from dignitaries. The day Micah stood before her, invested with his new lands and wealth, she wore this same shade of blue. It had been a jubilant day, celebrating the two strangers who played such a significant part in ending Maligon's rampage across their kingdoms.

Kassa shook her head. No one ever imagined one of those strangers would one day oversee Moniah as regent while the other ruled Elwar. That twist of fate kept the dissidents murmuring, giving

Maligon opportunity to strike. Thinking of the possible outcomes of the next few days, Kassa felt drawn to the window. What she saw could quell the unrest or raise it to a new level.

Having watched the two ride down from the hills, she turned from the window, whispering, "Finally!"

* * * * *

Chapter Thirty-Seven

The Kingdom of Belwyn

Empress Gabriella, overseer and protector of the kingdom of Belwyn, tried to focus on the complaints of two supplicants standing before her. She scanned the crowd of nobles and villagers gathered in the large Hearing Chamber, but her unexpected and unwelcome cousin, Maligon, did not stand among them. With many of her guard seeking out the ruffians who ransacked several villages, his arrival troubled her. He should reside below in her dungeons, but she feared the men who accompanied him might overwhelm what was left of her castle guard. The threat of his presence in the castle unnerved her, and his ever-congenial attitude disturbed her even more. She still didn't understand how he came to sit by her bedside before dawn two days ago. At least she'd managed to send Karyah with a message to Elwar in hopes of receiving aid.

The supplicants fidgeted, and she prepared to hear their complaints when the sounds of heavy boots marching down the corridor distracted everyone.

"Out of my way!" Maligon's loud voice echoed off the walls as he marched into the room, flanked by several soldiers.

Sir Jerold and a few of her knights stepped forward to block his path.

Most of her guard remained at their posts along the walls, their stances turned away from Gabriella's shocked face. She rose to her feet, displaying a calm she did not feel. Her cousin had finally given up on friendly pretense.

Maligon smirked at the men blocking his path. "So few to protect you, cousin?"

Sir Jerold stepped closer, his hand on his sword. "Why do you approach the Empress with her own soldiers?"

Gabriella searched the men with Maligon, her insides churning. Many of her guard stood among them.

Sir Jerold drew his sword. "Answer me."

The sharp sound of steal sliding from sheathes met his actions as Maligon's men stepped forward to confront Jerold.

Jerold confronted them, his voice coming out in a low growl. "Drop your weapons in the Empress' presence."

Maligon laughed.

Jerold held his stance and called for more guards to join him. Few did. Gabriella glanced around, horrified at the implications of her guards' inaction. Nobles crowded against the walls, shoulder to shoulder with commoners, eyes wide in fear.

"What is the meaning of this?" Gabriella asked, engaging full authority into her voice.

"I'm tired of pretending, Gabriella," Maligon said.

"Refer to her as Empress." Jerold pushed closer to the man.

"Must we do this?" Maligon gestured around the room at the cowering people and indifferent guards.

"Explain yourself." Gabriella gave the command, certain the answer would infuriate Jerold. How could she convince him to retreat without appearing to succumb to Maligon?

Her cousin grinned. "Belwyn's soldiers are tired of this farce. They wish me to wed you and share the throne." He straightened and squared his shoulders, grimacing as if his maimed shoulder still pained him. "As is my birthright."

"Such a minor request," Gabriella said forcing sarcasm into her tone while squeezing her knees together to quell the tremor in her legs. She turned and settled herself in the seat of royalty. "Share my throne? How much a fool do you think I am?"

"Well, that depends." He sauntered toward her, only to be blocked, again, by Jerold.

"Remove yourself before I do it for you," Jerold said.

Her cousin tilted his head, an amused gleam in his eyes. "I don't think you will."

Gabriella held her breath. Fear for Jerold's safety overwhelmed her. If he came to harm, all was lost.

As the young knight raised his sword, the few others loyal to Gabriella charged at the traitorous soldiers.

Maligon sighed and slid behind the protective barrier of his men who surged forward and engaged her knights.

Swords clanged.

The nobles screamed and scuffled back from the combatants. Gabriella leaned forward, her fingers digging into the arms of her throne, trying to choke down fear for Jerold. Too much had been sacrificed for his safety.

Jerold raised his sword over his head, pointed it downward like the tail of a scorpion. With a loud cry, he slammed the broad side of the sword on the top of a man's head. The man crumpled to the ground. Another soldier took his place.

Gabriella stared in horror as the small number of her loyal men fought multiple attackers from all sides. Jerold fought well, but four of her men lay on the ground wounded or worse. Only Jerold and two others remained to protect her.

The attackers advanced, encircling the trio who stood with their backs to each other.

"Stop!" Gabriella fought the urge to rush at Maligon, her fingers curled to scratch out his eyes. Men fell back except for Jerold who remained in a tight battle of strength against his attacker.

"Sir Jerold, stop."

"Empress!" Jerold's objection echoed in the sudden quiet, as he staggered back from the other soldier's sudden release of force.

Lips quirked in amusement, Maligon skirted the battle ground. He executed a mocking bow toward the throne.

Gabriella fought the urge to swallow or lick her lips, not willing to give in to his self-assured stance.

He sauntered closer, placed a foot on the step before her throne, and leaned in. "What's more important to you? Your pride or your people?"

Today, he wore his gray-brown hair pulled back in a fighter's tail. Life had been hard on him. The lines in his face ruined the beauty he had once flaunted in court. Fighting leathers displayed what his formal robes had hidden—a body, still lean and muscular, save for the deformities from injuries delivered by King Micah.

"Gabriella? What will you do? Shall we wed?"

Rumors of an attack on Teletia had coincided with Maligon's arrival, but her cousin assured her he returned from exile to protect Belwyn's throne. She knew better but had hoped to keep him preoccupied until help arrived.

"I must have an answer now." He gazed at her, unblinking.

Empress Gabriella surveyed the room. The entire court waited, eyes wide, mouths agape or set in firm lines. It came to this. Maligon chose to move against the four kingdoms through her throne, again.

If she acquiesced, they might gain some time, but she doubted that. If she declined? She wished she knew which answer would send help the fastest.

Directing a silent prayer to the Creator, Gabriella asked for protection and careful sight for the Watcher carrying the warning to Elwar. "No."

Soldiers seized her. A collective gasp hissed along the walls of the chamber. Jerold struggled to reach her, only to be pushed back by Maligon's men.

"Don't be a fool," Maligon shouted. "Stay out of my way and life goes on as usual in Belwyn."

* * * * *

Chapter Thirty-Eight

The Kingdom of Elwar

Cheers from the villagers outside Elwar's castle reached Kiffen. A roar from the crowds announced the king's arrival inside the city walls. Kiffen stood on a raised platform in the inner courtyard waiting for the Monian procession to enter the gates. The wind snapped the banners in the tower, a sharp sound over the murmuring of the people. He stared toward the gates until he heard a gasp from Leera. She stood at his side but turned away from the gates. He followed her gaze.

Adana floated across the courtyard toward the raised platform. She wore a ceremonial robe of Monian glimmer cloth. The soft blue of the material billowed in the breeze as she ascended the steps, and the wind molded the material against her body. He'd never appreciated the whirling gusts in the courtyard before, but now he thanked the Creator for the invisible hands taunting him with Adana's body. The memory of her scent, warm sun mingled with budding flowers, floated in the air as she took her place between his father and stepmother.

Before turning toward the gates, Adana peeked at him from lowered eyelids. He tipped his head in acknowledgement, and a pleased smile crossed her face.

The crowd outside the gates grew louder, signaling the Monian procession's arrival at the outer castle walls. Kiffen forced his attention toward the gates as the first of the Monians marched into sight.

At the forefront, clad in the brushed golden armor, horned helmet, and leather leggings of the First Soldiers, rode a solitary horseman carrying the Monian banner. One hundred men marched behind him. The banner carrier proudly held the black standard high, rippling in the breeze, the golden giraffe of Moniah depicted in full run.

The horseman paused before the platform and bowed his head to Adana. For a brief moment, Kiffen thought he saw the man's gaze skim toward Kassa with a look of longing, and the old Watcher returned the look with a smile. A rare sight.

As the soldier rode to the side of the yard, the troops of First Soldiers neatly divided and stepped sideways forming a wide corridor from the gates to the platform where Adana stood with Kiffen's family. Through this corridor marched ten rows of Watchers, ten in each row. They wore soft leather tunics of a sun-bronzed shade, similar to the one Adana wore during sword practice. Montee, as the First Vision, strode before them with precise steps and an unwavering gaze focused on Adana.

The Watchers' tunics hung at hip length, high slits on each side. Beneath the tunics, they wore tan leggings that clung to and outlined their muscular legs. Each Watcher wore a bow slung across her back. A sling and several knives dangled from braided belts cinching the waist of their tunics. Their hair, varying in shades of youth to great wisdom, lay neatly down their backs intricately braided with brown cord. Each Watcher stood taller than the women of Elwar as well as many of the men of his kingdom.

Watchers in full dress were nothing new to Kiffen, but seeing a large squad of them provided a reminder that Adana, although young, belonged among these soldiers. The waiting crowd murmured at the sight of the Watchers, struck as Kiffen was by their bearing. Quilla may have fought to extinguish the warrior in the princess, but he recognized much of her behavior in the stance of focus and attention these soldiers gave to their surroundings. What amazed him, as it had ever since he first met Adana, was their ability to watch everything without swiveling their heads. He couldn't see it, but he felt their heightened awareness of the surroundings.

The sound outside the gates rose in excitement, and everyone within the walls turned toward the gates. A gasp rippled across the courtyard when two giraffes, dressed in elaborate armor, glided through the gates. Kiffen studied the armor with surprise. When had the Watchers decided to cover their royal beasts in heavy leather?

The two giraffes walked through the human corridor, but the first one paused, head raised, eyes searching the platform. Kiffen and the crowd held their breath in awe when the giraffe slowly spread its forelegs and bowed low to Adana. He turned to look at her reaction. The rapture on her face added a flush of beauty even he had never seen before. It was as if Adana had become whole again. Why couldn't he bring that look to her face?

Queen Quilla's voice shattered the moment as she chastised Leera who bobbed and bounced to get a better view of the giraffes. "Be still, you are not a child!"

Kiffen stepped closer to Leera and gently touched her hand, the contact too brief for Quilla to catch and scold.

She turned toward him, her eyes shining. "Look how tall they are."

He nodded but turned his attention to the second, even taller giraffe.

"Why two giraffes, Kiffen?" Leera said, echoing his own thoughts.

He shook his head. The animal tugged at his memory. Six years earlier he and Serrin visited Moniah. On that trip, Serrin selected and bonded with Bai'dish. During that same visit, Am'brosia had been born. Could this be Bai'dish?

Serrin had decided to teach Adana to sword fight until Kassa came looking for her young charge. The two children hid their practice swords behind their backs, cowering under Kassa's disapproval. Kiffen, slouched on a barrel, had thanked the Creator he was not part of their scheme. He almost fell off his perch when Kassa turned on him, instead.

"Kiffen of Elwar," she raged, "you are the elder here. Did you not realize the heir could be harmed?"

That was one of the few times Kassa had startled him. The woman was tough, but except for that time, he never felt fear or discomfort in her presence. Adana and Serrin fought to suppress their giggles until Kassa's hawk-like stare turned toward them. She held them frozen like little rabbits for several breaths, then her countenance relaxed and her mouth crooked into something like a smile. "No matter. We have more important matters to attend to."

"She's birthing?" Adana dropped her practice sword and grabbed Serrin's hand.

Kassa nodded.

The young girl had locked her other hand into Kiffen's and then dragged the two boys to the paddock, nearly slamming Kiffen into the walls along the way.

Kiffen and Serrin soon lost interest in the labor of the mother giraffe and wandered the compound. One young male giraffe trailed them along the fence.

On that particular day, Glume, Moniah's giraffe keeper, spoke to Serrin. "I see you've found your giraffe, young master."

He felt sure the second giraffe in the procession was Bai'dish, Serrin's giraffe. Why bring him to Elwar?

"Kiffen?" Leera's voice brought him back to the present. "Why do you suppose they brought two giraffes? Could one be a gift?"

He shook his head. "I think the second one was Serrin's."

"Bai'dish?" Leera's blue eyes widened in surprise as small wrinkles creased her brow.

Kiffen scanned the other people on the platform for a clue. Pultarch stood on the far side of the platform, his gaze locked on the vision of Adana. Kiffen tried to swallow away the anger over his rival's blatant adoration.

A horn heralded the arrival of the Regent, and Kiffen turned back toward the gates.

King Micah cantered his black stallion through the column of soldiers, Watchers, and dignitaries. He rode at a slow, even pace, his face giving no indication to his thoughts. Micah wasn't born a king, not even a royal, but just like Kiffen's father, he resonated with regal nobility. Drawing to a stop before the raised platform, he dismounted in front of King Donel and climbed the steps of the platform. The old friends dropped their reserve and greeted each other, like smiles shining in their bearded faces. Donel grabbed Micah in a bone-crunching hug.

Micah pounded Donel's back in greeting, but then stepped back and bowed over Queen Quilla's proffered hand. Rising he said, "I trust my lady Adana has not been too much trouble these few years."

With a voice as smooth as honey, Quilla said, "She was a joy. I feel as if she's my own daughter."

Kiffen shook his head at his stepmother's response. He thought he heard Leera snort.

Then King Micah turned toward Adana, a look of wonder on his face. "You look just like your mother."

"Papa! I've missed you so." Adana threw herself into his arms.

Micah eventually released their hug and tilted Adana's chin up to peer into her face. The love and pride reflected between them touched Kiffen in a way he couldn't describe. He rubbed his lower lip and waited to greet the man who would give Adana away to some undeserving suitor. Instead of a formal greeting to everyone on the platform, Micah turned and waved the Watchers forward. The warriors approached the platform and, in unison, bowed before Adana, their bows rising from their backs like a small mountain range.

Adana approached Montee, the First Vision, and laid a hand on her shoulder. The Watcher rose and extended her right arm to the princess. They grasped each others' elbows. With a start, Kiffen realized that the two women stood at an even height, along with the other Watchers, a head taller than most of the women of Elwar. When had Adana grown so tall?

"Your watch remains steadfast. All is well." Montee made the formal pronouncement to Adana.

Joy flooded from the girl as she beamed at Montee.

"My lady, we brought the item you requested." Montee turned and motioned for the Watchers to rise. One stepped forward with a small parcel wrapped in a soft cloth.

Adana turned toward Kiffen, her gazing sliding past him, and beckoned to Leera. "Princess Leera, I requested a special gift from Moniah for you. I know it is not all you desire but maybe it will help."

Montee bowed low before Leera and then presented the parcel to her. "Welcome, Sister," she said.

"Welcome, Sister," echoed the rest of the Watchers.

Leera stared open-mouthed at the parcel.

"Open it," Adana said with a laugh.

His sister picked at the binding, mouth pressed tight as she struggled with the tight knots. The cloth fell away to reveal a Watcher uniform in green-dyed leather. Leera blinked several times, a flush painting her cheeks. A drop of moisture splattered on the leather.

"You are now an honorary Watcher. Never be caught with your eyes closed," Adana said.

Leera stroked the material. "It's green."

"Of course it is," Adana said. "Watchers must blend in with the environment, so I requested green to match the hills and trees of Elwar."

Queen Quilla's composure faded into a similar shade of green.

* * * * *

Chapter Thirty-Nine

Montee hesitated outside the door of King Donel's study. The tiny crack between the doors provided a view of Donel and Micah. Micah seemed to tower over his friend, not having succumbed to the wider girth of older men as the shorter King Donel had done.

"Any trouble during the journey?" Donel asked.

She waited, curious to hear what the two kings might discuss in her absence.

Donel poured himself another cup of ale. A log on the fire split and crashed as he set the cask back down.

Micah, goblet in hand, turned away making his voice harder to hear. "Troubles? No, but disconcerting information and events."

"How so?"

Shaking his head, Micah crossed to a chair and sat just out of Montee's line of sight. "I'm afraid Chiora set the wrong wheels in motion by sending Adana here. She should have been home, preparing to rule."

Montee choked down a snort of disgust. The fire crackled, and she watched sparks dance in the air before fading away. His daughter would be dead if she had remained in Moniah. Enough Watchers received that vision to know the truth of it.

King Donel sat forward. "I know. These raids on Belwyn's and Teletia's outlying villages disturb me. I've protected the princess so far, but how will you keep her safe on your return?"

This issue troubled Montee, and she and the regent had discussed it at length.

"It is a problem. We encountered refugees fleeing both kingdoms. They flock toward Moniah."

"Any inside Elwar's borders? The attacks haven't reached us." King Donel sipped his wine. "Yet."

Micah shook his head. "Elwar lies farther north. If we don't stop him…"

"Both Belwyn and Teletia declined their invitation to the celebration," Donel added.

Montee straightened at this turn in their discussion and entered the room. She inclined her head to the two of them. "Your Majesties." She then turned to Donel. "We heard of the declined invitations. I sent squads to investigate, and we increased our forces on this journey."

"Yes, I know." King Donel sighed. "A wise move. I told the queen that too many nobles together will tempt our enemies, but she insisted on following protocol." He held up the cask to Montee, an inquiring look on his face.

She shook her head.

"So what do you think?" Micah asked, an eyebrow arching sharply. "Do we continue with the plan?"

Montee frowned at his doubt. Men could be difficult, especially those not raised around Watchers. Visions came from the Creator, but still these men wanted to determine their wisdom.

King Donel answered the question with another. "Are the two of you sure of this vision?"

"You know as well as I do visions are confusing," Micah said. "It's hard to say, but I've never known one to be wrong."

"With hindsight, of course." King Donel rubbed his face and took another sip of wine.

"True, with hindsight, but some are as clear as day. This one, unfortunately, is not clear." Micah picked up his goblet but did not drink.

"Your Majesties," Montee said, "Adana experienced a prophetic dream. It matches my own, and Kassa's, too well to be anything else. To ignore it is unwise."

King Donel shook his head in frustration. "Those visions terrified me when we first came here. That's one of the reasons I chose Roassa rather than Chiora."

"You chose?" Micah chuckled. "Thank you, my friend. I needed a laugh. Chiora never forgot how she found you bellowing at the bottom of that mudslide. You were lucky Roassa never saw that."

Montee watched them both grin over the memory. The story was often told around the kingdoms, and Watchers loved to tell it when they felt frustrated with men.

The logs on the fire crashed, silencing the two men. Montee kicked embers into the hearth, watching the cinders brighten with heat and fade. That small, normal action was a Watcher's outlet to hiding emotions. She knew neither man recognized her frustration over their hesitation.

Kassa's warning voice rang in her head. *Never discount a man's opinions. The Creator did not make them Watchers, but he did give many of them strength and strategic thinking.*

She turned to the two kings and spoke with conviction. "We cannot ignore the vision. Not when three of us share it."

King Donel leaned toward her. "Do you understand it?"

Montee straightened in an effort to tower over the seated men. "I believe so. We need to protect the crowns at all costs."

"This image of my crown underground is disturbing." Donel nodded toward Micah. "At least you can swim."

Montee sighed at the man's interpretation. "Assuming we can take that part literally."

"So is Adana safer betrothed?" King Donel ignored her comment. "That's why you risked two giraffes on the journey, isn't it?"

Micah nodded. "The decision is even more important now."

"Are you sure we aren't playing right into the vision? Bai'dish did not choose any of Moniah's men. Maybe the timing is off."

A look of defeat crossed Micah's face. "Montee's vision indicates otherwise. Chiora always assured me Adana's reign would be intertwined with Elwar. She expected her to marry Serrin, though."

Sitting forward, Donel placed his ale on a nearby table. "I'm prepared to summon our eligible men, but we might want to consider her most attentive suitor, first. Pultarch. He's the son of the Earl of Brom."

* * * * *

Chapter Forty

Adana leaned on the fence of the giraffes' temporary corral in Elwar, Montee by her side. She held out a carrot to Am'brosia, who ambled over and curled her lips back to retrieve the gift. Adana watched the familiar sideways chewing of the giraffe, contentment stretching through the bond. Once Am'brosia finished the morsel, she nuzzled the girl's ear. Joy radiated from the animal.

"What are you and Father not telling me? Why is Bai'dish here?"

Montee stroked Am'brosia's neck. "She's missed you."

Watching her First Vision and Am'brosia, Adana sensed the presence of withheld secrets from both of them. She flashed a thought to Am'brosia, hoping her connection would provide some answers, and received an image of Bai'dish. He glowed and stood tall and strong. The giraffe's pull of attraction toward the male surged through the link. Am'brosia wasn't too young to mate, but the female's raw yearning caught Adana by surprise.

Frowning at the unhelpful giraffe, Adana turned to Montee, but paused when struck by the significance of Am'brosia's communication. Bai'dish was not in the corral when she arrived, and he was nowhere in sight. She started to comment on this when Montee finally responded to Adana's original question.

"I believe we covered everything in this morning's briefing—the raids, the refugees, Belwyn's and Teletia's declined invitations," Montee said. "Oh, and your night visitor. Any more thoughts on that one?"

"No." Adana waved away that subject, aware of the First Vision's attempts to divert her attention. Had everyone forgotten her impending authority? "Where is Bai'dish?"

"I believe Glume mentioned taking him to another area to keep these two separated for now. They've shown an interest in mating." Montee stroked Am'brosia's flank. "We don't need that to happen just yet."

"Yet?" Adana pulled back in surprise, gaze narrowing on Montee. "Do you still plan for Bai'dish to mate with her? That the bond created with Serrin still holds?" She shook her head and spun to face Montee. "What are you not telling me?"

"You have so many demands on you right now. Don't worry about something else." The Watcher looked at her, chest rising in a calming breath.

Why did she need to calm herself at this moment? She definitely hid something.

"I believe you agreed to meet Princess Leera for a walk in the gardens. Some friendly company might serve you well." Without another word, the First Vision turned and walked toward the castle.

Adana considered commanding Montee to return and answer her. Exactly the actions Quilla would take, and for that reason, she hesitated. Her father and Montee still regarded her as a child. Acting like Quilla wouldn't improve the situation. She could mention her dream, but, again she hesitated. Did she really want to know if they'd found an interpretation? Especially since she kept its frequency a secret. Her first prophetic vision was supposed to be exciting, not frightening.

"Are you coming?" Montee turned back, an eyebrow raised. "You promised the princess. Do you want me to give her your regrets?"

Adana gave Am'brosia one last look, sending a plea for answers through the link, then pushed away from the fence and followed the Watcher back into the castle.

A few moments later, she approached Leera, who sat by a fountain near the garden entrance. The petite girl flicked her fan in agitation, causing Adana to reconsider joining her, but the princess looked up and spotted her.

"There you are. For a moment, I thought you weren't coming." The fan snapped shut and Leera beckoned to her. "I have splendid news." She dimpled as Adana sat down on the bench beside her. "Pultarch is in the castle."

Adana regretted not escaping when she could.

Leera dragged her from the seat and linked her arm through Adana's, steering them toward one of the garden paths. "I was just finishing breakfast." She paused and gave Adana a scolding look. "You ate much too fast today, by the way."

Leera dimpled again and continued her chatter. "Anyway, I happened to glance up and see Pultarch walking past the conservatory door. Mother was distracted with the chamberlain and all her plans, so it was quite simple for me to waylay him before he disappeared."

Adana pictured the scene with Leera sliding from her seat and tiptoeing out into the hallway, glancing at her mother over her shoulder.

"He seemed quite surprised to see me, and," Leera frowned, "too hurried for proper manners."

Adana waited for Leera to get to the point. The girl loved drawing out the details, especially when building to something of great import, otherwise, she would have told Adana her news already.

"Maybe he was expected somewhere, and you were making him late."

Leera danced with excitement. "Oh, you already know! You wicked girl. Why didn't you tell me?"

"Tell you what?"

"Your father summoned Pultarch to the castle this morning."

Adana froze like a ground squirrel caught in the crosshairs of a hunting eagle. Her belly contracted. "Father? For what?"

"Do not be coy with me, Adana. To discuss your betrothal plans, of course."

Bile rose in Adana's throat and she reached out for Leera's hand to steady herself. Was this why Montee would not answer her questions? It made sense, but she'd hoped the concerns over Maligon might delay any decisions about a betrothal.

"Oh you poor dear. There's a bench right here." Leera fluttered around her while Adana flopped on the seat.

The warmth of the day overwhelmed her, and the droning of the bees pounded in her ears. *Breathe*, she thought. *Breathe. It will calm you. Will it? Could she do focused breathing for the rest of her life?*

Leera hovered over her. "You did not know? Oh how delightful I should be the one to tell you."

"What exactly did he say to you?" Adana fought to keep her voice calm and even.

"Of course, of course, you want to know all the details. I was sure of that, so I've been going over every last word while I waited for you. But most importantly, he wants to see you. He's coming here to the gardens once he finishes with your father."

Irritated at Leera's excitement, she turned on the girl. "Tell me what he said. How did father summon him?"

Leera frowned. "For someone who just learned that at this precise moment her father is arranging her marriage to a man who worships her, you are—"

"Leera. When did I ever suggest to you that I wanted to marry Pultarch?"

Breaths ticked by as Adana glared at the younger princess.

With a sigh, Leera folded her hands over Adana's. "I assumed your objections were an attempt to not reveal how much you wanted this ... in case he was not chosen."

Adana choked down tears. Why had she refused to acknowledge the obvious? Everyone expected this arrangement, but she never allowed herself to seriously think about it.

"He loves you, Adana." Leera handed her a handkerchief.

Adana stood and wiped at her eyes. "Forgive me. Too much is happening. Perhaps the summons was for another purpose."

"What other purpose could there be?"

"The Brom estate houses troops and an armory. With all of the border troubles, maybe they want to discuss security measures."

"Forgive me if I hope you are incorrect with that suggestion," Leera said, her eyes wide with distress.

"Of course."

Adana felt shame at the thought of preferring battle plans to a betrothal. Forbidden desires drove a person to ridiculous ideas. She knew better. Given the choice, she never would have come to Elwar in the first place or face this dilemma. A little voice in her head pointed out she wouldn't have fallen in love with Kiffen either. She swatted the voice away.

"Forgive me, Leera, I believe I need to take a moment to compose myself." Adana headed for the garden's entrance only to spot Pultarch hurrying toward them, a huge smile brightening his brown eyes.

A midnight-blue glimmer cloth cloak swirled behind him as he picked up his pace. Beneath the cloak, he wore a matching blue riding tunic and breeches. The Brom bear insignia clasped the cloak to his right shoulder.

Adana tried to observe him with new eyes. Other women gushed over Pultarch's thick, brown hair, broad shoulders, and boyish dimples. These attributes never swayed her. She didn't gush.

"Elwar's loveliest flowers bloom here on the path. Good morning Princess Leera, Princess Adana." He performed an elaborate bow.

Thanks to her Watcher training, Adana hid her impression of his overdone actions. One would hope he realized by now that his flourishes and grand gestures did not fit with her reserved demeanor.

Leera nodded in acknowledgement of his greeting then pressed a hand to her forehead. "Sir Pultarch, thank goodness you arrived in time. I'm afraid a headache drags me away from Adana's company." She glanced at Adana under lowered lashes. "I will leave you in capable hands, my lady."

With hurried steps, she headed toward the castle. Adana watched her go, considering how to return the favor in the future. The girl would pay for leaving her alone with Pultarch.

"A most joyous morning to you, my lady," Pultarch said as he bowed and kissed Adana's hand. His lips lingered on her hand.

Nothing, Adana thought. No thrill, no heat, no excitement from his touch, no flutter, just a slight dampness on the back of her hand. She discreetly wiped that away on her skirt.

"Shall we?" he asked extending his arm to her.

She grasped his arm at the bicep, noting he tightened the muscle under her touch, no doubt to impress her. Others would swoon at the implied strength. She found it ridiculous.

As they wandered the paths, he bragged of his latest hunting exploits, a dismal failure for once, but he told it with good nature and an attempt at humor. She forced herself to laugh at the right points and wondered if, maybe with time, she could learn to appreciate him, if not love him.

At the far end of the garden they entered a secluded rose arbor and sat on a bench. Adana closed her eyes and drank in the spring air and the rose perfume. She inhaled several breaths, reaching for her calm, then turned toward Pultarch. His stare unnerved her. His palm, when he reached for her hand, felt clammy.

The skin around his eyes and nose whitened against the flush of his cheeks. He looked away and swallowed hard, his Adam's apple bobbing several times.

"Pultarch, are you ill?" She stood intent on escape. "I'll fetch you some water."

He grabbed her hand and pulled her down next to him, a thin attempt at a smile stretching his lips. "No. I'm well. I want to talk to you about something."

"Of course." She took slow, deep breaths, praying he wouldn't mention the betrothal.

"I'm nervous." He laughed and raked shaking fingers through his hair, leaving tracks in the thick locks.

"Whatever it is, Pultarch, you can tell me." It took all of her disciplined training to encourage him.

"You will be returning to Moniah soon." He took her other hand.

Studying her hands trapped in his, she said, "Yes."

"I will miss you."

"We will surely see more of each other." Adana tugged on her hands, but he held them in a firm grip.

"No," he said, "that's not what I mean." Pultarch released her hands, but only to give her cheek a tender stroke. "I'll miss you."

The touch and the depth of his gaze left no doubt to his meaning.

Adana struggled to find a proper response. What if Leera's suspicions turned out to be right?

"Pultarch," she began, "I too will miss you. And your stories."

"Yes, but do you share my feelings?"

Adana looked away from him. What could she say? How did Queen Quilla teach her to respond to unsolicited affection? Compliment, as you turn the suitor down. But could she shun the man she might spend the rest of her life with? If only she knew her father's plans.

She forced calm into her voice, hiding a flash of irritation over needing to ask the same question of so many people. "Do you know something you're not telling me?"

He jumped up. "I should not speak of such things to you." Then he grinned at her, a spark of his nature returning. "King Donel invites me to speak with him often." He knelt before her, his gaze trapping Adana's. "We discuss my plans, my beliefs. My feelings for you. He knows I've prayed to the Creator for you, for this match."

"Prayed?" Adana drew back in dismay. She hadn't prayed since her mother died. What new punishment had the Creator released on her now?

"Yes, Adana."

Guilt washed over her as she realized how much he opened himself up to her, expressing his deepest desires. Never once had he spoken so candidly. Leera was right. Why else would he say these things now?

What would it be like to spend her life with a man she's fond of, but not in love with? Curious, she touched her hand to his hair. It was soft like a puppy's.

Before she drew her hand away, Pultarch grabbed it and pressed her palm to his mouth. His fleshy lips grazed over her skin. "I offer you my allegiance, Queen Adana. Whatever you desire I will give you."

"Sorry to interrupt." The two of them jumped at the sound of Kiffen's voice.

Adana stood, almost knocking over Pultarch in her haste. He rose and faced off against Kiffen, the contrast between Kiffen's lean musculature and Pultarch's broad build so distinct Adana forgot her embarrassment.

Pultarch took a menacing step toward Kiffen. "We wish to be left alone."

In that moment, she knew she could never love Pultarch, not the way she loved Kiffen.

"My lady Adana, Kassa has need of you," Kiffen said, his mouth curling in disgust.

She stared at Kiffen, feeling the heat rise in her face. Unable to bear the presence of both men, she fled toward the castle.

* * *

K iffen watched Adana rush away. She hesitated to ride his horse with him, worried about propriety, but here she was trysting in the garden with Pultarch?

He turned toward Pultarch. They once were close friends. When did that change?

Frowning at Kiffen, Pultarch's gaze drifted toward the retreating figure of Adana. Everything between them changed after the princess' introduction to court. Competitors in everything, this one they couldn't laugh off to fight again the next day.

He wondered if Pultarch knew what drove them apart.

* * * * *

Chapter Forty-One

Adana's clothing lay spread out on the furniture in her chambers. Kassa stood before two trunks folding their belongings. The sight gave Adana a pang of homesickness and despair. She was going home, leaving Kiffen behind. But taking Pultarch with her.

Kassa glanced up. "I see, once again, Prince Kiffen has found you. I wish I had known of his uncanny ability to locate you three years ago. It would have made my life easier."

Straightening, she turned to smile at Adana. Since the arrival of the Monian contingent, Kassa had returned to wearing her uniform. Adana was startled to notice how much the subdued colors revealed Kassa's age. Her thick black hair revealed more silver, now. Her suntanned face sported many more wrinkles around her mouth and eyes.

Had Kassa ever had similar problems with men, or was she too old to remember the frustration?

Kassa's smile faded to concern. "Child, what's wrong?"

Adana threw her hands up in frustration and plopped down on the nearest chair. "Nothing. Not a single thing."

The woman's gaze pierced Adana's core. "That's convincing."

She never spoke of Kiffen or Pultarch to anyone, but then her mother's voice sounded in her ears. *Don't hold everything in. Trust Kassa.*

She took a deep breath. Would Kassa understand or know what to do? She might approve of Pultarch or tell her father about Kiffen.

"So are you going to tell me what is bothering you?" Kassa crossed her arms.

She dropped her Watcher's façade, and everything spilled out. Montee and her father keeping secrets. Worries about Maligon. Leera and Pultarch hinting at a betrothal. Refugees seeking Moniah's protection. Pultarch in the garden. Before she could stop herself, she admitted her feelings for Kiffen.

"And he found us alone in the rose arbor, Pultarch down on his knees."

Kassa nodded. "Quite a problem, Maligon and the refugees, that is."

Adana glared at Kassa. "Have you heard anything I said? Kiffen found me with Pultarch."

"I did, but I wanted you to realize what really is bothering you."

Shoulders sagging, Adana fought the urge to whine. She didn't whine. She never whined. No one would change that. "I know I should focus on the kingdom's problems not love."

"Love matters. If it didn't, your mother never would have had to sentence Maligon for his crimes."

"If I choose incorrectly, I'll have the same problem."

"Maybe. Maybe not. What would you do if this were a political circumstance? Two different landowners wanting the same water rights?"

"Kassa, really, I'm not a water ditch."

A hawk-like stare pinned Adana to her seat.

Kassa expected her to carry out this charade. Moniah did have water rights problems, landowners fighting over the same well or irrigation channels. Until she had enough knowledge, her mother never exposed her thoughts or opinions to either side. To do so would jeopardize the final decision, which typically was easy to determine once all was revealed.

With a smile she began to recognize her advantage on both parts.

"Kiffen's interruption saved me from answering Pultarch's question. It couldn't have been timelier, although it was awkward. As for Kiffen, nothing really happened, and it is realistically no concern of his. At this point neither one of them knows of my true feelings."

"Remember, what they don't know is your secret to holding power." Kassa smiled her approval. "Since you did so well with that solution, we won't discuss how Kiffen managed to sneak up on a Watcher twice in as many days."

Adana frowned. She often wondered about Kiffen's ability to surprise her. At least Kassa did not know he had always done just that—caught her off watch.

"Now wash your face with cool water. It will refresh you. Then go to the queen. She sent for you some time ago. I imagine she's getting impatient."

* * *

No matter how hard Adana tried to follow Quilla's directives, she fell prey to the queen's sharp rebukes. Today, even Leera felt the sting of her mother's harsh tongue.

Proper etiquette meant constant summons to rehearse, repeat, and review any event at the castle. Today that meant going over every last detail and nuance of Adana's recognition ceremony.

At the end of the lengthy session, Quilla dismissed the two exhausted girls. They hurried toward the door.

"Adana, one more thing," Queen Quilla said.

Adana sighed and turned back toward the queen, hiding her amusement at the unladylike groan slipping from Leera's lips.

"I laid out several suitable dresses for you," the queen said. "Which one did you choose?"

After three years of the woman's strict treatment, she knew Queen Quilla's reaction before she answered. "None of them. I will wear my ceremonial Watcher uniform."

"What?" The queen's shrill voice echoed off of the walls. "This is a court event, not a call to arms!" Small in stature, her anger seemed to extend her height, the pins in her glossy brown hair springing free as she stalked toward them. "You cannot wear leggings and a tunic to my party!"

"Ballene's Fire," Leera whispered. "We were almost out the door."

Adana stretched to her full height, just as the queen had taught her, looked down her nose at the smaller woman, and said, "First, this is not your celebration. Second, I will be recognized by all of Elwar as the new Monian Queen. Third, all Monian heirs, for centuries, have worn their ceremonial uniform during this ceremony. So will I." Turning sharply on her heel, Adana marched out of the room with Leera scurrying after her.

* * * * *

Chapter Forty-Two

Winding stairs led down into the dark, unused dungeons of Belwyn. Sir Jerold fought to control his unease from the walls of earth closing in on him. In the distance, a light flickered. At last, the dark-skinned guard paused at a cell. His torch cast a dim light through the bars.

At first Jerold thought the guard was playing a game with him, but, as his eyes strained to see, he began to discern the outline of a shape huddled against the wall. The shape turned away from the light, blocking the beam with upheld hands. It cursed the guard in a strong, but feminine voice. Jerold stared harder into the dank cell, realizing the guard did heed his request. The voice was Gabriella's.

Laughing, the guard tracked the offending glow after the prisoner who tried to scuttle from its glare.

"Tch, tch. Are you harassing the Empress again, soldier?"

Jerold jumped as Maligon descended the last steps and approached the cell.

"Traitorous behavior is punishable by death." Maligon frowned at the guard. Then he peered into the cell and smiled. "My mistake! The Empress relinquished her throne days ago. She is nothing."

Distracted by Maligon's mocking, Jerold lurched backwards in shock as Gabriella lunged through the bars, her hands just slipping from the cloth of Maligon's coat. They had stripped her of her fine gown and left her in her underclothes. Her hair, usually a tumble of dark curls, hung in a tangled mass. Dirt smudged her face, but her eyes glittered with clarity.

"Blazes, Maligon! Have you no honor? Keeping her caged like a rat in this filth?" Jerold reached through the bars to comfort her. "My lady, what do you require?" Even as he asked the question, Jerold recognized how ludicrous it sounded.

"Are you pleased with your coup?" Empress Gabriella glared at Maligon. "Do you really believe you can rule? You, the illegitimate spawn of my cousin's rape?" She spat at him, the glob of spittle landing squarely on Maligon's forehead, where it dangled in a long slow drip that did not release to the floor.

Maligon struggled to wipe the spit away, but his mangled right hand could not properly perform the duty. He did not attempt to wipe the offending matter away with his left hand. Jerold suspected the scar tissue over Maligon's shoulder and back would allow it, but he had also seen how the man sought to hide the weakness in that arm.

Stomping his foot, Maligon summoned the guard. "Remove it!"

The guard obeyed, taking a pale white handkerchief out of Maligon's pocket and wiping the globule away.

The traitor eyed the Empress with a frown. "You do look a mess, my lady. Have your Ladies in Waiting abandoned you?"

"Enough!" Jerold fought to restrain himself. "Why is the Empress—"

"She is not the Empress!" Maligon spun toward Jerold.

"Why is she here?" Jerold fought the urge to take a step back from the pompous man. "You promised proper care for her."

"Jerold, you fool yourself if you trust his promises," Gabriella said.

Maligon shrugged. "Actually, I offered her more respectable arrangements."

"Respectable?" Gabriella pressed herself against the bars. "In your bed."

Jerold hesitated. Every nerve in his body screamed to attack. The stench, the damp air, the despicable nature of the man who controlled their lives, choked him.

In another place or time, he would have struck the man down, but he had already seen what happened to those who dared rebel against Maligon. Belwyn's walls sported their heads in gruesome splendor. He knew he must outwit this madman. His entire twenty-one years in disguise had been in preparation for this possible event. Breathing slowly, he waited until he knew his voice would not betray him. "My Lord Maligon, you promised me a private audience with the Empress. Am I to assume you will not honor that promise either?"

Maligon studied him for a long time. Jerold knew he was looking for signs of fear or anger. Most did not know his true identity as Empress Gabriella's son, and the young prince prayed to the Creator he could remain undiscovered until aid arrived.

"Give him a few moments." Maligon nodded toward the guard and turned to leave. The guard grunted and backed a few steps away.

"Have they harmed you?" Jerold took Gabriella's hand in his.

"No. And not important." Her gaze flicked to the guard and back to Jerold's face. She lowered her voice. "He has Watchers imprisoned here."

"Are you sure?" Jerold stepped closer and eyed his mother carefully.

She nodded.

"Impossible." He tried to imagine how Maligon could have managed the capture of a Watcher. Historically, they chose death over imprisonment.

"The guards brag about it." Gabriella shook her head. "They're blindfolded and bound all the time."

Jerold shuddered. Could those perfectly composed soldiers survive in the dark? The blindfolds would unsettle most, but could those women remain unwavering through the one situation they feared—complete loss of sight?

"Is Karyah here?" His thoughts turned to the Watcher who risked her life to get word to Elwar.

"I do not think so, but Jerold, the guards said a Watcher set the trap for them."

Darkness closed in tighter, choking him. He saw, again, the guards who stepped to Maligon's aid and turned their backs on his mother. Had this evil penetrated the most loyal soldiers in the four kingdoms, too? Who would turn from a Watcher's training?

As if she heard his thoughts, his mother said, "Maligon's daughter."

"He has a daughter?" Jerold shivered while recognizing the irony that his mother's efforts to hide her own son might be mirrored by Maligon.

"With Maligon, anything could be possible."

"Time's up." The guard stepped forward and grabbed Jerold's arm.

Jerold held tight to his mother's hand. Before the guard pulled him away, he looked back to her for guidance.

"You *must* go." Gabriella released her hold on him, but she held his gaze.

Jerold nodded in understanding and turned away. Her command was clear. He must find some way to reach Elwar or Moniah and enlist their help.

* * * * *

Chapter Forty-Three

The Kingdom of Elwar

From a hidden alcove high above the Great Hall, Adana observed the arrival of the first guests to her recognition ceremony. The concealed perch provided her with an ideal view.

At Quilla's insistence, she began dressing for the event just after the mid-day meal. The queen seized the extra time to push her dress preferences on Adana, yet again. After succumbing to all of the woman's demands for three years, Adana thrilled at her ability to stand firm against the queen. It felt good to feel like her old self, something Queen Quilla had stifled, and, of course, Adana finished dressing with hours to spare.

Leera was not as fortunate.

"But Mother," Leera said as an army of servants surged into her chambers, "I'm going to wear the uniform Adana gave me."

"Most certainly not. Now be still or you will disgrace us by missing the entire evening."

Neither noticed when Adana slipped out of the room.

In the hall below, many of the Elwarian landowners mingled while Watchers stood sentry. Lady Suppina Sarx, mouth gaping, stared after a cluster of Watchers strolling past. A swift elbow from her brother, Lord Sarx, caused her to close her mouth, but the lady failed to drop her shocked gaze from the tall women.

Lord Sarx exhibited an avid interest in the Watchers, too, but his face did not share the shocked expression of his portly sister. In fact, as Adana's gaze wandered over the guests, she realized all the Elwarian women regarded the Watchers with disapproval, while their male counterparts could not mask their fascination.

"What is bothering them?" Adana said to herself as she studied the guests. Except for the occasional Monian emissary, she doubted most of the celebrants had seen a Watcher up close or for such extended periods of time, but they weren't unheard of.

Two Watchers stood separate from the crowd, observing the arrivals through the main entry. Adana, even from the distance of the balcony, could see how the uniform sculpted to the Watchers' bodies.

Warmth rushed to her face as she recalled Kiffen's disdain every time she wore the uniform. She twisted and stretched to look at her own clothing. A belt of glimmer cloth accentuated her waist, and the ceremonial uniform glittered in the light from golden strands threaded throughout the black supple leather of her tunic. The tunic hung low enough to be considered modest in Moniah, however in Elwar, the view of any leg above the ankle labeled a woman as risqué. How many times had Kiffen proven this? True, her ceremonial uniform had leggings made of golden glimmer cloth rather than the usual leather. Tucked into soft leather boots, the leggings hid her flesh, but the material clung to the contours of her legs.

The lighter, close-fitting material gave freedom to the wearer, unlike the dresses Quilla forced on her. She tried to imagine a Watcher performing her duties in one of those dresses. Even one deemed appropriate for riding would disable a Watcher.

Surely, the ladies of Elwar understood the practicality of a uniform over elaborate dresses. She watched several Watchers prove her point as they moved cat-like throughout the crowd. *I have been in this kingdom too long, she chided herself. I am not Elwarian, but a proud Monian. The representative of my kingdom. I have no reason to be ashamed or embarrassed. People will stare at me no matter what I wear.*

She inhaled and nodded once in confirmation of her thoughts and turned her gaze back on the people below in time to observe the arrival of several Monian nobles. They wore their traditional flowing glimmer cloth robes, and the overwhelming presence of the diaphanous material distracted the Elwarians from the more revealing uniforms of the Watchers. Glimmer cloth accounted for half of Moniah's export income, and many of the neighboring kingdoms coveted the secrets of its creation.

Lord Sarx weaved his way through the gathering crowds of Elwarian women and approached the Monians. He stood before a gathering of the highest-ranking landowners, and his gestures, even from this far, implied the nobleman he conversed with did not agree with his comments. Rage seemed to cluster above Sarx as he turned and stalked away. She straightened. His walk matched the secret visitor's. Why would a friend to the king and queen feel the need to visit the castle in secret late at night?

As Lord Sarx disappeared into the crowds, Adana leaned over the railing and searched the crowd for Sinti, wondering if she had recognized Sarx. A small flutter of nervousness awoke in her belly. The room held hundreds of people. A Watcher lived a simple life, void of crowds. A queen did not receive the same luxury.

Tamping down that feeling, Adana continued to seek out Sinti, finally spotting her on the far side of the hall. The Watcher's position gave her unencumbered sight of the gathering. Would her Watcher's senses pick out Sarx and his distinctive walk?

"I knew I'd find you here." Adana jumped in surprise when Kiffen drew aside the curtain blocking the alcove's entry.

Thoughts of Sarx fled from her mind. Once again, the prince had caught her off guard.

Kiffen peered over at the gathering below, his body close behind hers. "It looks like the entire court has arrived."

Her stomach somersaulted over his presence, heat rising to her face. For a moment, she recalled the close contours of her uniform and wondered if that new consciousness or the memory of their shared ride exhilarated her more. She resisted two urges at once, one to turn to him and the other to hide herself in the curtains. She chose to remain focused on the crowd below.

Oblivious to her discomfort, Kiffen stepped closer. "Did you see Lady Suppina with her mouth hanging open like a fish?"

Stifling a giggle, Adana turned, surprised to discover how close he stood. Trapped between his body and the balcony rail, she teetered off balance, and he reached out and steadied her. He did not let go. Instead he gazed down at her, a look heated with attraction instead of the cool distance she'd become accustomed to. The kiss was sudden and unexpected.

Adana pulled away and slapped him.

His hand rubbed the spot, eyes widened in surprise.

"Just because I'm dressed like this, doesn't mean I'm available. I represent Moniah's Seat of Authority in these clothes, no matter how much you disapprove of them." She stood straight, not hiding any of her body, daring him to stare.

Stare, he did, but again, with the heat she saw just moments ago. "I like your uniform." He glanced at the floor, his mouth working to hide a smile. When he looked back up, a pleased grin spread over his face. "I've always liked your uniform."

What could he mean? She crossed her arms and glared at him, fighting the urge to squirm under his gaze. "Then why have you glared at me every time you saw me wear it?"

Kiffen took a step toward her. "Is that what you think?" A chuckle escaped his lips. "Is that why you glared back at me?"

"A Watcher doesn't glare. She hides her emotions."

His lips pressed together as if fighting another smile. "Of course. But you often appeared to glare at me. I must have misread you." He spread his arms to the sides. "As you misread me. I fought to hide my fascination with you. It didn't seem right because of my brother."

"Fascination?" Adana inched closer. "Fascination with me? Or my uniform?"

"Both."

Her heart thumped harder. He moved closer.

She tilted her head up and stared into his eyes. His gaze held hers, and she found herself placing her fingers on his arm. He cared for her. He liked her uniform.

The firm muscles didn't flex to impress her like Pultarch's often did. Kiffen's arm was solid, strong, and temptation led her fingers wandering up to his shoulder and neck until she traced along his fresh-shaven chin. He drew in a ragged breath.

Shyness overcame her. What was she doing? She stared at his chest rather than the deep brown of his eyes. "Then we both want … what's impossible."

Kiffen groaned and pulled her body to his. She leaned into him. This time their kiss lingered.

She pulled away. "This won't work. We only torture ourselves with something that can't be."

"How can this be wrong?" Kiffen bent to kiss her again.

It took everything within her to stop the advance, placing her hand on his chest. Beneath her fingertips, a steady heartbeat, warmth from his skin flowing through the thin cloth of his tunic. The longer her hand remained the faster it beat.

With reluctance, she stepped back. They had withheld many secrets from each other. "We should talk."

A small bench provided the only seating in the alcove, the similarity to the rose arbor she shared with Pultarch earlier struck Adana as they sat. "Kiffen, about Pultarch."

Dismay clouded his face and he rose to leave. "No, it's none of my concern. I have no claim on you. I shouldn't be here. Please forgive me."

He stood, one foot turned toward the alcove entry. The memory of his mouth on hers distracted her as she stared at his slim waist spreading upward toward broad shoulders. "Kiffen, please don't go. Not now." She reached for his hand. "I wanted to thank you for interrupting Pultarch yesterday."

"Thank me?" He twisted toward her. "Why would you thank me for interrupting such a special moment between the two of you?"

Adana flinched at the pain evident in his words. Shaking her head, she said, "*This* might be a special moment. *That* was an awkward one."

Hope flickered across his face.

Adana said, "Pultarch asked about my feelings for him. I didn't know what to say. How could I tell him the truth when he is the most likely choice for my betrothed?"

"Everyone believes you love him."

"What do you believe?"

"My opinion does not matter." Kiffen grimaced, his shoulders tense and wary.

She laced her fingers through his, then raised her gaze to his. "I don't love Pultarch. The decision would be easier to handle if I did." Her heart pounded at the audacity of her actions. This had to be the most foolish, and wonderful, thing she had ever done. "There's someone else."

"And this someone else?"

"Isn't it obvious?"

The air knocked out of her at the force with which he grabbed her up from the bench and hugged her. He kissed her hair, her forehead, her cheeks, her mouth. She gave in to the joy of the moment, marveling over his returned feelings, at his heart pounding in time with hers.

After several blissful moments, the reality of their situation filled her with worry. She groaned and pulled away. "What are we going to do?"

"Has your father or Montee discussed your betrothal with you?"

"No. Everyone avoids the topic, except Pultarch. That's what he wanted to talk about today."

"I've fought my feelings and tried to accept the truth." He ran a hand through his hair. "But these last few moments undid me. I'm afraid I made a mistake when I came for you by the pond. If I'd sent someone else for you, we wouldn't be here."

Adana sighed. "I don't know if that would have changed anything."

"We could try to talk to our fathers," Kiffen said. "Maybe they will listen to us."

"Maybe," she said, "but what about our people? So much is unstable. It would tear the kingdoms apart. One of us could abdicate if there was a reasonable heir, but they will never agree to us."

"It would have been easier if Serrin lived." Kiffen slid away from her. "You loved him, didn't you?"

"He was a good friend, but that's all it ever was. With time, I think I would have."

"Oh, you would. Everyone loved Serrin. If he had lived, Father would have assigned your protection to him instead of me."

"Protection?" Adana looked up. "What do you mean protection?"

"You may as well know." He leaned back against the wall. "Serrin asked me to protect you. His last words. When you arrived, Father made the same request. To make sure you were safe and did not get lost."

Serrin's last words were of her? A troubled guilt welled up in her chest, but Am'brosia pushed through the link. The giraffe revealed image after image of Kiffen watching over her. Realization hit.

"So when I ate the berries? Or yesterday? Or—" The number of times he appeared nearby overwhelmed her.

"I followed you everywhere. I always knew where to find you." He shrugged. "You did lose me a lot in the last year. I guess your Watcher training helped there."

"And the pond?"

"Watched you float around in that boat for three years."

"And all this time I never knew you were there."

She dropped to the seat, her thoughts jumbled, until an increased hum of voices from below warned her of the time. "I must go."

As she rose, he said, "Adana, we can try to get our fathers to see our way."

"How?" Despair surged in her chest.

"We can go to the temple. Ask the Creator." Confidence spread over his face.

"You mean pray?" Did he really mean to ask the Creator for such a selfish blessing?

"Yes, the Teachers are always telling us prayer leads to miracles."

"I don't think—"

"What if it works?"

"Do you believe it will?"

His nod seemed childlike and innocent. But the temple? She only entered that dark space of despair when required and did her focused breathing until time to leave. If it gave him comfort, she'd let him pray, though. "Alright. But not in the temple. I don't have time."

"Then here." He knelt and pulled her down to face him, hands clasped with hers. She fidgeted in the awkward discomfort of the submissive posture, aware the last time she knelt for the Creator her mother died.

Kiffen closed his eyes in meditation. Adana tried to form the words to the Creator, to plea for them, but her mind whirled in other directions. She had not prayed since her mother's and Serrin's deaths. The recollection of those fervent prayers made her heart pound in alarm. Prayer would not work. The pain afterwards, when she realized the Creator punished her, was unbearable. She and Kiffen were doomed. She wanted to scream at him to stop, but he opened his eyes, a smile on his lips.

It was done.

They would never be together.

"You're crying." Kiffen wiped a tear from her cheek. "Please don't. It will be alright."

She breathed to stop the tears and wrapped her arms around Kiffen for what she knew would be the last time.

* * * * *

Chapter Forty-Four

In her chambers, Adana found a frantic Quilla directing a maid to "find that girl immediately." The poor servant almost collided with Adana in her attempts to abide by her mistress's wishes.

Her father sat on the window seat, a suppressed grimace on his face. Kassa sat in a chair by the fire devoting all of her attention to polishing something that flashed golden in the firelight. Her Honor Guard of Watchers stood at the door, their faces a stoic mask of control.

"Ahh, she appears at last." Quilla crossed her arms and glared in Adana's direction. She stalked toward Adana and grabbed her by the shoulders. "I don't understand why you think you must—"

Her words choked off when the alert Watchers jumped to Adana's side.

King Micah chuckled, stood, and approached them. "Ah, Quilla," he said. "You really have treated her as one of your own, haven't you?" Mirth evaporated as he glowered at her. "Have you forgotten she is the lady Adana, soon to sit on the Seat of Authority and be crowned Queen of Moniah? You will not treat her as one of your servants."

"Micah," Quilla said, "I meant no harm. The child—"

"Child?" Her father's voice resonated around the room. "No child rules Moniah. Look at her."

With a nod of his head, the Watchers stepped back, but remained at attention.

Adana stood still and regarded the queen, amazed at her father's ease in challenging Quilla. At least, he acknowledged her approaching status, her growth over the years.

Quilla regained her composure. "Yes, I've looked at her, and I'm appalled she plans to appear formally in this!" She sneered at the garment, unaware of the bristling tension from the Watchers.

"Enough." Kassa wrapped the item she was polishing in the cloth and laid it on the table before her. She stalked across the room until she was chin-to-nose with Quilla. Looking down her hawk-like beak, she glared into Quilla's eyes. Adana held her breath, surprised to feel a brief twinge of pity for the queen.

"My lady Adana has behaved beautifully. She's performed as you've asked. You have done everything to undermine her training to provoke her to anger. Not once. Not even once has she complained. Few people in Elwar or Moniah have as much patience."

Micah laid a hand on Kassa's arm, and she relaxed, taking a few steps back. Her voice so quiet and controlled, everyone leaned in to listen to her. "I believe Adana explained to you about the uniform. As a member of your court, she abided by all of your rules and traditions, as have I. Well, today she does not represent Elwar. She represents the monarchy of Moniah. Behold our tradition."

With a sweeping gesture, Kassa stepped back to stand beside Adana. Montee took up a similar position to her right, and the other four Watchers fanned out behind them. Confronted with seven very tall women in full Watcher uniform, Quilla swallowed, nodded to them, and announced, "I see all is ready here. I'll take my leave of you now."

As the queen swept through the door, Adana heard her mutter, "Savages."

Adana laughed and hugged Kassa once the door closed. "That was wonderful. I didn't have to say a word."

"Maybe so," Montee said, "but be careful you don't create an enemy with this."

"I've never trusted her, but an enemy?" Micah frowned at Montee. "Did you have a vision?"

Sighing, the First Vision shook her head. "No, but I do not feel good about her."

"Very few people do," Micah said. "I never understood why Donel married her after Roassa died. There were several more amenable women of royal lineage than her." He shook his head. "Concerns for a different time. Today, we focus on brighter things."

Kassa returned to her seat by the fire, picked up the object she had been polishing and handed it to Micah. With a smile, she patted Adana's cheek, and left the room, followed by all of the Watchers except for Montee.

Micah motioned Adana to a chair.

Left alone with her father and Montee, a different tension filled the room. Mere breaths separated her from her future, but she sensed other things were at play.

"Tonight is an important night, Adana." Her father sat down in front of her. "Not just for you but for Moniah, too. It has been three years since your mother wore this pin." He held out his palm. Inside the cloth lay a pin of a giraffe in profile, its spots made of topaz, with an emerald for its eye. "It was a gift to her from Queen Roassa when Elwar's court recognized your mother as the rising Queen of Moniah. It represents your office as much as the crown and Seat will.

"Montee will use it to pin your cape on during the ceremony."
He held the pin out to her.

Speechless, she took it. When Adana was a child, her mother
used to let her hold the pin. She would tilt it in the sunlight and cast
reflections on the walls of her mother's chambers. It felt cool and
smooth to the touch. The last time she saw her mother wear it was
just days before she fell ill. Tears came unbidden to her eyes, and she
tried to wipe them away. Somewhere in the distance she felt the
comforting presence of Am'brosia. The animal sent her images of
sunshine glistening in the fountains of her home.

Montee left the window and moved to stand beside the king, her
face more closed off than normal.

"What is wrong?" Adana said, sitting on the edge of her chair.

"Nothing." Micah laid a comforting hand on her shoulder. "We
have one more thing to tell you before we go down to the celebration, though."

* * *

Adana reeled from shock. Alone in her chambers, she
awaited the summons to the recognition ceremony,
and, now she knew, the announcement of her betrothal. No more waiting, no more worrying.

After months of seeking answers from the Creator about
Bai'dish's survival, Montee received a strong and specific vision. She
saw Bai'dish during his bonding to Serrin, but the giraffe's gaze was
focused beyond the prince. Two cords connected to Bai'dish, one
disappeared as the vision of Serrin faded. The other cord grew
stronger as it connected to a man, his features unclear. Bai'dish had
chosen a different partner as a true match for Adana.

In Moniah they sought to find this man, but Bai'dish ignored each eligible candidate brought before him, leading her father and Montee to seek Adana's chosen in Elwar.

Letting the giraffe decide went against every tradition she knew. Adana shook her head. Her betrothed should select his own giraffe, one he felt a connection with.

Shame washed over her. Am'brosia tried to warn her through their link earlier in the day. Adana's inability to understand reminded her that her separation from Am'brosia, and the use of the potion, stunted the natural progression of bonding with the animal.

"Who?" Adana had asked, trying to control the tremble in her voice. "Who must I marry?" She knew it couldn't be Kiffen. He would have said so.

Her father patted her hand. "You must trust Bai'dish for now."

Then they left her alone.

* * * * *

Chapter Forty-Five

Frantic, Adana sought her connection to Am'brosia, sending the vision of Bai'dish standing before a line of Elwarian men. The response from the giraffe showed an image of Bai'dish gazing back at her.

Adana ticked off the names of the possible suitors in Elwar, trying to avoid the obvious choice. Pultarch came to the castle to be tested. He must have come straight from the selection. His confidence the day before told her all she needed to know.

"My lady." Montee entered the room. "It is time."

Adana followed Montee into the wide corridor, her mind swimming with thoughts of Pultarch and Kiffen. For once, the power and significance behind the approaching ceremony didn't weigh on her. Breathing deeply, she sought focused breathing, using it to strengthen her limbs, gone weak at the thought of life with Pultarch.

The laughter and chatter of people below dragged her to the present. She stood at the top of the marble staircase that led to the hall. A rustle of cloth from behind announced the arrival of Elwar's royal family. Adana turned and managed a tight smile for Leera. The princess' rose-colored gown, bodice shimmering in swirling designs of gold and pearls, transformed the young girl into a woman. Adana wondered if Leera knew about the selection process with Bai'dish but discounted the thought as soon as it came to her. Leera could not have kept that secret.

King Donel stepped forward to speak to King Micah, and Adana's breath caught in her throat at the sight of Kiffen. To see him standing mere steps away, and know he would never be closer, sent pangs through her core. She closed her eyes for a moment, centering her focused breathing. Once the pain lessened, she risked a second look.

His royal blue tunic shimmered with gold-embroidered lions. A black sash wrapped around his waist, a solid gold lion's head clasp holding it in place. A small gold circlet served as his crown, the symbol of Elwar's heir.

Kiffen caught her studying him, and a smile danced across his face. His eyes glistened with amusement, their brown depths causing her to draw her breath in discrete, but short, inhalations.

He was everything Pultarch wasn't, long and angular while Pultarch was broad-chested and powerfully built. Her mind flashed to the moment they shared on the horse and the time in the alcove earlier, his lean body firm as she rested against him. Through the pain of these thoughts, her eyes met Kiffen's. He winked at her, the change from his earlier coldness such a relief. She longed to speak to him again, to tell him their plea to the Creator came too late. The decision had already been made.

A trumpet sounded from below. The crowd hushed. Adana's heart hammered in her chest, and she turned away from the enticement of Kiffen.

"His Majesty King Donel and His Highness Prince Kiffen!" The chamberlain pounded his staff twice on the floor as the two descended the stairwell. Adana saw the edge of the crowd part and bow as royalty passed them by.

"Quilla, Queen of Elwar and the Princess Leera."

The two women who had monopolized the majority of Adana's time in Elwar, glided past her and descended the stairs, their elegance announced by the regal tilt of their heads and the daintiness of their size. In contrast, Adana's retinue would overpower as they walked, a purposeful stride meant to radiate authority and strength.

Below, King Donel lifted his hands to the crowd. His voice boomed across the room. "Tonight history is made in our kingdom. Tonight, two countries, two cultures, two friends, Elwarian and Monian alike, rejoice in the coming of age of the lady Adana of Moniah. Raise your voices in acknowledgement of the next Queen of Moniah, the lady Adana."

"The Heir of Moniah! The Watch of Moniah." The acclamations echoed off the walls as voices raised in the traditional greeting.

Adana laid her hand on her father's arm as Montee led the Honor Guard down the stairs, Adana and her father following them. For each agonizing step, she breathed in deeply and released the air in a measured stream through her nose. She kept her gaze distant as Queen Quilla taught her. *Descend the stairs first and then nod occasionally to dignitaries near the dais. Do not acknowledge those standing in the rear of the hall.*

Pultarch stood at the base of the stairs like a groom at a wedding. She felt his gaze envelop her as they reached the foot of the stairs, and he beamed at her with such joy and adoration that Adana paused. Her father looked at her with concern. To cover the error, she tilted her head in a regal nod and glided forward, unable to focus on any other person.

The room glittered with thousands of candles suspended from the ceiling in large arrangements and from candelabra placed along the walls. The dais, raised above the room by three steps, gave a commanding view of the Hall. Air rushed out of Adana's chest in relief as she reached it. On the dais stood two thrones, one embossed with lions, the other with giraffes. Elwar's royal family waited before the dais, King Donel in the forefront.

Adana's father stopped before them, then he stepped back and handed her over to King Donel. "King Donel of Elwar, Moniah expresses their deepest gratitude for Elwar's enthusiasm and duty to our heir, lady Adana. Today, on her eighteenth birthday, both kingdoms will witness the ceremony that recognizes her as the rising Queen of Moniah."

King Donel took Adana's hand and led her up the steps, turning her to face the crowd.

Adana looked over the faces of the people gathered to witness her promises to Moniah's main ally, Elwar. Recalling Kassa's advice, she turned and focused only on Montee who approached the dais and knelt before her. In her hands, she held a cloak made of glimmer cloth. It shone gold with a multitude of giraffes etched in black along its border.

"Arise Watcher." Adana breathed in relief. At least, she remembered her part.

Montee ascended the stairs and shook out the cloak. With a flourish, she sailed it into the air and released it. The glimmer threads flashed in the candlelight as the smooth material slid over Adana's shoulders. The First Vision then took the giraffe pin and clasped the cape to Adana's right shoulder. The pin stabbed Adana's flesh, and she flinched at the sharp sting radiating from the entry point.

"My apologies," Montee whispered. "This completes your bond with Am'brosia. I could not warn you or the potion would not work."

Adana sucked in her breath as the sting subsided and warmth radiated down her shoulder into her chest. Heat spread upward into her face and raced along her arms and legs, suffusing her with a temperate sense of power. In the forefront of her mind, Am'brosia pranced and danced. It felt like the giraffe smiled.

In a loud voice, Montee said, "May the weight of this emblem on your right shoulder always lead you to do right. May you never lose your sight and vision."

She knelt before Adana and everyone in the ballroom knelt with her. "May you never lose your sight and vision," all repeated.

Adana swallowed. Waves of warmth flowed from the pin prick, leaving her calm and relaxed, her hearing muffled.

"Arise, people of Elwar and Moniah." Her voice echoed throughout the hall. "Arise and hear my pledge."

The uneasy tension from earlier evaporated as if the puncture gave it an exit from her body. The room vibrated with color, and, for a moment, she paused in surprise. Whatever Montee had given her heightened her sight, revealing color auras over each guest, their expectancy in the air. She couldn't say why she identified it as expectancy. She just knew. The swirls of various bright hues glittered and spun around the room.

Staring across the sea of color, she stepped forward and addressed the crowd. "On my return to Moniah, I will carry your well wishes to my court. Once crowned, I will always seek sacred vision. I will never close my eyes to sight. My watch will protect the hallowed bond between Elwar and Moniah, keeping us all from evil and shame. The Creator is my witness!"

The Keeper of the Faith, Father Tonch, approached the dais, accompanied by his wife, Mother Sariah, the Protector of the Faith.

They both wore the white robes designated for their high offices. Sariah carried a cushion holding a small, but heavily jeweled, crown. The one Adana would wear until her coronation in Moniah.

Even though she did not trust in their Creator anymore, Adana felt a bubbling of happiness and peace flood from her shoulder as her childhood teachers joined her.

Father Tonch said, "All Monian queens enter into a sacred relationship with the Creator. Our lady Adana requests the Creator to witness her pledge, and the Creator does so. Now let's seek blessings for her reign. Please kneel in submission to the Creator."

Amidst a great rustling of clothing, everyone knelt. As Adana followed suit, she watched the difficulties the Elwarian women encountered while assuming this posture in their elaborate dresses. She thanked her ancestors for choosing more practical clothing, another reason to appreciate its revealing simplicity.

"Holy Creator, provider of blessings and honor," Father Tonch and Mother Sariah intoned together, their voices blending in harmony. "We kneel before you, not as two kingdoms, but as your faithful. We are thankful and joyous on this the eighteenth birthday of Adana, daughter of Chiora, daughter of Moniah. We humbly ask your blessings on this servant. She is descended from the great gifted ones, possessing your blessing of vision. Give her wisdom and patience to aid in the use of her gifted sight. Help her to know you intimately so she can properly lead all Monian people. Bless her rule in Moniah and bestow that blessing on her alliance with Elwar. Endow her with your supreme vision, so she may always seek and serve you until Vision's end."

Adana listened to their words, uncomfortable with the implication. The queen of Moniah was expected to hold a strong and intimate connection to the Creator. Had all queens done so? Was she the first to doubt the Creator's intentions? Her shoulder burned where the pin had pricked her, and she turned inward, using her focused breathing. With each inhalation, she sought to numb the puncture's effects while seeking to represent the proper spirit of obedience.

Father Tonch took the crown and placed it on Adana's head. The weight pressed down on her, adding to the heavy responsibility the blessing established. Mother Sariah helped her to stand, not releasing her arm until Adana adjusted her posture to find a proper balance. For the first time, she experienced the force of the crown and struggled to hold her chin uplifted in a regal pose.

Mother Sariah planted a kiss on both of her cheeks. "Bless you Chosen One," she said. The woman gazed at her with pride.

With each indrawn breath, Adana told herself the words of the blessing were as she had always seen them—part of the ritual, nothing more. With each exhalation she sought to extinguish the burning sensation in her shoulder.

Mother Sariah and Father Tonch guided Adana to King Donel who escorted her to the giraffe-engraved throne. He bowed to her as she sat, then he settled into the lion throne, signaling the end of the official part of the ceremony. Elwar's royal family and Adana's father joined them on the dais.

The crowd parted as a man rushed toward the dais, his multi-colored tunic and conical hat identifying him as the Memory Keeper. He bowed to Adana and Donel before turning and gazing around the Hall.

A hush fell over the crowd as they waited in anticipation of the story told at all recognition ceremonies, The Birth of the Kingdoms.

"Memory Keeper," Adana said, "what story might you share with us tonight?"

"One of a father's love for his daughters, Chosen One." The man bowed from the waist, his sweeping hand taking in the entire contingency of royalty gathered behind the thrones on the dais.

"Excellent," Adana said. "Rise and tell."

The Memory Keeper leapt into the air, causing the guests to jump backward. Twisting, he landed facing the crowd and proceeded to stroll around the suddenly cleared circle before him, a secretive smile on his face. After he completed his circuit, he halted in the center of the room and spread his arms wide.

"Chosen One, Kings, Queens, Princes, and Princesses! Nobles and kinsmen! For you today I offer a simple story. A touching story. One that happened hundreds of years ago but affects us to this day.

"Many generations ago, there was a kingdom known as Yarada. The king of this country was truly blessed with twin daughters. He doted on the both of them, and they grew to be beautiful young ladies.

"The first-born loved horseback riding and often rode through the mountains and forests of Yarada. She played the piano and flute with grace and sang like an angel. Her embroidery was second to none, except her mother's. But this young lady was not just talented in artistic measures. She loved the intrigue of court politics. She spent every free moment by her father's side as he held court or listened to the petitions of his people.

"The second-born preferred the outdoors. She could sew a straight seam if required, but she preferred purpose to luxury. This princess excelled in archery and her aim with a slingshot surpassed most men in the kingdom. Due to her expert marksmanship, she beseeched her father to allow her to learn the use of the sword, which she turned into her own special dance of skill. She spent more time in the

soldiers' training grounds or helping her father and his advisors with military strategy than in the formal courts.

"When she wasn't involved with military matters, this daughter took long excursions into the outlying lands of the kingdom. She loved the simplicity of nature and often returned from these trips carrying small, injured animals or birds to nurse back to health. After one of her excursions into the southern part of the kingdom, she returned with a young giraffe… and the story of a village of women with extraordinary vision and her new ability to communicate with this majestic animal."

The Memory Keeper bowed toward Adana again, and when he rose, he withdrew a wooden statue of a giraffe from the folds of his cape. The guests applauded as he knelt before Adana and presented the giraffe to her.

Adana took the statue, sliding her fingers along the raised nubs that the wood carver created to simulate the giraffe's spots. She paused at the extension of the neck, amazed to see the statue's spots matched Am'brosia's in location and shape. She bowed her head in thanks, and the Memory Keeper continued his storytelling.

"As the twins' father aged, he worried over his successor to the throne. Without a son to follow as king, one of his daughters must become queen. The first-born held the right by birth, but the king watched his daughters' growth, noting the differences in their skills and strengths. He worried whether mere order of birth should decide the future of Yarada.

"His advisors determined the right to rule fell to the first-born. The first-born understood court intrigue and politics well."

With another flourish, the Memory Keeper produced a statue of a young woman astride a horse, a representation of the first born. He presented this statue to Prince Kiffen, her descendant, causing the prince to step forward and stand beside Adana's throne.

She fought the urge to reach for his hand as it hung just to her side.

The Memory Keeper continued.

"The first-born negotiated with skill and the nobles of the land held her in great regard, but the second daughter held the loyalty of the armies in her hand. The soldiers respected her abilities and considered her worthy to lead them. Plus, her experience in exploring the far reaches of the kingdom gave her knowledge of the people of Yarada and neighboring lands.

"Over many nights, the king pondered this problem. With his health failing, he worried he might die without making the best choice. As word of his indecision reached the nobles and the army, each pressed for their chosen daughter to rule."

The Memory Keeper paused and glanced around the crowd, his gaze falling on Adana last. She felt the storyteller's curiosity in her and knew he must be recording everything he saw while this simple, well-known story unfolded.

"As typical among people, word of the king's concerns eventually reached the princesses. As different as they both were, they had the strong bond of love and companionship often found in twins. To them, the answer was simple, and they approached their father with a solution.

"He saw wisdom in their plan and asked his Chief Advisors to witness his decision. Within two months, the king died, his heart light and relieved that the matter was resolved."

The Memory Keeper paused, head bowed. Adana counted one, two, three breaths before the man lifted his head in triumph and projected his voice to the corners of the Hall.

"The king's decree divided the kingdom of Yarada in two. The first-born daughter, Elwar, wore the crown in the northern regions of mountains, hills, and forests. The second daughter, Moniah, wore the crown in the southern regions of the plains. To this day, Elwar and Moniah remain sisters, while still very different lands. Sisters in birth, they pursue different interests and cultures, just as the king's daughters of old.

"And that is why today, we in Elwar gather to recognize the Chosen One's right to rule the southern kingdom. She is heir to the second daughter, and we acknowledge her."

With a twirl and a bow, the Memory Keeper finished his story. The nobles applauded as he disappeared into the crowd. Adana watched him go, aware he would lurk around the edges of the gathering tonight, cataloging information for tonight's story. As the court's Memory Keeper, he had earned the right to be present where stories developed.

* * * * *

Chapter Forty-Six

At the end of the Memory Keeper's story, the clear notes of a flute trilled in the air. King Donel stood beside Adana, his arm extended to escort her to the first dance in the center of the room. They glided to the notes played by the solitary flutist, a representation of the musical talents of Queen Elwar of long ago.

When the dance ended, two Watchers entered the Hall, carrying a huge object draped in luminous gold glimmer cloth.

Montee joined Adana in the center of the room. "Your Highness, the Watchers of Moniah present the sacred head."

Adana caressed a corner of the draping amazed at the enhanced liquid feel of the material. Was it another effect of the potion? With a flick of her wrist, the cloth slipped off, revealing the large white skull of a giraffe. This skull was from the first royal giraffe and represented the Monians' respect for the noble beast. Possession of any other giraffe fossil was a traitorous offense punishable by death in Moniah.

Adana skimmed her hand over the smooth bone, gasping at the quick shock of joy and welcome radiating through her fingertips. She felt Am'brosia pull her into the link, but the view the animal shared was of Queen Moniah seated on the throne.

Adana stood in a trance until Montee's voice drew her back. "The sacred head of Moniah's first giraffe serves as the percussion for Princess Adana's dance with her father."

King Micah faced Princess Adana, and they waited for Montee to slap the skull in the first staccato rap. A sharp sonorous tone echoed throughout the hall, and Adana did a quick side-step and slide as she and her father stood back-to-back and circled each other, their faces staring out into the crowd. With each resonating tone, the steps grew faster as she and her father continued to slide, step, and circle the room, casting an ever-vigilant watch on the guests. The faster the beat, the more insistent the dance, feet slapping the stone floor in demand. Done properly, each observer would believe the dancers watched their every move, causing them to freeze in awareness. The dance ended when Adana and her father completed the circle and returned to their starting position.

As the last note resounded, her father whispered in her ear, "Your mother would be proud of you tonight. I feel her presence in you. Smile and enjoy this evening."

As he turned away, Adana spotted Kiffen across the hall. He strode toward her, but Pultarch appeared at her side, a proprietary hand on her arm. King Donel took Quilla by the hand and glided onto the floor as the musicians began the next dance. After the first few steps, other nobility joined them.

Adana glanced one more time toward Kiffen as Contina rushed to his side, curtsied, and extended her hand in expectation.

A sting of displeasure pierced her shoulder as she watched him enclose the woman in his arms while Pultarch pulled her into his. After a few moments of gliding to the light melody, Pultarch spoke. "You look so beautiful tonight. I am the envy of all the men here." Pultarch glanced around the crowd and then centered his gaze on her, pride lighting his eyes. "I'm going to enjoy that envy for the rest of our lives."

His words slammed into her. He radiated with self-confidence and had gone so far as to wear a coat embroidered with giraffes.

"You saw Bai'dish yesterday?" She waited, dreading his answer.

"Bai'dish?" He paused, a quizzical look crossing his face. "Oh. The giraffe? Amazing creature!" He spun her around on the dance floor, happiness flooding his face.

She fought to hold her head erect and keep the weight of the crown balanced on her head. Her neck ached as she forced herself to accept Pultarch's next words.

"That animal got so excited when I entered the pen. Remarkable. I had no idea giraffes possessed that kind of energy! They look so lazy."

"Lazy?" Adana bristled at the idea. Only a person unfamiliar with giraffes would perceive them that way. His comment on energy didn't sound like an accurate description, either.

"Oh yes," Pultarch said. "He pranced all over the corral when he saw me. Magnificent. You should have seen the amazement on everyone's faces. I knew then I was the chosen one. That gave me the courage to talk to you yesterday." His eyebrows drew down over his eyes for a moment. "I'm sorry I didn't tell you. I'm not supposed to know." Flashing his well-known smile, Pultarch said, "Forgive me?"

Adana blinked several times, her hand clenched within Pultarch's, squeezing with the force she reserved for her archery. He returned the squeeze, a quick excited pump of his hand. She swore to never let him know her true feelings and took refuge in breathing, nodding her forgiveness.

The young lord, her betrothed, she reminded herself, laughed in relief and embraced her, his chest slamming into hers. "We will be the happiest couple in all of the kingdoms."

Unbidden, the sensation of resting against Kiffen as they rode his horse toward the stable reared in her mind, contrasting his gentle strength with her partner's over exuberant actions. Pultarch crushed her closer and whispered in her ear. "You tremble. With eagerness for our betrothal?"

When the music ended Adana stumbled back and turned with relief to greet her next partner, noting with concern how Pultarch backed away, casting a scowl toward the man.

After each dance, Adana looked for Kiffen, but a bevy of young ladies flitted around the prince in hopes of a dance that might lead to a king for a husband.

Soon, the chamberlain pounded his staff on the stone floor to summon the guests to dinner. Adana held her chin up and fought a rush of disappointment when Pultarch offered her his arm. He had claimed three more dances that evening, including the last. Each time he grasped her hands, the puncture wound in her shoulder burned with excruciating heat.

Montee said the potion on the pin enhanced the connection to Am'brosia. The giraffe's presence hovered closer, but her emotions felt manipulated and amplified this evening. The lovely auras turned murky as she danced time and again with Pultarch, and the reassurance washing over her during the ceremony fled as she fought doubts about the Creator.

If Bai'dish chose Pultarch, why did pain slash her shoulder each time he touched her? What would be worse? Finding a way to accept marriage to Pultarch or living the rest of her life in unbearable pain?

Kiffen appeared by their side as Pultarch led her across the threshold of the Banquet Hall. "My apologies at my tardiness, Adana." He nodded to Pultarch. "Thank you for standing in for me until

I could reach the lady." Kiffen offered Adana his arm. "My lady, if you will allow me."

Relief flooded from the puncture wound, once again confusing Adana.

She cast a fleeting smile at Pultarch, who scowled at Kiffen but stepped back. "Of course," he said and bowed.

Adana laid her hand on Kiffen's arm and followed him into the room. "Queen Quilla didn't mention you were to escort me to dinner."

"No, she didn't mention it to me either." Kiffen grinned. "But Pultarch obviously doesn't know."

She laughed, joy tingling in her shoulder. "You sounded so official."

"One of the rights of titles, my lady."

She considered telling him about the betrothal but chose to keep this brief moment free of disappointment. At least for Kiffen.

Lavish tables filled the Banquet Hall. The head table stood on a raised platform facing the celebrants. Seated to Adana's left were King Donel, Kiffen, Father Tonch, and then Leera. Seated to her right were her father, Mother Sariah, Queen Quilla and Montee. Beyond Montee was an empty chair. Adana searched the celebrants for Pultarch, convinced he would soon occupy that seat, but she found him seated near the middle of the room, his gaze focused on Kiffen, his brow drawn down in a jealous stripe.

Before she could comment to her father about the empty seat, a line of servants entered the room. They carried heaping platters of sumptuous delicacies—roast turkey, duck, salmon, sweet pastries and fruits, and soufflés of carrots, potatoes, and cheese.

What food she managed to swallow lay in her stomach like a rock. Other attendants hovered nearby with imported Lisseme wines, rushing to refill any empty goblets.

Throughout the meal, nobles from both kingdoms came forward. Each one presented a gift to a servant who handed the tokens up to Adana. The Elwarian gifts tended toward jewelry, silver, gold, or marble, while the Monians prepared their next queen for defense with knives, exquisite arrows, and handcrafted bows.

With each presentation, the noble knelt before her in a pledge of support. Adana's shoulder responded in spasms that forced her to consider each person carefully. In many cases, the spasm resonated pleasure, but with a few of the nobles her shoulder ached in agony.

As she accepted jeweled gloves from Lord Sarx, the soreness in her shoulder sank deep into muscle and bone, sapping her mouth dry. She fought for composure and nodded her thanks. The pain reminded her she had not told Montee that Sarx was the secret visitor to the castle. Before she turned to the next person, Adana struggled with an impulse to reach for her finger bowl and rinse her hands clean.

As attendants cleared the final course away, a horn blew and the doors swung open. Eight servants stood in the archway carrying a massive tray between them. On the tray rested the largest cake Adana had ever seen. It stood several layers high, with glistening jewels of candy and flowers cascading down the layers. She swallowed at the sight—it was a betrothal cake.

* * * * *

Chapter Forty-Seven

When the cake appeared in the doorway, Kiffen fought the urge to escape the room. He grabbed his wine goblet and drained its contents in one gulp. With nothing left to distract him, he turned and drank in Adana's countenance. Pultarch had hovered near her all evening while a slow, overwhelming rage engulfed Kiffen. At least, his former friend didn't sit at the main table.

Adana sat forward, rigid and still, a fixed smile on her face. As the huge, tiered cake crept forward, her knuckles whitened around the base of a goblet.

The servants carrying the cake came to a halt in front of the royal table. Kiffen closed his eyes to the scene, but the sound of his father rising to his right forced him to gather his emotions and appear unmoved by the cake.

King Donel said, "Esteemed friends, we have an empty place at the royal table."

Everyone glanced toward the vacant chair. Kiffen suspected its presence worried the guests as much as it had worried him throughout the evening.

"This chair represents the absence of my beloved son, Prince Serrin." King Donel paused and cleared his throat, fighting emotions he only revealed at the mention of Serrin or Roassa.

"For years I anticipated this day and the joy of announcing Serrin's betrothal to my lady Adana. In acknowledgement of his brief life, I ask each of you to raise your cup to the memory of Elwar's departed son, Prince Serrin."

Guests saluted Serrin's memory with their cups. After the solemn toast, King Donel sank into his seat, a strange expression on his face. Micah rose and turned to address Donel.

"Indeed, it was a sad day in Moniah when we learned of Serrin's death, so soon after the passing of our beloved Queen Chiora." He paused and cleared his throat while he turned his attention to the gathering. His voice cracked with emotion when he spoke again. "From the first time they met as babes, all could see a bond between Prince Serrin and my lady Adana. Their betrothal seemed blessed by the Creator, but we didn't ask for guidance so missed what was meant to be."

The guests rustled and murmured to each other.

Kiffen studied Adana's profile, aware, in a few moments, his obvious attention would forever become unseemly. Sadness gripped him, and he willed her to look in his direction, but she continued to grip her goblet and stretch her lips in a parody of a smile.

Micah continued. "The unexplained survival of the giraffe, Bai'dish, added to our misguided plans. Never before has a giraffe continued to live and thrive if its human bond dies.

"As everyone knows, Watchers possess the gift of prophecy. Moniah's First Vision, Montee, sought the Creator for answers to this mystery."

The guests turned as one body and gazed at Montee. She sat unfazed, accepting their regard without acknowledgement.

"The Creator provided a vision. Bai'dish would select the proper man to marry Adana." Micah shook his head in wonder. "For the first time in our history, the giraffe chose the betrothed."

Kiffen turned and really looked at Adana. Her face registered acceptance, not surprise. When had she learned of this? Did she know this when he kissed her?

His stomach dropped and disappointment burned along his limbs as Micah descended the stairs from the main table and walked toward the center of the room.

And Pultarch. Pultarch straightened and smiled, aware many looked with expectation in his direction.

"Bai'dish did not choose any of our men in Moniah, so we came to Elwar and invited your men to meet our royal giraffe."

Micah paused and looked around the room. The guests waited; their breath held as one. Kiffen, unable to help himself, sat forward waiting for the inevitable.

"Bai'dish's reaction to one of Elwar's finest nobles amazed us. He swung his neck in sweeping arcs and kicked with more energy than any giraffe I've ever known."

Silence echoed in the hall as Micah paused. Adana looked pale but still held her head high. Kiffen wished to comfort her but knew his opportunity disintegrated with the coming announcement. He'd witnessed Bai'dish's reaction to Pultarch.

In a strong, firm voice, Micah said, "When the giraffe did not cease this frenzy, we became alarmed. We could not calm the animal and bade this noble to leave."

Pultarch straightened in his chair and smiled at the king, leaning forward to stand, but Micah's voice rose in distress. "Our caretaker prepared to give Bai'dish a sedative in hopes of calming him, but we hesitated. The sedative would render him helpless. The fall could injure him. Maybe kill him."

Micah walked back to the royal table, while Pultarch sank back into his chair, a look of bewilderment replacing the confident smile.

Awash in cool relief, Kiffen followed the king's figure as he turned and beamed at the guests, the concern on his face gone. "At that crucial moment, a young man we had *not* invited to the choosing arrived, as if Bai'dish's frenzy lured him. We watched in fear for this man's safety while he drew near and soothed Bai'dish. A miracle. Giraffes only allow those with a sacred bond or duty to touch them."

A murmur ran throughout the crowd, and Kiffen sat upright in his seat. When Pultarch left the compound the day before, a huge smile plastered over his face, Kiffen heard the cries of alarm and rushed into the corralled area. Men circled the frenzied giraffe, but none could draw close. As if other hands guided him, he had walked past the men and laid his hands on Bai'dish.

Could Bai'dish have chosen him?

Micah continued. "Once calm, Bai'dish spread his legs and lowered his head in a deep bow to the man. Bai'dish had chosen."

Adana darted an apprehensive look at Kiffen. He could not hide his smile. Her brow furrowed, and she stared back, uncertainty on her face.

Micah's firm, reassuring hand landed on Kiffen's shoulder. "Bai'dish chose Prince Kiffen."

The guests' shouts of surprise echoed off the walls, but Kiffen only saw the emotion that flickered over his beloved's face before she masked it in a Watcher's composure. The amazement in her expression, he knew, mirrored his own.

"Arise, Prince Kiffen, chosen of Bai'dish, and greet your betrothed, Adana, Chosen One of Moniah!"

Kiffen crossed the distance to Adana in two large strides.

"He chose you?" she whispered.

He smoothed an errant tear off her cheek. "Yes." He took her hand and kissed it, never looking away as her blue eyes lit up with a wonder he could not describe.

Adana laughed, a nervous smile flitting across her face. She blinked up at him, and he bent to kiss her. The touch of her lips shot through him, releasing a desire he repressed in her presence. Her body leaned toward him as they separated.

They clasped hands and faced the room. Elwarian guards and Monian Watchers stood in front of the royal table. Others moved throughout the crowd, alert and vigilant. Kiffen looked toward Pultarch's seat, but his rival had disappeared.

The Watchers before the dais bowed to the betrothed couple, and slowly the guests followed suit in an uncoordinated fashion. Moniah's Watchers then stood and declared, "Long live Queen Adana and King Kiffen!" The titles came prematurely, but after a few repetitions, most joined them in the tribute.

Kiffen felt Adana shiver and entwined his fingers with hers. He scanned the guests, noting malevolence on several of the faces, despite the continued tribute. Moniah had never had a king before, always a husband king. What did this mean for Elwar? Would both kingdoms accept him?

One by one, those who shared their table congratulated them. Kiffen turned expectantly when Leera approached, thankful they could rely on her support during the difficult months to come. But Leera would not look at them. She gave each of them a brief hug and a near-miss kiss on the cheek before turning away.

Queen Quilla advanced, her perfect face frozen in a forced smile. Cold ran through Kiffen's veins as she gave them each a stiff peck on the cheek.

As they turned back to the guests, Kiffen sought out the pleasant faces. More smiled than frowned, but even so, disquiet churned in his belly. This decision changed the world for them.

* * * * *

Chapter Forty-Eight

Sarx waited in the darkness of the silent corridor. The celebration and revelry over, only an occasional exhausted servant passed him by. None would notice or recall persons whispering together tonight.

Queen Quilla glided into the shadows and faced him.

"It's final?" he asked.

"Yes." An unladylike snort. "Everyone is furious."

"Yes," he agreed. "I'm amazed at their stupidity. Or blatant disregard for custom. Maybe they are more courageous than we expect."

"No." Quilla leaned in, mouth set in a straight line. "It's the Watchers. If not for Montee—"

"She will be dealt with. Do not concern yourself."

"Do they not realize the jeopardy they place the royal lines in? Any children," Quilla shuddered at the word, "will be half foreign blood."

"Only a quarter Elwarian and a quarter Monian. Don't worry. We are prepared."

"Everything goes as planned?" Quilla leaned toward him, excitement in her eyes.

"My men act as we speak. Soon, you and I will rule Elwar."

"And play puppet master to Moniah's throne." She laughed in triumph.

* * *

At the first opportunity, Leera fled the celebration for her rooms. The surprised chambermaid rushed in after her but scurried away quickly when Leera flung a vase at the door.

Choking back tears, Leera wiped her eyes and stared out into the night. The stars still twinkled in the sky. The moon cast a soft glow over the gardens. How could such light and beauty grace the night of this disaster?

The scene at the dinner played over and over in her mind. Her brother running into Adana's arms. The shock on Pultarch's and Contina's faces. Joy shone in Adana's face; her cheeks blushed a pink never revealed to any other suitor. The fools. How could they do this to her?

She jumped to her feet and paced the chamber, swinging at vases, candles, pitchers, trinkets, smashing everything to the floor. Finally, with nothing left to break, she flung herself face down on the bed and screamed into the bedclothes.

Leera cried herself out long before her mother rushed into the room. The queen sat on the edge of the bed and gathered Leera into her arms, rocking gently.

Memories of childhood comfort embraced Leera. Fresh tears flowed for a time, then she pulled away from the comforting shoulder to look up into angry eyes, surely a mirror of her own. "It's not fair, Mother. It's just not fair."

"Don't worry, dear." Her mother stroked Leera's cheek. "We'll correct this abomination. Don't worry."

* * *

"**A**nd when did you decide not to tell me?" Quilla stormed into their chambers, catching Donel in the act of pouring a goblet of wine. "Did you not think I needed to know? He is my son, too."

Sighing, Donel sat in a chair and sipped his wine. "Only a few knew. We needed the decision to remain secret as long as possible. You know the political unrest this will cause."

"You did not trust me to keep this confidence?" She stalked over to him and knocked the goblet out of his hand. "I am your wife. The queen. I should have known."

Donel straightened and looked at his wife. His sharp gaze pinned her to the spot where she stood. "You've never been one to hold onto interesting gossip for long, Quilla. Or have you forgotten how you managed to marry me?"

* * * * *

Chapter Forty-Nine

The young noble slammed down an empty tankard of ale. His head bobbled as he looked around for the serving girl. With a quick smile, Shana scurried over to refill his drink. When this gorgeous gentleman first entered the tavern with Lord Sarx, she shoved past the other girls before they realized the opportunity had crossed the threshold. She thanked her keen hearing for catching the formal sounds of his speech. Loud for a gentleman, but considering the part of the city, not unusual, his voice reached her ears before he pushed through the doors.

Except for Lord Sarx, not many of the king's court darkened the establishment of The Sleeping Dog. She had to take her chances when they came, even if it meant serving Sarx. The man's oily gaze made her desire a bath.

She graced the younger man with her most alluring smile as she brought more ale, aware her expression suggested many services, but the attractive nobleman seemed unaware. Lord Sarx raised his eyebrows in recognition of her invitation, though. He was much older and definitely not as magnificent to look at. Recoiling, she turned away from his glinting black eyes. Sarx might be wealthy, but a sleazy danger lurked within his gaze, similar to the street thugs who tried to monopolize the tavern. May the young one be her ticket out of this place. Not Sarx. He was not worth the humiliation.

"Will my lord be needing other services tonight?" She stood close to the man, her hip cocked to the side, supporting the weight of the tray she carried. Many men enjoyed this stance. It showed off her curves even more in the tight bodice and skirt she wore.

The young man, who had been staring at the amber liquid she placed before him, heaved his head up to look at her. "Her eyes are wrong." His voice slurred as his head bobbed toward the lord. "Don't you think, Sarx?"

The older man scrutinized her face. "They are similar, surely, and look at her hair. It's the same light shade you find so appealing."

Shana's heart skipped a beat. Nobles drowning their sorrows over proper ladies could mean money, lots of it if she pleased him. Arching an eyebrow at Sarx, she said, "A jilted lover?"

"An understatement, but yes." The man grimaced.

Shana laid down the tray and bent over to cup the young one's square, firm chin in her palm, just like her mother had done with her when she was a child. He stared at her, his brown eyes glazed with drink. Could he get her out of here? If she saved him, would he save her? He was obviously young and impressionable. His beauty just sweetened the task. And his eyes had drifted to her bodice.

She wrapped her arms around him, pulling his head to her waist.

With a groan, he threw his arms around her. "She was mine, all mine!" Then he started to sob.

* * *

Pultarch mumbled in his sleep and thrashed on the small cot. Sarx and the tavern maid stood watch over him. She shook her head. "She must have been quite remarkable."

Sarx smiled at her, enjoying the visible tremor that ran over the serving girl's shapely body every time he looked at her.

"No, nooo." Pultarch moaned and rolled his head on the pillow.

She knelt by the bed and smoothed the boy's brow, crooning a lullaby in the voice of an angel.

Sarx studied the girl. He had searched the local taverns for months before he found the one in the rumors. The one said to resemble Adana. The resemblance was uncanny.

Until Pultarch joined him this evening, she had always given his table a wide berth. Still, over several months, he learned she lacked the accent or demeanor of the streets. Very little polishing would be necessary, and he recognized the hunger in her expression. She could have a new life tomorrow if she cooperated.

He found her obvious dislike of him thrilling. Smart girl. But with Pultarch as bait, she'd do what he wanted. He felt sure she had mentally tallied up the boy's worth within minutes of their arrival at The Sleeping Dog. Sarx smiled as he imagined her reaction when she learned the truth of the riches he could send her way.

"Tell me, girl, what do they call you?"

"Shana, my lord." She stood up, smoothing her apron before she met his gaze. A drunken snore came from the bed.

"Ahh, a beautiful name." Sarx studied her, his head tilted to the side. "But tell me, how do you come by such proper speech? Your surroundings indicate …" He spread his arms and the gesture took in the barely furnished room, the sour smell of the tavern below, the rowdy noises that reached them through the closed door.

"Do I not belong here?" She took an agitated step toward him. "Do you think to judge me?"

"But you didn't always live like this?" He enjoyed the interlude. It was refreshing to deal with a woman who did not hide her dislike of him. She bristled every time he spoke.

Shana stared at him for a long time. Emotions played over her face, and he guessed she was debating how much to tell him. He had already implied she could live better than this. Would she take the bait?

"I used to serve as a lady's attendant."

"And?"

"And I lost my position." She looked away.

The silence stretched out for several moments.

"I see," said Sarx. He sat down in the only chair in the room, crossed his arms, and scanned her from head to toe.

Indignation crossed her face, but she faced him, chin held high.

He laughed. "I bet your lady did not appreciate the attention her man gave you, hmmm?"

Shana shrugged. "If that's how you prefer to view it, my lord."

"But still, you have not told me how you ended up here."

"I did not plan for this, if that's what you mean." She turned away from him signaling an end to her willingness to share.

Sarx smiled. She knew a better life than this. That's all the temptation he need offer when he had the handsome Pultarch to sweeten the bargain.

* * * * *

Chapter Fifty

Sergeant Markel of Elwar's Guard stared down the street outside the castle gates, his ears tuned to a rumble of voices that continued to grow louder, draw closer. Drunks celebrating the lady's birthday or reacting to the betrothal?

As approaching torchlight flickered on the walls of buildings, he called his men to arms. "Bar the gate. Arm yourselves."

He drew a breath and stepped into the street with a squad of men, prepared to stop the mob. The clang of a bar falling into place locked the gate behind him. His orders tonight were specific. Stop any trouble before it reached the castle.

When the rabble of men rounded the corner and saw the soldiers blocking their way, they roared and surged forward.

Markel raised his hand and the castle archers stretched their bowstrings, arrows aimed toward the street below. When the mob came within range, the guards rained arrows down on the men. Street thugs, for the most part, they did not turn and run. Anger seethed in their eyes, and they raced toward the soldiers, wicked swords or knives grasped in their fists.

Markel swore at their determination, wondering who held the power to drive them forward.

The first clang of sword against sword vibrated through Markel's body, a familiar sensation turned horrific by the anger and size of the mob. He thrust his sword past the man's untrained attack, cutting him down and jumping over the body to entangle the next one.

Around him men cursed, swords clanged, and bodies thudded against man and stone. Markel tasted the rusty tang of blood, igniting anger in his soul. He never expected to fight Elwar's own people, much less put them to the sword.

The smell of burning oil itched his nostrils, and he turned to find several men racing up the street carrying effigies of burning rags. They chanted in grating, steel-tones, "Long burn Kiffen and Adana."

The strength of iron shot through Markel's veins at the sight. He roared into the fray, killing traitors with swift strokes of his sword. "For Kiffen! For Adana!" The soldiers with him and those on the walls picked up the call and drowned out the sounds of the traitorous threats.

* * *

Adana ran over the hill and down toward the pond, her laughter trailing behind her. The moonlight danced over the water, and the boat bobbed in time to the music of her heart. Before she reached the water's edge strong hands grabbed her and spun her around. They both laughed as they tumbled to the ground.

She pulled Kiffen's face toward her and kissed him with the passion she'd withheld for so long. The contact thrilled her, and she pulled him closer with the thrilling, yet alarming, desire to feel his skin next to hers. The pressure of his lips drew her closer, against his hard chest, fingers wandering over shoulders and back.

She sighed with happiness but choked it off when something changed in the night. The bond with Am'brosia pulsed with tension and fear. Adana pulled back and stared toward the castle.

Kiffen grabbed her hand. The desire in his eyes burned her inner core, and she fell back into his arms. Am'brosia tugged. Adana sat up, panting in fear, attraction overridden by the giraffe's insistence. "We should go. Something is wrong."

"What could be wrong?" He sat up beside her, concern etched across his face.

"You don't feel that?"

"I feel a lot." He smiled and stroked her cheek.

"No. From Bai'dish. Don't you feel something?"

"I don't know." Kiffen tilted his head and held still. "What should I feel?"

Frustration overwhelmed her. How to explain the bond to someone who never knew he had it?

They jumped to their feet at the sounds of someone running toward them.

The Watcher Joannu crested the top, her face a warrior's calm. Adana ran toward her. "What is it? What's happened?"

Kiffen drew up beside her as the woman reported the news. "We're under attack. You must come with me."

* * * * *

Chapter Fifty-One

Karyah squatted by the lake as she dried the blade on her Watcher's tunic. She paused to stare across the water, checking that all was quiet and safe, then rose and returned to her small fire hidden behind a copse of trees. Even though the open expanse of the lake called to her, in Elwar the trees provided better protection, even if they blocked her view and made her uneasy at times. As a courier, she traveled between the kingdoms several times in a season. This secluded spot between the trees at the edge of the lake and forest helped conceal her.

She checked her dinner, thankful for the abundance of Elwar's wildlife, and turned the spit over the fire. The majority of Moniah's hunting fare for the solitary traveler provided very little meat. This rabbit represented one of the few bonuses to traveling in Elwar.

As Karyah pulled the spit out of the fire, a crackle of leaves caused her to spin in a low crouch and peer into the shadows. A pair of eyes glowed back at her, reflecting the fire's light. Keeping one eye on the intruder, she used her keen vision to search the surrounding trees, looking for a shift in the shadows indicating the presence of others. She could not sense anyone, but the trees hampered her ability to see as well as she would have preferred.

"Show yourself," Karyah said as she rose to her full height, knife drawn.

When nothing happened, she took a careful step toward the unblinking gaze. As she reached the perimeter of the clearing, the eyes blinked and a lone deer bounded away into the trees, its white tail visible as it fled.

Karyah shook her head as she sheathed her knife. "Maybe I don't like Elwar as well as I thought," she said. "Fearing attack from a deer." Chuckling, she picked up her rabbit-on-a-stick and proceeded to enjoy her dinner.

While she savored the meat, Karyah's thoughts returned to her mission. Except for watching for danger as she rushed toward the castle in Elwar, she had thought of little else. At least Maligon's traitorous soldiers had not thought to stop her as she left the city. That they let a Watcher sneak out of Belwyn moments before their attempt to overtake the throne amazed her, and she hoped it indicated poor training on Maligon's part. How had Empress Gabriella responded when confronted in her throne room? By the time Karyah became aware of Maligon's plan, access to the empress' court was blocked.

Once clear of the city, she had taken the road to Elwar. The message from the empress, combined with obvious signs of a military coup, confirmed the First Vision's earlier suspicions, and Karyah hoped she was not too late to pass along the warning.

Licking the last remnants of her dinner from her fingers, she extinguished the fire, and scattered its evidence, checking for retained heat. As candidates, all Watchers learned of the trainee, Ballene, and her carelessness with fire. Karyah shuddered at the thought of being remembered for two hundred years because of a mistake that destroyed Moniah's only forest. Not a Watcher's dream, by far.

Satisfied she would not join Ballene's questionable fame, Karyah climbed into a tree, tucked herself into the curvature between a large branch and the trunk, and fell asleep. After a few hours, she roused herself in the pre-dawn light and dropped to the ground. The tall woman stretched before walking through the forest and up the hill on the other side. At the crest, she paused within the protection of the tree line. Watching her breath fog in the morning air, the Watcher slowed her breathing to focused inhalations. She scanned the quiet countryside stretched out before her. Only wildlife inhabited the area. She broke into a trot. If Karyah paced herself, and avoided discovery, she would make it to Elwar's castle by late afternoon.

* * * * *

Chapter Fifty-Two

Adana ran her gaze around the people gathered in King Donel's smaller meeting chamber. Her honor guard, as well as Montee, Kassa, Kiffen, King Donel and his advisor, Simeon, and her father sat around the table, tense and drained from the night's attack. In the corner, almost hidden in the shadows, Father Tonch sat, eyes closed, his fingers steepled and pressed to his lips.

Simeon sat at the forefront of the gathering, his imposing figure solid and silent, his deep brown eyes now shadowed from lack of sleep. He'd lived his life in service to Elwar's crown and fought in the war against Maligon, saving Donel's life in the final surge of battle. Every time she saw him, the man looked serious. She didn't know him well but felt comfort in his presence.

Montee closed the door to the chamber after asking the guards to admit no one. Once she sat, Simeon leaned forward. "Last night's armed riot supports our worst fears. The news of your betrothal created problems that we expected and are prepared to face."

Adana stiffened beside Kiffen.

Simeon gave the two of them an unwavering stare. "We need to remove the two of you from court by tomorrow. Without notice. The people need to believe you are still here."

Montee looked down the table at the two of them. "From this point forward, you will be accompanied by a guard. Adana, your

339

Honor Guard will serve for you. Kiffen, Simeon has volunteered as part of your guard. He is in the process of selecting the rest."

A hard knot of dread formed in the pit of Adana's stomach. "The riot. I have yet to hear a final report."

"Does it matter?" King Donel said. "You need to leave. That's what's important."

Kiffen jerked as if to rise to his feet.

Adana laid a comforting hand on his arm. "Yes, it does matter. We are no longer children. We have more to consider than our own protection."

"She's right." Kassa gave a nod of approval. "They are no longer the future. They are the present. We told the kingdoms so last night."

Silence infiltrated the room. Adana glanced toward her father for any clue of his thoughts, but he was turned toward Donel. Donel, in turn, looked toward Montee and Simeon. An almost imperceptible nod passed between the two advisors. Who was in charge here?

Simeon's face turned graver than normal. "We suffered several injuries last night. But no casualties on our side. Many of their men died."

Death, the result of her happiness. She swallowed and rubbed the ache in her shoulder.

"The effigies concern me most." Her father spoke at last, his face drained and pale like it was after her mother's death.

"Effigies?" The word bled all of the moisture from Adana's mouth.

Montee placed a firm hand on Adana's arm. "They burned two effigies. One for you. One for Prince Kiffen."

Her concerns over this betrothal resurfaced. Why had she let desire take control? Their dream had burned away like the morning's dew conquered by the sun.

"Removing us in secrecy won't stop any uprisings." Kiffen reached under the table and squeezed her hand.

"Kiffen's right." Adana stood up, pulling away from the physical draw of Kiffen. She didn't dare look in his direction. "We should renounce the betrothal."

Ice engulfed her heart at the words. It shattered into tiny fragments when Kiffen stood beside her.

"By announcing our betrothal, you endangered Adana, as well as both kingdoms. I agree. We must renounce it."

Disappointment enshrouded her, choking the air from the room, and placed a gap between them she couldn't cross.

Pain shot through her shoulder, and she gasped, massaging harder. "I must consider the welfare of Moniah. And Elwar." Her voice faded, and she paused, chin down, but she forced her voice to ring strong when she looked back up. "I can't let this decision threaten Kiffen, either."

The others remained silent, whether in agreement or disagreement, she couldn't decide.

Kiffen's father struggled to his feet and approached them. He took Kiffen's and Adana's hands in his. "The future of Elwar and Moniah lies in your hands. This decision stands. You will marry."

"Why?" Adana pulled her hand away.

"Bai'dish." Montee's voice rang clear and strong. "The vision was clear."

"And Queen Roassa." King Donel paused and peered into his son's eyes. "Kiffen, your mother told me the original story of Yarada.

It speaks of a reunited kingdom. The Memory Keepers stopped telling the true end many years ago."

"You want us to combine the kingdoms?" Kiffen said.

Even with the betrothal, that idea had never occurred to Adana. She gulped, considering the complications. Who would rule? Where would they live? Would Kiffen expect her to remain in Elwar? Could she expect him to live in Moniah?

Her father leaned forward, his hands clasped between his knees. "Your mother spoke of the reunited kingdom, too. She said the Creator would tell us when. And that time is now. With Belwyn and Teletia absent last night, we fear situations are worse there, as they may become here."

"You will both go to Moniah," Montee said. "Kiffen, with your father continuing to rule here, you will have time to learn your new responsibilities."

Had that been a tremor rippling along Kiffen's shoulders? Did he recognize the unspoken truths in Montee's words? As long as his father lived, there would be two kingdoms, but when he would need his father most, he would be alone. Adana knew that devastation well.

"Do we suspect anyone? Do we know who led this attack last night?" Adana's voice rang sharp in the silence. A desire to strike out at their betrayer overwhelmed her.

Each face registered the truth. No one knew. She leaned forward and caught Kassa's eye. "We have to consider the possibilities, don't we? Do you suspect anyone?"

"There is a list." Kassa spoke in the quietest voice Adana had ever heard from her.

"But we don't want to jump to conclusions." Donel turned toward her, frustration in the set of his eyes and mouth.

The night visitor surfaced in Adana's thoughts. "The night before father arrived. Did any of you receive Lord Sarx? In the middle of the night?"

Kassa studied her closely. "It was him?"

"Yes." She turned to Donel and Simeon. "Did you receive him? Because a man entered the castle late that night. I saw him in the shadows. Someone let him in, and someone stood at the door when he left. A woman."

Stunned silence ran around the table like a banquet disturbed by the arrival of a mouse scattering crumbs in its path.

"He is on the list." Simeon eyed her carefully. "You're sure it was him?"

Adana recalled the night. She glanced at Sinti, whose face registered comprehension as she identified the man. The Watcher nodded in agreement.

"It was Sarx."

Beside her Kiffen groaned. "Contina's uncle is under suspicion? Who can we trust?"

"I believe I can answer your question." Father Tonch rose from his seat in the corner, his presence calm in their midst. "There is unrest. Evil forces seek to destroy us. Last night's attack reinforces our concerns. You must give trust sparingly.

"To appease those who will note your absence, we will say the two of you seek religious contemplation after your betrothal. It's a common practice. No one but the Teachers of the Faith have access to those couples. To all outward appearances, you will do just that."

The Keeper of the Faith approached the couple, his face somber. "The love between a man and a woman can be powerful when united to protect those they care about. If you don't marry, then we will fail. A house divided, falls."

* * * * *

Chapter Fifty-Three

The pain in Adana's shoulder lessened after Father Tonch's words, as if her shoulder recognized the truth behind the Keeper of the Faith's statement. As she walked along the corridor surrounded by her requisite guard, she tried to recall the moment of the puncture and Montee's odd apology. With a tight circle of Watchers around her, she felt safe asking Kassa about it.

"What did Montee mean when she pricked me with the pin? She said it wouldn't work if I knew."

"Ah, so you do recall that part." Kassa checked the corridor, and Adana followed suit. They were the only ones in this section of the castle. "The pin represents more than a gift from Elwar."

"I remember it. I used to sit in Mammetta's room, catching the stones in the sunlight making it dance colors along the wall."

"It kept you content for long stretches of time." Kassa nodded. "But the pin is more than adornment. The gold is infused with a potion from every giraffe bound to Moniah's queens. Since the very first one."

"Impossible." Adana tried to count the many giraffes over the ages. "Wouldn't the tears have dried up?"

"It's not the tears. It's the horn residue."

Adana's eyes widened at the mention of the greatest secret in her kingdom, the source of the glimmer cloth. She smoothed her hands over the soft glimmer material of her outfit.

Each year, just after mating season, the giraffes' horns oozed with a gelatinous substance. This gel, cooled to a gooey consistency and infused with tiny ground flecks of Moniah's sandstone, created a mixture in which cloth was submerged for ten days. After it dried, the weave of the material took on a glistening, smooth quality that caressed the skin of its wearer. Any material soaked in the mixture became fireproof, while the original gooey substance, if not treated with sandstone, burned brighter and hotter than any other substance known throughout the kingdoms.

"Your pin came from Roassa, but Moniah provided the mixture of gold and glimmer liquid." Kassa paused as they passed some servants in the corridor. After rounding a corner, she waited until halfway along that stretch of hall to speak again. "With time, the power leaks out of the pin. That's what happened to your grandmother's, so Roassa made a new one. The only giraffe whose residue did not go into the making of this one was—"

"Am'brosia." Adana smiled as she felt a nudge of fondness through the link.

"Yes. Since she hasn't mated yet, I polished it with Am'brosia's tears."

Adana had taken little notice of Kassa polishing the pin the night before, thanks to Quilla's behavior.

"What does it do?" she asked

"It's different for each queen," Kassa glanced around as they entered the stairwell. She motioned for Adana to wait until they reached the top. At the landing, she started along the carpet runner lining the stone floor, glancing about for any signs of people within earshot. "How did it feel when Montee stuck you?"

"It stung." Adana recalled the sudden burning that went beyond the normal pinprick.

"What else did you feel?"

"Happiness. For a while." She thought of the burning sensation when she listened to Father Tonch and Mother Sariah's prayer. "Then it burned."

Kassa paused in an area where no one could approach without being seen. "It strengthens your bond to Am'brosia and the Creator. Your mother often felt sensations in her shoulder. She called them warnings."

Memories of her mother rubbing her shoulder came to Adana. She often attributed them to sore muscles or the strain of ruling. She slid her hand under her clothing and felt for the puncture wound. A tiny depression met her finger. At the moment it felt calm.

Before heading to her chambers, Kassa grasped Adana's shoulders and examined her face. One of her fingers brushed the puncture spot, and it tingled. "Glume spoke to Suban. He told me you over-used the formissa plant while here. This should help counter the buffer, but you will need to discuss each sensation with Montee until you determine how your shoulder works for you. Together, you will discover if the plant in your system has altered the effects."

Through the bond, Adana saw Am'brosia crushing the leaves of the plant under her hooves again. Anger welled up within her. Hers or the giraffe's? Distracted by the sensation, she started to enter her room but pulled up short as Kassa blocked access to the chamber door.

"One of your guards must clear all rooms before you enter."

Adana crossed her arms and waited outside with Joannu and Veana while Kassa and Sinti entered the chamber

"What are you doing in here?" At the sound of Kassa's raised voice, Joannu pushed Adana against the wall while Veana rushed into the room.

"Honestly, it's not like you don't know me!" The agitation in Leera's voice rang clear.

Adana pushed past Joannu, glad to see her friend.

Elwar's princess sat in the window seat holding a cup of tea. She bared her teeth at Adana in a smile. "What's this? Do you fear repercussions from last night's fiasco?"

Kassa stiffened at the comment, but Adana placed a restraining hand on her arm. "I'm glad to see you."

"I should think so." Indignation radiated around the petite woman. "After that horrible announcement last night."

Turning to leave, Kassa paused and frowned at Leera's comment. "Joannu and Veana will be just outside the door should you need them."

As the door closed behind the Watchers, Adana collapsed in the chair by the fireplace. She peered at Leera and chuckled. "Ballene's fire, leave it to you to be the first to test my new guard."

Leera placed her cup on the window ledge. The fresh scent of mint tea floated across the room to Adana. "Blazes. What is going on?"

"Did you hear about the attack last night? They burned effigies of me and Kiffen." Faced with her closest friend, the full measure of the rebellion sank in. To steady her nerves, she rose and poured herself a cup of Leera's mint tea. The bright aroma steadied her, and the flavor washed the horror from her mouth. So much had happened. She longed to tell Leera everything, but Simeon cautioned them not to discuss any details with others. No matter how much you trusted someone, he had stressed, they may not be worthy of that honor. And if the sudden sting in her shoulder meant anything, it agreed.

"How awful for you." Leera settled back in her seat. "It would have been easier if your father had done the right thing and betrothed you to Pultarch."

"I don't think so." Adana perched on a chair and tried to ignore the continued stinging in her shoulder. "I'm relieved he didn't."

Leera paused in stirring her tea and put the cup down. "Do you love my brother?"

"Yes."

Jaw clenched, Leera's lips barely moved. "You never told me."

"I didn't tell anyone."

"Does he love you?"

"Oh Leera," Adana smiled at the ability to say so. "Yes, he does."

"You should have told me."

Adana crossed the room and wrapped her arms around Leera's small shoulders and hugged her rigid body. "How could I? Tradition doesn't allow it. I didn't even know he loved me until yesterday."

"But we were friends." She pulled away from Adana's embrace. "I told you everything. I should have known."

Adana hesitated at the betrayal evident in Leera's eyes.

Leera smoothed her skirts, picked up her cup, and stared into its contents. "No." She set it down again with a clatter. "Why did you allow Pultarch to hope?"

"I never suggested I had feelings for him."

"And I never saw you as the flirtatious type." Leera shook her head. "Poor Pultarch, you just dangled him along. Never intending to marry him."

They had laughed and cried and shared everything for three years, but, at that moment, it felt like Quilla sat before her. Closing her eyes, Adana took a deep breath and tried to reason with Leera. "I did not dangle Pultarch along. And I would have married him if chosen."

"Ah, but he wasn't. You got just what you wanted—my brother and rule over both kingdoms."

"What?"

"I wish I'd realized your plan sooner. Our friendship never meant anything to you, did it?"

"Leera, you don't know what you're saying. I love you like a sister."

"Well, you made sure we would be sisters, didn't you?" Leera cocked her head to the side, a Quilla smile on her face. "Mother was right about you after all."

"What can I say to you? I made no plans. I couldn't. Like you, I assumed it would be Pultarch."

"Poor Pultarch." Leera shook her head, a distant look on her face.

"What? Have you seen him? Did you speak to him last night?"

"Don't you know? He left after the announcement. I wouldn't be surprised if he killed himself."

"Killed himself? He wouldn't do that." Alarm clutched Adana's stomach.

"Are you sure? He loves you very much."

"All this talk of killing. I'm in danger. Kiffen is in danger. Now you want me to believe Pultarch is capable of killing himself?"

"You could fix this easily." Leera flicked at an imaginary spot on her skirt.

Adana waited. The anger and pain had vanished from Leera's face replaced by a calculated expression. An expression Adana knew well.

"How?"

"Marry Pultarch."

A bitter laugh escaped Adana's throat. If she hadn't already used a similar argument that morning, she might be tempted to listen. "I can't."

"We'll see." In a rustle of skirts, Leera rose and glided out of the chamber.

Dumbfounded, Adana watched her closest friend disappear. How could this have gone so wrong?

"Blazes!" The realization hit her. The Creator never gave her what she truly needed. Rather than deny her desires, she got exactly what Kiffen had prayed for. What a horrible sense of humor the Creator must have. She rubbed her shoulder in anger. It burned worse than the night before.

"What do I do now?" Her voice echoed off the walls.

A trunk lay open beside her bed, a few items already packed. She yanked dresses out of the wardrobe and stuffed them in the trunk. With each violent jerk or shove, she fought to ignore the hollow feeling in her shoulder and heart.

Montee entered the room and studied Adana for a moment. "I understand you had a visitor?"

"Just Leera."

"Veana reported shouting."

"Yes." Adana shoved a clump of clothing in the trunk.

Montee watched her. "You won't be taking the trunk. You must travel light."

"Fine." Adana slammed the lid shut.

"My lady, what happened?"

"I would prefer not to discuss it." Adana rubbed her shoulder

"Does your shoulder bother you?"

Adana shook her head. She didn't want to discuss her shoulder.

"We need to take note of it. Kassa tells me you asked her about the pin." Montee sat on the edge of the bed. "You used to talk to me. Remember?"

"Yes, of course I do, but this is different." She turned on Montee. "You know nothing of my friendship with Leera."

"So tell me."

"I just lost my closest friend." Adana returned to the trunk, shoving more clothing inside. "This should be the happiest day of my life, but it's not. Forgive me if I don't feel like confiding."

Shaking her head, Adana continued to sort through the clothing in her wardrobe. The task was futile, but she could not look at Montee. Her shoulder burned, and she cursed the Creator for granting her dreams.

* * * * *

Chapter Fifty-Four

Sarx sat in a back corner of the Sleeping Dog's common room. "Something amiss?" he asked the hooded and cloaked woman who joined him there.

"Yes," Quilla said as she sniffed in disdain and perched on the edge of the chair. "They claim Adana and Kiffen plan to seek religious seclusion, contemplating their nuptials."

"And?"

She snorted. "That girl might appear faithful in public, but it's an act. She doesn't have a religious thought in her braided head."

"Really?" Sarx tapped his forefinger against his lips. With whiplash action, he grabbed Quilla's arm and twisted it. "How long have you known this? We could have used her false faith to our advantage."

"Unhand me. Do not forget who I am." She pulled away, fury flashing in her eyes. "Has everyone lost their senses? *What* I share with you is *my* decision. It doesn't matter. I'll still control her in the end."

"Only if he does what we ask of him." Sarx glanced upstairs toward Pultarch's room.

"Did you find the girl?" Quilla scanned the inhabitants of the tavern, her face scrunched in distaste.

"Yes, she bears a remarkable resemblance to Adana. Even our dear pet saw it." He smiled at the thought. The interchange between the drunken lord and the wench had provided him much amusement.

"How is the fool?"

"Terribly hung over, I'm afraid. He will be as obedient as a puppy, though, if he can have his love back."

"You will send him to me?"

"Naturally. The jilted lover plans to save his lady love from her marital disaster. You are his only hope." Smiling, he added, "He really believes she loves him."

* * *

The celebratory mood in the castle vanished in the wake of the previous night's riot. In an effort to draw focus away from the riot, Quilla scheduled an engagement celebration—a mid-afternoon picnic in the gardens the next day. She presided over the remaining guests, overdoing her feigned joy of the upcoming nuptials.

An irresistible desire to irritate Quilla and forget her own troubles plagued Adana. She begged the Memory Keeper for a story and selected the tale of her father's and King Donel's arrival in the kingdoms. Quilla hated the story since it belonged to a series that included an account of how Donel fell in love with and married Queen Roassa. What better way to aggravate the queen?

Olaf, the Memory Keeper, yawned and waved Adana's entreaty away. He stretched out on the blanket where he sat and began to snore loudly, but, of course, this was part of the entertainment. Since it was a popular tale, her request generated encouragement from the guests, and Olaf's antics made many people laugh for the first time that day.

Finally, he stood, stretched, and yawned in a great show of exhaustion. He swirled his cloak around him and, in a sudden reversal of mood, bounded to a spot beneath a tree, his face dappled with the shadows of afternoon sunlight streaming through the leaves.

A hush spread over the picnickers. Except for bird calls and a gentle breeze rustling in the trees, the crowd fell silent.

"Our esteemed Queen-To-Be has requested the story of The Two Young Men from the North," Olaf said as introduction. He executed a sweeping bow toward Adana and added, "It's my honor to comply."

The slight man took a deep breath, and began:

The village slept. Mud flew from the horses' hooves as two young men galloped away from the only home they had ever known. In tradition, they left without speaking to their families, but on the edge of town, they stopped at the village bakery.

The two stomped into the shop, startling the short, round man behind the counter. "You two are early today," he said as he turned to check the ovens.

The aroma of baking bread, cinnamon, and other delectables sweetened the air. The red-faced baker, Smitty, returned to the counter and noted their travel attire. The pleasant expression slid from his face. "So, this is the day?" he asked.

Micah, the taller boy, nodded. His friend Donel eyed the fresh breads and poflas on the counter.

Smitty began to select a few small loaves, "Well then, you'll want some provisions for your journey, won't you?"

"Some poflas, too," Donel suggested. "I could eat a dozen!"

Olaf paused as a titter ran through the crowd. Laughing himself, King Donel patted his widening girth and gestured for Olaf to continue.

At the young man's suggestion, his friend, Micah, frowned. "We can't afford poflas. We've not even left the village yet, and you're spending all of our coin."

Smitty ignored Micah's complaints and tucked several of the fist-sized pastries into their pack. He placed the supplies on the counter and said, "My gift." The man studied the two young men, his face drooping in sadness. "Won't you reconsider? My business isn't much, but it's enough to live comfortably. You know I have no children to leave it to."

Donel and Micah shook their heads.

The baker bowed his. "I will miss the both of you. You head north to the king's army?"

"No," Micah said. "Everyone goes north. We're going south."

Smitty's eyes widened. "No one returns from the southern mountains. It could be dangerous."

Donel grinned. "We hope so."

Sons of wealthy landowners, Micah and Donel could remain in the village working for their eldest brothers. Both, born the last of several children, held no right to inheritance. With little chance of ever owning land or livestock, neither boy had a stomach for this service.

Beyond working for their brothers, their options were limited—a life devoted to faith.

Olaf folded his hands in a prayerful pose.

An apprenticeship.

Olaf feigned hammering a nail.

Or the journey.

Olaf marched around in a circle, his hand shading his brow as he searched the horizon.

Smitty offered another option to these young men—frequent visitors to his bakery—but adventure ran in their veins. Today, their journey began.

For the next few weeks, they rode from village to village, fed by local farmers in exchange for news.

Olaf shrugged his shoulders in despair.

What little news there was.

As the season turned toward summer, they found themselves deep in the foothills approaching the southern mountains.

A few days earlier, they had shared a campfire with a trapper who scratched out a crude map for them and told them to sell their horses before they attempted the mountains.

"Be wary," he warned in his gruff voice. "It may be summer here, but those hills don't know it yet."

As they sold their mounts and marched toward the looming mountains, Donel said, "Maybe this journey will finally turn interesting."

The higher they climbed, the cooler the air became. The trapper's warning held true as they trudged up muddy tracks cluttered with washed-away debris from the spring thaws.

After two grueling days, they found the narrow trail through the pass.

Micah stared at the trapper's map. "We would never have found this without that old man's help."

Donel only nodded, his breath heaving from the steep incline.

Again, the crowd chuckled, and King Donel waved his hand in dismissal. "Pure storytelling, for entertainment, of course." He jumped up, and to Adana's surprise, he trotted over to her father and challenged him to a footrace.

"No thank you. I'd hate to overtax you." Her father's eyes crinkled with amusement. "Or turn my ankle in front of this fine company."

Donel nodded and leaned up against the tree beside his lifelong friend. He gestured for Olaf to continue.

A few days later, Micah and Donel reached the cave.

"The trapper cautioned us to stop here for the night," Micah said, calling Donel back to the cave.

Donel stared into the valley below. "It's only mid-day. And look, it's down-hill from here. He probably expected us to reach this cave during a rainstorm."

The man had a point. For the first time in four days, the sun shone on them, and only a few distant clouds gathered on the horizon. Micah's clothes felt almost dry, so he agreed and followed Donel down the path.

The error of their decision became clear soon. The path turned steep, rocky, and slippery, making the descent to the valley floor a longer, more difficult trek than expected. With only a few hours of daylight left, they decided to return to the cave.

Neither man noticed the gathering clouds until the first few drops of rain splattered the path. As if on cue, the wind rose, and rain pelted them.

Donel grabbed for a nearby tree, barely bigger than a shrub, trying to maintain his stance against the mountain's riverlike onslaught. He grasped Micah's arm and pulled him beneath the tree. The two peered up the hill, streams of rain washing over them.

Micah searched for signs of the cave above, but visibility was limited. He studied the steep ascent, eying the few stalwart trees along the treacherous path. "Do you think we could pull ourselves up by those trees?"

Donel turned and studied the mountainside. "If they can withstand this storm, surely they can hold us."

Despite his inclination for baked goods, young Donel was fit and muscular. Often the champion in wrestling matches, he enjoyed a quiet grace of motion and could catch his opponents unaware with his swift moves. If anyone could scale the slope in these conditions, it was Donel. Micah was several inches taller, with a leaner build. His strength lay in his quick mind and the trust people placed in his bright blue eyes which shone in contrast to the grime now streaking his face.

Leaning into the wind and rain, they tied a rope around their waists.

Donel pulled his ax free. "Maybe I can dig it in deep enough to keep us from sliding away." Before he ducked out from underneath the bush, he turned to Micah and said, "I'll give two tugs on the rope when I'm ready to pull you up. Whatever you do, don't slip. We'll end up at the bottom."

Olaf bent over and staggered forward, feigning a slow struggle against the elements. He shouted the next part of the story, as if the rain drowned his voice out.

They inched upwards, slithering and lunging for any possible handhold. Water ran down their backs and churned the path into a slick mess. Finally, they reached the last tree, but the path above them was gone, washed away, leaving a vertical cliff to the cave above. Both crouched under the tree, studying this new obstacle.

"If you climb up on my shoulders, do you think you can reach the top?" Micah said to Donel as he untied from the rope.

Micah braced against the tree and gave Donel a hand up, trying to maintain his balance while the other man writhed on unsure footing.

Olaf staggered under the tree, holding imaginary feet on his shoulders. He turned his head toward the sky and shouted.

"Hurry up."

Donel grappled with the cliff. "I'm trying."

Micah clenched his jaw, digging in his heels.

"What the—" Donel exclaimed, and Micah stumbled from the sudden absence of weight on his shoulders.

He turned to stare up toward the cave. When Donel's round face did not appear over the edge, Micah called, "Donel? Are you alright?" Thick rain drops pattered on Micah's face and the leaves in the silence.

Olaf held his hands out in a gesture of confusion. Worry creased the storyteller's face.

Exhausted and wondering if he could climb to the top on his own, Micah leaned against the tree. As he breathed heavily and tried not to succumb to frustration, the rope's end tumbled back down the bank. With relief, he secured it around his waist and tugged it, gasping as Donel yanked him up and over the ledge.

Olaf flung his body to the ground and shook his head in confusion. He continued the story while pantomiming out Micah's next actions.

The rope fell slack when Micah landed on the ground outside the cave. He rose to his hands and knees, bent over trying to catch his breath.

The soft leather of a small boot edged into his vision. Micah shot backward and groped for a knife. Donel sat on a rock eying two young soldiers guarding him at sword point. A soldier grabbed Micah's arm and shoved him against the wall in the cave.

Ten soldiers, close in height to Micah, surrounded them. One spoke. The two men shook their heads and wondered whether excitement and adventure was a good thing. As strange as the language was to them, stranger still were these soldiers. They wore leather tunics and leggings…and definitely were female.

Bowing, the Memory Keeper indicated the end of his story.

"Please tell the next one?" Leera leaned forward with a pout.

Olaf gave her a wary glance and looked sideways toward Quilla's look of displeasure. "It's a cliff hanger," he said.

Someone in the crowd called out, "I'll tell it. They help win the war against Maligon and marry the queens!"

Laughing, King Donel saluted the young man. "Give that man no more to drink. He's obviously had too much." He rose, the action dismissing the guests. The picnic was officially over.

* * * * *

Chapter Fifty-Five

Adana and Kiffen stayed in the garden long after their guests wandered back to the castle. Although she enjoyed the picnic and story telling, Adana still could not shake the gloom of this day. Never in her wildest dreams did she imagine the day after her betrothal to be so full of danger and desperation. She looked around and sighed, noting their newly appointed guards.

"This is absurd." Kiffen scowled. "I want to take you riding or to the pond or anywhere without them. And the last thing I wanted to do was spend all day in meetings or with our friendly guards."

"I know," she said. "We've got to do something. I feel so restless."

"We won't get far with your Watchers hovering. Any one of them could run me down in a matter of seconds."

Adana laughed at the thought, and after a few seconds Kiffen joined her.

"I wonder what would happen if we wandered into a private corner of the gardens?" Adana's thoughts ran to the night before. "Do you think they'd follow or leave us alone?"

"Here comes Montee." Kiffen straightened as the Watcher marched toward them.

"Excuse me, my lady." Montee bowed her head in greeting. "Prince Kiffen."

"Yes, Montee?"

"You appear at a loss for something to occupy your time." The Watcher smiled. "I have a suggestion."

Adana felt Kiffen straighten beside her and shake off his melancholy.

"Good," he said.

"Both of you could use some sword practice." Montee eyed Kiffen for a moment and then turned her gaze on Adana.

"Wonderful." Adana jumped to her feet. She winked at Kiffen and leaned close to his ear. "You can feel the kiss of my sword instead of my mouth."

He growled something under his breath about his sword, but she ignored him, suppressing the urge to shock Montee.

"I do need to get in some practice." Kiffen rose and stretched his arms over his head.

"Funny," Adana said, poking him in the ribs, "we use to spar often, but we haven't done so in quite some time."

"Once you became more to me than a little girl, well—" Kiffen leered at her.

"Ahh, so you realized I might outwit you?"

"Hah! Never. I merely sought to protect you."

They teased all the way to the sparring yard. Adana smiled. This was just what she needed. A way to burn off the energy of her attraction to Kiffen. Her grin widened at the knowledge that Quilla would disapprove.

* * *

The sparring yard provided a squared-off area, surrounded by the stables and soldiers' quarters. A paved, stone tunnel ran below the gardens, connecting the yard to the main castle. As the two took up swords and the first clangs rang out, the few guests still idling in the gardens above rushed to observe. They chattered and argued over why the newly betrothed couple was clashing swords. The consensus was Kiffen and Adana fought in anger. The Elwarians, so unaccustomed to women soldiers, could not fathom the possibility that this was no different than two men practicing.

Montee chuckled with amusement at the scandalized glances the Elwarian women threw Adana when she tucked the skirt of her dress into her belt, creating a billowing pair of pants. Several noblewomen slapped at their daughters' hands as they fingered their own skirts with speculation. Adana's ankles flashed as she danced around Kiffen, striking at and dodging his blows.

She pressed an early advantage and pushed Kiffen against the gathering crowd who had wandered into the yard. The young ladies cheered, and Adana turned to acknowledge their approval with a sweeping bow, causing the young men to scoff at Kiffen's refusal to seize the opening to attack.

The prince held back, Montee noted with scorn, probably in a misguided fear of hurting his betrothed. She decided to let this last a few more moments, and then she would step in and show him what Adana really could do.

Just then, an enraged shout echoed through the tunnel. "What are you doing?"

Montee tensed into a protective stance, placing herself between the sparring circle and the tunnel.

Pultarch stalked into the afternoon sunlight. The crowd parted as he pushed his way toward the pair. Usually tidy and well-turned-out,

Pultarch showed the signs of a rough night: wrinkled clothing, blood-shot eyes, and an unhealthy pallor to his skin.

Montee hesitated before allowing him passage but followed close in his wake.

Pultarch glared at Kiffen. "Not only do you take her from me, you seek to harm her too? Why? Why would you?" Then he slowly turned, accusation in his eyes, as he met the uncomfortable faces of the onlookers. "Why? Why? Why?" His last word came out in a strangled whisper as he halted in front of Adana.

Panting from exertion, Adana approached him, pushing sweaty hair out of her face. "Pultarch. Don't."

The pity on Adana's face concerned Montee. Pultarch's ego suffered and pity wouldn't fix that.

For a moment nothing happened. The crowd hovered, waiting. Simeon had materialized on the other side of the circle. Montee met his wary gaze.

"I'll fight you!" Pultarch spun away from Adana and faced Kiffen, his eyes blazing.

Kiffen crossed his arms and studied Pultarch. Montee braced herself. Pultarch acted on emotion, making him all the more unpredictable.

Adana stepped between them. "No, Pultarch, it's not—"

But Kiffen did not let her finish. "Get him a sword."

"No." Adana tried to push them apart. "Don't."

Montee and Simeon moved as one between the two young men, gauging their moods and level of control. She cast a questioning look toward Simeon. This would be a nasty fight, but better it happened under controlled circumstances rather than later.

"With practice swords only," Simeon said.

Both young men glanced toward him and nodded. More people joined the spectators in the practice yard, their agitated hum buzzing with speculation on the outcome.

Adana pushed past Montee and planted herself before Kiffen. He glanced at her as he adjusted his gloves, his eyes just slanting away from Pultarch for a brief moment.

"No, Kiffen. Don't do this. He's hurting."

Montee wondered how she could miss the obvious signs. Whatever stood between these two men stemmed from something larger than the both of them. This inevitable clash must have brewed for a long time.

Montee's thoughts turned to her own bout with unrequited love. Heightened emotion blocked a Watcher's senses. Prevented by their high rank, neither she nor Linus had been willing to sacrifice their service to Moniah. In the weeks that followed her promotion, she had missed many clues and details evident to a Watcher's eyes, especially Samantha's pain over not being chosen as First Vision. Their lost friendship weighed heavy on Montee's heart. She hoped it never came to combat like these young men.

Even though Adana's and Kiffen's situation bore little resemblance to her love with the Commander of the Soldiers of the First Sight, the effect was the same. Adana's heart blinded her to the reality of the feud between the men.

Montee laid a gentle hand on Adana's arm. "They must do this."

* * * * *

Chapter Fifty-Six

Micah heard the crowd's noise from the courtyard a few moments before Queen Quilla rushed in and demanded they do something to stop Adana and Kiffen. Rather than respond to her demands, he and Donel hurried to watch, but as they reached the courtyard, a guard hailed them. "A Watcher approaches, sires."

Disappointed, the two kings returned to the castle to receive the Watcher's report in Donel's chambers.

Ostreia, a Squad Leader sent to determine the situation in Teletia, arrived, dusty from the road, breathing heavily from exertion. At the sight of the two kings, she knelt before them. "Sires, I bring ill news."

"We must hear your report, Ostreia, but first let me send for some sustenance," Micah said, and then turned to a page. "Please bring some drink and food for the Watcher."

The young boy scurried away.

Once he was gone, Ostreia said, "A force of soldiers, some from within King Ariff's guard, broke into Teletia's castle and kidnapped the royal family. His remaining guard fought them, many losing their lives."

"Wait," Donel said. "Some of Ariff's guard assisted in this attack? Turned on their king?"

Her green eyes troubled, the Watcher nodded.

Micah watched Donel's tongue slip along the edge of his lower lip, a nervous tick he'd had since childhood.

"When did this happen?" Micah said.

"Three days ago. The majority of King Ariff's army was deployed outside the castle. Hunting bands of ruffians. There've been several attacks on small villages and farms along Teletia's borders."

Micah nodded recalling the refugees he encountered between Moniah and Elwar.

"Yet you managed to escape?" Donel said, curiosity in his gaze.

"No one cared about a peasant girl leaving the kitchens. Once I knew I could not help the king, I disguised myself and came here." Ostreia held her gaze steady on King Donel. Micah felt pride in the Monian Watcher's loyalty. With this level of allegiance, Adana's chances of surviving these new obstacles increased drastically.

"Did you try to track them?" Micah said.

Before she could answer, the page returned with a decanter and a platter of fruit, bread, and cheese. Silence fell in the boy's presence. As he turned to leave, Donel called him back. "Boy? How goes the sparring between the prince and the lady Adana?"

Ostreia straightened from the platter. Her stance shifted, ready to run to her ruler's aid if necessary. Micah waved his hand at her, shaking his head with a smile.

The young page turned back to his king, his brown eyes dancing with excitement. "Your Majesty, it appeared an even match, but some say that the prince was holding back in order to not hurt the lady Adana."

Micah snorted. He hadn't watched his daughter spar in some time, but the reports Kassa sent him indicated her skills were exemplary.

Donel chuckled. "Really? How interesting." He leaned forward. "So it's over then? Who won?"

The boy's voice squeaked with excitement. "Neither sire. Sir Pultarch interrupted them, and now *he* is fighting Prince Kiffen."

"Pultarch of Brom?" Donel exchanged a worried glance with Micah. "Your name boy?"

"Catch, sire."

"Catch? An odd name." The boy appeared ready to explain, but Donel halted him with a wave of his hand. "Catch, I need you to bring me word once this sparring ends. Make sure you can report on any injuries." He paused and thought a moment. "Send Sir Simeon to me once his duties to the prince permit."

"And the First Vision," Micah added.

Delight over his assignment flushed the youth's face as he scurried from the chamber, only remembering to stop and bow before racing through the door.

Donel turned to Micah. "What do you make of this?"

Micah shook his head. "It doesn't sound good, but Montee and Simeon won't let it go too far."

Ostreia, choked down the last bit of bread and gulped the cup dry. "Sires?"

They returned their attention to her, aware this news was more important than a spat between jealous youths.

"I attempted to track the kidnappers, but the castle was in an uproar. I left three Watcher units to search for the king."

"Do you know who led the attack?" Donel said, "Who controls the castle?"

Ostreia's green eyes darkened. "Sire, I'm not positive. I heard Maligon's name a few times. I never saw him."

Ostreia hesitated a moment, bowing her head. Her body rose and fell in a large intake of breath. Then, she squared her shoulders and looked back up at the kings. "I left my fourth unit inside the city to verify if it's Maligon."

* * * * *

Chapter Fifty-Seven

Kiffen heard Adana's plea to stop and briefly reconsidered his decision to fight Pultarch. He had Adana's love, so why rise to this challenge? Then he remembered Pultarch by her side over the last three years, in the rose arbor just days ago, and for most of the dances last night.

He pushed past Adana.

She spun toward Pultarch. "Please Pultarch, it's me you're upset with. Please. Not him."

"I love you," Pultarch said and turned away. He reached for the practice sword that one of the guards handed him.

Montee pulled Adana out of the way. "They must do this. If not now, then later. I will not let it go too far."

"Nor I." Simeon stood beside her.

Kiffen nodded to himself, relieved at the presence of the two warriors. Montee and Simeon had read the situation well.

Guards formed a boundary separating the onlookers from the combatants. He and Adana had sparred in fun, but the guards knew this swordplay would be different.

Kiffen stepped into the center of the circle and waited.

Pultarch, using little regard for style or form, flung himself forward, swinging his sword at Kiffen's head. The sloppy approach gave Kiffen ample time to dodge the intended head ringing.

Thrown off balance, Pultarch stumbled through his missed attempt, caught his footing at the edge of the circle, and whirled around. He straightened and turned toward Kiffen, his demeanor shifting in that moment. The brown eyes his sister, Leera, often compared to a precious puppy's cooled from a furious red glare to icy calculation. Several people stepped back, pulling capes tighter.

Kiffen nodded at the change. He could beat Pultarch if his rage persisted, but it would be a bitter victory. If Pultarch lost his temper later, then so be it, but Kiffen wanted to start on equal footing.

The two circled each other while the crowd waited, silence thick around them. The missing years in friendship had turned the two men into strangers on the practice field. The last time they fought, they laughed and enjoyed the exercise. Evenly matched, they never declared a winner.

Both men struck, the echo of their wooden swords thumping throughout the sparring yard. Kiffen struck and counter struck, relaxing into the rhythm of the exercise. Neither of them stood out as the expert or superior fighter.

Then Pultarch spun in an arc that placed him behind Kiffen. His stroke slammed into the back of Kiffen's legs.

Sprawling forward, Kiffen fought to regain his balance. He narrowly avoided Pultarch's downward strike.

He pivoted, regained his footing, and looked into the smug smile on Pultarch's face. "That's new."

Pultarch hacked out a laugh. "A lot is new."

With renewed energy, Pultarch rammed into Kiffen locking their swords. "She wants me." He spat in Kiffen's face. "You are nothing."

Kiffen remembered this part of Pultarch's strategy—menace the opponent with painful words. How Pultarch managed to convincingly threaten his opponents in the sparring ring when he never exhibited this behavior in social circles confused him. Was this the true Pultarch, while an actor walked the gardens with the ladies?

Kiffen pushed forward, struggling to release his sword from Pultarch's. Pultarch leaned his weight into the struggle, bearing down on Kiffen. With Pultarch's weight pressing heavily into their locked swords, Kiffen relaxed and stepped aside. Pultarch stumbled off balance. Kiffen shoved him sideways and jumped away from the arc of Pultarch's sword as Pultarch hit the ground. He sprang back to his feet with a snarl. The two circled each other, glaring, waiting for the next move.

As the fight wore on, Kiffen began to feel his lack of rest over the past few days.

Pultarch appeared to be fully energized. He sauntered around Kiffen, throwing taunts. "I'll take her from you." He spun completely around daring to bare his back to Kiffen. When he met Kiffen's gaze again, he barked out a laugh. "She'll have a real man. Not a boy!" He strutted back and forth. Kiffen waited, gauging when to strike.

Pultarch paused near Adana and cocked his head at the crowd. "Look at her, she's mine."

Adana reached out her hand, despair on her face. "Pultarch?"

Kiffen hesitated. Did she love Pultarch?

With a shout, Pultarch grabbed Adana's hand and dragged her into an embrace. "This is mine!" He kissed her square on the mouth.

Before Kiffen or Montee could act, Adana shoved Pultarch toward Kiffen. "Unhand me." She leapt backward, hands raised in a defensive stance.

Kiffen rushed forward, concern for Adana conflicting with an urge to pummel Pultarch.

Pultarch grinned and faked a lunge at Adana.

Adana spun sideways and kicked out high, hitting him in the jaw.

Kiffen swung into the melee, narrowly missing the rebound of Adana's foot. He hooked his left arm around her waist and swung her toward Montee. Sword raised to strike, he spiraled toward Pultarch. With a solid thud his sword met Pultarch's temple and the man went down. The crowd fell silent.

Montee and Simeon ran forward and knelt by Pultarch's unconscious body. Kiffen stepped back, breath heaving in his chest. Euphoria flooded his veins until he caught sight of Adana hurrying toward the tunnel. He glanced back at Pultarch's still form. Time dragged. What if the blow to his head killed the man?

Simeon motioned several of the guards over. "Take him to Suban's chamber. He will have a nasty headache when he awakens."

Kiffen breathed in relief. He had not killed Pultarch. His shoulders drooped in exhaustion, and his cheeks ached from the gritty tension of the fight. He stretched his jaw, absorbing the pain in the only way he knew how. A smile.

* * *

Micah leaned back in his chair and ran his fingers through his beard. Maligon. If these strikes came from Maligon, matters were getting dangerous. Many lives could be lost. Were they right to match Adana to Kiffen? Ashamed for questioning the Creator, he rubbed his temples and sent up a silent prayer of apology.

A guard entered the chamber. "Sires, another Watcher has arrived."

At Micah's silence, Donel said, "Send her in."

Karyah entered the room, nodded to Ostreia, and bowed before Micah.

"Karyah, please tell me you have good news," he said, fighting the exhaustion resonating in his voice.

"I'm sorry, Sire, I don't. Maligon has overtaken the Empress Gabriella's palace and guard."

Donel rubbed his eyes. "Are you positive it is Maligon? Or is this rumor?"

Micah studied the Watcher and held his breath. No Watcher would state information as a fact unless she held proof.

"It is Maligon. The empress warned me."

Anger seethed through Micah's body. He and Chiora argued over her decision to leave the traitor's fate to the Creator. She was gone, but once again, he must face this fiend.

"What do you know of the Empress' situation?" Donel asked.

"Sire, I left during the coup. Word is Maligon marched right into Belwyn's throne room and took over. I could not save her." Accepting wine from Ostreia, Karyah continued before taking a drink. "The Empress managed to speak privately with me the day before."

"What did she tell you?" Micah asked.

"Maligon arrived a few days ago. He's followed her everywhere out of concern for her safety."

"Safety? From what?" Micah sat forward.

"Outlaws attacking the villages, refugees fleeing to the city for her protection."

"And her forces are scattered around the kingdom trying to restore order?" Micah finished for her.

"Yes. Maligon brought his own men and offered protection if she would marry him. She expected her soldiers to return yesterday, overtake and imprison him, but several of her own men turned against her."

The page, Catch, rushed into the chamber. Noting the somberness of the four adults, he skidded to a stop.

Agitated, Donel turned to the boy. "Yes, what is it?"

Unable to contain his excitement, even in the strained atmosphere, the boy chirped his news. "Prince Kiffen won, Your Majesty. Sir Simeon and the First Vision approach."

Micah exhaled. "Good. At least some things are as they should be. Send Kassa here, too."

The boy turned to leave, but Donel stopped him once more. "Wait, Catch."

"Sire?"

"What of the injuries?"

Catch swaggered with pride. "Sir Pultarch will have a nasty headache when he awakes."

* * * * *

Chapter Fifty-Eight

Leera sat in a chair beside a cot in the apothecary's quarters. She glared at Pultarch's unconscious form, her fan beating an impatient rhythm on her knee. The young lord lay on fine sheets as pale as his skin, his hair matted with sweat. A large purple bruise shaded his temple.

Pultarch roused as she snorted with disgust. Groaning, he struggled to sit up, but fell back onto the pillows.

A tentative hand probed at the injury on his head. When he moaned from the effort, Leera fought the urge to slap him. How could such a magnificent specimen of the male species look so thoroughly awful? Every fiber of her being begged to scream at him to act like the noble he was, but she recognized her mother's influence in this urge. For three years, she had watched Adana conduct successful negotiations by showing concern and compassion toward others. Leera resolved to try this foreign approach, afraid her mother's tactics would not yield the proper response from Pultarch.

She moved to his side, laid her hand on his, and spoke in a gentle voice. "Pultarch? How do you feel?"

He peeked through his left eye. Moving slowly, he managed to sit up this time. Leera assisted him, adjusting the pillows and smoothing the sheets.

"Water?" he croaked.

Grinding her teeth, Leera held a cup to his lips, tilting it just enough for a small trickle to flow into his mouth.

He gulped, forcing her to let him drain the cup and then wiped at his mouth, glancing around the room. "Where is Adana?"

Leera snorted. "After that show, do you really expect her to come rushing to your side?"

Pultarch bowed his head. "I don't know why I acted that way. The queen told me they were fighting. I'm such a fool."

A tear trickled down his cheek.

How could he cry over his own stupidity? Well, if he was too emotional to fix this, she wasn't. She needed to help him find his strength, not defeat. Some of the ruthlessness he exhibited in the sparring yard would help right now.

Suppressing her anger, she said, "We'll fix this. We just need a plan."

Pultarch looked hopefully at Leera as he dashed away his tears.

"First of all," Leera said, wrinkling her nose in disgust, "we need to clean you up. You look and smell despicable."

Pultarch relaxed. "When do you think I can see her?"

* * *

Adana sat on the fence of the giraffe enclosure watching Am'brosia pull leaves from a basket positioned at the height of her head. The giraffe's long tongue rolled out as she wrapped her lips around the food. With each bite, she bobbed her head and worked her mouth sideways as she chewed. Watching this simple action soothed Adana. She had rushed here in humiliation, thankful for the calm greeting provided by her graceful giraffe. She had felt no tension from the animal during the swordfight. Was Am'brosia so sure of Kiffen?

Am'brosia stopped her grazing to glance toward Adana. Was there satisfaction in the animal's eyes?

The scene with Pultarch replayed in her mind, and she seesawed between wishing for her mother's presence and being thankful her mother never witnessed this embarrassment. How could she lead a country when she could not prevent an unwanted embrace? This day was collapsing around her.

She slid down from the fence and walked with Am'brosia into the middle of the enclosure. Resting her forehead on the giraffe's chest, she breathed deeply, seeking her center. Am'brosia, in tune with Adana's pain, hugged her back in the only embrace she could offer, curling her long neck around the girl, leaving a short space between her heavy head and Adana's shoulder.

They stood together for a long time before Adana heard the gate swing open and someone approach. "I want to be alone."

"I know, child," Kassa whispered. "Your guards still maintain their distance." She ran gentle fingers through the strands of Adana's unbound hair.

The action reminded her of her mother. Leaning against the giraffe's broad foreleg, she said, "I failed."

"Your mother always found comfort with her giraffe when displeased with herself." Kassa stopped the gentle strokes and moved to Adana's side.

Adana shrugged. "She never failed, though."

"She thought she did many times."

"Thought and did are two different things," Adana said. "Not only did he catch me unaware, I stepped right into his reach!" She tightened her hands into fists. "I'm a Watcher. I should have sensed his intent."

"It doesn't always work that way." Kassa stepped back and crossed her arms, her hawk-like stare making Adana squirm from its intensity. "You are not invincible, and no one expects you to be. You know what happened after your mother captured your father."

Adana knew, but it didn't matter. "He helped her defeat Maligon."

"Before that."

"We're not talking about Maligon. This was Pultarch, a supposed friend. How could I not see his intentions?"

"Your mother held your father captive at first. Do you recall that bit of history? But he still managed to prevent Maligon from abducting her. It wasn't until after he saved her that she trusted him to help her defeat Maligon."

This discussion seemed pointless, but she knew that Kassa would not stop until she made her point.

"She did not foresee the danger, either. Your father did. Even though he risked his life to do so, he escaped Watcher guards to stop Maligon. Not a single Watcher foresaw what was about to happen. Only your father."

Adana could not shake her feelings of failure no matter what Kassa said. "War makes situations difficult to read."

"Yes, it does," Kassa said. "A perfect reason why you should not blame yourself."

"We're not at war."

"Close enough. Maligon has moved again."

Adana's hand paused on Am'brosia's neck. "You speak as if it's a fact."

"It is. Word from Empress Gabriella confirms it. You leave for Moniah tomorrow. There is no time for secret departures."

"Where's Kiffen?"

Kassa looked across the yard. He strode toward them while Bai'dish hurried to the fence in a mirror image of the prince's behavior. When Kiffen climbed the fence, ignoring the gate, Bai'dish nudged at him, almost toppling him backwards.

"Whoa, give me a moment," Kiffen said.

Bai'dish backed away.

The prince paused, one leg over the fence. "Did he understand me?"

"Probably," Kassa said.

He jumped to the ground and reached his hand out to stroke Bai'dish's nose, a smile of wonder on his face. Bai'dish herded him closer to Adana.

"Are you hurt?" Concern etched around Kiffen's liquid brown eyes. "I was afraid he had hurt you."

"No, Kiffen. Just my pride."

He pulled her into his arms, and Adana stiffened for a moment, unwilling to admit she longed to lean on him. Kiffen pulled back and searched her face. "I will never let anyone hurt you."

The tender way he looked at her pinged a note of pleasure from her shoulder. She relaxed against the gentle comfort of his chest, listening for the thump of his heart. Am'brosia and Bai'dish moved in to surround them in a protective barrier.

Too soon, Kiffen separated from their embrace and turned to Kassa. "Have you told her?"

"Only that she leaves tomorrow due to Maligon."

"I'm going with her." He stared at Kassa, a challenge in his eyes.

Kassa said nothing about his claim. "They are waiting for us."

Kiffen nodded. "First, we must speak to Pultarch."

Angry nausea rolled in Adana's stomach. "No."

"Adana, we must. He's awake now, and I think we should put an end to this misunderstanding."

She didn't know how to respond. She knew Kiffen was right, but shame and irritation with the man beat in her chest.

"We must try," Kiffen said, taking her hands in his. "He may have his faults, but he cares for you, and he was my good friend once."

She sighed. Nobility couldn't hold small grudges. "A brief visit."

Adana ran her hand along Am'brosia's side, reveling in the solid strength of the giraffe's mammoth bulk. Then she followed Kiffen and Kassa back into the castle.

* * * * *

Chapter Fifty-Nine

Adana and Kiffen found the Earl of Brom in the infirmary lecturing his son. Conrad of Brom's life consisted of burying one wife after another, each with a stillborn baby. Pultarch his only surviving heir, Conrad never remarried but fastened his hopes on his only son.

The elderly earl tried to rise from his seat in order to bow properly, but Kiffen and Adana rushed over, settling him back in the chair.

"Please don't," Kiffen said.

Pultarch had not moved to assist his father or show his allegiance to Kiffen. Instead, the young lord stared at Adana with shame, yet adoration.

"Prince Kiffen, my lady Adana, I must apologize for my son's brashness," the earl said. "We were discussing his imminent appeal to King Donel and King Micah for an appropriate penalty for this unfortunate incident."

Pultarch shifted on the cot and dropped his gaze. His hand stroked a large, swollen bruise on his temple. In this room, with the pale sheets as background to his washed-out pallor, what remained of Adana's anger gave in to pity.

The earl cleared his throat, and Pultarch glanced at his father, guilt flashing across his features. Conrad tilted his head toward the couple, his mouth in a firm line.

His son struggled to sit upright on the cot. "Prince Kiffen. Please accept my sincere apology. My behavior was unforgiveable."

After several tense moments, Kiffen waved the apology away. "It is forgotten."

"And my lady Adana," Pultarch choked out, then stopped. After a few agonizing moments, he slid off of the bed to kneel before her. "Please forgive me for my rude and bold actions." He looked up with his huge brown eyes. "I do not know what came over me."

The room turned silent, distant voices in the courtyard below sounding clearly on the air. Adana glanced at Kiffen. His jaw muscle pulsed, but nothing else showed in his face, which told her he fought to hide how troubled he was by the passion of Pultarch's act of contrition. The temptation to pat the young man's head came over her, just like in the rose arbor a few days earlier, but recalling her previous anger, Adana took a step back to provide a proper distance.

Glancing at the earl, she felt his expectation bore through her. "Sir Pultarch, your actions disregarded proper respect due to a lady. *Any* lady." She paused.

At the sound of her formal tone, Pultarch's shoulders sagged in dismay.

"Since you've previously behaved with the utmost kindness and respect, I will forgive you. Now please get up and let's put this behind us."

"Agreed," the Earl of Brom said and clapped his hands together. "That comes as welcome relief. I thought my son had lost all sense. I feared much worse from Lord Sarx's message. It sounded like my dear son had tried to start a war."

At the mention of Sarx, Adana exchanged a worried glance with Kiffen. Why had Sarx sent a message to the earl?

As if he heard their unspoken question, the earl continued. "Lord Sarx has kindly kept me up to date on court events during my illness.

He knows I find it difficult to venture out, and I still hold quite an interest in court activities." He gazed fondly at Pultarch.

"Oh, and my pardon!" The old man raised sparkling eyes toward them. "Congratulations to the two of you."

"Thank you." Adana smiled and bent to kiss his cheek.

While Kiffen accepted Conrad's congratulations, Adana turned to Pultarch. "How is your head?"

"It's not bad." He refused to meet her gaze. "I've had worse before."

"Worse or not, you should put a cool cloth on it to help with the swelling." She peered at the large knot on his temple, just beginning to show the purple and red of a bruise. "It looks awful."

"It's nothing," Pultarch said, sitting up straighter.

After Kiffen and Adana took their leave of Pultarch and his father, Kiffen wondered aloud, "Do you think Brom never expected you to marry Pultarch?"

* * *

Lord Sarx peered through the door and watched the royal couple disappear around the corner. He slipped into the corridor and turned to assist the young lady from the small room. Ignoring her haughty glare, he checked her appearance and grinned with pleasure. Shana, once properly attired and groomed, held a remarkable resemblance to Adana. He still could not believe his good fortune in finding such a close match, especially since Adana's coloring was so unusual. This acquisition, if properly handled, could make the tasks Maligon had given him much easier to carry out.

Pleased with the girl's appearance, Sarx quizzed her, "What is your name?"

"Lady Elayne of Glenhaven."

"Why are you here?"

"My mother, your cousin, sent me to you in hopes of finding a suitable marriage from the noblemen at court."

He had chosen Glenhaven because she knew the place even though it had not been her home in five years. And then only as a lady's maid.

"And what do you say if someone recalls an acquaintance you do not know?"

"I've spent the last few years in seclusion caring for my grandmother. It was her dying wish I be given an introduction in court. Before that I was too young to be introduced to any person of consequence."

Sarx smiled his approval. "You are quite good." He stroked her cheek, enjoying her flinch at the touch. "It's a shame I can't keep you for myself. Pultarch is such a bore."

They entered the infirmary quietly.

The Earl of Brom, dozing in his seat, snorted awake at their arrival and sat up with concern. "My lady, you've returned so soon. Is something amiss?"

At the sound of his father's voice, Pultarch rolled over on the cot to face them, his eyes widening at the sight of Shana.

Sarx chuckled with satisfaction. "My dear Conrad, my cousin and I have only just arrived. How could she be returning?"

The earl stuttered in confusion and then peered closer at Shana. "Remarkable."

Sarx led the tavern maid forward. "My lord, may I present my cousin, Lady Elayne of Glenhaven." Shana curtsied to the aging earl. "Lady Elayne, may I present the Earl of Brom and his son Pultarch."

Pultarch stared in fascination. Lady Elayne smiled at him, but her smile faded as she noted his injury. "My lord, what has happened to you?"

Pultarch continued to stare at her, a dumbfounded expression spreading over his face.

The earl answered for his son. "Nothing more than a sparring incident, my lady. I assure you he is quite alright."

Ignoring this exchange, Sarx addressed Conrad. "I just learned the lady Adana has been summoned home early. Some border troubles, I understand."

"Really?" Conrad wondered aloud. "How odd she did not mention it."

Sarx sneered. "Not odd at all. I'm sure Micah and Donel want little fanfare."

The earl nodded in agreement. "It would be wise if the rumors you've told me are true."

"'Tis a pity. I thought you might like to offer my cousin as a companion to the lady during her last days here."

"An offer like that would ease our guilt over today." He shook his head sadly. "Too late, I'm afraid."

Sarx waited while the old man suffered in his regret, and then he suggested an alternative. "I truly want to aid you in this predicament, Conrad." Stroking his beard, he squinted at Shana. Unease flashed in her eyes, amusing him. He loved pushing people off balance.

"I promised the Lady Elayne a life at court, but why not Moniah's court? Soon it will be one and the same."

* * * * *

Chapter Sixty

Simeon wasted no time outlining the news about Belwyn and Teletia. The same group from the morning had gathered to discuss strategy. "We need more time to muster proper security for your departure, my lady. And we'll need more supplies for a larger force."

Kiffen drew breath to speak, but Simeon kept talking. "Kiffen, we want you to lead one of the security flanks."

Kiffen frowned, a confused expression on his face.

"There is still danger of an ambush; therefore, several squads of soldiers will flank the lady Adana's caravan. I want you to lead one of the rear squads."

Montee continued this line of information. "The Watchers will depart with Adana's caravan, but several will join each of the squads once we've traveled a day's journey."

Adana had other concerns. "What of Belwyn and Teletia?"

"Elwarian troops prepare to leave as we speak," Simeon said. "Our main concern is your safe return and protection of both kingdoms. We suspect Maligon will try to attack one of us very soon."

"Do you think he has enough men to attack? He's already overtaken two kingdoms in the last few days." Kiffen studied the map laid out on the table. "We are much larger and definitely more fortified."

"With our forces divided between Moniah and here?" Micah said. "I assure you, Maligon's timing coincided with our absence on purpose."

* * *

A dana sat in her rooms and stared unseeing at the cold supper before her. She wanted to race home across the plains of Moniah and leave these troubles behind. Not that they wouldn't follow her there. The best she could do was flee to her rooms. Kiffen had stayed to discuss plans with Simeon and did not seem to mind her desire to be alone.

Except she wasn't alone. Her mind still reeled at that interesting turn of events. Who would have believed the Earl of Brom's embarrassment over his son's actions would force Kiffen to accept Pultarch as his personal companion?

Sighing, Adana regarded Brom's other surprise, the Lady Elayne of Glenhaven seated by the window. Their supposed resemblance caused quite a stir, but Adana's Watcher intuition anticipated complications from this unexpected gift. Her shoulder remained calm, though, not reacting to the lady's presence. Could she trust it? Kassa implied her use of formissa berry might have complicated the potion's abilities.

Lady Elayne was taller than the average Elwarian woman, but Adana still had the height advantage. Adana's hair was tawny, a mix of brown and gold, while Elayne's a shade darker and reflecting a slight reddish tint. Lady Elayne did appear to take in more detail than the average person, but Adana suspected a different purpose behind the girl's watchfulness.

Pushing her plate of food away, Adana stood and paced the room.

Elayne looked up from her needlepoint. "My lady, do you need anything?"

She wandered over to examine the crooked stitches in Elayne's handiwork and laughed. "I'm not sure I believe the opinions that you look like me, but your needlework is almost as bad as mine."

Elayne put down the stitchery. "I never did master this." She regarded Adana. "You are tense."

Adana flopped back on her chair. "Your powers of observation are remarkable."

"Would you like to discuss what's on your mind?"

She sat up and shook her head. "You must realize my position will not allow me to share my thoughts with you."

Elayne nodded but did not drop her searching gaze.

The stare unnerved Adana, and she decided to find out more about this unwanted gift. "When did you arrive?"

"At the castle?"

"No, the city."

"Oh," Elayne said. "A few days ago. Everyone talked of your birthday."

"You've heard about last night?"

Elayne shrugged her shoulders. "Silly gossip."

"For example?" Adana held her breath, curious about the rumors.

"Some people claim you became hysterical when your father announced your betrothal."

She laughed. "Really? Do they say I threw quite a tantrum?" She leaned forward. "What else do people say?"

"Some say you refused to accept the betrothal. That you prefer another."

"Do they say who?" Adana asked, anticipating the obvious answer.

Lady Elayne paused and bit her lip.

Adana waited, surprised at the girl's reluctance to speak. She noticed a slight intake of breath followed by compressed lips, indication the girl hesitated over the choice of words. She waited through two more breaths for the lady to answer her.

"Most people claim you prefer Pultarch."

"Ahh." Adana nodded her head. "They would."

"Do you?"

"Prefer Pultarch?" She sighed and shook her head.

Elayne's shoulders sagged in relief, a reaction that surprised Adana. "Then you love Prince Kiffen?"

"Yes."

A huge smile spread over Elayne's face, transforming her into someone Adana could like. "That is wonderful news!"

Confused, and a little curious at Elayne's relief, Adana stood and approached her. Elayne lowered her gaze.

"Why would you care if I love Kiffen?" She had heard that Elayne met Pultarch earlier today. Like any other lady in court, she probably swooned over his boyish charm. "Has Sir Pultarch's appeal captured you, too?"

Elayne turned away but not before Adana noted the alarm on her face.

"I've troubled you. I promise I'm not teasing you. I just couldn't help but think..." She paused and knelt beside her. "It would be a relief if he returned your feelings."

"It feels wrong that you kneel before me." Elayne pulled back.

"It most certainly does," Kassa voice caught them by surprise as she entered the chamber.

Adana sighed and counted to five. Could she not have a conversation without interruption?

"Lady Elayne is quite correct." Kassa stood over her, forehead creased in a frown. "You must never kneel before a subject. It implies weakness and subjugation."

Adana rose to her feet, the action slow and deliberate. "I will choose what is appropriate or not. If I choose to comfort someone by kneeling beside them, then I so choose. My mother never forgot that compassion goes a long way. Neither will I."

Kassa nodded. "Good. A queen's response." Without another comment, she turned and walked from the room.

"What was that about?" Adana wondered aloud as the door closed behind Kassa.

"She is pleased you stood up to her."

Elayne squirmed under Adana's direct, searching gaze. Could she read Kassa so easily? She had only met her today.

Adana whispered, "Who are you?"

A small spasm rippled along Elayne's mouth. She tightened her lips, evidence that she stopped herself from licking them. She picked up her needlework again, intent on the pattern in the cloth.

The Lady Elayne hid something. Was it of peril to the kingdoms? Her actions reflected a heightened awareness and tension. The puncture in Adana's shoulder tickled as if she was brushing up against something. Were these signs latent indicators the woman was a Watcher? Maybe Elayne's family refused to acknowledge a Watcher's skills in their daughter. Some families feared the service.

Should she have her tested? A sparkle of energy ran through her shoulder to her fingertips. The bond with Am'brosia skipped in response.

"We must have you tested. You're a little old, but if you have the sight, we need to train you."

"Tested?" Elayne's voice squeaked.

"As a Watcher," Adana said.

"A Watcher, whatever for?" The girl ignored her needlework, again.

"You demonstrate a few of the skills. Have you ever known something before it happened?"

"Of course, everyone has, but—"

"Have you ever dreamed something that happened later?"

Lady Elayne bit her lip and fidgeted, her gaze shifting toward the door and back to Adana.

Adana forced a hard gaze toward Elayne, the same gaze Kassa used that resembled a hawk studying its prey. With a stronger mental push, a hypnotic effect could hold a person in place. Urge them to respond.

Fear crossed Elayne's face, and her voice trembled. "My lady?"

Adana relaxed the pressure a little but not all the way, giving Elayne some freedom. "I need you to answer my question." A tinge of guilt tickled her shoulder, but she shrugged it away. Royalty had to use firm methods at times, and she needed to practice this skill.

"What question was that?" Elayne glanced around the room.

"Have you ever dreamed something that came true?"

"Dream?" Elayne's posture slackened. Her face took on a distant look. "Maybe. I'm not really sure."

"Have you ever known someone was there before you saw them?"

"I'm sorry, I don't think I understand." Strain showed in Elayne's neck muscles as she struggled to lean back in her chair. Shoulders stiffened, she ripped her gaze away.

A jolt rippled through Adana's body as Elayne broke free of the hypnotic hold. Frustrated, she moved closer to Elayne and pushed with her questions. "For example, when Kassa came through the door a moment ago, it surprised us. Have you ever known someone was coming, but there was no apparent reason for you to know?"

Elayne looked at the floor, her head shaking.

"Think hard," Adana pressed, convinced Elayne hid something of importance. "It may have been years ago or yesterday. Has it happened before?"

When Elayne gave a short, reluctant bob of her head, Adana's heart jumped with excitement.

"I knew I was coming here," she said, voice just above a whisper. "Not to my uncle's, but somewhere more important. I knew it."

Adana nodded. "We must have Montee test you."

"No, she can't." Elayne pressed her hands to her mouth.

"The idea troubles you? Don't worry, Watcher testing is harmless. You may become a Watcher candidate if you pass."

A curious look crossed the lady's face. She bit her lip. "I'm sorry, my lady, but what exactly would that mean?" She nodded toward the door. "I've seen them, but I'm not sure I really understand them."

"A Watcher is freedom," announced Adana, the exhilaration of that truth flooding through her for a moment. "You will not have to rely on anyone for your life and protection. It is freedom and knowledge."

Tears welled in the Lady Elayne of Glenhaven's eyes.

* * * * *

Chapter Sixty-One

Under a clear blue sky, Adana's entourage rode through the palace gates and began its slow descent out of the city. Cheering crowds lined the streets. Adana breathed a sigh of relief. These crowds appeared amiable, not hostile. She had spent the night imagining enemies lurking in the shadows, but it looked like the Elwarian guard had things under control. As her horse wound through the streets, she sought her connection with Am'brosia, sharing the animal's alert tension as well as the view from above the crowds.

The last time Adana ventured outside of the city was to visit the Earl of Brom's holdings, Pultarch in attendance.

At the thought of Pultarch, Adana's mind turned to the few moments she and Kiffen had shared in the stable yard before her departure. Their bodyguards and companions kept a discreet distance, which meant that Pultarch lurked nearby, now a member of Kiffen's personal entourage.

Although he no longer glowered at Kiffen, the young lord still stared nonstop in their direction. Adana searched Kiffen's gaze. "Do you think it's wise to have him nearby?

Kiffen shook his head at her inquiry. "He acts committed to our safety. There's no sign of his anger…or jealousy, now."

"Do you trust him?" she asked.

"Hardly," Kiffen said. "That's why I'm keeping him in sight. How about your companion?"

Adana shrugged her shoulders. "I feel like she's hiding something."

Kiffen watched the Lady Elayne approach Pultarch. "She does look like you. You're always hiding something." He nodded toward the two companions. "Maybe Pultarch will notice the resemblance."

"She's already smitten by his charms."

Kiffen leaned in and whispered in her ear. "And why were you not smitten?"

She laughed as they forgot their companions.

Kiffen's squadron left Elwar through the east gate of the city as Adana rode through the south. She wished he rode beside her but recognized the wisdom in separating them, dividing Maligon's targets.

They traveled throughout the warm day, pausing to water the animals and eat a light meal. During these rest stops, Adana watched Elayne for signs of fatigue. Most ladies did not travel well unless they rode in a carriage and stopped for meals. The urgency of the situation and the blessings of good weather prevented such pleasantries. Elayne did not balk or complain about the long hours in the saddle. At least her companion might not become a burden, but this, also, caused Adana to wonder.

From habit, Adana looked for signs of approaching riders. Soon, they would enter the forest and the Watchers would have to rely on the surrounding troops to maintain a safe perimeter. At this thought, Adana looked around for Montee. She stood with Glume watching over the giraffes, inspecting and adjusting their armor.

Am'brosia searched to the west while Bai'dish finished drinking. Adana sought the link, marveling at the view. What would it be like to see from that height all of the time, without walls or tree branches in the way?

Two Watchers stood beside Am'brosia and Bai'dish and scanned the horizon. Additional Watchers stood guard along the camp perimeter, side by side with Elwarian and Monian soldiers. In all, there were fifty Watchers and two hundred soldiers in her escort. With her father, Montee, Elayne, various servants, and a few Monian nobles, they made a sizable group.

* * *

On the second day, Adana walked with the giraffes and Montee. Am'brosia swaggered beside her. "I think she's gloating to Bai'dish that I'm here while Kiffen isn't."

Montee laughed. "Or she's adjusting to walking with her new armor."

Adana eyed the leather that covered Am'brosia and Bai'dish from the hump at the base of their necks down the length of the animals' backs. A fine mesh of metal links connected the gear underneath the giraffe's girth.

"I'm thankful for their protection, as much as I dislike being the first queen to require it. They move well with it, almost like wearing a second skin. It's well-thought out."

"You can thank Glume for that. Once he knew of the danger posed to the giraffe in the wild, he devoted weeks to creating this protection. He's been working on an idea to add blades to their rear legs. So far, he's not satisfied with the results. He's concerned they'll cut themselves instead."

"Does he really believe they need blades? Their hooves are lethal alone."

A kick from a giraffe could kill. Adana had seen a lion after a pride unsuccessfully tried to take down a giraffe calf. The mother crushed the skull of the largest lion, and the rest scattered after that.

Montee smiled. "Glume wants to ensure their complete safety. But yes, he's admitted their hooves might be enough."

They walked a while longer. Adana scanned the horizon, checking the landscape in between. Her gaze fell on Elayne's reddish-brown hair blowing behind her as her mount maintained their brisk pace.

Studying Adana, Montee asked, "How are you managing with Elayne?"

She shrugged, a motion she never used before meeting Leera. "I don't know if manage is the word for it, but we're getting along. Have you learned anything about her?" Inquiries into Elayne's background went out the moment she arrived in the castle.

"We found nothing." Montee frowned. "It's as if she never existed three days ago."

"No background? No acquaintances? No family?"

Montee shook her head. "Normally, I would send a squad to Glenhaven to track down her family. We just don't have the numbers to do that now. No one in Elwar or the surrounding countryside knows her except the Earl of Brom, Pultarch, and Sarx."

Adana pondered this news. "Brom did say she spent the last few years tending to an ailing aunt. Maybe there truly is nothing to know."

"If so, I would breathe much easier."

They walked on, inspecting the horizon and everything in between by habit. The forest loomed ahead, but still most of a day's travel ahead. Rolling hills appeared to fade into the green trees like waves of wind across the prairie grasses of Moniah.

Recalling her discussion with Elayne on their last night in Elwar, Adana stopped walking. Montee continued a few paces before turning in question.

"I want Elayne tested."

Montee raised an eyebrow. "Watcher tested?"

"Yes, and soon." Adana resumed walking. "She said some things. It made me wonder."

"Why didn't you test her?"

"Me?" The thought had never crossed her mind. "I've not reached my full potential."

Montee chuckled. "No Watcher ever reaches their full potential. Until you die, you still have potential."

"I know, but am I truly capable of testing? I've not even dreamed yet."

Was that true? Adana held her breath, wondering if Montee would take the opportunity to discuss her strange dream with her. When Montee continued walking without comment, Adana asked, "Have I?"

"You tell me."

"You sound like Kassa."

"Well?"

"I didn't see this betrothal." Adana slowed her steps, stalling, unsure if she wanted to explore her dream, again.

Montee maintained her pace for a few steps then quickened her steps. Her straight back as she left Adana behind said all the princess needed to know. You couldn't hide from reality, especially with the responsibilities she faced.

She hurried to catch up to her advisor. "Kiffen muddles my vision."

"Men usually do." Moments passed without comment. "You haven't answered your question."

Adana seesawed. To tell Montee about the changes in her dream would mean admitting to the danger. Unbidden, she felt the water swirl around her and saw the crown floating away.

Aware others kept watch, she felt safe enough to close her sight to her surroundings and pursue the image of her dream. She took a deep breath, let it expand in her chest, and released it in a slow breath through her lips. She breathed again, sinking into the memory of the dream.

Water swirled around her. Teachers called to her from the bank. The crown floated before her.

"What are you counting?" Montee's voice snapped her back.

Surprised, Adana looked down to see she was ticking off on her fingers. "I think I'm pacing. On my fingers."

Montee regarded her. "Any clues in those fingers?"

Hands held out before her, she stared at them as if they spoke their own language. "I've already told Kassa about my dream. She didn't comment."

"She thought not to frighten you."

"Frighten me?"

"Neither of us knew what it meant."

"Neither?"

"Kassa and I had the same dream. An evident warning, but we don't know how to interpret it."

The dream had been given to others? The images felt so real. Moniah's crown drifting in the river. The beast. Elwar's crown buried away from the light of day.

"Someone's going to die?" she asked.

"Possibly," Montee said.

"Who?"

"There is the problem. Is the underground crown a reference to Serrin?"

Adana shook her head. "He died before I received this dream."

"Then King Donel or Prince Kiffen."

She stopped walking. Every time she considered the dream might refer to Kiffen, she forced her thoughts in another direction. A queen could not ignore the implication of a vision, no matter how painful. Her mother faced the prophecy of her own death. Adana must determine the prophecy behind the dream. Without knowledge, she was like other people, blown by the wind that scattered dry dirt along the prairie. She needed to understand the warning if she wanted to change things.

"Montee, visions are only a warning. The outcomes can be altered, correct? There would be no purpose to them if we couldn't somehow change them."

The Watcher nodded, but her face took on a stillness as she answered. "There are rare instances where actions changed the prophecy's message, but usually a vision gives us the time to prepare for the inevitable. You recall the first lesson of dream visions?"

"The meaning is not immediately clear, and often we must wait until the event unfolds to recognize the true prophecy."

Montee nodded. "Worrying about King Donel or Prince Kiffen will not help us. That may feel harsh. It never changes, but you need to face these issues as a Watcher and queen. Fear will not solve anything. The Creator gave you this gift. You must honor the blessing by exploring all possible meanings."

Adana nodded, ignoring the reference to the Creator. "It was easy to be distracted in Elwar, but Kassa never let me forget my responsibilities." She halted. "You sounded a lot like her, just then. A true First Vision."

Montee had mastered the art of keeping her emotions hidden. It was one of the skills she was known for. But for a fleeting moment, Adana saw satisfaction skim over the First Vision's face and a brief spark of pleasure dance in her eyes.

Regaining their stride, Montee said, "You will test Lady Elayne when we camp tonight."

* * *

The test was a dismal failure. Elayne did not exhibit any distance perception or respond correctly to her visual memory when asked questions about the areas they passed through during the day. The easiest details eluded her. At the end of the test, Montee said, "Lady Elayne, we apologize for wasting your time. You are not Watcher material." This was the prescribed statement for any failed candidate, but today it disheartened Adana.

"I don't understand," she said to Montee after Lady Elayne walked away. "She accurately recognized truth from gossip. She knew details only a Watcher or an informed person would notice."

Montee shook her head. "Luck? Experience? Or she's not who she says she is."

* * * * *

Chapter Sixty-Two

That night, Adana's caravan camped on the edge of the forest, the entire group subdued and silent before the monstrous trees. As Adana walked to her father's tent to meet with him and Montee, she couldn't help but recall her last time in the forest. The trees still rose in an ominous wall for as far as she could see. Would she recognize the spot where they buried Hunter? His family had retrieved his body, so she knew it wasn't there but wondered if his soul remained among the trees. She wished the man were still alive to help protect her people against Maligon.

Inside her father's tent, they reviewed the plans for the next day.

"What news do we have from our flanks?" Adana asked.

"All clear. No signs of disturbance anywhere." Montee leaned over the map without looking up as she gave her report.

"No signs?" Adana asked, concern rising in her mind. "What became of the refugees I heard so much about? Have they disappeared?"

"No, my lady," Montee straightened. "Elwar sent out their guard to assist them in relocating. Most of them are secured for now."

"When did this occur?"

"Two days ago. I thought you had enough concerns at the time, so we did not mention it in your briefing."

Adana stared at Montee and her father, fighting displeasure over their decision. Her absence had prevented full participation in her kingdom's interests, but Kassa made sure she knew everything in their briefings. "Sir Micah, why was I not informed?" It was time her father and Montee saw her as the queen she would soon be. They needed to realize she was capable.

Her father's eyes widened at her use of the title he would wear after her coronation. Montee shifted her stance, a slight motion. Neither answered.

"What else have you kept from me?"

"Nothing but the details we are briefing you on now," her father said.

Adana nodded. "Do not forget, in two weeks time, I will be queen. Now is a perfect time to start thinking of me in that regard. I will not permit you to determine what I do and do not need to know."

"I am not accustomed—"

"Become accustomed."

He gave a brief nod.

"Good." She sat in the only chair in the tent. "Continue."

"The forest will be too dark in the morning," her father said, "so we plan to wait until mid-morning to enter. If all goes well, you will be home in five or six days."

Adana nodded her agreement. "Thank you. Is there anything else?"

"Yes." He came to stand before her. "You will be queen in two weeks if we transport you safely. You must stay in the center of our formation the entire time we are in the forest."

As she had off and on all day, Adana recalled her last trip through the forest. "I suppose I deserve the warning. I will remain with my guard; you have my word on it." Adana rose, but she paused at her father's side before ducking out of the tent. "You will remain by my side. I still need you if I am to be as great a queen as mother."

She looked into his eyes, fighting the sudden sadness washing over her. She wished her mother were there, had joined in the celebration in Elwar, and helped her adjust to the changes in her life.

Turning away, she exited the tent, shoving her wistful thoughts away.

Silence settled over them until she and Montee reached her tent. The Watcher stopped just inside the entrance, letting the flap fall closed behind her. "My lady?"

Adana accepted a glass of wine from Elayne and sat on a cushion. Gesturing for Montee to join her. "Yes, Montee?"

The woman remained where she stood. "You were correct to reprimand us. I will not forget you are queen. Several times today, you have shown me the proof of your ability."

A pleased glow spread through Adana at Montee's words. "I am glad we understand each other. Now join me for dinner. I believe we have a long night ahead of us. A storm is coming."

Elayne turned at her pronouncement. "Has it reached us? I was sure it was at least a few hours away, yet."

Adana sat forward with a frown. "How did you know the storm was coming? I thought you stayed in the tent."

Elayne blinked. "I did stay inside."

"Then how did you see the lightning in the distance?" Adana had noticed a flash just as she reached her tent. The clouds had not gathered around them yet, but any Watcher knew the distant almost imperceptible flash meant lightning too far away for most to see.

"No, Lady Adana." A confused look crossed Elayne's face. "I've remained in the tent as required."

"Then how did you know a storm was coming?"

"I've been hearing the thunder for some time now. Haven't you?"

Montee opened the tent flap, stared outside a moment, then let it drop back into place. "I can barely make out the lightning in the distance. I haven't heard any thunder."

"I don't hear any thunder, either," Adana finally said.

A platter of fruit in her hand, Elayne settled on a cushion near Adana's chair. She kept her eyes downcast. "I'm sorry that you don't hear it. I thought everyone could."

As predicted, the rain began to fall soon after they finished their dinner. Adana listened to its drumming on the tent, thankful her position allowed her the privilege of shelter. Her Watchers, except for Montee and Veana, camped in the rain. She considered asking Sinti and Joannu into the tent, but Montee squelched the idea. "You must have your guard's presence on the outside of the tent. The storm is nothing. They've trained in worse conditions."

Montee's final remark bothered Adana. She did not want to sleep in the rain again, but she knew the time approached when she must spend her time in the Watcher lifestyle.

As rain poured down, her thoughts tumbled over all of the changes of the last few days. Could she really rule as well as her mother? Some said Queen Chiora had been the best queen in centuries. But she wouldn't rule alone. Her marriage to Kiffen would combine the kingdoms. She had no idea how to accomplish joint rulership. Did her dream foretell a life of misfortune for the both of them? She tossed and turned until the storm died down to a light drizzle. Just before dawn she drifted into a restless sleep.

Morning arrived cool, cloudy, and wet. Rain still sprinkled the camp but tapered off by breakfast. While the travelers sloshed through the puddles and assembled their gear, a wind swept through the clearing, peppering everyone with water. Adana, accompanied by Samantha and Joannu, ventured out as the sun began to break through the clouds. The wind plucked at her braid and billowed her cape behind her. Lifting her face to the wind, Adana embraced the cool, fresh air after the smoldering smoke in the tent. The aroma of coffee and hot oats mingled with the loamy smells of damp ground and vegetation. The sun's warmth began to penetrate the drenched camp, steam rising from the sodden clothing of the soldiers and the bodies of the horses.

Around her, people worked with precision, ignoring nature's interruption. Adana first visited her horse and gave him a brisk brushing, enjoying the horse's snort of gratitude and his coarse hair under her fingers. Then she turned her attention to the giraffes. Fighting to keep her balance against Am'brosia's indignant, but gentle, head butts, she attended to Bai'dish first. Bai'dish chewed on leaves, ignoring the other giraffe's reaction, a flicker of amusement in his eyes so much like a look she often saw from Kiffen.

By mid-morning, the sun burned away the damp chill, and the wind died down to a gentle breeze. Reluctantly, the caravan left this improved weather for the darkness of the forest. The sunlight diminished and then almost vanished as the trees thickened. Beyond the first few trees on the edge of the wood, all evidence of the night's storm disappeared. The forest floor was dry.

"Isn't it beautiful?" Elayne rode next to Adana, a blissful smile on her face.

Adana arched a brow at her, but Elayne's enraptured gaze was tilted up toward the treetops. The trees towered so high, the lowest branches were well above Am'brosia's and Bai'dish's heads. As she looked upwards, Adana began to notice birds flitting about in the canopy and an occasional squirrel intent on some pursuit.

She laughed, an odd sound ringing among the silence of the caravan. "I never considered it might be beautiful."

Elayne gave her a shocked look. "Why ever not?"

"I can't see far beyond us. What's ahead, behind, beside us." Adana gestured toward the branches above. "But, you're right, the view is quite incredible."

Elayne peered upwards. "I meant the birdsongs." She tilted her head back, her eyes closed. "The wind blowing through the trees, the animals scurrying away from our path." She opened her eyes. "Listen."

Adana halted her horse and strained to hear. Sounds of the caravan greeted her ears—the clop of horse's hooves, a quiet word muttered between a couple of soldiers, and the jangle of harnesses and weapons. She strained harder, holding her horse and body as still as possible, and detected the faint sound of wind blowing through the treetops, the branches creaking and leaves rustling in the breeze. As if from a great distance, she eventually heard a bird chirping. "I can barely hear it," she said. "You can hear more than one bird? Animals?"

"My mother used to call me "big ears." Elayne's hands flew up to sides of her head and she blushed. "I could always hear more than others."

"Like the thunder last night." Adana pondered this for a moment. "What is that like? To hear so well?"

"I have nothing to compare it to." Elayne rode beside her in thought, silent long enough that when she spoke again, she startled Adana. "It is helpful to hear so well, for instruction and correction, but it can be difficult when there is a lot of noise."

That thought, she could relate to. "Probably how I feel when there is too much to look at or block my view. Like this forest."

Close to evening, they stopped in a clearing. As they set up camp, Adana tried to familiarize herself with the surroundings and imprint the details on her mind. She was glad to see it didn't look like the spot where they stopped on her way to Elwar, but without the view of the setting sun, she struggled to distinguish direction.

Montee interrupted her, "Look for the moss on the trees."

"How did you know?"

"Your face betrayed you. You looked like a trapped Watcher. I've seen it hundreds of times." Montee walked away, calling to one of the Watchers to gather wood for a fire.

* * * * *

Chapter Sixty-Three

Donel sat in his library, watching the flames dance along the logs in the fireplace. Silence pervaded the castle, the only sound coming from the pop and crackle of the logs as the fire ate away the pulp. Sighing, he took another sip of wine, recalling the strategy meetings he and Roassa had held with King Ariff of Teletia to defeat Maligon.

Roassa's gaze during those meetings always turned bright as she planned their troop movements. Even in her frailty, she had blossomed when in command, the color rising in her cheeks, reaffirming her name. The same look appeared in Kiffen's eyes this past week. The boy had always been more Roassa's son than his, and he was glad of it. Roassa had been the better ruler, had seen more easily the truth behind the façades presented in court, and had known what her people needed before they even knew it.

Donel's worst mistake came from his own inability to read people. He shook his head as he considered his biggest error in that regard.

After Roassa's death, hard drink became his friend, his effort to fill the emptiness. Many times, he awoke in odd parts of the castle, no memory of the previous night. Quilla took advantage of this behavior in her search for power. His surprise when he awoke in her arms, her later claim of a pregnancy, and his marriage to Quilla was set. When Leera was born ten months after their wedding, he knew his new queen had lied about his drunken actions, but it was too late to change anything.

Donel drained his glass and flung it into the fire, crying, "I was such a fool!" The glass popped and shattered, but he never saw it.

"Yes, you were a fool." Quilla smiled as she plunged a dagger into his neck, grimacing at the effort.

Donel stared in fascinated shock at the spurt of blood. In slow motion he watched Quilla hand the dagger to a soldier.

As his life seeped away, he heard her say, "Sound the alarm. Someone has murdered the king." She smiled one last time into his eyes, then leaned close to his ear and whispered, "Long live Queen Quilla."

* * *

Darkness enshrouded the mountain. King Ariff of Teletia scanned the countryside one more time before returning to the cave. His wife, Morana, and son, Navon, huddled under a musty blanket, collapsed in exhausted sleep. He reached down and stroked a dark tendril of hair from Morana's face. Even in restless slumber, she looked fifteen instead of thirty. The joy of her life, their son Navon, snuggled in her arms. They had waited a long time for the blessing of this child. Ariff's memories turned to three other children, dead before their first breath.

He sighed as he stroked the curly brown locks from the five-year-old prince's face. The fate of Teletia rested on this small boy's survival. His lips pressed in grim determination at the thought. The child may be young, but they survived Maligon's surprise assault thanks to Navon's imagination.

Just before Maligon's attack, with a few moments of free time, they had given in to Navon's pleas to play a game of hide and seek. He had a remarkable talent for locating odd hiding places. A useful skill once Maligon's men locked them in a rarely used chamber in the castle's west tower. In a flash, Navon found a hidden doorway that Ariff, in his forty years, had never known existed. Never again would he object to Navon's inquisitive nature.

Exhausted, King Ariff slid down to a seated position against the hard cave wall. This cave, well-known in stories, still provided a perfect hiding place from Maligon. It was the very cave where the Watchers first found Donel and Micah. Few people knew its actual location. Common belief placed it much further south, closer to the Monian border. Those who knew the truth encouraged this misunderstanding, realizing secrecy provided a safe haven in unusual times.

Now, we must wait, he thought. Soon, someone would think to check the cave. Until then, his family was safe.

* * * * *

Chapter Sixty-Four

Deep in the forest, Adana's caravan set up camp for the night. The cook and watch fires gave scant light in the heavy darkness. Adana and Elayne were attending to their horses when Montee approached.

"When did you last sleep in a tree, my lady?"

Adana paused and looked at her First Vision, frowning over the idea. "I believe it would be two years ago. Queen Quilla was horrified. I scratched up my arms and had to wear long sleeves for a week." She shrugged her shoulders. "After that, Kassa and I decided to put a halt to that practice while in Elwar."

Montee studied the tree canopy, walking between the trunks. Occasionally, she lightly slapped one.

"What is she doing?" Elayne asked.

"Selecting a tree."

"What does she mean?" Elayne whispered in a confused burst. "She expects you to sleep against a tree?"

Adana smiled at Elayne and followed Montee to the towering tree she had stopped beside.

"Why did I choose this tree, my lady?" The Watcher's hand rested on the trunk. Elayne stood beside them, her face screwed up in confusion.

Adana's fingertips trailed along the tree's circumference. It felt smooth and cool, but not damp, beneath her hand. At least, Montee had not chosen an uncomfortable tree. She gazed into the branches, checking for knots, identifying supportive limbs and formations to cradle her for the night. Her first tree had been covered in scratchy, scaly bark. In addition, rain had poured down for days before that exercise. Her companion trainees claimed Samantha, the Watcher in charge of their training, selected uncomfortable trees for their first experience out of meanness. Later, they learned the choice was deliberate in order to show them how a poor selection could rob them of a night's rest.

Wrinkles of consternation creasing her brow, Elayne crossed her arms, fingers clenching her forearms.

Adana answered Montee but kept her gaze on Elayne. "The tree provides easy access to its supportive branches. The bark is smooth and cool to the touch. About twenty spans up is a nice cradle formation to prevent me from falling."

Elayne stared at the tree. "I climbed trees as a child, but I see no footholds."

Adana guided Elayne's hand to a spot on the tree. "Slide your fingers along here." When Elayne reached a short bump in the bark, Adana said, "There. Do you feel that knob?"

Elayne nodded. "Surely, you cannot expect—" She stopped as Adana grabbed the knob and scaled the tree.

Adana smiled down at Elayne. "There's room for two. Would you like to join me?"

"No." Elayne took a step back.

"Then you can enjoy my tent tonight. Goodnight."

Adana felt Elayne's gaze on her until she lay completely hidden in the branches. She peered through the foliage and watched the lady stumble after Montee. "Excuse me, but do you truly expect royalty to spend the entire night in a tree?"

Montee turned. She and Elayne stared at each other for a few moments, and then Montee asked, "Our methods do not meet with your approval?"

"No…well, I do not understand."

"True. You do not understand. It will be up to my lady Adana to determine what you need to understand. For now, know that this practice has saved many lives." Montee turned and marched away.

Hidden in the branches, Adana smiled. Elayne felt concern over her welfare. Maybe the woman would prove trustworthy, after all.

* * *

K iffen stared into the small campfire while his mind wandered toward the location of Adana's camp, ahead somewhere within the forest. He felt an unfamiliar pull from that direction and guessed it was part of his connection to Bai'dish. Montee had given him a musky fluid to drink each morning, and the awareness became stronger with each dose. There hadn't been time to learn how to use the connection, so it hovered in the back of his mind like a gnat, pulling him toward Adana's camp.

At least their route had been clear and safe, but the forest presented many hazards. As a boy, he enjoyed trips into the forest. He and Serrin hunted with their father, creeping along the trail of their prey. These experiences taught them the dangers of the area. An entire army could ambush the caravan without warning. He prayed to the Creator to help the flanking troops protect her. Sighing, he went to check the sentries' reports and try to get some sleep.

* * *

Kiffen jerked awake at the sound of the tent flap being drawn back. A soldier knelt beside him. "Prince Kiffen, one of the Watchers reports horses approaching from the north. Elwarian."

Kiffen rubbed his face and rolled from his bedroll. "How far?"

"About a league."

The prince splashed his face with water. "Send the Watcher to me."

The soldier gave a short bow and left the tent. Kiffen kicked Pultarch's sleeping form. His presence galled Kiffen, but he preferred to keep him nearby. "Wake up."

Pultarch stretched and sat up. "What is it?"

"You sleep too well. Did you not hear my soldier's report?"

"Riders?"

"So you were awake." Kiffen wondered why Pultarch feigned sleep only to admit to it.

"No," Pultarch said as he strapped on his sword. "A report in the middle of the night? What else could it be?"

He glared at the man. How could he ever trust him? "I need you to wait outside. Send Simeon to me."

"You don't want me to hear this report?"

"You are not here by any choice of mine. I abide your presence because the alternative is to trust you. Please remove yourself until I summon you again."

As Pultarch ducked out of the tent, a Watcher entered. Kiffen turned, trying to recall her name. Failing to do so, he said, "Good, you are prompt. You spotted the riders?"

"Eight soldiers wearing Elwar's full battle gear approach on horseback. I believe one of them is the sergeant of the castle guard."

"Markel? Why would he leave the castle?" Kiffen dropped into the only chair. He could think of no reason for his father to send Markel. "What do you make of this?"

A flash of concern crossed her face. A Watcher's face remains impassive to most people, but Kiffen's experience in observing Adana made him more alert to the slight shifts in a Watcher's body language. He waited to see if the woman's words would match the concern she tried to conceal.

"They ride with agitation. I fear the news is bad."

Simeon entered the tent. "The riders have arrived."

"Send Markel to me, alone."

Sergeant Markel entered the tent and bowed low before Kiffen. He was a solid, square-built man. His dark beard and moustache could not hide the exhaustion in his eyes or the hard set to his jaw. Kiffen had only seen this expression on the sergeant's face twice in his life—first, when his mother died and second, when Serrin died. Simeon stood beside Kiffen's chair, resting a supportive hand on his shoulder.

"Your Highness…Prince Kiffen…" Markel paused and took a deep breath. "King Donel has been killed, and Queen Quilla has claimed the throne in your absence."

Cold prickled down Kiffen's back as he flew up from his seat. "What? How?"

"Your Highness," Markel looked down for a moment but returned Kiffen's gaze before continuing. "His throat was slit. A maid found him sitting before the fire in his private chambers."

Kiffen stumbled backwards, grasping behind him for the arm of the chair, his mind struggling to understand the simple words. This could not be true. His father murdered? Why? He stared at the three people gathered in his tent aware what they must think. His betrothal to Adana killed his father.

"Sire," Markel interrupted his thoughts, "I apologize, but there is more."

Weariness washed over him as he waved his hand at the man. "Continue."

"Queen Quilla has claimed your throne. She denounced your title and ordered the castle guard to remove those who support you. We fought our way out. Most who support you are dead or fleeing."

Kiffen's mind flew over the words, unable to grasp the stark truth. Several moments passed.

Simeon placed his hand on Kiffen's shoulder. "Sergeant, you are to be commended for your courage and dedication. Your men? Can they be trusted?"

"Sworn to silence until the king decides on an action."

Kiffen's head jerked up. King! The title raced through his veins calling him to the role of his ancestors. A flood of responsibility rolled over him, and he realized what he must do.

"Sergeant Markel, you honor me with your loyalty. Summon your men." He stood. "Simeon, find someone to bring them a meal. We have much to do." He turned to the Watcher and said, "You are?"

"Rolanna."

"Rolanna, summon your squad. We must warn the lady Adana."

Within moments, the soldiers and Watchers gathered in the tent. Kiffen studied a map of the forest, pinpointing the location of Adana's camp.

"Quilla will not stop with my father. We must warn the lady Adana before Quilla's men reach her." He pointed to the soldiers and three Watchers. "We will leave immediately." He indicated a location on the map southeast of his camp. "Princess Adana's camp should be here. Rolanna, you take the advance, so we do not alarm them. We must reach her first." He turned to the guard. "Send word to the other flanks. But you remain here in my tent. Put Pultarch in my bedroll. If Quilla sends assassins after me, let them find Pultarch instead."

The guard nodded. "It will be a pleasure."

* * * * *

Chapter Sixty-Five

The dream returned. Adana bobbed in the rapids, her crown taunting her. She reached for it, but it sank from sight and resurfaced down river. Shouts of men, Teachers of the Faith, came from the far bank. They beckoned to her, but the current dragged her farther away, toward a rock protruding from the river. She slammed into the rock. Darkness fell over her.

Adana jerked awake. Sounds of clashing swords and shouts rang from nearby. Her head throbbed where she'd hit the rock in her dream. In her lap sat a small stone. Picking it up, she tried to shake the vision's effects and focus on the sight below her.

"My lady, Adana. Please wake!"

Adana twisted in her perch, spotting Elayne's upturned face at the foot of the tree. Too much firelight flickered over the scene below. "What's happening?"

"We're under attack."

Adana twisted and dropped quickly from the tree. Through her link to Am'brosia, she felt the animal's agitation. For a moment she felt their consciousness leap forward like it did the day Am'brosia dragged her across the plains into the sight of other giraffes. But the connection disintegrated.

Elayne pushed a parcel into her hands. "This is all I could gather before they swarmed your tent."

The bundle included her bow and quiver along with her sword and small pack. An urge to run struck her, and she recognized it as

Am'brosia's thoughts. "Where is Montee?" Adana started to trot toward the fighting.

Elayne grabbed her by the arm. "Montee instructed me to help you escape." She began to drag Adana behind her.

"Nonsense. I must fight with my people."

"Not this time. Montee was very specific. You will come with me."

Against her will, Adana was pulled in the direction of the horses and giraffes. Should she trust her? Elayne's strength surprised her. The ladies she met in Elwar would not have the muscle to pull her.

Just a few spans away, Adana saw one of her men fighting a soldier, their faces contorted in the struggle. She pulled free from Elayne to draw an arrow. The pair tumbled sideways, and Adana saw the face of the other man. One of her guard, too. She lowered the bow in confusion.

"My lady." Elayne's breath came hot on her face the woman stood so close. "We must go."

Adana raised her bow and sighted along the shaft, letting the focus carry her into her breathing. The two men twisted in their struggle. One man faced her, his face contorted in fury and defense. Her true man?

The other man shoved him, and the two stumbled toward a tree. The second man's eyes registered triumph, and he raised his knife to strike a killing blow.

Adana released the arrow into the second man's arm, unwilling to kill, yet.

The man staggered under the strike, but his downward stroke plunged into the chest of the first man.

As he fell, the first's gaze connected with hers, alarm and warning in them. Over the noise of battle, she couldn't hear him, but his lips said, "Run."

She released a second arrow dropping his attacker and turned toward the sound of pounding feet. A soldier raced toward her. He shouted in triumph.

Her third arrow flew.

The connection from Am'brosia slammed back into focus as the man fell, the shaft protruding from his chest. The giraffe's message rang clear. *Leave.*

Adana turned toward Elayne. The woman gripped a knife in her hand, her eyes wide in fright as she scanned the forest around them

"Come. Stay close." Adana turned and ran toward the horses.

The battle raged to her left, and Adana skirted the trees, keeping a close watch on Elayne. She kept pace with Adana's long-legged gait.

A sharp cry served as the only warning. Adana tumbled to the ground under the weight of an Elwarian soldier. She twisted, forcing one leg free. A swift kick to the man's shin did nothing, and she clamped her teeth down on his arm.

An unearthly howl escaped the man's lips, ringing in Adana's ears. He fell limp, the fight out of him. She pushed his body away.

Elayne stood over them, her knife dripping blood. "I…I may have killed him."

Blood soaked the man's coat, seeping from the knife wound.

"Good. Thanks." Adana turned to Elayne. Shock glazed the lady's eyes.

Adana grabbed her arm and dragged her in the direction of Am'brosia. The connection was fading in and out as they encircled the camp.

Joannu's urgent voice reached her out of the gloom. "We must hurry. The fighting is close."

Adana could barely make out the form of the Watcher standing by three saddled horses. Relieved, Adana jumped into the saddle.

Before she could spur the horse into a run, Joannu grabbed the bridle. "We must move quietly, so as not to alert them to our departure." Carefully, she guided the horses through the trees.

"You released Am'brosia and Bai'dish?" Adana searched for the connection, feeling it rise and fall in her mind.

"Can you sense them? We should follow."

"The connection is fading. We must hurry if I'm not to lose her." Adana closed her eyes and sought to hold the link, feeling the bond tighten with stretched tension.

Joannu nodded. "Slowly, until we put some distance between us and the camp."

* * * * *

Chapter Sixty-Six

Kiffen's patrol pulled up short as Rolanna ran back into their midst. "They're under full attack."

Through the trees, fire flared and men's shouts intermixed with the clang of swords.

Turning to his men, Kiffen said, "Find the lady Adana and the regent. Get them to safety." Without waiting, he spurred his horse forward, his men spread out and raced into the battle

The fighting swarmed toward Kiffen. Light filtered through the trees, shadows jumping as soldiers clashed. Adana's tent would be in the center of the camp.

Before Kiffen could dive into the midst of the fray, Simeon's horse plunged in front of his, cutting him off. "Stop."

Kiffen growled at Simeon. "Out of the way!"

"Stealth, my lord. You cannot reach her if you plunge into that madness."

"I will not stand by while she's slaughtered."

Simeon dropped from his horse. "And neither will I. Come. This way."

Kiffen slid from his horse and followed Simeon. His heart pounded in his chest. What if she was fighting for her life this very instant? Could he save her?

Both froze at the sound of running feet. Two soldiers ran across their path. Kiffen raised his sword and started toward them. Both men dropped suddenly to the ground, arrows sticking out of their backs. Behind them, Montee stood among the trees her bow ready.

"Montee," Simeon said as the First Vision rushed toward them.

"You are off track," she said.

Kiffen ignored her comment. "Why aren't you guarding Adana? Where is she?"

Montee nodded in the direction the two men had been running. "Joannu escaped with her a few moments ago." She looked at Simeon. "You must take the prince to the Border Keep before they discover him."

Kiffen felt his body turn cold. "You will not send me away from her. I must protect her."

"She can protect herself," Montee said. "I will follow her as soon as I can. You must go another way. There are too many of them for us to fight."

"Montee," Simeon said, "where is Micah?"

She hesitated, but her gaze met Kiffen's without flinching. "They hit from too many directions at once. They got him first."

"Micah is dead, too?" Kiffen said. He staggered backward as if hit.

"Too?" Montee stepped closer, her Watcher's gaze alert.

Kiffen swallowed bile. "My father was murdered this night in the castle."

Montee's chin jerked up. Her eyes blazed in the dark. "Both of them? You must return to your throne immediately."

Simeon shook his head. "Quilla claimed the throne. Elwar is too dangerous." A brief silence stretched between them. "We will cover your tracks, Montee. Follow lady Adana."

"You must leave, before it's too late. We will head for Moniah if it is safe." She jogged in the direction Joannu had taken Adana.

Kiffen turned to follow her, but Simeon grabbed him. "Don't."

He shoved Simeon's hand away. "She's all that matters. She must live."

"So must you."

The sounds of fighting had faded to the north. Kiffen and Simeon walked into the remains of Adana's camp, stepping over bodies. Simeon stopped at one. Rolanna, a look of shock on her still face. They edged closer to the camp. All was quiet except for the roar of fire eating several tents.

Simeon approached a large blue tent, the cloth collapsed and dragging the ground. A hand stuck out from under the material as if reaching for something. He lifted the edge of the tent and stared into the unseeing eyes of Adana's father. Both men fell to their knees beside the body.

Sergeant Markel found them in that position.

"Blazes, no!" The sergeant collapsed beside the regent king. After a few ragged breaths, he reached down and closed Micah's eyes. A few more soldiers approached, Monian and Elwarian both. As truth and exhaustion overcame them, each knelt behind Kiffen.

Kiffen roused himself to find soldiers and Watchers gathered behind him. He stood and each one focused on him with expectation.

"We must honor the fallen today, but we cannot remain here. The woods will reclaim them, but the regent king must be moved."

Without comment, several First Soldiers stood and wrapped Micah in the blue cloth of his tent. Kiffen watched them, noting the first rays of sunlight filtering through the trees.

A new day had come.

* * *

nger shrouded Adana as she fled east. Why had her soldiers attacked each other? Flashes of the battle in the forest played in her mind. Shouts, the flash of swords in firelight, the crackle of multiple fires eating away the tents, the smell of burning wood and canvas. Who attacked them and how? She didn't need to ask why. Too many people objected to the plan to unite her kingdom, Moniah, with Elwar through marriage to Prince Kiffen.

Sometime later, the horses emerged from the forest, and the three women urged them into a gallop. Joannu rode on Adana's left flank, Elayne on her right, the thuds of the horse's hooves the only sound in the night. When they reached the top of a slight rise, Adana slowed her horse and twisted in the saddle to check behind them. A half-moon shone across the landscape. A slight breeze lifted the hair pulled free from her braid and stung at scratches on her arms from the struggle with the soldier.

No one in sight.

The forest trees lined the horizon for as far as she could see. Would the fires set by her attackers destroy the forest?

"Ballene's fire!" She huffed the expletive, her concerns jumping from alarm over the night's attack to concern over a large-scale fire. At least no smoke trailed into the sky, and it appeared they hadn't been followed.

She kicked her horse into a gallop again.

How far had they ridden? Rolling hills rose up to meet the horses' hooves as they put distance between them and their attackers. Her mind flew along her connection to Am'brosia, trying to determine the location of the giraffe she had been bound to for six years. Am'brosia led the way, along with Bai'dish. The two beasts held a large lead on her small band. Adana felt the rocking sway as Am'brosia raced across the land without hesitation. The clarity of the image conveyed confidence in their direction of escape. The landscape the giraffes now passed through resembled the plains around Adana, the hills dwindling into the flat grasslands of her kingdom, an occasional small herd of animals grazing in the distance. The giraffe's assurance spilled through the link, a calm awareness of a plan. They knew a safe place to stop and wait for Adana to join them.

The route continued many leagues east, away from Adana's View, Moniah's royal fortress and her original destination. Concern over how far off track they might be chilled Adana, but her mother always told her to trust the giraffes' instincts.

There were greater concerns for now. Where might Maligon's soldiers lurk in the distance? Nothing disturbed the scenery, seen through her eyes or through the giraffe's, but, after last night's surprise attack, she didn't trust her sight as well. An odd thought for a Watcher, blessed with the gifts of vision, much less the rising heir to Moniah's Seat of Authority.

As the sun peeked above the horizon, warmth crept over her body, a welcome relief to the horrific night. Joannu and Elayne slowed their horses, murmuring sighs of thanks in response to the light of day. None of the three had spoken since the first hurried words outside the camp, hours earlier. The sun might provide comfort, but still the trio remained silent and vigilant in their flight.

The ground flattened out, with an occasional rolling hill interrupting the landscape, and Adana's heart gave a double-beat of hope. She was in Moniah.

* * * * *

Cast of Characters

Adana	Heir to the throne of Moniah, trained as a Watcher
Am'brosia	Giraffe bonded to Adana
Ariff	King of Teletia
Bai'dish	Giraffe bonded to Serrin
Barlo	Kiffen's horse
Chiora	Queen of Moniah, Adana's mother
Conrad	Earl of Brom, Pultarch's father
Contina	Niece of Lord Sarx
Donel	King of Elwar
Father Tonch	Keeper of the Faith, married to Sariah
Gabriella	Empress of Belwyn
Glume	Giraffe Keeper
Halar	Kassa's husband, 2nd in Command of the Soldiers of the First Sight
Jerold	First knight of Belwyn
Joannu	Watcher
Ju'latti	Queen Chiora's bonded giraffe
Kalara	Watcher
Karyah	Watcher Envoy to Belwyn
Kassa	First Vision under Chiora's reign
Kiffen	Heir to the throne of Elwar, son of King Donel and Queen Roassa
Leera	Kiffen's half-sister, daughter of King Donel and Queen Quilla

Linus	Commander of the Soldiers of the First Sight
Maligon	Traitor exiled by Chiora after Maligon's Rebellion, believed dead
Markel	Sergeant in Elwar's castle guard
Memory Keeper	Storyteller
Micah	Husband King of Chiora, Father of Adana
Montee	High-ranking Watcher
Morana	Queen of Teletia
Mother Sariah	Protector of the Faith, married to Peter Tonch
Navon	Prince in Teletia
Ostreia	Watcher Envoy to Teletia
Pultarch	Son of the Earl of Brom
Quilla	Queen in Elwar, 2nd wife to King Donel, mother to Leera
Roassa	Queen in Elwar, 1st wife to King Donel, mother to Kiffen and Serrin
Samantha	High-ranking Watcher
Sarx	Elwarian noble
Serrin	2nd son of King Donel and Queen Roassa
Shana	Tavern maid
Simeon	Advisor to King Donel
Sinti	Watcher
Suban	Apothecary in Elwar
Suppina Sarx	Sarx's cousin
Va'lent	King Micah's bonded giraffe
Veana	Watcher

* * * * *

Author's Note

While the giraffes in this story are fictional and exist in my imagination, and hopefully in yours now, I hope you'll take the time to find out more about the plight of real giraffes and the efforts the Giraffe Conservation Foundation (GCF) is taking to save them. Giraffes suffer from a silent extinction because they do not receive the publicity other endangered animals receive. According to GCF's website, giraffe numbers have declined by almost 30% in the last three decades to approximately 111,000 in the wild. It is likely that giraffe numbered ten times as many only a century ago. Please check out https://giraffeconservation.org and help if you can. By purchasing this book, you've already helped because I will donate 5% of the book's profits to GCF each quarter.

* * * * *

About the Author

Barbara V. Evers began storytelling at the age of four. She couldn't read, yet, so she roped her Aunt Vivian into taking dictation for her. She is an award-winning author and Pushcart Prize nominee with short stories and essays appearing in several anthologies.

When she's not writing, Barbara is a professional trainer, speaker, and freelance writer/editor. Outside of work, Barbara loves reading, photography, and exploring wildlife and the great outdoors.

Barbara lives in Greer, SC, with two of her grandchildren, her husband, Bruce, and a rescue dog named Roxy.

You can find out more about Barbara's upcoming books and sign up for her newsletter at www.BarbaraVEvers.com. Also, you can follow her on Facebook @BarbaraVEversAuthor.

* * * * *

The following is an
Excerpt from Book One of The Balance of Kerr:

Burnt

_____

Kevin Steverson &
Tyler Ackerman

Available Now from New Mythology Press

eBook and Paperback

Excerpt from "Burnt:"

Tog shrugged. "I like chicken," he said as he pulled out his dagger. Standing nearly seven feet tall and weighing nearly three hundred and twenty pounds, a dagger for him was a short sword to most men. He cut a piece off. He didn't bother blowing on it and poked it into his mouth. There was instant regret on his face. He began breathing through his teeth with the piece of meat between them, the sharpness of his incisors giving away that he was half Orc, if his size didn't already reveal it. He grabbed his mug and drained it.

Kryder shook his head, cut another piece for himself, and blew on it. Before he took a bite, he said, "If I had a copper for every time I've seen you do that, I could exchange them for a piece of gold. I'm talking about a whole coin and not a quarter piece."

Tog wiped his mouth with the back of his hand, ignoring the remark, and said, "So when are we going to be contacted? Besides the cost of mugs, this place isn't cheap. It's not like we have coin to spare. We should think about an inn more in line with our coin purses."

"I don't know," Kryder answered. "The old man said someone would contact us here. If we go across town, whoever it is may not find us."

"Well I…" Tog started to say when he was interrupted by a loud voice two tables away.

"Look here, halfbreed," a man dressed similarly to them, in leather armor covered with a travel cloak and a sword on his hip, said loudly. One side of his face had a scar stretching from eyebrow to lips. He was speaking to them. "I don't eat with such as your kind."

The three men sitting with him laughed. One wearing a half-helmet with leather flaps hanging on each side added his own loud insult, "Since the rape didn't kill his mother, surely bearing an Orc bastard did the deed." The group laughed even louder.

Kryder reached down to his side and drew another smaller, more ornate dagger with his free hand. He laid them both on the table. He stood, turned around, and looked at the four men. Tog, on his feet nearly as quickly, reached over his shoulder and grabbed the axe strapped to his back with one hand. It was dual-headed and meant for two hands when used by a normal-sized man. He placed it on the table beside his own large dagger. A hand's length of the worn leather-covered handle hung over the edge.

The four men realized the object of their harassment and his companion didn't intend to leave. They meant to fight. They scrambled to their feet, knocking over chairs. Several groups stood and moved away from the center of the room, while others left the tavern completely.

The owner's sons looked toward their father. He shook his head. Fights happened, even in his establishment in the better part of town. Usually he had his boys put a stop to it. This time, the insult thrown at the large patron was more than he could tolerate. He decided to let the man demand his apology, even if it meant he had to beat it out of the four. It was an easy decision.

* * * * *

Get "Burnt" now at:
https://www.amazon.com/dp/B0861FRWFH/.

Find out more about Kevin Steverson & Tyler Ackerman and "Burnt" at:
https://chriskennedypublishing.com/imprints-authors/kevin-steverson/burnt/

* * * *

The following is an
Excerpt from Book One of The Milesian Accords:

A Reluctant Druid

Jon R. Osborne

Available Now from Blood Moon Press

eBook, Audio, and Paperback

Excerpt from "A Reluctant Druid:"

"Don't crank on it; you'll strip it."

Liam paused from trying to loosen the stubborn bolt holding the oil filter housing on his Yamaha motorcycle, looking for the source of the unsolicited advice. The voice was gruff, with an accent and cadence that made Liam think of the Swedish Chef from the Muppets. The garage door was open for air circulation, and two figures were standing in the driveway, illuminated by the setting sun. As they approached and stepped into the shadows of the house, Liam could see they were Pixel and a short, stout man with a greying beard that would do ZZ Top proud. The breeze blowing into the garage carried a hint of flowers.

Liam experienced a moment of double vision as he looked at the pair. Pixel's eyes took on the violet glow he thought he'd seen before, while her companion lost six inches in height, until he was only as tall as Pixel. What the short man lacked in height, he made up for in physique; he was built like a fireplug. He was packed into blue jeans and a biker's leather jacket, and goggles were perched over the bandana covering his salt and pepper hair. Leather biker boots crunched the gravel as he walked toward the garage. Pixel followed him, having traded her workout clothes for black jeans and a pink t-shirt that left her midriff exposed. A pair of sunglasses dangled from the neckline of her t-shirt.

"He's seeing through the glamour," the short, bearded man grumbled to Pixel, his bushy eyebrows furrowing.

"Well duh. We're on his home turf, and this is his place of power" Pixel replied nonchalantly. "He was pushing back against my glamour yesterday, and I'm not adding two hands to my height."

Liam set down the socket wrench and ran through the mental inventory of items in the garage that were weapons or could be used as

449

them. The back half of the garage was a workshop, which included the results of his dabbling with blacksmithing and sword-crafting, so the list was considerable. But the most suitable were also the farthest away.

"Can I help you?" Liam stood and brushed off his jeans; a crowbar was three steps away. Where had they come from? Liam hadn't heard a car or motorcycle outside, and the house was a mile and a half outside of town.

"Ja, you can." The stout man stopped at the threshold of the garage. His steel-grey eyes flicked from Liam to the workbench and back. He held his hands out, palms down. The hands were larger than his and weren't strangers to hard work and possibly violence. "And there's no need to be unhospitable; we come as friends. My name is Einar, and you've already met Pixel."

"Hi, Liam." Pixel was as bubbly as yesterday. While she didn't seem to be making the same connection as Einar regarding the workbench, her eyes darted about the cluttered garage and the dim workshop behind it. "Wow, you have a lot of junk."

"What's this about?" Liam sidled a half step toward the workbench, regretting he hadn't kept up on his martial arts. He had three brown belts, a year of kendo, and some miscellaneous weapons training scattered over two decades but not much experience in the way of real fighting. He could probably hold his own in a brawl as long as his opponent didn't have serious skills. He suspected Einar was more than a Friday night brawler in the local watering hole. "Is she your daughter?"

Einar turned to the purple-haired girl, his caterpillar-like eyebrows gathering. "What did you do?"

"What? I only asked him a few questions and checked him out," Pixel protested, her hands going to her hips as she squared off with

Einar. "It's not as if I tried to jump his bones right there in the store or something."

"Look mister, if you think something untoward happened between me and your daughter –" Liam began.

"She's not my pocking daughter, and I don't give a troll's ass if you diddled her," Einar interrupted, his accent thickening with his agitation. He took a deep breath, his barrel chest heaving. "Now, will you hear me out without you trying to brain me with that tire iron you've been eyeing?"

"You said diddle." Pixel giggled.

"Can you be serious for five minutes, you pocking faerie?" Einar glowered, his leather jacket creaking as he crossed his arms.

"Remember 'dwarf,' you're here as an 'advisor.'" Pixel included air quotes with the last word, her eyes turning magenta. "The Nine Realms are only involved out of politeness."

"Politeness! If you pocking Tuatha and Tylwyth Teg hadn't folded up when the Milesians came at you, maybe we wouldn't be here to begin with!" Spittle accompanied Einar's protest. "Tylwyth? More like Toothless!"

"Like your jarls didn't roll over and show their bellies when the Avramites showed up with their One God and their gold!" Pixel rose up on her toes. "Your people took their god and took their gold and then attacked our ancestral lands!"

"Guys!" Liam had stepped over to the workbench but hadn't picked up the crowbar. "Are you playing one of those live-action role playing games or something? Because if you are, I'm calling my garage out of bounds. Take your LARP somewhere else."

"We've come a long way to speak to you," Einar replied, looking away from Pixel. "I'm from Asgard."

"Asgard? You mean like Thor and Odin? What kind of game are you playing?" Liam hadn't moved from the workbench, but he'd mapped in his mind the steps he'd need to take to reach a stout pole which would serve as a staff while he back-pedaled to his workshop, where a half-dozen half-finished sword prototypes rested. From where he stood, though, he didn't feel as threatened. He knew a bit about gamers because there were a fair number of them among the pagan community, and he'd absorbed bits and pieces of it. Maybe someone had pointed Liam out to Pixel as research about druids for one of these games—an over-enthusiastic player who wanted to more convincingly roleplay one.

"Gods I hate those pocking things," Einar grumbled, rubbing his forehead while Pixel stifled another giggle. "Look, can we sit down and talk to you? This is much more serious than some pocking games you folk play with your costumes and your toy weapons."

"This isn't a game, and we aren't hippies with New Age books and a need for self-validation." Pixel added. Her eyes had faded to a lavender color. "Liam, we need your help."

* * * * *

Get "A Reluctant Druid" at
https://www.amazon.com/dp/B07716V2RN.

Find out more about Jon R. Osborne and "A Reluctant Druid" at:
https://chriskennedypublishing.com/imprints-authors/jon-r-osborne/

* * * * *

Made in the USA
Monee, IL
04 February 2021

58602570R00252